Darius was still fighting a man from the last rush. He gave a shout and his opponent screeched as Darius cut off his hand. The man backed away, blood spurting from the stump, and the three spearmen lost several heartbeats as they tried to cover him.

'Sword!' Kineas said. He put his hand back.

Darius slapped his own sword into the open hand.

Just like that.

Kineas stepped forward, took the lead man's spearhead on his shield where he could feel it and *pushed*, fouling the man's weapon. The man set his feet and pushed back, his mates helping him. Kineas felt the strain and tilted his shield, bent his knees and rolled low, passing his shield under the lip of his opponent's, kneeling on the damp flagstone. He cut low, felt an impact and stood up, pushing with his legs as Darius came up to guard his back, and the lead man staggered back, shouting that he was cut, and the rest broke, fleeing as best they could from the terror of the darkness and the blood.

Darius rose next to him, having found the sword of the man whose wrist he'd severed.

'Thanks,' Kineas said. The *daimon* of combat left him, and his knees began to shake. He was *alive*! He almost fell. His chiton was drenched in sweat.

'Think nothing of it,' Darius said in court Persian. He was grey, but he managed a smile. 'Could I have my sword back, do you think?'

Christian Cameron is a writer and military historian. He is a veteran of the United States Navy, where he served as both an aviator and an intelligence officer. He lives in Toronto, where he is currently writing the next novel in the TYRANT series while working on a Masters in Classics.

By Christian Cameron

Tyrant
Tyrant: Storm of Arrows

TYRANT

STORM OF ARROWS

CHRISTIAN CAMERON

An Orion paperback

First published in Great Britain in 2009
by Orion
This paperback edition published in 2009
by Orion Books Ltd,
Orion House, 5 Upper St Martin's Lane
London WC2H 9EA

An Hachette UK company

3 5 7 9 10 8 6 4

A CIP catalogue record for this book
is available from the British Library.

ISBN 978-1-4091-0366-0

Typeset by Deltatype Ltd, Birkenhead, Merseyside

Printed and bound in the UK by
CPI Mackays, Chatham ME5 8TD

The Orion Publishing Group's policy is to use papers that
are natural, renewable and recyclable products and made
from wood grown in sustainable forests. The logging and
manufacturing processes are expected to conform to the
environmental regulations of the country of origin.

www.orionbooks.co.uk

For Sarah

ἔλθε μοι καὶ νῦν, χαλεπᾶν δὲ λῦσον
ἐκ μερίμναν ὄσσα δέ μοι τέλεσσαι
θῦμοσ ἰμμέρρει, τέλεσον, σὺ δ᾽ αὔτα
σύμμαχοσ ἔσσο.

Sappho, Hymn to Aphrodite

GLOSSARY

Airyanām (Avestan) Noble, heroic.

Aspis (Classical Greek) A large round shield, deeply dished, commonly carried by Greek (but not Macedonian) *hoplites*.

Baqça (Siberian) Shaman, mage, dream-shaper.

Daimon (Classical Greek) Spirit.

Epilektoi (Classical Greek) The chosen men of the city or of the *phalanx*; elite soldiers.

Eudaimia (Classical Greek) Well-being. Literally, 'well-spirited'. See *daimon*, above.

Gamelia (Classical Greek) A Greek holiday.

Gorytos (Classical Greek and possibly Scythian) The open-topped quiver carried by the Scythians, often highly decorated.

Hipparch (Classical Greek) The commander of the cavalry.

Hippeis (Classical Greek) Militarily, the cavalry of a Greek army. Generally, the cavalry class, synonymous with 'knights'. Usually the richest men in a city.

Hoplite (Classical Greek) A Greek soldier, the heavy infantry who carry an *aspis* (the big round shield) and fight in the *phalanx*. They represent the middle class of free men in most cities, and while sometimes they seem like medieval knights in their outlook, they are also like town militia, and made up of craftsmen and small farmers. In the early Classical period, a man with as little as twelve acres under cultivation could be expected to own the *aspis* and serve as a *hoplite*.

Hyperetes (Classical Greek) The *Hipparch*'s trumpeter, servant, or supporter. Perhaps a sort of NCO.

Kopis (Classical Greek) A bent, bladed knife or sword, rather like a modern Ghurka knife. They appear commonly in Greek art, and even some small eating knives were apparently made to this pattern.

Machaira (Classical Greek) The heavy Greek cavalry sword, longer and stronger than the short infantry sword. Meant to give a longer reach on horseback, and not useful in the *phalanx*. The word could also be used for any knife.

Parasang (Classical Greek from Persian) About 30 *stades*. See below.

Phalanx (Classical Greek) The infantry formation used by Greek *hoplites* in warfare, eight to ten deep and as wide as circumstance allowed. Greek commanders experimented with deeper and shallower formations, but the *phalanx* was solid and very difficult to break, presenting the enemy with a veritable wall of spear points and shields, whether the Macedonian style with pikes or the Greek style with spears. Also, *phalanx* can refer to the body of fighting men. A Macedonian *phalanx* was deeper, with longer spears called *sarissas*, which we assume to be like the pikes used in more recent times. Members of a *phalanx*, especially a Macedonian *phalanx*, are sometimes called *Phalangites*.

Pous (Classical Greek) About one foot.

Phylarch (Classical Greek) The commander of one file of *hoplites*. Could be as many as sixteen men.

Psiloi (Classical Greek) Light infantry skirmishers, usually men with bows and slings, or perhaps javelins, or even rocks. In Greek city-state warfare, the *psiloi* were supplied by the poorest free men, those who could not afford the financial burden of *hoplite* armour and daily training in the gymnasium.

Sastar (Avestan) Tyrannical. A tyrant.

Stade (Classical Greek) About 1/8 of a mile. The distance run in a 'stadium'. 178 metres. Sometimes written as *Stadia* or *Stades* by me. 30 *Stadia* make a *Parasang*.

Taxeis (Classical Greek) The sections of a Macedonian *phalanx*. Can refer to any group, but often used as a 'company' or a 'battalion'. My *taxeis* has between five hundred and two thousand men, depending on losses and detachments. Roughly synonymous with *phalanx* above, although a *phalanx* may be composed a dozen *taxeis* in a great battle.

Xiphos (Classical Greek) A straight-bladed infantry sword, usually carried by *hoplites* or *psiloi*. Classical Greek art, especially red-figure ware, shows many *hoplites* wearing them, but only a handful have been recovered and there's much debate about the shape and use. They seem very like a Roman gladius.

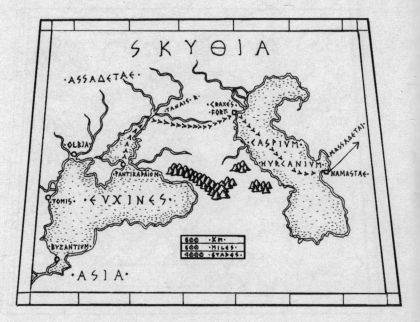

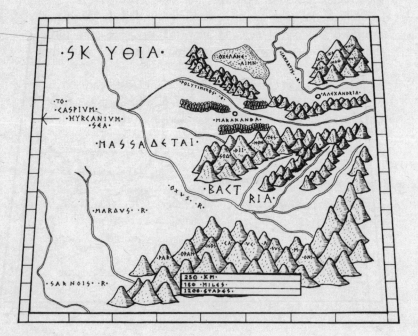

The conqueror of Asia stalked into his tent and tossed his golden helmet at the armour stand by the camp bed. It hit the wooden post with a bronze clang. The servants froze.

'Where the *fuck* are my recruits?' he yelled. 'Antipater promised me eight *thousand* new infantry. He sent three thousand Thracians and some mutinous Greeks! I want my Macedonians!'

Members of his staff followed him into the tent, led by Hephaestion. Hephaestion was not afraid of his royal master, certainly not his master's temper tantrums, and his bronze-haired head was high. He was smiling.

Behind him, Eumenes and Callisthenes were more hesitant.

Alexander scratched his head with both hands, trying to get the sweat and the dirt out of his hair. 'Don't stand in the doorway like sheep. Come in or get the fuck out.'

Hephaestion handed him a cup of wine, poured another for himself. 'Drink, friend,' he said.

Alexander drank. 'It's not fair. If people would just do as they were told …'

Hephaestion raised an eyebrow, and they both laughed. Just like that.

Alexander swirled the wine in his cup and looked at Eumenes. 'Did he say why?'

Eumenes – shorter, not godlike in any way – accepted a goblet from Hephaestion, who rarely served anyone but the Great King himself, and met his lord's eyes. They were mismatched, blue and brown, the blue eye ringed in black and opened just a little too wide. Eumenes sometimes thought that his master was a god, and other times that he was mad. Either way, Eumenes, a brave man and veteran of a dozen hard fights, disliked meeting Alexander's eyes.

Eumenes of Cardia was a Greek and not a Macedonian,

which made the bearing of bad tidings all the harder. Men competed to bring Alexander good news. When the news was bad, men conspired to avoid being the goat. Eumenes, the foreigner, the smaller man, was the goat.

'Lord,' he said carefully, 'would you like to read the letter, or shall I tell you what I think?' In the right mood, Alexander craved straight talk. Eumenes lacked Hephaestion's touch with his lord, but they had an emergency and he needed Alexander to act like a king.

'Just tell me,' Alexander shot back.

Eumenes looked at Hephaestion and received no sign at all. 'Reading between the lines, I would say that Antipater sent an army to conquer the Euxine cities – and perhaps the Sakje tribes.'

'Sakje?' Alexander asked.

'The Western Scyths,' Callisthenes answered.

'Amazons?' Alexander asked.

Callisthenes snorted contemptuously. Alexander whirled on him. 'Why are you here, sir?' he asked.

Callisthenes raised an eyebrow. 'Because you can't tell the difference between a Scythian and an Amazon.'

Alexander seemed pleased with this remark. He flung himself on a couch. Hephaestion came and lay with him. Servants brought food and more wine.

'So Antipater made a campaign against the Scythians,' he said.

'Not in person. He sent Zopryon.'

'Shit for brains,' Alexander said. 'I assume he cocked it up?'

Eumenes nodded. 'I think that's where we lost our missing recruits.'

Alexander snorted. 'They're off chasing Amazons, eh?'

Eumenes shook his head. 'No, lord. If I'm right, and my sources are firm on this point, all our recruits are dead.'

Alexander rolled off the couch and stood. 'Zeus Ammon my father. Zopryon lost a whole *taxeis*?'

'Zopryon lost a whole army, lord.' Eumenes waited for the explosion. 'And died himself.'

2

Alexander stood rigid by the couch. Hephaestion reached out and put a hand on his hip, but Alexander struck the hand away. Hephaestion frowned.

'They almost defeated my father. Philip, my father. He was wounded – wounded badly.' Alexander was speaking very softly.

Eumenes could remember it. He nodded. 'Yes, lord.'

'And Darius – these Sakje defeated Darius.' Alexander's face was immobile. He stood like a schoolboy reciting for his tutor.

Callisthenes shrugged. 'Not so much defeated as avoided, if Herodotus is to be believed. They made Darius look like an ass, though.'

Alexander glared at him.

Callisthenes raised a shaggy eyebrow. 'Of course, it took Athens to *defeat* Darius.'

Alexander's face burned as the blood rushed to his cheeks. 'Athens *checked* Darius. Sparta *checked* Xerxes. *I* conquered Asia. Macedon. Not Athens and not Sparta.'

The philosopher glared at Alexander, who met his look and held it. Long seconds passed. Then the philosopher shrugged again. 'As you say,' Callisthenes said, with a nod.

A tense silence filled the tent. Outside, the new recruits could be heard being shepherded to their quarters in the sprawling camp – a camp so big and so well built that men already called it a city.

Alexander sat on the couch again. 'And Cyrus,' he said, as if continuing an earlier conversation.

They all looked at him, until understanding dawned on Callisthenes. 'Yes,' he said. 'Yes, as you say, Alexander. Cyrus lost his life fighting the Massagetae. Well to the east of here.'

'Massagetae?' Alexander brightened. 'Amazons?'

'The Massagetae are the Eastern Scythians,' Callisthenes said. 'Their women do fight, and they sometimes have warrior queens. They pay tribute to the King of Kings. There are Massagetae serving with Bessus and with Spitamenes. The queen of the Massagetae is Zarina.'

Alexander raised his goblet in salute to Callisthenes. 'You

do know some useful things.' He drank, staring out of the door of his tent.

Eumenes fidgeted after the silence stretched on too long. Callisthenes didn't fidget. He watched Alexander.

Alexander ran his fingers through Hephaestion's hair. Then he watched a Persian boy retrieve his helmet and polish it with a cloth before hanging it on the armour stand. Alexander gave the boy a smile.

Callisthenes continued to watch him.

'Antipater has cost us more than a few thousand recruits,' Alexander said some minutes later. He leaned back so that his golden curls mixed with Hephaestion's longer hair. 'Our own legend of invincibility is worth a pair of taxeis and five hundred Companions.'

'You are invincible,' Hephaestion said. From another man, it would have been fawning. From Hephaestion, it was a simple statement of fact.

Alexander allowed himself a small smile. 'I cannot be everywhere,' he said. He rolled off the couch again and motioned to the silent slave who waited at the foot of the bed. 'Take my armour,' he said.

The silent man opened his breastplate and put it on the armour stand. Alexander shrugged out of his tunic and stood naked, the marks of the armour clear on his all-too human flesh.

Naked, neither tall nor especially beautiful, Alexander picked up his wine, found it empty and held it out for a refill. Slaves tripped over themselves to correct the error.

Callisthenes laughed at their eagerness and their fear. Alexander smirked. 'Persians make such *good* slaves,' he said. He drank off the whole cup and held it out again, and the pantomime was repeated. Even the Cardian had to laugh. The slaves knew they were being made game of, and that made them more afraid. Wine was spilled, and more slaves appeared to clean it up.

'I can't be everywhere,' Alexander repeated. 'And Macedon cannot afford to appear weak. These Scythians must be punished. Their victory over Zopryon must be made to look the stroke of ill-fortune that it was. When Bessus is brought to heel, we should spend a season crushing the Massagetae.'

Callisthenes sensed the dismay of the other men. 'Alexander,' he began carefully, 'the Massagetae live far to the north and east, beyond the Kush. And they live on the sea of grass, which Herodotus says runs for fifty thousand stades. We will not crush them in one season.'

Alexander looked up and smiled. It was a happy smile, and it removed years of tension, war and drink from his face. 'I can only spare them a season,' Alexander said. 'They're just barbarians. Besides, I want an Amazon.'

Hephaestion struck the king playfully, and they ended up wrestling on the floor.

PART I

FUNERAL GAMES

1

The sun shone on the Borysthenes river, the rain swell moving like a horse herd and glittering like the rain-wet grass in the sun. The Sakje camp was crisp and clean after days of rain, much of the horse dung vanished into the the general mud that filled every street, the felt yurts and the wagons bright as if new-made. Kineas had taken the sun as a sign and risen from his bed, despite the fresh pain of his wounds and the recent fear of death.

'You should find the stone,' the girl said. She was eleven or twelve years old, dressed in caribou hide, with a red cloak blowing in the wind. Kineas had seen her before around the camp, a slight figure with red-brown hair and a silver-grey horse from the royal herd.

Kineas crouched down, wincing at the intense pain that shot from his hip, down his leg and through his groin. Everything hurt and most actions made him dizzy. 'What stone?' he asked. She had big eyes, deep blue eyes with a black rim that made her appear possessed, or mad.

'It is a *baqca* thing, is it not? To find the stone?' She shrugged, put her hands behind her and rocked her hips back and forth, back and forth, so that her hair swayed around her face. She was dirty and smelled of horse.

His Sakje didn't run to endearments for children. 'I'm sorry,' he said. 'I don't understand.'

She favoured him with the look that children save for adults too slow to understand them. 'The *stone*,' she said. 'For the king's barrow.' Seeing his incomprehension, she pointed at an old barrow, the kurgan of some ancient horse-lord that rose by the great bend. 'At the peak of every barrow, the baqca places a stone. You should go and find it. My father says so.'

Kineas grinned, as much from pain as from understanding. 'And who is your father, child?' he asked, although even as he said the words, he knew where he had seen that long-nosed profile and the fine bones of her hands.

'Kam Baqca was my father,' she said, and ran away, laughing.

He knew as soon as she spoke that he had seen the stone in dreams – seen it and dismissed it. He feared his dreams now, and denied them if he could.

But he gathered a dozen of his Sindi retainers and a few Greeks: Diodorus and Niceas because they were friends, and Anarxes, a gentleman of Olbia, because Eumenes was wounded and Anarxes had the duty. Together, they rode down the river a dozen stades.

'What are we looking for?' Diodorus asked. He, too, was recovering from a wound, and his red hair gleamed where it emerged from a bandage that swathed his whole head, under a Sakje cap of fox fur and red wool. Temerix, the Sindi smith, rode over.

'We're looking for a stone,' Kineas said.

'For kurgan,' Temerix said, as if this was the most natural thing in the world. 'Lord Kineas sees it in dreams. We come find it.'

Young Anarxes' eyes were as wide as funeral coins at this open talk of his hipparch's godlike powers.

Diodorus raised an eyebrow and nodded slowly. He reached into his cloak and produced a clay flask, from which he took a long pull. He offered it around. 'Did it ever occur to you that life was simpler when we were just mercenaries?' he asked.

Kineas and Niceas exchanged a look.

Diodorus pointed with the fist that held the flask. 'Look. Kineas is wearing a Thracian cloak. Anarxes here, as fine a wrestler as we've ever seen – an Olympian, by Apollo – is wearing Sakje *trousers* as if that were the most natural thing in the world. All our men wear their caps.' Diodorus touched his bandages and the Sakje cap perched atop them. 'Are we even Greeks any more?' he asked. He took another drink of wine from his flask and handed it to Kineas.

Kineas shrugged. 'We're still Greeks. Did travel to Persia make you Persian?'

Diodorus was serious. 'It made me a lot more Persian than I

was before I went there. Remember Ecbatana? I'll never think of Greece the same way again.'

'What are you saying?' Kineas asked.

'There's a rumour that you and Srayanka aim to take us all the way east to fight Alexander,' Diodorus said. 'I've heard you talk around it. You mean it, don't you?'

Kineas shook his head. 'Lot is insistent and Srayanka wants to support him. The queen of the Massagetae has sent messengers to the Assagatje. They had another yesterday.' He drank.

Diodorus grunted. 'Hey! Hey, that's my wine!' He seized the flask. 'We have unfinished business before we go riding off to fight the boy king. The tyrant, for instance.' He looked out at the horizon. On their right, the Borysthenes flowed down to the Euxine Sea. On the left, the sea of grass rippled in the wind as far as the eye could see, and then another forty thousand stades, or so Herodotus claimed. 'I don't want to fight Alexander. I don't want to see more fascinating barbarians. I'd like to retire to Olbia and be rich.'

Kineas rode along, hips moving with his mount. He hurt, and despite weeks in a cot in Srayanka's wagon, or because of them, he felt sore in every muscle. 'Things change,' Kineas said.

Diodorus nodded. 'Too true. The peace faction took over in Athens while we were winning this campaign.'

Kineas laughed, which also hurt. 'Athens seems very far away.'

Diodorus nodded. He handed his flask to the silent Temerix. 'That's what I mean. When I left Athens with you, I thought my heart would break. When we were cracking Darius's empire, I used to dream of the Parthenon. Then we fought this campaign. Now Athens is too far away to remember and I'm a gentlemen of Olbia. Now I dream of finding a wife and buying a farm on the Euxine.' He paused. 'I'm afraid that I'll end up in a yurt on the sea of grass.'

Kineas had stopped his horse unconsciously. He was looking straight at the stone he'd seen in his dream, and the day seemed colder. 'Hera,' Kineas said. He spoke aloud a prayer for divine protection.

Diodorus was looking at him.

'It's just as I dreamed it.' Kineas's voice was hushed. 'The stone is broader at the top. When we dig it up, the bottom will be shaped like a horse's head. We'll flip it over and the horse head will mark Satrax's grave.'

Diodorus shook his head, but as the Sindi dug away at the deep soil around the stone, he became thoughtful, and when the shape of the stone's hidden base was revealed, he rubbed his beard in annoyance.

'Remember when we were just mercenaries?' Diodorus said, again.

They buried the king in the old way. It was the last act of the army that had won the battle at the Ford of the River God, and even as the men cut turf in the rain, Kineas could feel the spirit that had animated them flowing away like the rising river at their back carrying the rainwater to the sea.

The Greeks did their part. Diodorus, Niceas, Philokles and Kineas cut turfs side by side, their cloaks soaked through and the rich loam under the grass turning to sticky slime on their hands and feet. Around them, for stades, Sakje and Greek worked together, every warrior cutting enough turfs to cover a man and his horse. Then the cutters carried the turf to the builders, almost all of them Sindi tribesmen from the farms up the river – earth people, the Sakje called them – or dirt people. They dug out the chambers of the barrow and reinforced them with heavy timbers floated down the river from the forests in the north.

Once, Satrax had stood at this ford and asked Kineas if he would like to go north to see the forests.

And now the king was dead. Kineas shook his head at the ways of the gods, at Moira and Tyche, fate and chance. He straightened and rubbed his hip, which hurt like fire with every trip he made back to his own pile of turf. He could only carry one block of earth and grass at a time – his right shoulder was better, but the long cuts on his bridle arm and his left leg still gave him trouble.

Diodorus and Niceas and Philokles had wounds too, and

they were working by his side. Kineas was determined to do his part without complaint, but on his next trip his left forearm hurt so much he had to put his turf on the ground and sit in the rain. 'I want a bridle gauntlet,' he said. 'Parmenion had one.'

Philokles nodded. 'I suppose Temerix could make you one,' he said. His tone expressed his view that too much armour was effeminate.

'Look at that,' Niceas said, pointing at the new kurgan.

At the mound, Marthax, the old king's warlord, and Srayanka, the old king's niece, were bickering, their fists raised and their voices audible across half a stade.

The two had shared the burden of design and construction, but they could agree on nothing. They quarrelled about the kurgan's size and shape, about the location of the internal chambers, about the orientation of the door and their own roles in the final rites. When Kineas saw Srayanka, whether in fleeting assignations or carefully arranged chance meetings, she smelled of loam and spoke only of Marthax's perfidy. She tried to hide her anger, but out on the plain, the warriors knew too much of the quarrels of their leaders. They cut the turf, and mourned, and worried about the future.

In addition to turf, each warrior was expected to bring a gift to the king's barrow. Around the base of the square of earth, more Sindi dug a trench. A long row of tethered horses – most of them chargers, all brilliantly accoutred – waited to be slaughtered for the burial.

The battle had cost the allies thousands of men, but the campaign as a whole had bound them together, Sakje and Sauromatae and Euxine Greeks. Today, they all laboured together, almost without orders, to build a mighty grave for the dead king of the Sakje. The turf bricks rose from a wall to a block and then to a squat pyramid of grass as ten thousand men and women made their offerings of earth and gold. And as the afternoon dripped into the evening, the clouds began to break and the weeks of drizzle gave way to a soft evening. The last courses of turf went up to the truncated top and torches were lit, then Kineas and a dozen of the lesser baqcas of the various clans hoisted the stone he had chosen and dragged it up to the top of the kurgan and positioned it carefully. None of the baqcas questioned his choice or his right to be there, and they were a silent and worshipful coven as they did their work.

By the time the stone was in place and a song had been sung over it, darkness had fallen, and more torches were brought forward. Even as Kineas walked on a pair of trees laid as a bridge, the horses in the trench below began to shy and call. They were afraid. They were right to be afraid.

Marthax and Srayanka took turns pulling the chargers down, first grabbing the headstall and then giving the killing blow with a short sword, slashing the beasts across the neck where the muscle was soft and the artery close to the skin. They shared the task as cousins and priests, but Kineas could see the iron in Srayanka's spine and the careful set of her shoulders, and a season in the saddle shared with Marthax allowed Kineas to recognize the same tension in the big Sakje warlord.

Each was resolved to be seen to be worthy ... of kingship. The competition had started. Kineas wished they could settle it quickly. The Euxine Greeks had other concerns, and they needed a steady hand out here on the plains.

Kineas wished that he was sure that Srayanka was the queen the Sakje needed. Or even that Marthax was fit to be a king. He wished that the boy, for all his failings and his desire to take Srayanka for himself, had lived.

He wished that many men had lived – Nicomedes and Ajax, priestly Agis, Cleitus and his son Leucon, Varô of the Grass Cats, and countless others, many of them friends and companions. Laertes, whom he had known from boyhood, who had followed him across the world and back. But of all of them, Satrax the king was the one whose death affected every man in the army. Satrax was the man who bound the army together, and his death signalled an end.

The torches flared and spat in the last of the rain. To the west, stars were appearing in the sky. The ground stank of horse blood, and the light of the torches glared fitfully on gold and iron and wool.

Marthax wore red, as was his right as the commander of the dead king's bodyguard. He had the king's sword across his arms, and with it he climbed the pyramid of earth and grass until he stood on the top.

Srayanka, dressed from head to foot in white skins decorated in blue hair and gold cones, climbed behind him, carrying the king's helm. This she placed with reverence at the very apex of the pyramid. Then she took the sword from Marthax. She raised it into the darkness.

Thunder rumbled in the distance, and the crowd of warriors made a noise like the sigh of the wind over the plain of grass.

'Victor in two great battles, hammer of the Getae, lord of ten thousand horses,' she called. Kineas understood her slow Sakje well enough. He had heard her practise this chant for ten nights.

Again, the warriors seemed to sigh.

'Young like a god, swift in battle, terrible to his foes, life-taker, lord of ten thousand horses,' she called, and again they sighed.

Marthax stood behind her, his arms crossed.

'Wise like a god, gold-giver, great in peace and council, lord of ten thousand horses,' she said, the sword in her hand unmoving. She had arms like bundles of iron rods, as Kineas now had reason to know.

Satrax had helped to unite them, but he had also been a reckless adolescent intent on taking Srayanka for himself. Kineas was not altogether sorry he was gone.

'He was the king of the Sakje!' she shouted, her voice suddenly deep and wild. And at the last word, she reversed the blade and plunged it into the grass.

The warriors gave a great shout, a bellow of sorrow and anger and victory and loss, and then they turned away to the banquet that awaited them, a feast on the new mound, a last feast with the old king. They ate and drank and wept, and bards sang songs of the battles. And they were like brothers and sisters, all the Greeks and the Sakje and the Sauromatae.

One last time.

*

15

Ataelus, the Massagetae warrior who led Kineas's scouts, introduced the messenger from the east with a sweep of his arm.

'Fifty days' ride to the east on a good horse, with five more horses for changing – beyond the Kaspian, farther than the Lake of the Sea of Grass, farther than Sauromatae – for riding fifty days, and not for resting – there is the queen of the Massagetae.' Ataelus's eyes roved around. The open tent was packed, and there were more Sakje all around. He stood straight, fully conscious of the importance of the occasion. 'This man for being my cousin. Qares speaks for the queen.' Ataelus stepped back.

The messenger of the Massagetae was shorter than Ataelus and had something of his look – black ringlets like a Spartan, a wind-burned face and a round nose like a satyr. He wore a red silk robe over silvered-bronze scale armour that winked like a hot fire in sunlight. In his hand he held a short Sakje sword with a hilt of green stone. He brandished it at the council of chiefs and Greek officers who sat in the fire circle in front of Satrax's empty wagon.

Sakje rules of council allowed any interested person to attend, so hundreds of men and women, many armed, and dozens of children gathered on the council hill. They were never fully quiet, and the murmur of their comments and the sigh of the wind forced the speakers to shout to make themselves heard. The messenger of the Massagetae had a deep voice and it carried well.

'Keepers of the western gate!' he shouted, and Eumenes, still stiff from wounds, interpreted in a tired voice. 'Queen Zarina, lady of all of the riders of the east, calls upon you to come to the muster of all the Sakje! Iskander, who the Greeks call Alexander, King of Macedon, threatens war on the sea of grass! Zarina requests the aid of the Assagatje!' He waved the sword. 'She sends this, the sword of Cyrus, as a token of her need. Let Iskander hear the thunder of your hooves and feel the taste of your bronze arrows.'

Srayanka stepped forward and accepted the sword. There were cheers from the crowd of onlookers, but also hisses of disapproval.

'Let Zarina fight her own war!' shouted a young war chief of the Standing Horse clan. He tugged at his braids in annoyance. 'And who are you, Cruel Hands, to take the sword of Cyrus? Eh? Eh? Give it to Marthax!'

Parshtaevalt, one of Srayanka's chiefs, clouted the Standing Horse on the shoulder. 'Silence!' he roared. 'Srayanka is the king's heir.'

Kineas listened to the dissenting opinions and wriggled on his stool.

Next to him, Philokles sharpened a twig with his belt knife. 'They've just had a war,' Philokles said quietly. 'They don't want another.'

Srayanka held up the sword and waited for silence. 'I accept the sword of Cyrus for the Assagatje,' she shouted. 'We will not send ten thousand riders to the east. Tell Zarina we have already fought Iskander in the west.' She turned to the crowd. 'But will we leave our cousins alone to face the monster? Did the east not send us Lot?'

Lot shouldered forward. The Sauromatae prince was tall and blond and pale-eyed, past his first youth but still in his prime. He had a new scar that ran across his face from his right eye down to the left corner of his mouth. When he came up to Srayanka, he reached out and she handed him the sword. He raised it over his head and the crowd was quieter. When he spoke, his excitement and his thick eastern accent made him difficult to understand.

'Just as you needed our horses,' he called, 'now Queen Zarina asks in her time of need. Even a tithe of your strength would help. I promised Zarina when I rode west that I would bring the Assagatje back with me. Will you make me a liar?' He turned to Kineas. 'And will our Euxine allies desert us? Olbia and Pantecapaeum and all the cities of the Euxine have benefited from our alliance. Will they stand by the tribes in turn?'

Eumenes had to speak quickly to keep up with Lot, and the effort of translating the difficult dialect was exhausting the young man. Kineas put a hand on his shoulder and felt the heat of fever in the bare skin. He turned to Philokles.

'Take this young man to his bed,' Kineas said. 'Shush!' he ordered Eumenes. 'My Sakje is good enough for this!'

Despite his claim, Kineas glanced around for Ataelus. Ataelus's Greek wasn't of the first order, but he could translate well enough. Ataelus pushed forward with his wife, Samahe.

'Lord?' he asked.

'Help me speak,' Kineas said.

Ataelus took a stand by Kineas's right shoulder.

Kineas rose. 'I am *not* the lord of the Euxine Greeks,' he shouted. Ataelus translated. Kineas went on, speaking slowly, half-listening to Ataelus's version. 'I cannot speak for Olbia or Pantecapaeum. When the phalanx of Olbia has settled the affairs of our own city, we will be ready to listen to plans for alliance and war in the east. We *are* faithful allies. But we are not yet ready to talk.'

Prince Lot shook his head and this time he spoke more carefully, his accented Sakje coming out in a rhythmic cadence as if he declaimed an epic poem. Ataelus still struggled to keep up. 'For being noble allies. For holding field – brave! Standing fast! But now, he says, no king of Sakje! No army of Sakje! No allies to go east to Massagetae, fight monster. Says he is for weeping.'

Marthax rose. He walked to the centre of the circle, but he did not ask for the sword of Cyrus. He was a big, heavy man with a ruddy blond beard and a big belly. He was the best-known war leader of the Sakje, the king's cousin, his sword arm. And one of two possible contenders for the kingship.

'Of course they are for going home,' he said, with Ataelus trailing his words.

Kineas was adept enough at listening to Marthax, and he followed the Sakje directly, listening to Ataelus with half an ear to check his own translation.

'My people are going home to bring in the harvest and ship it down the rivers,' Marthax said. 'Satrax dreamed of taking an army east to the Massagetae. He was a great king, but he was also a boy in his heart. He wanted a great adventure. Now he is gone.' Marthax crossed his arms on his chest and looked at Prince Lot. 'Things change. Seasons change. Before Zopryon came, perhaps we could have sent warriors east to the sun to help our cousins of the eastern gates. But that cycle did not come to pass. Different suns rose and sank, and now we must fill our wagons with grain and prepare to survive a winter on the plains. Perhaps next spring we could send a tithe of our young warriors east to Queen Zarina and the keepers of the eastern gate.'

A junior lord of the Standing Horses stood to speak – the same man who had shouted at Srayanka. Marthax bowed to him and went to sit, and the young warrior, his arm in a sling, came to the centre of the circle.

'I am Graethe of the Standing Horse,' he said. He had the accent of his clan, which Kineas had come to know as the northern Sakje accent. But he spoke slowly, as was the custom in council, and Kineas could understand him well enough. 'My lord has taken our warriors out on the sea of grass to pass the summer on the wind, and to watch our Sindi. If he were here, he would say that Zopryon was not the only wolf to threaten our herds, but only the strongest. The Standing Horses will not cross the sea of grass to go to the eastern gate. Let the Massagetae see to themselves.'

Kineas's eyes were drawn to a young woman, or perhaps a child, who sat behind Marthax, playing with a bow. Children were everywhere among the Sakje – they were allowed un-limited freedom. But this was the girl who had called herself Kam Baqca's child.

Instead of shooting toy arrows, she had wrapped the bow-string around an arrow, and she was using it to twirl the arrow faster and faster. Kineas had seen a jeweller in Athens using a bow-drill, and he wondered if the girl had devised the tool herself. She was using it to bore holes in Marthax's great shield of rawhide and wooden slats, the bronze arrowhead cutting at the bronze binding and rawhide strings until the whole structure was about to give way.

Kineas reached out a hand to stop her, and her eyes met his. They were old eyes for such a young face, deep and blue like cold water, and he stopped the movement of his arm as if he had been stung by an insect.

She smiled. She was a child on the edge of womanhood, and her smile was equal parts mischief and wickedness.

The Standing Horse droned on in the same vein. Marthax watched him with drooping eyelids. Srayanka, on the other hand, watched the young man as if she might leap at him. When he drew breath for another foray, she stood up and put out the hand with the sword to forestall him.

'Great is the wisdom of the Standing Horse,' she said. 'We understand that they took their place in battle, and that they will not go east to the support of the keepers of the eastern gate. Have you more to add?'

The young man bowed his head and said nothing, but he glared.

'We welcome your words, Graethe.' She pressed a strong hand on the young man's shoulder, and he sat. One of Srayanka's young leaders, Bain, laughed and gave a wolf call, and Graethe flushed.

Srayanka turned and glared at Bain. 'Silence,' she said.

Bain's face burned with adolescent wickedness. But he subsided when Urvara rose to her feet. Daughter of Varô, the lord of the Grass Cats who had died in the great battle, Urvara had her own scars – she was a bow-maiden, and Kineas could remember her rallying her people to support his final charge. She was just sixteen or seventeen, with heavy brows and full lips and arm muscles like the cords on a siege engine. Bain loved her.

'The Grass Cats look to the rising sun,' she said, pointing her riding whip out to the east. Her voice was deep and calm for such a young girl, and Kineas had to admit that Srayanka was no fluke – the Sakje formed remarkable women. Amazons, he thought.

'We will go east to the rising sun and lend our aid to the keepers of the eastern gate,' she said simply.

'Your clan lands are to the east,' Marthax said without rising. 'Your homes are on the way.' His tone was dismissive.

'We came here,' she said simply. 'My father died for the king of the Assagatje. I know what you think, Marthax. I care not.' She sat.

Srayanka's eyes turned to Kineas, and he rose. Most of the men around Marthax made growls in their throats.

Before he uttered a word, Marthax rose as well. He was almost a foot taller than Kineas. 'You have no place speaking here,' he said.

Kineas caught his eye and held it. 'My "clan" is the largest here,' he said. He looked around the tent. Some eyes were openly hostile – Graethe's, for instance. Others were friendly – Parshtaevalt of the Cruel Hands nodded, as if to make him speak.

Kineas stepped up to Marthax. 'We died for you,' he said. 'We stood at the ford and held Zopryon until you came. My people died. My friends died.' He raised an arm that was covered in scars from his part in the fighting and looked around the tent. 'My city is still held by the tyrant and his garrison of Macedonians, and I must see to it, or my "clan" will be living among you for ever.' He shrugged and turned his back on Marthax, which made the skin between his shoulder blades itch as he faced the crowd, and he thought, When did I cease to trust the warlord? 'We must be allowed to go and reclaim our city before the citizens despair and take a rash action.' He whirled on Marthax. 'And you cannot pretend to give me orders and then silence me in council. You were Satrax's warlord. Who are you now?'

Marthax had not expected Kineas to attack him. Nor had Srayanka, who had the worried look of a woman who doubts her man's wisdom. Marthax stepped back as if stung, and his face became as red as his jacket.

'Who am I?' Marthax asked. 'I am the king of the Sakje!' he bellowed.

Pandemonium. The clan leaders all rose to their feet, some denouncing, others cheering or shouting to be heard.

Marthax seized the moment. 'I am the cousin of Satrax, and I was his warlord. I have commanded all the tribes in battle, and emerged victorious in every contest. I led the expedition against the Getae, when we slaughtered them in battle.' He reached behind him and brandished his shield. 'I am the strong shield of the Sakje!' he roared.

It dropped to pieces in his hand, and silence fell on the tent – the silence of terror and omens.

A high voice came from behind Marthax, like a man's falsetto, or the voice of a young child.

'*You may be king until the monster is dead, and the eagles fly,*' it said.

Marthax threw the shards of his shield to the ground and reached for the girl, but she rolled under the edge of the tent and was gone.

2

'You are beautiful,' Srayanka said. She was stretched by his side in a welter of furs. Rain made a seashore sound on the roof of her wagon, and her calloused hand stroked him with lazy familiarity.

The language barrier kept him from responding in kind. He could tell her that she was beautiful; he could say that her breasts were beautiful, her legs were beautiful, a catalogue of physical attributes; but none of them would catch his meaning. In Greek, he would say that her beauty amazed him every time he saw it unveiled, that he would never tire of watching the complex curves where her hard stomach met the rise of her hips, that the lush velvet of her skin and its contrast with the fighting leather of the palms of her hands excited him as no other woman ever could – but her Greek was still limited to fifty verbs and a few hundred nouns, and the sort of subtlety that made compliments accurate and personal was as far beyond her as the comedy of Aristophanes – so far.

Their lovemaking was occasional, often hurried and always secretive. That they were partners was suspected – and resented – throughout the dwindling camp. And especially tonight.

The Sakje were riding away. The council had ended in division and anger before Srayanka had been formally recognized to speak so that she could lay her own claim to kingship, but the sides were drawn.

All of them together – the Sakje and the Olbians – had fought a great battle, the greatest battle any of them could remember. Ten stades north of the wagon-yurt where Kineas lay entwined with Srayanka, the field of the Ford of the River God was still an unquiet grave three full weeks after Zopryon's army had died on it. More than twenty thousand Macedonians and their auxiliaries and allies had perished – and almost a third that number of Sakje, and a thousand Euxine Greeks.

The dead outnumbered the living, and the rain that fell like the tears of repentant gods rotted the corpses so fast that men feared to touch or lift them. Carrion creatures still thronged the field, feasting on the Macedonian dead who lay defenceless, their armour stripped off.

Men said the field was cursed.

Kineas felt it like an open wound, because the unburied dead haunted his dreams, demanding burial. It was beyond his experience, that one army might be exterminated and unable to bury its dead. It frightened him. As did the voices of the many dead.

'What are you thinking, *Airyanām*?' Srayanka asked. She propped herself on an elbow. She was naked in the damp heat, and not so much shameless as unconscious that anyone would wear clothes on such a hot night. Inside her wagon, she disdained clothing as long as the damp and the heat prevailed.

Kineas forced himself away from the battlefield in his mind and back into the wagon with her marvellous, god-given body and her ambitions and her caprice. But he was honest. 'I'm thinking of the unburied dead,' he said.

'Food for crows,' she said with a shrug. She made a gesture to avert unwelcome attention from the creatures of the underworld. 'Naming calls, Kineax.' She put a finger to his lips. 'Don't speak of the dead so lightly. They were enemies. Now they have passed beyond. The field is cursed, and the Sindi will avoid it for a generation. And then the grass will grow greener for the blood, and then the grain will grow. That is the way. And the Mother will take their unquiet spirits down to her breasts, and in time, all will be healed.'

He watched her, sitting like a statue of Aphrodite, ticking off her points about the dead on one hand as if she was a scholar in the agora. 'You should be queen,' he said. 'You have the head for it.' He rubbed his untrimmed beard and scratched his head. 'I should not have spoken today. I spoke out of turn and I fear—'

'Hush,' she said. She shook her head, her unbound hair swaying. 'Marthax is stronger than I, Kineas.' She watched him for a moment in the light of the single oil lamp. 'I will not lead my people to war against each other. Marthax will not be a bad king – you know him. He does as he thinks he must.' She sighed. 'I worked hard to prepare the people to accept you as my consort.' She shrugged, and her heavy breasts rose and fell, and the sheath of muscle moved from her hips to her neck, and he wanted her. But he was a disciplined man and he kept his hands to himself.

She turned to face him. 'Instead, they fear you.'

'Because I am foreign?' he asked, tracing a finger along her flanks.

'And because you are baqca, and because you love me. You are like a creature from a song of heroes, and you bring change.' She kissed him. 'Because you could rule them with a rod of iron, and they fear that.'

He shook his head. 'I have no desire to rule,' he said.

'But you would, if you thought it was for the good of all.' She rattled off the phrase 'good of all' in his own intonation.

He shrugged. 'Listen, my love. Together, we could force the will of the army. Make it your army.' There, it was said. His own officers wanted to be gone, but he had to offer – to support her claim.

She took his head in her hands and kissed him. 'No, Airyanãm. I thank you, but no. It was Satrax's army – and he is dead.' She made a motion with her hand indicating the unknowable will of the gods. 'If he had lived another year, I would have been his heir – *we* would have been.' She shrugged again. 'I will not pit Greek soldiers against clansmen.'

Kineas sat up with her. 'What will you do?' he asked. 'What will *we* do?'

She was silent for a long time, and they could hear thousands of horses cropping grass – the ever-present sound of the Sakje camp. Somewhere, men shouted by a fire.

'I will go east,' she said. 'Many of the younger warriors are still willing – even eager – to fight the monster in the east. I will tell Marthax that I will lead them, and he will accept, because that path avoids war.'

Kineas had felt the decision coming. He had known from the first that Srayanka favoured sending an expedition east to

25

support the Massagetae. He hadn't imagined that she would go herself.

'But ...' he said. And stopped himself. *But what of us?* was too selfish for him, or for them. Her choice was clear, and she had made it like the hero she was. Could he do less?

'I must seize Olbia from the tyrant,' he said. 'Then I can join you.' Just like that – and the future was set. *Join you* echoed in his head – echoed in the world of dreams, like prophecy, and suddenly he was cold.

She shook her head. 'No. That is – what is the Greek word? Folly? Madness? You Greeks have so many words for stupid thinking. You can be the tyrant of Olbia – you can be king. *They worship you like a god.* You have made their city some-thing, and your army is now a strong one. The grain will make you rich, your hoplites will make you secure and your alliance with the Sakje will make you great.'

Kineas knelt and took her hands. 'I don't want to be rich,' he said, and even as he said the words, he knew that they were as true as they were trite. The image of a long trek east to fight Alexander at her side stretched away like a dream, and beside it, the day-to-day world of patronage and politics seemed like a nightmare. 'I don't want to be tyrant, or king. I want you.' He grinned like a boy. 'I have had a dream that I will defeat Alexander.'

She smiled then, and he feared her a little, because it was not the smile of love, but the smile of triumph. 'Then you shall have me, Airyanãm. And we will go far,' she said, and put her lips on his. 'Even to the mountains of the east, and Alexander.'

When they had made love again, she wrapped herself around him despite the damp heat and their sweat, and together they fell asleep. And no sooner had he acknowledged the pleasure of such sleep, her smooth, hard leg pinned between his, than instead he was ... *astride the tree, a branch clenched between his legs. Farther along the branch, two eagles demanded food from a nest between Srayanka's thighs. Their screaming demands drowned out her words. When he reached out to her, the larger chick nipped him, and he fell ...*

He glanced around, and all the warriors behind him were strange, all Sakje, in magnificent armour, and he himself wore a vambrace of chased gold on the arm he could see through the slits of his helmet. He was dry, sitting tall on a horse the colour of dark metal, and the battle was won, the enemy broken, and across the river, the survivors tried to rally in the driftwood and by the single old dead tree that offered the only cover from the bronze rain of Sakje arrows, and he raised Srayanka's whip, motioned three times and they all began to cross the river. He was ready for the arrow when it came, and he almost greeted it, he knew it so well, and then he was in the water – hands grabbing at him ...

He was dead, and walking the battlefield, but it was another battlefield, Issus, and the dead were rising all around him like men woken early from rest. And then they began to walk, rubbing at their wounds, some stuffing the intestines into their guts. They tried to speak but failed, and many shrugged, and then, Greek and Persian, they all began to walk away from the battlefield ... and they were joined by the dead of Gaugamela, more Persians and fewer Greeks and Macedonians, all shuffling along in a column of the wretched dead.

A single figure emerged from the column. He had two deep wounds, one in his neck and another under his armpit, and his breastplate was gone, and his face was slack and empty of feeling, rotted and black, but Kineas could recognize Kleisthenes, a boyhood friend who had fallen in a nameless fight on the banks of the Euphrates. Kineas could feel that Kleisthenes was sad. Indeed, sadness came off him like heat from a fire. His jaw, almost naked of flesh three years after his death, was working, but no sound emerged. He reached out a hand and rested his finger bones on Kineas's deeply scarred forearm.

'What?' Kineas demanded. 'Speak!'

Kleisthenes' jaw worked again, more like a man chewing meat than a man attempting to speak. His mouth opened, and sand came forth. The rotting figure gathered the sand as it vomited from his mouth, catching it in his hands. He held it out to Kineas as if it was a payment, or an offering.

Even in a dream, Kineas was terrified. He stumbled back.

'Wake up now, or die in your sleep!' said the voice of Kam Baqca ...

Noises in the dark, and too much motion, and the wagon moving as if a man was climbing aboard. Kineas rolled off the furs and his hand was on his sword as the heavy felt that covered the wagon was ripped back and an arrow skidded along his back with a line of pain. There were torches in the dark, and the glint of weapons.

Srayanka was just coming to her knees and he pushed her down as another arrow bit deep into the wood of the wagon bed. Kineas roared 'The dead!' in Greek.

A black shape came up on to the wagon bed with a sword in each hand. Kineas was still half asleep, his mind in another world.

The creature's face was black. The thing hesitated – an all too human reaction – and then he swung both weapons together. The fog of the dream dropped a little more from Kineas's eyes and he saw that his opponent was a man with charcoal on his face. Even as he realized this, he sensed that the man's clumsy attack was a distraction, and as he ducked and parried he turned his head to see another black figure at the other end of the wagon, illuminated by the oil lamp. It was raising a bow, also hesitating, as if unsure what to shoot.

Kineas didn't hesitate. He cut at his first adversary, a long overhand cut with a wrist rotation at the end, so that the man's clumsy parry failed to stop the reversed curve of the Egyptian blade from cutting into his neck. He fell without a cry, his head half severed and black ink pouring out in the light of the moon.

Kineas leaped back and cut at the archer, and his blow severed the bow at the grip. One end of the cut bow snapped back and raked his hand, making him drop his sword with the pain, and the other end slashed across the bowman's face. Kineas kicked him and the bowman fell back off the wagon. Another arrow whispered out of the darkness and passed between Kineas's legs.

'Alarm! Attack!' Kineas shouted in Sakje. He could hear sounds of movement from the fires around them, and shouts in the distance, but the attackers were silent and otherworldly, and the hair on Kineas's neck began to stand up.

Even in the darkness, he could see the hilt of his sword gleaming against the carpets of the wagon's floor, and he bent and seized it. The grip was slippery with blood from his wound, and he bent to wipe his hand. Srayanka rose with her naked back to him, a bow in her hand, and shot before ducking again behind the cover of the benches.

Out in the dark, a *man* urged a general attack. Kineas could hear him demanding that they all 'go together'. And argument – in Sakje. Human. Kineas took a deep breath and steadied himself, the last fumes of his dream forced down.

His brain was working. They were men – mere men, not vengeful spirits who would have no need for weapons and orders. And they cared nothing for him – they were here to kill Srayanka. That was the only explanation for the hesitation of the first attackers.

It appeared that Marthax had found a solution to the succession problem.

The plan and its execution followed each other in two breaths, and Kineas leaped down from the wagon bed and charged straight at the voice in the darkness. The Egyptian sword cut down a man who was just turning to confront his rush, and he pushed past the collapsing body and ploughed straight into a man in full armour. The man cut at him and their blades rang together as Kineas parried.

Kineas stepped back, placing the armoured man between him and a fire, so he could see. The man he'd cut down was screaming (no monster from the dark world, then), masking all other sound. The armoured man swung at him and Kineas retreated, ducking the heavy blows, but his ripostes fell on thick scale armour. He didn't have enough light for fine work, and he felt the press of time – at any second, he could get a blade or an arrow in the back, and his naked flesh made a better target than these black-painted attackers.

He caught the next swing on his sword, pushed the other blade high, and stepped inside the man's guard. Then he grappled the armoured man around the waist and threw him to the ground, where every scale on the man's armour scraped against his naked chest. This was the fighting that Greeks trained for, and Kineas knew there was no Sakje who could stand against him. Down to the ground – fingers in the nose, thumb in the eye, knee in the groin – a spatter of blood, the smell of shit and his man was dead. Kineas listened while he wiped off the gore of the man's eyes on the tunic under his armour and his gorge rose, because it was one thing to practise killing a man so close, and another to do it.

The wounded man was still screaming, and off to the left, closer to the wagon, there was fighting. He lost precious seconds finding his sword again and ran, terrified that he had taken too long and she was dead.

She was not dead. She was on the wagon, shooting down, and just below her, Philokles the Spartan stood with his heavy black spear. He had an arrow in his shoulder and another in his lower leg, and two dead men at his feet. A ring of adversaries stood beyond the reach of the black spear. There were more on the other side of the wagon, where Srayanka was shooting.

Kineas came up silently and cut, the Egyptian blade going cleanly through the man's neck, and then he cut again, low, severing the tendons in a man's legs. Then he bellowed 'Athena!' and Philokles made two rapid lunges with the spear. A man slammed into Kineas's side and he was suddenly in a mêlée, blades all around him.

'Apollo!' from the other side of the wagon. Diodorus's voice.

Kineas fell, both feet sliding out from under him – blood on wet grass – and a blade whistled through his hair. He rolled towards Philokles, rose to his feet and cut at a new adversary, who parried and came in close to grapple. Kineas caught at his sword hand and froze – it was Parshtaevalt.

'Kineas!' he said, and fell back. Then the two fought back to back for an eternity – perhaps a minute – their backs touching, the warmth of that touch meaning life and safety.

'Apollo!' again in the darkness, and then another and another, and the pressure on Kineas was lifting. He cut low – always dangerous in the dark – and his man went down with a grunt. Kineas leaned back until he felt Parshtaevalt's back, and then took a deep breath. 'Athena!' he called.

'Apollo!' came the cries – and then they were all around him. He pushed through them, a horde of Greeks and Sakje mixed. Urvara stood, as naked as Srayanka, a bow in her hand, with a ring of Grass Cats around her. Behind her, Bain, the young war leader of the Cruel Hands, stood with a bow, covering Urvara. He threw back his head and howled like a wolf.

Kineas had no time for them – he ran for the wagon.

Srayanka still stood in the wagon, beautiful and terrible by the light of the oil lamp. She had a shallow cut on her neck and it had seeped blood all down her right side, so that she seemed to be a statue in black and white.

'Marthax did this,' she said.

'You're alive,' he said.

'Marthax did this,' she repeated. 'He means war. Fool! Fool – why did he not talk to me?'

'He fears us too much,' Kineas said. He was conscious that they were both naked – indeed, everyone but the dead and wounded attackers was naked.

She nodded. 'Get me the chiefs who are loyal to me,' she said to Parshtaevalt, who had come up.

Kineas turned to find Niceas at his shoulder. The man was shaking his head.

'What do you intend?' Kineas asked the women he loved.

'To take the people who will go, and run,' she said. 'Otherwise, there will be war when the sun rises, and the Sakje will never unite again.'

'He betrayed us and his guest oaths,' Urvara said.

Srayanka shook her head. 'Perhaps.' She spoke rapidly in Sakje – too rapidly for Kineas to follow, and the younger girl nodded.

To Kineas, she said, 'Either this attack came from one of his men, and he will be forced to accept it in the day – or he planned it himself, and he has another thousand horsemen waiting to fall on us with the dawn. I am taking my people and the Grass Cats and any others who will come.'

'Now?'

'Now. I go north and east. I will ride north to the City of Walls. If they admit me, I will take money and grain. From there, I will follow the sea of grass.'

Kineas stood in the dark, still fogged from sleep, with the sick-sweet wash of combat in his veins, and tried to think. 'I will never see you again!' he said.

She smiled at him, and climbed down from the wagon to embrace him. 'That is the will of the gods,' she said. 'But I think that we are not two clansmen, lost on the plains. You are baqca and I am a priestess. You will see me,' she said. 'Go and reclaim your city. Then, if you wish it, follow me. You can go by sea to the Bay of Salmon – any Euxine Greek can show you the way. We will be slow – we will have many horses, and wagons, and children. If you miss us on the sea of grass, find us at Marakanda on the trade road. It is the greatest city on the plains.'

'Marakanda?' he asked. A city of myth. He shook his head. 'If I can catch you, so can Marthax!' Kineas said. His wounds hurt – the new ones, and the old ones more. But what she was saying made sense. And the plains were not as empty as he had once thought. There were roads and paths.

'Marthax will not want to catch me,' she said. She grabbed his head and pulled it down and kissed him until, despite his wounds and the blood on her, he was conscious of their nudity and the darkness.

'I must be the Lady Srayanka!' she said, breaking the embrace and pushing him away. 'Go!'

'Listen to me,' he said. 'Listen, my love – I can rally my men in an hour. Marthax will *never* stand against us – the Grass Cats and the Cruel Hands and my phalanx will break him in the dawn. You will be queen.'

She smiled – a smile that showed him that she had thought all of this through, and didn't need his political guidance, however much she loved him. 'I would be queen of nothing,' she said. 'This way, my child will be king. Now go.'

'Child?' he said, dumbstruck, as she pushed him away and yelled for Hirene, her trumpeter.

And then he was no longer a lover or a warrior, but a

general, and he had work to do. Srayanka's column, with herds of horses, goats and sheep, and a hundred heavy wagons, moved east just after dawn. Kineas's Greek cavalry shadowed their departure, and Ataelus's scouts watched Marthax.

Marthax was mounted, the rising sun flashing on his gold helm and his red cloak, and his warriors had their bows in their hands, but they didn't move.

The sun was high in the sky by the time Kineas's hoplites marched south, but they were going home and they were happy to be moving. They sang the paean as they marched past Marthax's men. They had fought Macedon together, and neither side seemed interested in conflict.

Kineas ignored Diodorus's hand on his bridle and his admonitions and rode clear of his column. He trotted up a short slope to where Marthax, massive and red, sat on his war charger – a great beast easily two hands taller than any horse in the army. Around him sat his knights and his leaders. Kineas knew them all. They had been comrades, until yesterday.

'Are we enemies?' Kineas asked, without preamble.

Marthax looked sad. He shrugged. 'Will you marry her?' he asked.

'The Lady Srayanka? Yes, I intend to marry her.' Kineas had a linen sack in his hand, and he toyed with the knot of the string securing the neck of the bag.

'Then we are enemies,' Marthax said slowly. 'I cannot allow you – the king of Olbia – to wed my most powerful clan leader.'

Kineas met his eyes, and thought of the last year – planning a campaign and executing it, with this man at his side, his humour, his great heart, his invincible size and clear head. 'You are making a mistake,' he said quietly. 'I am not the king of Olbia. I do not want your throne – and nor do you.'

Marthax – a man who never quailed, who knew no fear – glanced away, looking over the plains. 'I will be king,' he said. 'And I am not Satrax, to tolerate her scheming. She will wed me, or no one.'

Kineas shook his head. 'You are being a fool. Who is giving you this advice? She will not marry you – you don't even want

33

her! And her claim to the kingship is better. The first time you make a mistake, the tribes will desert you.'

Marthax turned slowly back to him. He shrugged. 'I have spoken my words,' he said. 'If she returns from the east, she will be my subject, my wife or a corpse.'

Kineas opened the sack and dropped the contents on the ground. 'She was almost a corpse last night,' he said.

Around them, the knights shifted and a murmur of discontent came like a breeze over grass.

Marthax looked at the head lying there. 'You have murdered one of my knights,' he said, but he appeared more confused than angry.

'This one attacked her yurt in the night,' Kineas said, pointing at the head of Graethe. 'He had fifty men. They are all dead.' Kineas looked around. 'You are making a terrible mistake, Marthax, and someone is leading you to it.' Kineas raised his voice. 'Let me be clear. You – and you alone – have split the clans. This one paid for his attempt to murder the lady. Now she is riding east, to fight the monster. You will let her go. *You will let her go.*' He took a deep breath. 'I am the lord of the walking spears, and of the flying horses. And I am baqca. Harm her on her march east, and I will burn your City of Walls, and no merchant will ever come to the sea of grass again.'

'Go and fuck yourself, Greek,' Marthax said, rising to his full height in the saddle.

'No gold. Nowhere to sell your grain. The end of your way of life. How long will you be king, Marthax? Will you last out the summer?' Kineas rode his horse right up close. Marthax towered over him, but Kineas was too angry to be afraid.

'Go, before we do you harm,' Marthax said through his teeth.

And then the child was there, pushing between the horses unseen. She stood by Kineas. '*He will pretend to be king until the eagles fly,*' she said. '*They will pick his bones.*'

'And take this carrion-imp with you,' Marthax said.

Kineas scooped the girl up, turned his horse and rode back to his column. She squirmed for a while and then dropped off his lap to the ground.

'I must get my horses,' she said.

Kineas let her go. A Scythian – even a child – was nothing without her horses, and Kineas understood the pull. Even as he watched her running across the grass towards the royal herd, he saw Prince Lot and the Sauromatae mounting up. They had fewer remounts and no wagons, and lived in tents made of heavy felt. There were two hundred of them, with another fifty wounded on travois dragged behind spare animals.

Prince Lot saw him and approached. His Greek was terrible and his Sakje stilted. After a minute, Kineas had gathered that the Sauromatae wanted to travel with the Greeks. Kineas rode on, calling for Eumenes. The boy – scarcely a boy now – had three wounds and was still in a wagon, but he was well enough to sit up and translate.

'He says, "I wish to travel with you. I spoke to the lady – she rides too fast for my wounded." He says, "Srayanka said that you would follow her by the Bay of the Salmon." He says, "I can show you the road, and my wounded will have more time to rest."' Eumenes listened to Lot's last phrase and gave a weary smile. He pointed at the fading dust cloud that was Srayanka and her clans. 'He says, "She should have been queen."'

Kineas smiled at the first good news of the morning. 'I will be delighted to have you with us,' he said. He repeated this until Prince Lot smiled broadly.

Kineas also had a handful of Sakje *prodromoi*. Ataelus had recruited them – almost twenty now – with liberal promises of horses, and made them into his own small clan, including his new wife. None of them had deserted, even the two Standing Horses, and they gave Kineas eyes far in advance of his little army wherever they marched. Another of old Xenopon's recommendations, even though the man had probably been too conservative to approve of Kineas's use of 'barbarians' for the role.

Kineas waved Ataelus in from his intense watching of the main Sakje host, and told him to include the Sauromatae in his calculations. Ataelus grunted. He rode over to the column of travois, where the adolescent girls rode lighter horses, with their bows in their hands.

'For them, for scouting,' Ataelus said. He spoke to Lot, who nodded.

Kineas turned to leave them to it, and started for the head of the column, but suddenly Ataelus's wife screamed a war cry, and other scouts were shouting. He turned his horse in time to see the lanky figure of Heron, the hipparch of the *hippeis* of Pantecapaeum, bringing up the rearguard. He wore his perpetual scowl as he watched his troop ride by.

There was movement from Marthax's camp. Out on the plain of grass, a dozen horses ran. Behind them came a troop of Sakje, all in armour. They were slower than the horses they pursued, and they were losing ground. Farther back, Marthax's main line had begun to move forward.

'Shit,' Kineas said. He knelt on the back of his ugly warhorse and tried to see through the dust already rising over Marthax's line. The man had three thousand cavalry – no more – and he couldn't hope to win a pitched battle against Kineas's hoplites and his Greek cavalry. But he could do a lot of damage by harrying Kineas's march. He could force Kineas to waste weeks. He could cost Kineas the city of Olbia and leave the army stranded on the plain, at the mercy of the winter.

It all went through Kineas's head in a few seconds as he watched a little girl on a white horse galloping towards him with a dozen more pale horses following her. The riders pursuing her were abandoning the chase as Heron's rearguard blocked their way, contenting themselves with curses and bow-waving. Heron himself continued to scowl as he shouted orders to his *hyperetes*.

Lot had formed the Sauromatae into a block and wheeled them into line with Heron's troop. The hoplites were already deploying to the right. Philokles the Spartan had taken his young men out of the line and was running to Heron, his transverse scarlet plume bobbing as he ran. The Greeks had been at war all summer. They could form line from column in any direction, at speed, without wasted orders.

Marthax's line halted well out on the plain, a good two stades clear of the Greeks and the Sauromatae.

Ataelus had an arrow on his string, and he was looking

at Kineas. Kineas shook his head and rode to the girl. 'What the fuck have you done?' he shouted at her, harsher than he meant.

'Taken what is mine, and what is yours,' she said. Around her milled two dozen horses, all white and flashing silver.

'You have stolen the royal chargers?' Kineas asked.

'My father said that after Satrax you would be king,' she said with the simplicity of childhood. 'Satrax is dead. They are yours – except for the white foals. Those are *mine*.'

Kineas was tempted to put her over his knee. 'Ares and Aphrodite. Heron – give me four men with a flag of truce to return these horses.'

Heron told off troopers, who looked afraid. He rubbed his forehead and allowed his bronze Boeotian helmet to dangle on its cheek strap. 'I prefer to be called Eumeles,' he said. 'At least in front of my men.'

Kineas smothered annoyance. Heron took himself very seriously, but when he wasn't acting like an ephebe with his first lover, he was becoming a fine officer. 'Very well, Eumeles,' Kineas said.

The Sakje host sat silently at a distance.

Prince Lot took Kineas's arm. He spoke quickly, emphatically, gesturing at Marthax in the opposite line.

Ataelus kneed his horse forward and translated. 'For saying, Marthax not king. Give horses, Marthax for being king. You for *making* him king.' Ataelus nodded.

The girl laughed. 'You don't want to be the one who makes Marthax king of the Sakje, do you?'

Kineas sat and cursed, but he didn't want to offend Srayanka. He wished she was there to advise him.

The two forces watched each other for an hour, and then the Sakje began to trickle away. They had discipline when they needed it, but Marthax's force was not as unified or as singular of purpose as Kineas had feared. Before his eyes, men and women rode off, collected their camps and departed – small lords first and then great lords. In three hours, Marthax had just two thousand horsemen.

At that point, Kineas ordered his line to form column.

He briefed his officers – Memnon and Philokles for the foot, Diodorus and Heron and Lot for the cavalry. They were careful and slow – forming a hollow square from a line was not child's play – and they marched with the spears on the outside and the cavalry in the middle with the wounded and the baggage.

It was late afternoon when Kineas began to believe he had broken contact. He knew how quickly Marthax could be on him if he wanted to move. The rain had started again, thunderclouds racing over the plains and pausing to soak the whole column and fill the river over its banks, so that brown water ran among the trunks of trees and washed more bodies off the battlefield, the ugly, bloated things passing down the river next to them.

'The glory of battle,' Philokles said by his side. He was watching two bodies bob in the current.

Kineas had halted his horse on a rise, just twenty stades south of the great bend. Philokles stepped out of the ranks of the phalanx to stand with him. In the distance, half a dozen Sauromatae girls sat their horses in a rough skirmish line on a river bluff, watching their back-trail.

Philokles pulled off his helmet and ran his free hand through his hair. Kineas ignored the Spartan's mood. 'If Xenophon had had a dozen Sauromatae girls, he'd never have had to worry about scouting.'

'And he'd never have written *Anabasis*,' Philokles said. His voice was flat.

Kineas laughed – his first real laugh of the day. 'I've spent all day thinking about Xenophon,' he said.

'Because we have to get to Olbia alive?' Philokles asked. 'Marthax won't follow us. His army is going home.'

'I saw,' Kineas said.

'You saw, my friend, but did you think? Marthax went to council to represent the faction that demanded that the war be over. Now he pays the price – even if he wanted to fight us, or Srayanka, he couldn't.'

Kineas hadn't thought of it that way. 'I knew I kept you around for a reason, Spartan.'

'I'm an Olbian citizen now,' Philokles said. 'Don't you forget it.'

They stood together as the army passed, on their way home at last, and the rain fell.

3

The late summer rain flattened the sea of grass and filled the rivers to a depth that only a mounted man could cross, even at the best fords. It washed away the blood and carried the glut of corpses at the Ford of the River God down to the sea, where the people of the city of Olbia watched them float by, bloated, gross and stinking. Being merchants, most of them kept a rough count of what they saw, and smiled grimly.

The rain fell for days, so that every hearth was wet and there was no place in a Greek house that was really dry, as woollen blankets and woollen tunics clung on to the damp. Smoke rising over the city told of fitful fires from sodden wood, and the scent of woodsmoke competed with the reek of wet wool and the underlying itch of wet manure.

Those who counted the corpses in the river looked at the gates and the roads beyond and wondered what had transpired on the sea of grass. They waited for word from their brothers, fathers, sons and husbands, lovers – virtually the whole free male population. A few had floated by. Women wept. Men looked at the citadel above them, with its Macedonian garrison, and their curses rose to heaven.

As the days passed and the rain continued to fall, the curses flowed like the rain. The imprecations began to flow by day and by night. A pair of Macedonians – farm boys, really, for all their airs – were caught in the agora and beaten by slaves. The garrison commander, Dion, responded savagely, throwing two-thirds of his garrison into the market at dawn and killing a dozen men, including a citizen.

After that, the city was quiet. Dion told the tyrant that he had the city cowed.

The tyrant called him a fool, and drank more unwatered wine.

Next evening, another Macedonian farm boy had his throat cut. The fools that did it dumped his body at the gate of the citadel. Dion gave his orders – in the morning, he'd make them rue it.

The rain had made the city wall slick. The men climbing along the wall in the damp darkness were grateful for the heavy hemp rope with knots every span, and even more grateful for the strong arms of their friends and slaves at the top of the wall. They were up in a few terror-filled moments – embraced – and gone into the dark.

'We're too far from the gate,' an older man said. His recent wounds pained him, and his temper – never really quiet – was savage. 'If they have archers on the walls, we're all dead.'

The men around him were leaning forward, keen as hunters, listening for any sound from the city below them. The nearest walls were two stades away. Every man stood at the head of his horse, both hands up, ready to stop a whinny or a neigh.

'Shut up,' the hyperetes said. 'Watch for the torches.'

'They ought to be in there by now.'

'Caught on the wall, maybe,' someone else said.

'*Shut the fuck up.*' The hyperetes' whisper carried all the savagery of his full voice.

Feet pounding through the lower city – too much noise, and no help for it. Wood slamming on stone as a woman leaned over her balcony to see what the fuss was and, seeing bronze, slammed her shutters home.

Breath hoarse, legs pumping, feet splashing through the wet ordure of the city without care for the slime. Shields pounding away against backs, the straps cutting a man's wind and leaving bruises on his shoulders. Eyes straining to follow the man in front, turn after turn, so that the long file of men wound like a worm through the slave quarter where most free men went only to get a quick fuck against a house, if that. Not this time.

The citadel – another wet wall of rock towering into the dark. And no ropes. No friends inside.

Of course, that was not exactly true.

The postern gate was open.

Dion could feel that the city below him was restless. He expected resistance. He was glad of it. Time to clean house.

'Follow me, boys,' he said to his men, a quarter taxeis of raw Macedonian recruits – just enough professionals to act as file-closers. There'd been talk – ugly talk – about the number of Macedonian floaters coming down the river, but he wouldn't hear it. Dion had his orders.

As his duty men opened the citadel's main gate, he turned to address those behind him. 'Kill everyone you find in the streets,' he said. His voice carried well in the rain, so that even the men pressed flat against the gate towers could hear him clearly. Their faces would have made studies for statues of Furies.

At a wave of his hand, their heavy sandals rang out on the citadel's arched roadway and Dion's garrison trotted into the lower city. Off in the murk towards the east, the sun was rising. Men could see the shields carried by the men in front as they ran, their heavy tread carrying a sound of menace.

A beggar was caught at the entrance to the agora and his guts tumbled out in his lap as Dion's sword opened him.

The pair of torches rose above the dolphin gate like a pair of red stars rising in the morning.

The horsemen mounted in seconds, vaulting on to their mount's backs with the practice of a summer of hard riding, no longer concerned about the sounds their horses might make. After a month, the time for waiting was over.

'Now,' ordered Kineas.

They rode down the long hill by the inner harbour and then straight through the gates, which stood wide open. There were bodies on the ground, but the horses didn't shy. The horses had seen corpses before. Their hooves pounded the ground and they were louder than the tramp of Dion's men, and more deadly, and where they passed they left only the silence of expectation.

*

In the citadel, no sooner had the garrison passed the gates than the men pressed against the wet rock walls leaped into the courtyard and butchered the watch. The men coming off the walls had been as raw as their victims once, but that was months ago, and the Macedonian farm boys died with as little regard as lambs at a sacrifice. A few had time to scream and one file-closer tried for the gate. He died with a heavy black spear through his back plate of tawed leather.

Dion cleaned his sword against the beggar's rag of a cloak and led his men into the clear space of the agora. He was intelligent enough to wonder why the agora was empty – not even a single merchant opening his stall – but the cowards had to know that he would come for blood. He formed his men in a tight phalanx. Their motions masked all sound, but something made him uneasy, and as the last man fell into his place, Dion called for silence.

Hoof beats.

Dion was just turning to bellow an order when a spear punched under his armpit. The point emerged through his neck and he lived only a few seconds – just long enough to watch the wolves fall on his phalanx. They looked like wolves ...

'Kill them all,' Memnon bellowed as he ripped his spear out of the corpse.

Kineas led his men up the road that ringed the citadel, still expecting a shower of arrows or red-hot sand, but there was a torch waving enthusiastically from the great tower over the arched gate and then he was in the echoing tunnel, his horse's hooves beating hollowly against the paving stones. Then into the citadel itself – new blood in the courtyard, a dozen Macedonians dead in their armour and Philokles with his twenty picked men facing fifty Keltoi of the tyrant's bodyguard across the courtyard.

In the cold iron dawn, Kineas could see the tyrant and his Persian minion at the back, shoving more Keltoi out of their barracks.

Kineas turned to Antigonus, Eumenes' hyperetes and one of Kineas's few original troopers. Antigonus was a Gaulish Kelt himself. 'Tell them to step aside and we'll accept their service. Or they may stand and die.'

Antigonus rode into the relative silence of the palace courtyard. Resignation could be read on every face – even the tyrant's.

The citadel had fallen. The sounds of a successful escalade were the background to Antigonus's voice. The road to the agora was full of city hoplites hunting the last of the garrison. The screams of the farm boys could be heard all the way across the river, and Dion's head was already on a pike over the main gate.

Antigonus spoke in the Keltic tongue of his fathers, gesturing repeatedly with his spear at the men behind him, and once at the tyrant.

The leader of the Keltoi, a tall, thin man in a heavy golden torc and massive gold bracers, stood forth, his heavy Thracian sword held comfortably in both fists. He had tattoos in heavy blue that ran up his legs, under his tunic, and emerged again at his neck to cover his face. He nodded easily to Antigonus and then to Kineas.

When he spoke, his voice was sad. His Greek, while accented, was good. 'We eat his food. We take his coin. We swear oaths.' The heavy Kelt shrugged. 'We die here.' He pointed with his sword at the cobbled courtyard of the citadel.

The tyrant laughed. It was a bitter laugh. He stood straight and came forward – a little drunk, as was his wont. 'Well, some things are worth buying,' he said from the safety of the last rank of the Keltoi. 'You came for my city after all,' he said to Kineas.

Kineas felt the rage of gods grip him. But for this man and his plotting, Agis and Laertes would still live, so would Nicomedes, and Ajax, and Cleitus. *And the king.* 'I came for you, traitor,' he said thickly.

The tyrant shrugged. 'Odd how the public interest and self-interest coincide. I don't imagine I could offer you gold to let me live?'

'Fight me man to man,' Kineas said. 'If you win, my men will set you free.'

He began to ride around to the left, to get a clearer look at the tyrant. At his knee, another horseman moved with him.

It was a foolish challenge, and he felt like a fool for making it. He could barely stand after his wounds at the Ford of the River God and the attack in the dark. Single combat was for young men who wished to be Achilles, not middle-aged men in love.

The tyrant glanced around and laughed grimly. 'No. I think not. Even if I won, these folk would butcher me like a heifer.'

Kineas shook his head in denial. 'Only a dishonest man fears the dishonesty of others,' he quoted.

The tyrant spat. 'Spare me your philosophy. And the rest of you – you plan to follow *him*? Will you be as loyal to him as you were to me? Eh, Kineas? Ready to ride the lion?'

Kineas sat straighter. 'I have no intention of taking control of the city,' he said stiffly.

The tyrant smiled. 'You lie.' He shrugged. 'But what do I care? Your ignorance will bring about the deaths of every man here – but I'll be dead. My share in this story ends here, doesn't it?'

The hippeis were calling for the tyrant's death. They began to chant. The Keltoi readied their shields.

'My ignorance?' Kineas said. 'Ignorance? I am ignorant of what sort of man would betray his own city to a foreign garrison! And I did not come to bandy words with such a traitor.'

The tyrant stood up straight, like a soldier on parade. He stood out from his Keltoi. 'Listen to me, you aristocratic bastard,' he said. 'The world is about to go to *shit*. When Alexander and Parmenion go to war – listen! The monster has lost his mind. We need Antipater! It will all come apart now – everything the boy king did will collapse like a cheap market stall in a wind – and all his wolves will fight over the spoils. Are you ready for that?'

Behind Kineas, Antigonus translated the exchange. The Keltoi chieftain listened patiently, his sword cocked back over his shoulder, a pose he could apparently hold for hours.

Behind the Keltoi, on the steps of the palace, the tyrant's Persian steward produced a bow – an elegant recurve bow that glowed with wax. He raised it at Kineas, but before he could shoot, he took an arrow in the chest and a second in the groin and he fell screaming. His squeals pierced the morning damp and made men – even hard men – flinch. The tyrant turned to glance over his shoulder. He grinned – a mad, death's-head grin. Then he seized a dagger from the belt of the Kelt nearest him and flourished it high like an athlete.

'Your turn, Kineas!' he shouted. 'By all the gods, Hama, I release you and your men from your oaths!' And so saying, he plunged the dagger into his own neck.

Close at Kineas's side, awaiting his chance, Ataelus the Scyth put his knees to his charger and it rose, rearing and punching both hooves like a boxer. At the top of its attempt to climb the heavens, he leaned out over his charger's neck and fired two more arrows over the Keltoi.

Unlike the Persian, the tyrant went down without a sound.

Antigonus spoke again in the guttural Keltish tongue. The chieftain, Hama, spared the tyrant's twitching corpse a respectful glance, and nodded.

'I think we live,' he said, and placed the point of his sword carefully on the ground. 'Our oath dies with him.' Around him, the Keltoi sheathed their weapons or laid them carefully on the wet paving stones.

Philokles walked over to the tyrant's corpse like Ares claiming his spoil. 'He died well,' the Spartan said.

'May I do as well,' Kineas agreed.

Kineas managed to order a guard to protect the Keltoi from harm before a mob of his own soldiers put him up on a shield and carried him off to the agora. And even as the city rang with his acclaim, he thought of Srayanka, already out on the sea of grass, travelling east.

Taking the city had been the easy part. Because Satrax the King was dead, and the Sakje alliance was shattered, and Alexander the King of Kings was out on the sea of grass, and the old gods of Chaos were laughing.

4

The funeral of Cleitus was a city-wide occasion. Almost every household had dead to mourn, between the battle at the ford and the storming of the city and the tyrant's excesses. The dead of the great battle were long since buried, and the trophy long since raised at the edge of a field of unburied enemies – a cursed spot to any Greek, and an uncomfortable thought – but the dead were still fresh in the memories of their city, and needed words said in public to mourn them.

Cleitus, who had once been the city's hipparch, and remained the leader of the aristocratic faction until his death, remained unburied, because the tyrant had denied his family the right to conduct the funeral. He had feared the public reaction.

Now Kineas had the tyrant's ivory stool. He did not wear a diadem and he did not reside in the palace – instead, he awoke as usual at the hippodrome barracks, where the tyrant's ivory stool leaned against the wall like a reminder, or an accusation. He was in some middle ground between the absolute power of the tyrant and his old role as hipparch and *strategos*, or military commander. He ordered that the funeral be a public occasion, and he was obeyed.

The army had been in the city for five days. There were Athenian ships in the harbour demanding grain, and the first boats full of grain were on their way down the raging river to the port. The autumn market was opening on the plain north of the city, although it would be weeks before cargoes could be gathered for the Athenian merchants, who owned the largest ships in the world. On the third night, he had gone to the stables and bridled the Getae mare and ridden her out of the dark gates, past all the farms, to the beginning of the sea of grass. As the sun rose, he sat at the edge of her world, and he reached out like a baqca ...

Across the plains that rolled under the new sun, past the camp

47

where Marthax chewed on the ruin of his plans, then north and east around the Bay of Salmon, and there she was, rising in the dawn, naked to the waist, cleaning her teeth with a twig, and she gave a start as he came near and grinned ...

He awoke cold, and tired like a drunkard, but he was happy again.

The next night, Kineas dreamed of Srayanka's tribes and their horses riding over the sea of grass, and of the dead, and of the tree. He tried to banish his dreams. He longed to be away into the dawn.

On the high ground north of the market camped the little army of Sauromatae. City slaves had built them cabins against the late summer rain, but Prince Lot's presence at his side served to remind Kineas, if he needed any reminder, that the sailing season was closing in, and he needed to leave soon if he was leaving at all. Five days in Olbia had revealed a host of reasons why he could not leave. The assembly had met twice and both times he had risen to announce his departure, and both times he had instead spoken of how many of the tyrant's laws had to be repealed, and how essential it was that the rule of law be restored.

On the fourth day, the assembly made him *archon*.

He went back to the barracks and talked with Philokles and Diodorus for hours, and then he sat on the ivory stool in the agora and announced the funeral of Cleitus.

The funeral day promised to be warm and sunny, and the procession began to form under the stars of earliest morning, the first stars and clear sky they had seen in days. Diodorus had the hippeis mustered before the first blush of dawn on the sand of the hippodrome. He had good officers under him, veteran hyperetes, and every man in the ranks had served in a battle – some in three.

Niceas grunted. 'They don't look the same as they did last year,' he said.

Kineas rubbed his chin. It was not a day for laughter, but he smiled. 'No,' he said. As he grew used to power, he was learning to say less and think more. 'No, they don't.'

Niceas grunted again. 'Weather looks better. Sky is clear.'

48

Behind him, the hippeis were falling in. Where five hundred had mustered on the morning of the great battle, fewer than four hundred would answer today.

The survivors of Cleitus's fourth troop – now under Petrocolus's command – were the strongest. They had come late for the battle and ridden only in the final charge, and despite having the oldest men, experience and fine horses had kept most of them alive.

But Nicomedes was dead – and his hyperetes for the third troop, Ajax of Tomis, lay in a canvas shroud, sewn tight, awaiting shipment to Tomis to be buried by his father. Their troop had fought alone against a tide of Macedonian horse, and died almost to a man. The survivors made a silent file in second troop.

Leucon had died in the rain and confusion of the night action, and Eumenes, despite three wounds and the treason of his father, sat at the head of first troop with Cliomenedes. Eumenes' father, Cleomenes, had been instrumental in handing the city to the Macedonians – either for personal gain or because he truly believed that Macedon promised the city a richer future. He had died out on the sea of grass, leaving his son a rich man, and a deeply unpopular one.

Clio was the youngest of their officers, Petrocolus's adolescent son, who had commanded the troop through the harrowing last hour of the great battle, and he was struggling to maintain authority despite his popularity and obvious courage. The two young men had all the youngest cavalrymen and his troop had seen the longest fighting, if not the hardest. The homes of the wealthy up by the statue of Apollo were still full of wounded from this troop, but for the moment, only twenty troopers sat behind them,

Only second troop, commanded by Diodorus and now holding all the mercenary cavalrymen, looked prepared for another day of battle. A summer of campaigning had made Diodorus into a fine commander, and Antigonus the Gaul was the complete hyperetes – calm, authoritative and efficient. His appointment made the integration of the tyrant's former bodyguard simpler, because he spoke their language and could claim some birth that impressed even Hama, their chieftain. There were almost a hundred of the Keltoi, and they were natural horsemen. Recent enmity meant nothing to them – more important were their endless taboos and rituals. A Greek officer might quickly have fallen foul of them. Antigonus had no such troubles. But for political reasons, only Hama and a dozen of his Keltoi rode in the second troop today. The rest were in their barracks. This was a parade of the victors.

And there was Heron. The tall young man was no less gawky in the saddle than walking the grass, and even the tallest of the captured chargers was too small for him. His troop – men of Pantecapaeum, a neighbouring city, and not really under Kineas's command – had also taken part in Nicomedes' desperate defence on the left of the army. They had been luckier – and broken earlier – and fifty saddles remained filled. But their victory was bitter-sweet. They were now exiles. Victory in the great battle had empowered the democratic faction in their city, and the troop of rich men – aristocrats to a trooper – was no longer wanted at home.

Kineas and Diodorus had been the victims of just such an event. They knew the sting of exile – the humiliation and the endless small slights that citizens imposed on stateless men. But Heron was a prickly fellow at the best of times, and he sat in his resentment, disdaining attempts to improve his lot, and his men followed his lead. They remained with Kineas because most of them had nowhere else to go.

Finally, formed on the far left of the line of hippeis, there were Ataelus's twenty Sakje, half of them women. They wore odd combinations of Greek and Sakje armour, rode expensive horses and were covered in gold. They were exotic and dangerous and they would march in the procession, despite the protests of certain city factions, as would the Sauromatae.

All the survivors had benefited from the battle by acquiring the very best of the Macedonian armour and the heavy Macedonian chargers. On the day of battle, the Macedonian horses had been starved and tired – but a month on the grass, even in the rain, had restored some of their spirit, and five days' access to the granaries of the city meant that every man was mounted like a prince.

Diodorus cantered up and gave a precise salute, his fist clenched on his breastplate. Kineas returned it.

'Rain's stopped,' Diodorus said. He grinned, his sharp features and freckled cheeks glowing with pleasure. He enjoyed command, and he worried less about the future than Kineas. 'Maybe there's hope after all,' he added. 'You look beautiful, I must say.'

'Why are you so fucking cheerful?' Kineas asked.

'I'm tired of rain. And Coenus is better this morning. His fever broke in the dark. He ate.' Diodorus tilted his helmet back so that his red hair showed at the brow. 'You have to see him. It's a gift from the gods.'

Kineas felt his mood lighten immediately. Coenus – one of his oldest friends, one of his best men, a scholar and a fellow exile – had been given up for dead.

So Kineas had a different look about him as he took his place at the head of the hippeis and led them out into the streets, through the gate and along the edge of the market to where the priests of Apollo waited with the phalanx – all the men of the city. There were gaps in the phalanx just as there were in the hippeis, but in his present mood, Kineas was glad to see that there were also men back standing in the ranks who had ridden into the city in the wagons of wounded.

Every morning another two or three of the wounded tried on their armour and either crept back to their pallets defeated, or fought their way through a fog of dizziness and weakness to attend the musters. The recoveries had peaked now. Kineas, who visited the wounded twice a day, had little hope for the men who continued to lose weight, or whose wounds were still fevered.

Sitalkes, the Getae boy, was one. Coenus had been another – with light wounds that had suddenly festered – and he had been down since the army left Marthax. If he had recovered, there was still hope for the rest.

Movement in the Sauromatae camp roused him from thought. Prince Lot was mounting a captured Macedonian mare. He waved to Kineas, and Kineas waved back. A glance over his shoulder showed him that Memnon was some minutes from having the phalanx in order. He pressed his knees against his own captured Macedonian charger and cantered painfully across the short-cropped grass, his hip burning with the rhythm of his unnamed charger's hooves.

Lot raised a fist in greeting. 'Rain stops!' he said in Greek. He pointed to the sky over Kineas's shoulder, where dark blue could be seen at the base of the sky in the east like the glaze on an expensive cup.

'Rain stops,' Kineas agreed. The Sauromatae had fought in every action that Kineas had led. Their superior armour and battle skills had kept many of them alive despite a battering, and most of their saddles would be full if they mustered. Their horse herd, bolstered by their share of the Macedonian and Getae spoils, numbered almost a thousand, guarded by shifts of well-armed young women, and they were eating Olbia's farmers out of their grain, yet another problem Kineas had to face.

'Rain stops and ground hard again,' Lot said. 'Hard ground makes good road east.' The Sauromatae prince leaned close. 'Need to ride – need to be home.'

Kineas switched to Sakje, a language where he was stilted and Lot was more fluent. 'At least a month until we ride, cousin.' Kineas had adopted the habit of addressing the senior tribal officers as cousins, elder or younger as age and rank dictated.

Lot had a magnificent, if barbaric, blond moustache, and his right hand parted his moustache and then twirled each end, a habit that was sometimes imitated behind his back. 'Need to ride,' he said in Sakje. 'My nephew worries me.'

Kineas shrugged. 'Nephew?' he asked, wondering which of the many Sauromatae or even Sakje counted as his nephew.

'My wife's sister's son. My heir. He worries me.' Lot stared out over the sea of grass as if he could see the man riding in the distance. 'Never thought to be gone so long.' Lot looked chagrined. 'Didn't know the sea of grass was so *big*.'

Kineas raised a hand to forestall him. Lot had done his

share – far more than his share – to win the victory at the Ford of the River God. Since that day, Lot had never ceased to press the Sakje and the Greeks to follow him east, where his tribe and the others of the Massagetae confederacy – the eastern Sakje – were hard pressed by Alexander. And the five days of waiting at Olbia was making him edgy.

'Patience,' Kineas said. 'Today we mourn our dead.'

Lot bowed his head. Then he waved to his own nobles, who began to file out into the column. Niceas had kept a space for them – they were aliens, but they were allies, and with Ataelus's little troop of prodromoi, they represented the whole realm of the Sakje out on the sea of grass.

A realm that might now be an enemy of Olbia. Kineas shook his head to clear it, because this was the day of mourning, and politics would have to wait.

Helladius, now chief priest of Apollo, joined him. Helladius was an old and very conservative priest, but he had held his ground in the phalanx. Memnon had noted that the old fool had ended the battle in the front rank and done his part.

'You will lead the procession?' Helladius asked.

Kineas shook his head. 'No. We will return to the ways of the city before the tyrant came. The priests of Apollo will lead, followed by the hippeis and allies and the phalanx, and then Cleitus's body and his honour guard. I will ride with them.'

Helladius nodded. 'The god smiles on you, Archon,' he said. 'I have interpreted the omens for you all summer, and I say that you are beloved of all the gods, but of Apollo and Athena most of all.'

Kineas narrowly avoided a cynical reply. Hubris was never becoming, and Helladius was not a sanctimonious fool. Or not entirely. 'Thank you,' he said carefully.

The funeral procession marched on time, because the army had a summer of campaigning behind it. The priests sang, and the phalanx caught the tune and sang with them, scandalizing the younger priests who had not served with the army. And then, as the procession entered the gates, Helladius began the paean, and all the soldiers took it up, thousands of throats straining to praise Apollo, the same chant that had settled their nerves in the last seconds before the Macedonian charge. Dolphins of gold rose on either side of the gate, and the temple of Apollo was visible at the end of the long street of the gods, and still the paean lifted to the heavens with its song of reverence and victory. Kineas found that he could not sing for the tears in his throat, and when he turned his horse to see the column he could see that many men were weeping openly as they sang, and yet the power of the paean waxed as if all the missing voices were there too, and for a moment the distinction between the world and ... *the world blurred and Kineas heard Ajax beside him, his pure voice full of pride, and Nicomedes' harsh croak in his ear, and Agis, who so revered the god, and many others.*

When the paean ended, so many men were weeping that it sounded as if the god was mourning, the sound of their laments echoing from the temple and across the agora, the sound magnified by the men too wounded to march but standing in orderly ranks at the foot of the temple steps, and the women, mothers and sisters and lovers and wives.

The troopers carrying Cleitus's ashes climbed the steps and placed the ashes where Kineas and Petrocolus had placed a bronze statue of Nike from Nicomedes' house. The priests sacrificed in the temple and blessed the people and the city, and then Helladius raised his arms and turned to Kineas.

Kineas dismounted from his Macedonian charger and walked up the steps, his thigh burning at every step and making his climb painful and slow. He stopped below the statue of Nike, so that her wings were over his head, and turned to the crowd.

'I speak to the whole city, the citizens and the wives and the mothers and the farmers and the smiths and the Greeks and the Sindi and even the slaves,' he said. A year of speaking in public had improved his manner, and the occasion gained him their utter silence.

'Nothing I can say will make the dead greater in the eyes of the gods,' he said. 'Cleitus, who gave his life to save you from the tyrant, failed because he was one man. But all the dead, together, drove the Macedonian from the field and slaughtered him. And all together killed the tyrant and freed the city. All the dead sacrificed themselves equally for the triumph of the city.'

He looked out over the agora with the feeling that he could see many men who were dead, and perhaps even some who were not yet alive. 'When we faced Zopryon in battle, no man flinched. The Sakje stood and the Greeks stood. The hippeis stood and the hoplites stood. The citizen and the mercenary stood together. Indeed, the slaves stood their ground, and this city has twice a hundred free men today because as slaves they did not cower.

'Virtue – freedom and liberty – is the concern of every man, not a few politicians or a few soldiers,' he said. 'I will chide you, Olbia, in full view of all the gods. You allowed a few men to make your laws and paid a few men to guard your walls, and those few became your rulers. Politicians and mercenaries!' he bellowed, and his words echoed off the walls.

'Cleitus died to pull down the tyrant – and failed, because he was one man, murdered for his voice. We waded in blood to stop Macedon – aye, and lost hundreds of the flower of this city's best men. But on our return, we overthrew the tyrant in an hour with a thousand willing hands helping us into the city and into the citadel. Women threw down ropes to the army. Slaves led us to the open postern of the citadel. Never let this lesson be lost on you, citizens of Olbia! Women of Olbia! Slaves of Olbia! In your hands are the keys to the city and the keys of your own chains!'

Chains chains chains echoed off the walls.

'Had Cleitus lived, he would now be archon,' Kineas continued. 'He was an honest man, a powerful speaker and a trained lawmaker. But he is dead.' Kineas paused, and then pointed at another Nike, also from Nicomedes' house, beside him on the steps. 'Had he lived, Nicomedes might have been archon. He desired the role with all his ambition, and he had the talents to lead the city to greatness. But he fell in the battle.'

Kineas looked out over the crowd, where men shouted 'Lead us, then!' as if they had been paid. He shook his head.

'I have acted as archon for a few days – to see the dead

buried, and to see good laws passed. But I will not be tyrant. And if I stay, either I will make myself your lord, or you yourselves will make me take the power. I must go east – to fight against Macedon, and to preserve the liberty you have just won. Our allies on the plains still need our help, and I will go with them. And when I return, you will be a strong state, with a free assembly, and I will vote my vote and grumble when my motion is defeated, drinking my wine in a wine shop and cursing that my side had the fewer voices.'

Then he told the story of the campaign, from the first rumour of Zopryon, to the assembly voting for war, through the campaign against the Getae and on to the last battle – a long story, so that his voice was hoarse when he reached the end. He named as many of the dead as he could – from young Kyros, who had been a great athlete, the first to fall in combat, to Satyrus One-Eye, who died in the courtyard of the tyrant's palace. He recounted their names and their deeds, until the crowd wept again that so many had fallen. And as he spoke, the sun rose to its full height in the sky.

When he fell silent, Helladius saluted the disk of the sun, and all the people cheered, and then they sang:

> I begin singing of Demeter,
> The goddess with shining hair,
> And Persephone, her daughter, fair—
> Slim-ankled, too. Hades took her,
> Zeus gave her to his brother,
> Far-seeing Lord of Thunder.

They sang the hymn to the end, and another to Apollo, as the sun rose strong on their faces. And then Kineas raised his arms for silence and summoned the assembly for the next day. He bowed to the grave markers of Cleitus and Nicomedes as if the men were standing with him and then he limped down the steps of the temple, mounted his horse and rode away.

That night, Kineas dreamed again of the column of the dead, and again a dead friend vomited sand – this time Graccus, a long-dead boyhood friend. But the tone of the dream changed, so that he was less afraid. And then a woman came to him.

'I have come to offer you a choice,' she said. She had the white skin of a goddess and she looked like his mother – or like someone else, someone as familiar as his mother.

He smiled at her in the dream because it was such a Greek dream, a welcome relief from the strain of the tree and the animal totems and the alienness that had infected his dreams since he came to the plains. She was dressed in a peculiar garment, a bell-shaped skirt and a tight jacket that bared her breasts. Kineas had seen such a costume on a priestess once, and on old statues.

'State your choice, Goddess,' Kineas said.

She laughed when he called her goddess. 'If you remain here, you will be king. You will rule well and wisely, and your city will be the richest in the circle of the seas.'

Kineas nodded.

'If you travel east, your life will be short—' she said.

Kineas interrupted her without intending it. 'This is Achilles' choice?' he asked. 'If I go east, I will live a short life, but a glorious one? And all the world will know my name?'

She smiled, and it was an ill smile, the sort that terrified men. 'Do not interrupt me,' she said. 'Hubris has many forms.'

Kineas stood in silence.

'If you go east, your life will be short, and no one but your friends and your enemies will know your name.'

Kineas nodded. 'It seems like an easy choice,' he said.

The goddess smiled. She kissed his brow …

He awoke to ponder the meaning of the first dream – a true one, he was sure. He needed Kam Baqca to interpret it, but it occurred to him that Helladius was not such a fool as he sometimes acted. The second dream needed no interpretation.

Kineas arose with the kiss of the goddess still lingering on his forehead and a sense of well-being, a very different mood from the day before. The sun was shining on the sand of the hippodrome. And down the hall, Sitalkes sat up in his bed and Coenus asked for a book, and the mood of the barracks changed as if the sun had come inside. Indeed, Kineas wondered if men were simpler creatures than he had supposed, that a day of sunshine could so change their mood, or serve to mend wounded men who had abandoned hope and turned to the wall, expecting to die. Men recovered in the citadel, and in their homes, as if the touch of the sun on their skin carried the healing of the Lord of the Silver Bow.

Kineas had a morning meeting arranged with the Athenian captains in his role as the acting archon, but well before that he donned his second-best tunic and a light *chlamys* and slipped out of the barracks alone. He purchased a cup of fruit juice from a stall in the agora, ate a seed cake in front of a jeweller's stall, purchased a fine gold ring for Srayanka and then climbed the steps of the temple of Apollo just as the morning prayer to the sun was finished.

Kineas waited until the last of the singers were clear of the vestry before he approached the priest, and he was surprised to see the young Sakje girl walking with the maidens.

The priest was putting away his shawl, examining the fine wool for cleanliness as he folded it.

'Helladius,' Kineas said. 'The Lord of the Silver Bow has seen fit to restore the sun.'

Helladius nodded. 'My lord withholds his anger.'

Kineas raised an eyebrow. 'Anger?'

Helladius shrugged. 'Who can know the thoughts of the gods?' he said. 'But I imagine that my lord was less than pleased at the unburied bodies at the Ford of the River God and withheld the sun, just as the Lord of Horses sent his waters to cover the death at his ford.'

Kineas nodded slowly. His mother and his uncles had been such believers – those who saw the hands of the gods in everything. 'It might be as you say,' he admitted.

'Or not,' said Helladius. 'I commit no hubris. What brings you here to honour my morning prayers?'

'Who is the Sakje girl?' Kineas asked.

'Her father was a priest – a great seer, despite being a bar-barian. His daughter is always welcome here.' Helladius smiled at her retreating back.

'You knew Kam Baqca?' Kineas asked.

'Of course!' Helladius said. 'He travelled widely. He

wintered here with us on several occasions.' He took Kineas's arm and led him into the temple.

'I think of Kam Baqca as a woman,' Kineas said.

'We knew him before he made that sacrifice,' Helladius said, and then shook his head. 'I don't think you came here to discuss a barbarian shaman, no matter how worthy.'

'I have a dream,' Kineas said.

'You have powerful dreams, Archon. Indeed, I saw when the Sakje treated you as a priest.' Helladius turned and began to walk towards the temple garden. 'Come, let us walk together.'

Kineas fell in beside him. 'Yes. The gods have always seen fit to provide me with strong dreams.'

Helladius nodded. 'It is a great gift, but I feel the gods' will towards you, and it is strong. I don't need to be a priest to tell you that the interest of the gods is not always a blessing.' He gave a half grin. 'The poets and playwrights seem to be in agreement on that point.'

Kineas stopped and looked at the priest as if seeing him for the first time. Helladius was hardly a humble man, and the wry humour he had just showed was not his public face.

Helladius raised his eyebrows. 'Do you receive more than dreams, Archon? Does the will of the gods come to you awake? Or the voices of the dead?'

Kineas rubbed his chin. 'You make my head spin, priest!' He looked around the quiet temple. 'I do not – how can I say this – I am not aware of other messages from the gods. But perhaps I do not pay attention properly. Tell me what you mean.'

Helladius rubbed his chin. 'Listen, Archon. You have priestly powers. I have seen this happen elsewhere – among the Medes it is common. Not every man with priestly powers becomes a priest. Do you know of all the types of divination?'

Kineas shook his head. He felt like a schoolboy. His tutor had taught him about divination. 'There are three types, I think.'

'You were tutored by a follower of Plato? Not a Pythagorean, I hope. There are as many types of divination as there are birds in the air, but I will tell you a little of the three main types so that you may be on your guard.' His voice took on a professional tone. 'My father taught me that there are three types of divination. There is natural divination – the will of the gods shown in the flight of birds, for example. I perform this rite every day. Or perhaps in the entrails of a sacrifice, such as I performed for you in the field. Yes? Then there is oracular divination – the will of the gods spoken directly through an oracle. These can be difficult to interpret – rhymes, archaic words, often they sound like nonsense or leave the hearer more confused by a riddle than ever he was by the question. And finally, there is the divination of dreams – the will of the gods spoken through the gates of horn into our sleeping minds.' Helladius shrugged. 'The dead may also speak in any of these ways, or rather, we may divine their speech. For instance, there is the *kledon*, where a god – or the dead – may speak through the mouth of a bystander, or even through a crowd, so that a priest may hear the speech of the god in random utterings.' He smiled. 'I am waxing pedantic, I fear. Tell me what you dreamed.'

Kineas told him his dream about his dead friends.

Helladius shook his head. 'I have seldom had such a strong dream myself,' he said in irritation. 'I see why the barbarians treat you as a priest. And you have had this dream twice?'

Kineas nodded. 'Or more.'

Helladius furrowed his brow. 'More?'

Kineas looked away, as if suddenly interested in the mosaics of the god that covered the interior walls of the temple garden. He didn't want to say that he had had the dream every night since the attack on Srayanka. Or that he *had* heard voices in the mouths of other men – the kledon.

Helladius rubbed his hands together. 'It seems possible to me,' he said carefully, 'that the dead of the great battle wish to be buried. And they speak through your old friend.'

Kineas nodded. 'I wondered. But I cannot arrange the burial of ten thousand corpses – even if I could call on the labour of every slave in this city. And today it seemed to me that Kleisthenes was offering me a gift, if only I had the wit to take it.'

Helladius nodded. 'My first interpretation is the obvious one. I am sorry to say that I cannot dismiss it just because its achievement is impossible – the gods make great demands. On the other hand, your thought about the gift is interesting. I shall pray, and wait on you later in the day.'

Kineas bowed. 'Thank you for your help, Helladius.'

The priest walked with him to the top of the steps. 'The former archon never came to the temple without fifty soldiers and a bushel of scrolls containing new orders and taxes,' he said. 'I wish you were staying.'

Kineas shook his head. 'I meant what I said, Helladius. It would start well. But in a year I would make myself king, or you would demand it of me.'

Helladius stood at the top of the steps, his pale blue robes blowing in the August wind. 'May I advise you, my lord?' he asked, and then, taking a nod for permission, he carried on. 'Men like you – it grows. The voices come more often, and the dead haunt harder.' He shrugged, as if embarrassed to admit even this much.

'What can I do?' Kineas asked.

Helladius shook his head. 'Obey the will of the gods,' he said.

Kineas nodded slowly. 'I do, to the best of my ability.'

'That is why you would have made us a great king,' Helladius said. He waited until Kineas was halfway down the steps, just even with the *stele* for Nicomedes. 'The gods love you!' he called, so that every man in the market on the temple steps heard him.

Kineas let a smile wrinkle his mouth. He didn't answer openly. Quietly, to the stele of Nicomedes, he said, 'The gods loved Oedipus, too.' He shook his head at Helladius. To no one at all, he murmured, 'Look how that turned out.'

5

His first official meeting of the morning was with the Athenian captains. He unfolded the ivory stool and took it outside to the sands of the hippodrome so that he could watch the morning drills while he heard the captains, and Niceas and Philokles stood on either side of him. The admiral of the allied fleet, Demostrate, stood to hand. He was a native of Pantecapaeum, a wealthy merchant, a former pirate and a pillar of the alliance that had defeated Macedon. And like Kineas, he knew that the war was not over.

The Athenian captains were cautious and deeply respectful, which made him smile.

'Archon,' their spokesman, Cleander, began, 'the blessings of all the gods upon your city and your house.' Cleander knew Kineas of old – they had shared a tutor during early boyhood. But he seemed to feign ignorance, either from respect or fear.

Kineas inclined his head, feeling like an imposter or a play-actor. 'Welcome to Olbia, gentlemen,' he said. 'May Apollo and Athena and all the gods bless your venture here and your journey home.'

They exchanged platitudes, religious and otherwise, for several minutes before Cleander got down to business.

'We know how hard the war has been on your city,' he said carefully.

Kineas fingered his jaw. 'Yes,' he said.

Cleander glanced at his companions. They were powerful men, the captains of Athens's grain ships, with large investments in their cargoes, even though none of them was an owner.

'We ask – respectfully – whether sufficient cargoes to fill our ships will be gathered before the end of the sailing season.' Cleander flicked a glance at the citadel, which loomed behind Kineas. *Do you have enough grain to feed Athens?* That was the real question.

Kineas nodded. 'The war has slowed the flow of grain from

the sea of grass,' he said. 'Many of the farmers had to leave their farms when the Macedonians advanced. And the allies needed grain to feed their army and to feed the horses of the Sakje.' This oblique hint – just the lightest suggestion of an alliance between the Euxine cities and the Sakje – caused a rustle among the Athenian captains. 'Despite this, I am confident that we will raise enough grain to fill your holds. The main harvest will not be in for a month. Your eyes must have told you that the war never came here – that our fields are full of grain, as are the fields on both banks of the river as far north as a boat will float. The grain coming to market now is last fall's grain, whose sale was interrupted by early storms and the rumour of war. It will trickle in, but the trickle will become a rush after the feast of Demeter.'

Demostrate cleared his throat, and then smiled when he had their attention. 'All the grain from the Borysthenes will come here to Olbia,' he said. 'And my city, Pantecapaeum, will have all the grain from the north that is brought down the Tanais river into the Bay of the Salmon. We are gathering our cargoes even now.'

Cleander smiled, as did the other captains. 'That is good news indeed. But a month is a long time for our ships to sit idle at wharves. Can you arrange for the grain to come more quickly? In past years, we have filled our ships *before* the feast of Demeter.' His tone carried the conviction that for the grain fleet of Athens, no favour was too small.

Kineas locked eyes with Cleander. 'No,' he said. 'There is not enough grain to fill your holds now.'

Cleander spread his hands. 'Archon, we are not fools. Even now, your market sells grain to the barbarians who camp north of the market – allies from the war. And you buy grain yourself. Send them home, and let us buy the grain. Athens needs the grain – right now.'

Now Kineas smiled. 'No,' he said. 'I'm sorry, Cleander, but I think I know more about what Athens needs than you. Athens needs a steady, strong ally on the Euxine, and she needs Alexander kept in his place – not looming over the sea of grass and all the eastern trade. My army needs to eat.'

'But our ships sit idle,' Cleander said. 'Perhaps,' and he smiled like a man of the world, 'perhaps you would prefer to sell us some of your private store of grain? You've been purchasing it for weeks.'

Kineas appeared to consider this for a moment. 'That is the city's grain, not my own. Or rather, the army's grain, purchased from the sale of the army's share of the loot of our victory.'

'Which you could now sell to us at a profit,' Cleander said.

'Except that I need that grain to feed the army,' Kineas countered.

'The army is home,' Cleander said. 'The need for grain is past.'

Kineas frowned. It was deliberate – he meant to intimidate, and he did. All the Athenian captains stepped back.

'You are in danger of telling me my business, Cleander,' Kineas said. 'I need that grain. And ...' he paused for effect, 'I need your ships.'

Cleander choked.

Kineas smiled and stood up. 'Cleander. Don't be a fool. I was born and bred in Athens and I would never harm her or her grain fleet.'

Cleander gave a sly smile. 'I knew who you were before I left Athens,' he said. He shrugged. 'Your Athenian birth might serve only to make you a worse tyrant. Think of Alcibiades.' He reached into his cloak and produced a scroll. 'I have a letter for you.'

Kineas frowned. 'From Lycurgus?' he asked. It was his faction, and Demosthenes', that had exiled him and arranged for his service to Olbia.

Cleander shook his head. 'From Phocion,' he said. Phocion was Athens's greatest living soldier. As a general, he had defeated Philip of Macedon, Thebes, Sparta – he was one of the finest soldiers in the world. And he was a friend of Alexander. Kineas had learned his swordsmanship at Phocion's hands.

He took the letter with something close to reverence.

Cleander laughed. 'Your father and Phocion were the leaders

of the faction that favoured Alexander,' he said. 'Imagine! And now you've destroyed a Macedonian army!'

Kineas shrugged. 'Phocion fought Philip, and they were guest friends,' Kineas said.

Cleander gave a wry smile. 'What would Polyeuctas say?'

Kineas grinned. Their tutor Polyeuctas, a pupil of Plato, had never ceased to harp on the evils of unfettered Macedonian power – and on the treason of Alcibiades. Despite being a venal man who took too many bribes, he had been a good teacher and an able politician. 'I think about him all the time,' Kineas said.

'And then we heard you were dead,' Cleander said.

'Pah! Not so dead,' Kineas said, and they embraced. 'Now that I seem less the foreign tyrant, perhaps you would care to lease your ships to me for a month,' he said. 'I have a great deal of Macedonian gold at my disposal.'

He outlined his proposition and the Athenian captains began to haggle – he was offering them good money for their time and adding to the value of their cargoes as well, but they saw further margin for profit, and the risk to their ships was real.

Cleander attempted to demand a reduced tax on grain at the dock, but Kineas wouldn't budge. The grain tax was the city's greatest revenue, but the possibility of loading large cargoes of the purest Euxine fish sauce fresh from the Bay of Salmon and the guarantee of escort from the navarch of Pantecapaeum sealed the deal. Cleander offered his hand, and they all shook.

'I hate transporting horses,' Cleander said, and the other captains agreed.

'I'm worried about the depth of water at the entrance to Lake Maeotis,' said another.

'Gentlemen,' Kineas said, rising from his ivory chair, 'those are professional problems, and I expect you to resolve them. We are agreed?'

Cleander shrugged. 'You drive a hard bargain – like an Athenian.'

Kineas laughed and they retired. Kineas grinned at Diodorus, who grinned back.

'You win the benevolent despot award,' Diodorus said. 'Played to perfection. I'll get you a mask and you can play all the tyrant roles in the theatre.'

'I'll settle for a cup of wine,' Kineas said.

His second official meeting of the morning was with Leon, Nicomedes' former slave. Leon waited for him in the portico of the barracks, leaning against one of the carved wooden columns and watching while the Athenian captains haggled. Indeed, he had gone inside and tasted the soup that simmered on the hearth, added a spice and brushed Kineas's cloak before arranging it neatly over the armour stand while he waited. Kineas caught his eye several times in an attempt to apologize, but Leon smiled wryly each time and found himself another small chore.

When Diodorus had brought Kineas a cup of wine and departed to see to some horse training, Leon finally stepped forward. 'Archon,' he said. 'I greet you.'

Kineas rose from the ivory stool and grasped his hand. 'Free man Leon,' he said. 'Citizen, if I understand yesterday's assembly!' The assembly had moved to make all two hundred of the army's freed slaves into citizens, less a patriotic gift than an acknowledgement that the holes in the phalanx and the economic life of the city needed to be closed up immediately.

Leon smiled. He was dressed in an elegant tunic, a fine piece of wool with a narrow green stripe at the bottom edge. It was a valuable garment, but it was also one he had owned when he was a slave. 'Nicomedes left me half his fortune,' he said without preamble.

Kineas put his hand on the big African's shoulder. 'Welcome to the hippeis!' he said. 'Can you ride?'

Leon met his eye. 'He left you the other half,' he said. 'In the event that Ajax died.'

'Oh,' said Kineas. 'Oh.'

Leon handed him a scroll. 'We are to divide his goods between us.' Leon looked away and then back. 'I *am* eligible for the hippeis. That is – very good. And yes, I can ride.' Despite his serious news, he smiled. 'In fact, all Nubians can ride.' His smile faded and became a frown. 'I cannot manage his business. He did business based on his own web of friends

– men who owed him favours, men who wanted his patronage. I inherit his money, but not his power.'

Kineas was still struggling with the shock of sudden wealth. 'You must be very rich.'

Leon shot him a look, even as he began to polish a helmet that had been left on a bench. '*We* are very rich.'

'He must have loved you,' Kineas said.

Leon rolled his shoulders as if shrugging off an uncomfortable cloak. 'I might say the same of you.'

'He loved Ajax,' Kineas said.

Outside, Diodorus and Niceas were shouting at each other about horses. Philokles pushed past them. Wearing a simple linen *chiton* and cloak, with a broad straw hat and a satchel of scrolls over his shoulder, he looked like a philosopher. Only the width of his shoulders and the exaggerated muscle lines on his arms suggested the monster he became in combat.

'He made me slave,' Leon said, and his voice quavered for the first time. 'And now he has made me rich.'

Philokles crossed the floor of the barracks to the heavy pitcher that was always filled with cheap wine and poured himself a cup. Then he poured a second and brought it out to Leon on the sand of the hippodrome. 'You look like you need this,' he said. 'I heard about your good fortune in the agora. Both of you. There's a certain amount of ... ill feeling.' He shrugged. 'But it is not universal.'

'I want to leave Olbia,' Leon said. 'I am sorry to intrude on you, Archon.' He drank the wine, flicked his eyes over Philokles and back to Kineas. 'I had to inform you, sir.'

Philokles dragged over a stool and forced Leon to sit. 'Drink your wine. The archon can spare you some time. You are, after all, one of his men.'

Kineas was still wrestling with the riches he had suddenly inherited. Leon's internal crisis was almost easier to bear. 'He says he can ride,' he said, and realized how inconsequential that was to Leon's revelation.

'I want to leave,' Leon said. 'I can't remain here, in his house, with his patrons and his relations.' He shrugged. 'It is not the life I want.'

'What do you want?' Philokles asked. He pulled up a stool and sat.

Kineas was staring at a wall-hanging, trying to estimate the value of Nicomedes' wealth and wondering what he would do with it. Leon's reaction was understandable – no man wants to be a slave, and Leon was clearly not slave-born – but Kineas found it difficult to understand the man's lack of feeling. He had never worn mourning, never appeared downcast, and Nicomedes had been a very popular man.

'I want to come east with you – with the army,' Leon said. 'In return, I will help to support the costs.' To Kineas, he said, 'Before I was taken as a slave, I was a warrior.' He gave a hesitant smile. 'And perhaps in the east I can make trade contacts of my own.' His face shut down, as if at a bad memory. 'Or find – a life.'

Kineas poured himself a cup of wine and drained it. 'Leon, you helped to save my army. You will always have my – obligation. Why ask me? Of course you can accompany the army – you are among the hippeis, now. You probably own more warhorses than a Sakje.' He shrugged.

Leon's mouth trembled. His eyes were full of tears and Kineas turned away to spare the man embarrassment.

Philokles put his arm around the former slave. 'Say your piece, Leon.'

Leon stood taller and shook his head. 'No. I am no weakling.'

Philokles drank off his wine. 'How old are you?' he asked.

Leon shook his head. 'Perhaps twenty,' he said.

'There is no shame in asking for protection. Kineas, pay attention. Leon needs your help, and he's too proud to ask.'

'Like some Spartans I have known,' Kineas said.

'It's an epidemic among Greeks, I find,' Philokles agreed. 'A pity it has spread to Africa.' He pushed the younger man forward. 'Speak your piece, boy.'

Leon took a deep breath. 'Nicomedes' lawyer wants me to divide the estate. I think he means to cheat me. As a former slave, I have no friends – slave or free. You are a fair man.' He glanced at Philokles. 'As are your friends.' He paused. 'I *have*

68

thought this through. I want to go east. But I want my fortune to stay here, and not vanish. I want to be a citizen when I return. If we hold things in common – your name and mine together – no man will steal from *you*. And they will think twice before they murder me.'

Kineas had never been a fan of slavery in any form, but Leon's description – understated as it was – that, left alone, he would lose the fortune and perhaps his life – brought home just how effective slavery was at robbing men of their dignity and rights. 'Murder you?' he asked, surprised. 'Slaves are freed and become rich all the time.'

Philokles snorted like a warhorse. 'No, my gullible Athenian friend. People talk about slaves being freed and becoming rich all the time. Such slaves are the supposed cause of bad politics and the butt of comedians – but have you ever met one?'

'Thais was a slave, before she became a *hetaira*,' Kineas said. He shook his head. 'Point taken.' He looked at Leon. 'I knew I disliked slavery. Very well – are they really proposing to murder him?'

'Nicomedes' nephew, Demothenes, was just discussing it in the agora,' Philokles said. He gave Kineas a serious look, which Kineas interpreted correctly.

'Very well,' Kineas repeated. He felt a vague anger, the sort of feeling he had when he was cheated in the agora, lied to about the quality of wine or the age of some fish. He rose and took Leon's hand. 'Philokles has been a lawyer. Let him draw up a document of alliance. I seem to remember that you have some skills at mathematics?'

Leon inclined his head. 'I do. And hard won they were.'

'Help me compose a *logistikon* for this little army,' he said. 'And then you can help me spend some of our money.' He put his hand on the boy's shoulder. 'Welcome to my staff.'

His third meeting was the hardest in every way – harder still for being so unexpected. Leon had his head down over a scroll of numbers and Philokles had gone to shelve the works he had purchased in the market when Sitalkes, still hobbling from his wound, leaned in the door of Kineas's private office, where the archon sat with his own bag of scrolls.

'There is a gentleman to see you,' he said. He was afraid, or deeply moved.

Kineas could see Arni, another former slave, past Sitalkes' shoulder. He rose, but he was unprepared for the man who entered.

'Isokles!' he said. Isokles was the father of Ajax. Ajax, who was dead, his body wrapped in linen, embalmed. Who had died serving Kineas, fighting for Olbia, a hero.

The man's face was red from grief, his eyes haggard. 'Kineas.' He stood silently in the door. 'My son is dead.' The words tailed off, and the man stepped forward and put his arms around Kineas, and wept.

Niceas, who had also loved Ajax, took the father away and left Kineas in peace, so that he could read the letter from his boyhood hero.

Phocion of Athens to Kineas, son of Nicocles, greeting,

Fate, which cast you as a soldier of Macedon and then as an exile, now has raised you high. We hear the reports of your generalship for Olbia, and of your defeat of forces sent by Antipater to conquer the Euxine cities.

Fools here prate of war with Macedon. The notion that Athens is a power in the world dies hard, and men, whether old or young, will deceive themselves about the power of their city, even when I offer them the example of Thebes.

I write to you not as a supplicant, nor as a friend of Macedon, although either role might suit me. Instead, I write as the man who taught you to use a sword. The anti-Macedon party claims you as if you were their possession, their slave, and claims all of your actions as their own. They will ask you to gather your army and march into Thrace against Antipater.

When they exiled you, and then sent you to Olbia, you were a tool – a sword. But now that you are a commander, you are the man who holds the sword. Beware what you cut.

Please send my greetings to young Graccus, and to Laertes, son of Thallus, and Diodorus, son of Glaucus, and Coenus the Nisaean.

Kineas read Phocion's letter with pleasure, because he could hear the man's growl as he said the words aloud, and he could see on the scroll where words had been scraped out and others added with care. Phocion was the greatest Athenian soldier of his generation, perhaps of all time, and one of his father's closest friends and political allies.

The second scroll was from Lycurgus, or rather from a scribe in his service. It had no greeting, and no salutation.

Your exile will be lifted immediately. Consider the restoration of Amphipolis your next task, and Athens will again be great.

Amphipolis was an Athenian colony in Thrace, long since taken by Macedon. The recovery of Amphipolis – an old ambition of the Athenian assembly – would require the complete overthrow of Macedon as a power. Kineas made a face.

Diodorus came in from the exercise field fingering a bruise on his arm. 'Ares is my witness, I need more time to heal. Little Clio just pounded me on the palaestra floor.'

'The summer has put muscle on the boy, and you are getting old,' Kineas said.

Diodorus winced.

'Here is something that will lift the sting,' Kineas said, holding out the letter from Phocion. Diodorus read it while drinking wine, then sat and drank again. 'He can't have known of the battle yet,' he said.

Kineas handed over the other message. 'It is not a long journey from the battlefield to this city by river. Nor to Athens, by sea, for a swift ship.'

Diodorus shook his head. He began to read.

Kineas rubbed his beard. 'Something going on here that is beyond me,' he said. 'Amphipolis? Are they insane?'

Diodorus put down the second scroll. 'Yes,' he said. 'I fear that Demosthenes and Lycurgus are so desperate to restore their party that they will dare anything. And we cost them nothing. They can cast us as dice and pay no political cost.' He looked at the scroll. 'Did they lift all of our exiles, or just yours?'

'All of us,' Kineas said. 'Poor Laertes.'

'He'd have done anything to win praise from old Phocion,' Diodorus said, and then he grinned. 'So would I.'

Kineas nodded. 'I thought it would make you feel better.'

'You won't take us to war in Thrace?' Diodorus asked.

Kineas shook his head. 'I'm going east,' he said. 'And if I can find the money and the men, I'll take an army.'

Diodorus picked up the letter from Phocion and pointed it at Kineas. 'Against Alexander?'

Kineas narrowed his eyes, squinting against an invisible sun. 'Against Alexander,' he said. And then, because he and Diodorus were closer than most brothers, he grinned and said, 'To Hades with Alexander. I want Srayanka, and to keep her, I'll war down invincible Macedon. I swear that I would storm Olympus.'

Diodorus grinned, and put a hand on his knee. 'We all know,' he said, and then avoided Kineas's blow.

Isokles' enduring grief did not pass in a day. Kineas sent the prodromoi out to find the best landings on the Bay of Salmon, and still the man grieved. Kineas began the complex problem of moving men and horses by ship, sending grain and cash to the selected landing sites, and still Isokles grieved. He moved listlessly around the barracks until Leon moved him to Nicomedes' house – Kineas's house, now. He came to the barracks every day and sat with the veterans to hear tales of his son – tales every man had to tell. Ajax and his relentless heroism were part of the tradition of the company. The boy had been reared on the heady wine of the Poet and the feats of Achilles had fired his blood. He had left a trail of single combats and brilliant exploits across that bloody summer, and his father heard them all, embellished by the passage of time, until Ajax seemed ready to take his place with the heroes of the *Iliad* – a place accorded to him by every trooper in the hippeis.

But after three days of hearing his son praised and drinking wine, Isokles pushed his way into where Kineas was surrounded by his staff, reading lists of goods to be shipped with his little army, and exploded like a nest of wasps hurled on to the floor.

'He didn't *need* to be a hero!' Isokles shouted without preamble.

Diodorus sprang to his feet – Isokles had the gait and the look of a madman, his eyes were wild and he had a sword.

Kineas put a hand on his friend's sword arm. 'It is grief,' he said.

Isokles was yelling, the sword almost forgotten as he shouldered his way towards Kineas. 'He was handsome and young! He was well loved, smart enough at business! I sent him to you for a single summer, to knock the foolishness from his head, and he is *dead*. Dead for ever! Dead in a war that was nothing to him!' Niceas grabbed him from behind, pinning his arms, but Isokles thrashed, nearly breaking Niceas's grip – not an easy thing to do. Philokles tackled him around the waist and Isokles hammered his elbow into the Spartan's face, breaking his nose in a fountain of blood.

'You killed him! All of you, with your talk of glory and honour!' Isokles spat the words *glory* and *honour* like poison.

Kineas considered reason. He had warned Isokles that his son might die, a year or more ago at a pleasant symposium in Tomis. But Isokles was beyond reason. And although Kineas had a lifetime of practice at watching those he loved die, and moving on, the death of the golden Ajax had cut at him too, so that he could seldom pass the room where the man's body lay wrapped in linen without touching it or shedding a tear.

'We all loved him,' Kineas said quietly.

'If you *loved* him he wouldn't be *dead*.' Isokles came to a stop in the middle of the room, with Niceas pinning his arms and Philokles, his face a mask of blood, hanging gamely around his waist. 'You *used* him for his heroism like other men use a prostitute for her sex.' He wept bitterly.

That was a charge that bit deeply. Ajax's relentless heroism had been a foundation of the *daimon* of the hippeis.

Kineas was silent. He didn't have an answer for Isokles' grief, and he felt the justice of the man's charges. He had never wanted to take Ajax, but he had wanted the boy's youth and enthusiasm for his company and for his own morale.

Isokles had stopped struggling now. He stood in the middle of the barracks floor, weeping. 'All of you have stories of his heroism. He might have died in any of them. You revelled in it – you stood back and *watched* as he threw himself at death.'

Niceas was right at Isokles' ear – he had the man's arms from behind. 'Your son was a great man,' he said. 'But you're a fucking idiot.' He took a deep breath. Isokles sagged in his grasp. 'We told your son every day to keep his head down and stop pushing himself at the gods.' Niceas's voice broke, and he, too, began to weep. 'How many times?' he cried, as he shook the father. 'How many times did I tell him to watch his own back and mind his place in line?'

'The night before the great battle,' Philokles said, his nasal consonants broken like his nose, 'Kineas told him to grow up and stop acting like an idiot.'

Leon, who had known the boy in a different way, spoke with the hesitation of a former slave. 'My master – Nicomedes – asked him many times to take care.'

'If Nicomedes were alive, I would kill him,' Isokles said. 'He bears the responsibility above all.'

Philokles, who had worn the wreath as the army's hero himself, rose to his feet. 'He burned very bright,' he said. 'He burned bright in virtue and honour and died young, and he will live for ever with the gods.'

Isokles, turned sane and grief-wracked eyes on him, the orbs white stele in the red wreck of his face. 'Keep your philosophy, Spartan. He is dead. He might have lived and burned just as bright, growing wheat and rearing children in the sun.'

Philokles nodded. 'Or disease might have crippled him, or accident. Or he might have drowned on a ship. He chose his way, Isokles, and despite all your sorrow, you are unjust to us who were his friends. He chose the manner of his life and death – more than most men, almost like a god. I honour him.' Philokles shrugged. 'He loved war. It is a terrible, stupid thing to love, and it showed its true face by destroying him.'

Isokles and Philokles stood nose to nose, the one crying tears from red eyes, the other still pouring blood from his nose so that he seemed almost to cry tears of blood.

And then Isokles fell forward into Philokles' arms.

And they all wept together.

6

After grief, the hardest part was arranging who would go and who would stay. Many citizens – most of the hippeis – had little interest in further campaigning. For rich men, they had seen more war than they ever expected. Like most veterans, few of them had any inclination for more. Among the officers, all were either men of consequence or young men likely to rise as a result of their military service. The campaign against Alexander would do nothing to add to their civic laurels and their fathers were not eager to see them march. Indeed, it was only as a tribute to Kineas's service to the city that the assembly voted to allow the expedition at all – and more than a few men rose to speak against it, led by Alcaeus, who bore Kineas ill will for his discipline during the campaign. For the first time in months, Kineas was referred to as an adventurer and a mercenary – charges that he met by rising and publicly renouncing the archonship. The city demanded that the army be sent 'to open trade routes in the east'. But the men who were going called it what it was.

'We're going to fight Alexander,' they said in the agora.

In the end, the expedition received the grudging sanction of the city, and later that of Pantecapaeum, Olbia's sister city to the east.

Among the younger sons, there were quite a few who were willing to follow Kineas anywhere, and all of Kineas's professional soldiers were content to go – soldiering was what they knew, and there was not likely to be another conflict around Olbia in the near future. Rumours from the plains came down the river with the grain, suggesting that Marthax no longer had any force in the field, and that every chieftain had gone home to see to his farmers and his grain as Philokles had predicted. It was also said that Macedon had a war against Sparta to prosecute, and no men to spare to avenge Zopryon.

Best of all, in the eyes of the assembly, Kineas proposed

to take the Keltoi with him. That they yet lived was a sore subject to the more democratic elements in the city, as they had been the tyrant's tool of oppression for five years and more. Many felt that they should have been massacred with the Macedonian garrison. Their presence in the hippodrome was more fodder for Alcaeus and his new allies. They were big men, Gauls and even Germans among them, and they scared the Greeks and the Sindi.

Memnon's original three hundred, the first mercenaries the tyrant had hired, were all citizens now – but citizens without a trade. Memnon remained the commander of the phalanx, and he had told Kineas privately that he intended to stay behind, but that he had no hesitation in allowing his lieutenant Lycurgus or any of his men to sign on for the expedition to the east. The mercenaries had been hired to oppress the population, and later kept on to stiffen the raw men of the town. But the men of the town were all veterans now, and the mercenaries had little to do and no one to oppress.

And of course, some of the poorer citizens, or men just on the edge of poverty, saw the expedition as a chance for regular pay and a life they'd grown accustomed to in the summer.

Kineas had seen it all before, all his life. War begat war, and men with a taste of victory and plunder took to the life of the soldier eager for more easy gold, casually forgetting the nights in the rain and the pain of wounds and the constant fear.

In the end, he mustered three hundred 'Greek' horse under Diodorus, well mounted and well led, a better force than any squadron of mercenaries under the circle of the heavens, with the Keltoi in the ranks and all of Heron's exiles. He had another three hundred infantry – all hoplites – under Lycurgus, with Philokles refusing rank but accepting some nebulous role. The loot of Macedon allowed Kineas to mount them all on mules, and the riches of Nicomedes allowed him to imagine that he could keep them all fed.

He also had fifty Sindi, the survivors of the company that Temerix had formed and still led. They were *psiloi*, armed with Sakje bows and heavy axes, tattooed men who feared nothing and looked for death and served as skirmishers for the phalanx.

Then there was Prince Lot and the Sauromatae, two hundred knights in the heaviest armour on the plains.

All told, with the inevitable tail any army carried, he had almost a thousand mouths to feed and more than two thousand animals to move. Only an Athenian grain fleet had the capacity to carry so many and the food to supply them, even for a week. Luckily, he had one to hand. He still worried about food and fodder for the march, and despite some chests of gold and a great deal of silver, he knew that eventually he would be forced to seize food to continue – a prospect that frightened him.

He had already sent Ataelus with his scouts and a dozen Sauromatae in a galley to locate camps on the shore of the Bay of Salmon and to pick a route inland. Before the assembly met, he sent Eumenes with Arni and a dozen Keltoi troopers to visit Pantecapaeum, Gorgippia on the east coast of the Euxine and even Dioskurias to the south by ship, with orders to buy cattle and get them driven to the Bay of Salmon. Eumenes needed to be out of the city anyway – the political factions were out for his blood because of his father's treason, or so they said. Every day there hurt him more, and his presence was being used against Kineas politically. Someone was aiming at Kineas.

Already.

Some days he wondered why he was going, and why he was leading a thousand men to the same fate. He was rich, and powerful – in the way that Greeks accounted power. He could be tyrant. He could be king.

And his death awaited him in the east.

But so did Srayanka. And the sniping in the assembly was already getting to him.

The Battle of the Ford of the River God was only two months past, and already the assembly had returned to its traditional bickering, the unanimity of the early summer vanished with the threat of Macedon. Because Kineas had already relinquished the title of archon and the possibility of being tyrant, smaller fish began to circle the ivory stool, looking for power. Kineas said as much to Philokles.

'Fish, you say,' Philokles responded. They were seated together in the assembly, which had gathered in the hippodrome because of the seating – and because the balance of power of the city had shifted away from the citadel. 'Vultures, more like.'

Demosthenes, Nicomedes' nephew, had performed the political acrobatics of converting himself, overnight, from an aristocratic snob who used his power to avoid military service, to a full-blown democrat bent on restoring complete power to the assembly. The fact that the man had avoided service with the hippeis and had seen no action over the summer sat ill with many of the assembly, but political memory was short and Demosthenes promised action on a number of fronts that would please the voters – the men in the phalanx. And when Alcaeus denounced Kineas for his anti-democratic harbouring of the Keltoi and 'Cleomenes' traitor son', it was Demosthenes who rose to his feet amidst the hissing to support him.

One of his first proposals was that Kineas's expedition to the east be held back until Kineas had cleared his accounts with the city. This proposal was met with another chorus of hissing when he first proposed it, but by the third meeting of the assembly, enough wine had passed enough lips for the idea to appear to have some merit.

Kineas sat and writhed like an unhappy child through the rest of the day. The resolution to call for his accounts failed by a good margin – but it had not been hooted down.

'Ares and Aphrodite!' Kineas said as he threw his cloak at his bed. 'Accounts? What accounts?'

Philokles smiled, rubbing his beard. 'I imagine that the honoured Demosthenes knows full well that we kept no accounts.'

Diodorus came in with his hetaira, who called herself Sappho, on his arm. She was an elegant woman of thirty, with good bones, a long nose and an imperious air that belied both humour and real learning. Diodorus had purchased her contract with his loot from the battle, and seemed satisfied with the exchange. 'Bad day in the assembly?' Diodorus asked. His freckles burned as he grinned.

'Why don't they ask at the citadel for accounts?' Kineas said, his voice as close to a whine as his men had ever heard.

Diodorus shrugged. 'Demosthenes doesn't want to see the accounts. He wants to hold you and your expedition hostage until you give him something.'

Kineas poured wine from a ewer and drank it off, glaring at all of them.

'His uncle's inheritance, perhaps?' Sappho asked. Her plucked eyebrows lifted. 'Would someone pour *me* a cup of wine?'

'Well, I am an idiot,' Kineas said, brought up short. 'Of course that's what this is about.'

Philokles looked at him as if he had two heads. Diodorus cocked his head to one side as if he was a dog examining a particularly good bone.

Kineas shook his head. 'No, I didn't get it.'

Diodorus shook his head. 'Sometimes, I think it's good for all of us that you chose not to be tyrant.'

Kineas felt the chagrin of a man who had failed to see a fairly simple stratagem. 'I've had a great deal on my mind these last two weeks.' It sounded weak, even to him. 'Can he carry the assembly?'

Diodorus snorted and Philokles echoed the sound. 'If you continue walking around with your head in the clouds, looking hurt and being silent, then yes, I suspect he will eventually carry the assembly. On the other hand, if we lay out a few silver owls on wine for the voters and start reminding them that Demosthenes is a coward and a pompous ass, he'll probably fade away. Hell, they all served with Alcaeus. They'll remember that he was an idiot without much prompting.'

Philokles shook his head. 'Demosthenes won't simply fade away. He's already got his claws into the traitor Cleomenes' political patronage – and he inherited a great many of Nicomedes' clients, even if he didn't get the money.' He paused. 'Not that I'm against what our fox here suggests. When

Odysseus says to make fire-hardened sticks, mere mortals don't refuse to build a fire.'

Sappho drank her wine, watching them. Kineas barely knew her – Diodorus had introduced her, and she sometimes sat in a chair during their symposia and sang or played on the kithara, but he only guessed at her intelligence. She was another Theban – sold into slavery by Alexander. She was quiet, and her flows of good humour could be interrupted by sudden moments of deep unhappiness. But something in the way she looked at them across her wine cup suggested wisdom.

'You have a suggestion, Despoina?' Kineas asked.

She shook her head. 'It is not my place,' she said carefully.

Diodorus came up and took her elbow. 'Sappho is as wise as any woman I have met – before she was enslaved, she was the daughter of a boeotarch of Thebes and the sister of another.'

Philokles smiled. 'I am from Sparta, where women speak their minds and men listen,' he said.

Sappho held her head up, thanking Philokles with a small smile. 'Well, then – Demosthenes has help. And money. Deeper pockets than yours, lord, even with the money that Nicomedes left and with your share of the spoils. And he seeks to prevent the expedition because someone behind him wants it stopped.' She regarded Kineas, and the weight of her eyes reminded him of Scythian women. He couldn't remember a Greek woman holding his eye in such a way. 'I have reason to hate Alexander, and I will do my all to see that he goes down choking on blood and cursing the gods. If I can be of aid against a slug like Demosthenes, pray command me.'

Kineas stroked his chin. 'So if we spend money on buying votes, he'll outspend us.'

Sappho shrugged. 'I think he's a deeper player than you think – or his master is. I think that he seeks to provoke you. He doesn't expect to win this round, although he'd like to. He probably *wants* you to go on this expedition – while you remain, he'll never have any power here. But it will be enough for him to start a story to your discredit, which he can use against Petrocolus and his son Clio when you leave.' She raised a plucked eyebrow. 'Am I not correct in assuming that you intend Petrocolus and his son to hold power here in your absence?'

Diodorus nodded. Kineas noted that although Sappho looked as if she had more to say, Diodorus cut her off without a second thought. Kineas saw the cloud pass over Sappho's features even as Diodorus began.

'Yes!' he said. 'Whatever Sappho thinks – and I'm sure she knows a great deal – Demosthenes is the sort that Pericles called an "idiot". Out for himself and only himself. He seeks to discredit you so that, when you are gone, he can work to reclaim the inheritance – and perhaps use the case as a step-ping stone to fill Petrocolus's sandals.' He turned to Sappho. 'Who is the man's master? Surely not Alcaeus?'

Sappho shook her head. 'I do not know. But Alcaeus's wife is Penelope, and she inclines – how may I say? – to the company of women. Through her I have learned what I have said. If I learn more, I will see to it that you gentlemen are informed.'

Diodorus gazed at her with unfeigned admiration. 'I have always fancied political women,' he said. 'The company of women, indeed.'

Kineas rubbed his beard and looked at Philokles.

Philokles shrugged. 'Spartan solution,' he said.

Kineas looked a question.

'Kill him,' Philokles said.

Everyone in the room breathed in sharply, except Philokles, who poured himself more wine and chuckled. 'A few days ago you held ultimate power in this town. In point of fact, you still do. Don't play Athenian games with the wanker. Summon him for military service, and if he refuses, get the assembly to vote a punishment.'

They all spoke together. Diodorus shuddered at Philokles' high-handed measures, and said so. 'Anti-democratic!' he shouted.

Niceas had just come in from drilling in the fields north of town. He listened to them, drank wine and grinned, a look that made him appear to be a demon or a monster. 'Just threaten him,' Niceas said into a lull.

Diodorus spoke dismissively. 'In politics, never threaten. Only act.'

Niceas shrugged and held Diodorus's eye until the other man's air of superiority melted away. They were old friends – and sparring partners – and Niceas was reminding the other Athenian that for all his aristocratic airs, he didn't have a grasp of assembly politics. And he managed it all with a raise of the eyebrow and a sneer.

'Demosthenes is a fucking coward who ducked military service this summer. He's afraid of his own shadow. I don't mean an empty, blustering threat. I mean a little fucking terror and the promise of more.' He looked right at Diodorus. 'Let me arrange it.'

Kineas ran fingers through his beard – a habit he meant to break – and promised himself a shave and a trim. He finished his wine and grinned at them.

'I think you are all right. I have to tell you what a pleasure it is to have such friends, and such advice.'

'Beats moping and suffering in silence, doesn't it?' Philokles quipped.

Kineas ignored him. 'Philokles, get some cash from Leon and put it out on the street. Niceas – give Demosthenes some idea of my unhappiness with his actions. Don't get caught.'

'Tonight?' Niceas asked.

'Can you arrange it?' Kineas asked.

'Give me another day,' Niceas said. 'And Temerix.'

Kineas nodded. 'And Diodorus, perhaps you would invite the man himself to pay us a visit – perhaps the day after to-morrow.'

Diodorus fingered his red beard. 'I don't like it. If Niceas is caught, we're giving him what he wants.' He shrugged, glanced at Niceas and smiled. 'If only Kineas was tyrant.'

Philokles snorted again. 'If he was tyrant, we'd be doing this every day, putting the screws to every man in the city.'

Sappho laughed. 'That must be why it is called democracy,' she said.

7

The next evening Kineas hosted a symposium. The attendees were mostly his friends and officers, although after the campaign, neither group was as exclusive as it had been before.

Diodorus shared a couch with Sappho, the first time he had done so in public. He received some glances – Olbia was an old-fashioned city, and even in Athens the presence of a woman, any woman, at a symposium threatened a debauch – but his place as a hero of the city was so secure that glances were inevitably followed by smiles.

One of those smiling was Petrocolus, who lay with his son, Cliomenedes, trying to ignore the presence of the woman. Cliomenedes couldn't ignore her, as he had to lean over her to talk to Diodorus, whom he idolized. Instead, he asked her about her life, her hairstyle, her role as a courtesan, and she answered him with clear, direct, intelligent answers.

Philokles shared his couch with Kineas. He was particularly well dressed in a beautiful wool tunic and fine dark leather sandals, and he smelled like a talent of gold. Kineas wondered whom the Spartan sought to impress, and even tried to make a joke about it – a joke that fell flat.

Niceas shared his couch with Sitalkes, the Getae boy's first symposium. He was still a recovering invalid, and had a cup of heavily watered wine to keep him from excess. Past him, Memnon shared his couch with Craterus, a city hoplite who had made a name for himself during the campaign and now bid fair to replace Lycurgus as Memnon's lieutenant. Lycurgus lay on the next couch with Heron of Pantecapaeum – two taciturn men who were likely to remain silent throughout the meal. But they were both officers, and both had agreed to go on the eastern expedition. Lycurgus was the oldest man present save Petrocolus, with a beard that was mostly grey, pale skin and pale eyes. His beard had white streaks where it sprouted from the scars on his face. His feet and lower legs were blotchy with the ingrained dirt of twenty campaigns. Heron, by contrast, was young and dark-haired, wore no beard and was ruddy-skinned like the Sindi, and his legs were unblemished.

Coenus shared his couch with young Dion, the heir to the political family formerly headed by Cleitus and Leucon. Dion had served with honour if not distinction throughout the summer, and his father's death at the battle left him heir to three fortunes. He was close to Cliomenedes in age and temperament, and Kineas had assigned Coenus to woo him for their faction and for eventual office. Coenus, with his education, flawless manners and aristocratic habits, made easy work of the boy's affections.

Lykeles, another of Kineas's old companions, lay alone, still too pained by wounds to make an easy companion at dinner. He would not be going east because his days as an active soldier were probably over – and the angry marks at his neck and shoulder suggested that even routine motions might hurt for years to come. But he smiled as often as pain would allow, glad to be alive. He would be left behind to help Cliomenedes manage the hippeis – and to maintain the company's communications with the city. With Arni as a factor, he would manage their fortunes and their estates, plead their lawsuits, and keep the wolves from their various doors. He had the experience of city politics to manage such a job, and Kineas hoped that he had enough reputation from the summer to keep the likes of Demosthenes from becoming too bold.

The two Gauls, now both men of property, shared a couch. Andronicus, the larger of the pair, had blond hair and blue eyes, while Antigonus had dark hair and green eyes and tattoos just visible at the neck of his tunic. Both of them had practised for a year to attend a symposium, with Philokles and Diodorus as the drillmasters, and they could hold both wine and discourse, although Antigonus's more limited command of Greek tended to leave him smiling genially rather than conversing.

Leon lay just by them, and completed the circle of couches by lying close to Kineas and Philokles as well. Crax shared his couch. The Bastarnae had also begun his life with Kineas as a slave, and he, too, was now free and richer by a string of horses and a shelf full of gold cups made in Macedon. Crax had taken many blows in the great battle, but none had broken his skin, and he was the healthiest of all of them. Every other veteran present bore wounds, and they lay on their couches in comfort that verged on somnolence. Alone of all of them, Lot sat in a chair, uncomfortable with Greek dining but happy with a cup at his elbow and men he liked all about him. He raised the first toast, offered libation to his own gods and thanked his host.

'Who is closer to me than my battle brothers?' he said. 'Who could be closer than men who will follow me east to fight Iskander?'

Lot's bold assertion silenced them for a while, and when talk restarted, it was light and seldom dwelled long on any subject, and only the efforts of Sappho at one side of the circle and Coenus at the other end – both, in their own way, masters of social intercourse – kept the gathering from silence.

The dinner itself was superb, the product of Kineas's kitchens and Leon's cooks – or vice versa. They had not divided their fortune, and so far owned Nicomedes' property together. Neither seemed in any hurry to divide the estate, as such a division would only serve to make lawsuits easier.

The dinner featured more *opson* than Kineas liked – fish followed fish, oysters in sauce, lobster in more sauce, bits of bread that looked more like decorations than the main course – but there were no Athenian moralists there to decry the decadence, and given the way they'd all eaten during the summer, no one could really accuse them of wanton luxury. Every man ate to surfeit. Lot spilled lobster on his fine silk robe and laughed, and Philokles, already a little drunk, tripped with a ewer of wine and spattered half the room. By the time the last mutton went round and the last flatbread to wipe up the last of the fish sauce, they were all a little greasy.

As the meal went on, they discussed matters of the city, such as lawsuits and politics, and listened politely to Sappho as she played on her instrument and sang. When the main courses were done, they pulled their couches closer and drank together, the wounded men more quickly flushed, but soon they were all redder of face and louder, and Sappho smiled and withdrew.

Diodorus tried to restrain her, holding her hand. 'Stay!' he said. 'You are no Greek matron, to be shocked at what men say with wine in them.'

She shook her head, and her smile warned him that he had wounded her. 'I am a hetaira,' she said with grim courtesy, 'not a flute girl.'

When she was gone, Diodorus looked ruefully at Kineas. 'Who knows?' he asked.

Kineas knew, but he rubbed his beard and made a mental note to explain to Diodorus sometime what was plain enough to him – that in her mind, Sappho was still a matron of Thebes. Ill usage, slavery and worse had not broken her notions of proper behaviour. He honoured her for it.

When Sappho was gone, the talk grew louder, the jokes a little wilder, but every speaker seemed to be waiting for something, and the party lacked focus until Kineas rose to his feet. Kineas waited for a pause in the noise and raised his cup, and they all raised theirs, as if they had been waiting all evening for this moment.

'I want to talk about the expedition to the east,' he said. He gave them a grin. 'Against Alexander!'

They sighed together, as if relieved. Lot gave a shrill *yip* like a Sauromatae war cry.

'Are we allowed to say that aloud?' Philokles asked.

Kineas was sober and serious. 'I am going east because I need to be out of this city, and because my destiny is there. Moira awaits me in the east. I cannot be plainer with you than that.'

Around him, the men who knew of the power of his dreams nodded, all gaiety gone, while others looked puzzled. Memnon laughed.

Kineas ignored him. 'I must go. That is not true of you. Many of you – all of you, now – have property here and reasons to stay. Every man of you can settle to a farm and a wife. And I am too fond of you to force you to come. Indeed ...' His voice choked a little and he faltered. He drank some wine to cover his confusion, and then said, 'Indeed, I don't expect to return. And I do not wish that to be your fate.'

They looked at him with questions, their eyes brimming with misgiving, and he saw the hesitation he sought. He had considered the matter for days, and decided he would do his best to make the ones he loved most stay in Olbia.

But Philokles made a mocking noise with his lips and then laughed. 'Your life or death is with the gods,' he said. 'And the same can be said for every man among us.'

Kineas shot his friend a look, but Philokles ignored him, as he often did.

'Our fearless leader believes that he goes to his death in the east,' Philokles said in a mocking tone. 'Of course, he was equally certain that the recent action on the Borysthenes would be his death. It would appear that the dreams sent to him by the gods were mistaken.'

All the men laughed, because there was no mockery more precious to them than the rare moments when Philokles turned his tongue, sharp as bronze, on Kineas. It was precisely because Kineas was their leader – in many ways, the best man among them, and every one of them conscious of his advantages – that they enjoyed it the more when he was the butt of humour.

Kineas pointed to the Spartan. 'You mock sacred things,' he said.

Philokles grinned. 'No, my lad, I mock *you*. Unless, like the tiresome boy king, you have appointed yourself a god?'

Kineas narrowed his eyes, red tingeing his vision as rage threatened him. He rose from his couch and began to stalk towards his friend. 'I do not want to drag my friends to their deaths!' he bellowed.

Philokles drew himself up to his not inconsiderable height, as if to remind Kineas that his rage might accomplish nothing – and laughed again. 'Your friends will follow you to the ends of the earth,' he said, 'if only to see what you do next.'

The party cheered him, and Kineas deflated, pleased that so many of them clamoured to go, and touched – and bemused – by Philokles' tone. 'And I call you my friend,' he said.

'You get too much worship and insufficient straight talk,'

Philokles said in a low voice, his tone covered by the laughter. 'You need us. And I'm damned if I'll let you go off and find a way to die.' Then he turned to the others.

'Hear me, men of Olbia. Kineas of Athens marches east, not to open a road for trade, but to make war on Alexander, king of Macedon. He makes this war not for his own profit, but on behalf of every man in Greece. If there was a lion loose in a nearby town, would you not pick up your spear and go to kill it? So, then – take up your spear and go with us, for the monster is loose on the sea of grass.'

And then they rose from their couches and crowded around, and Kineas embraced them amidst a storm of affection, and was humbled.

In the dawn of the next day, while the guests of the symposium slept in drunken fitfulness, Demosthenes awakened at a loud noise. He shouted until his slaves were awake, and he made their lives more unbearable than usual seeking explanations for the dead frog in his water cup. He scared them sufficiently that it was several hours before any of them dared to tell him that he had a long mark in red ochre drawn on his throat like a giant grinning mouth.

He fainted.

He did not appear when invited for dinner at the barracks, and his excuses were sketchy.

Later, Kineas spoke to the survivors of the symposium in the barracks. They were quieter from the results of the night's debauch.

'This will be the largest expedition of its kind since Darius crossed the plains,' he said, tapping a copy of Herodotus – Isokles' copy, in fact. 'The difference is that we'll have the cooperation of most of the tribes, or at least we won't have their outright enmity. But the major issue will not be hostile action. It will be food.'

He gestured to Leon, who sat with Niceas. 'We have worked out a logistikon based on a thousand men and two thousand animals,' he said. 'All of you served enough with the

Sakje last summer to know how they live on the plain. With our own scouts and the Sauromatae, we should never lack for grass or meat.'

The cavalry professionals all nodded.

'But we will lack grain for the chargers and bread for the troops. Greek soldiers eat bread. Opson is all very nice, but it is grain that we need. And it is easier to buy it as we go than to try to carry it with us.'

Philokles raised his hand. 'Grain is so cheap here,' he said. Other men nodded in agreement. Olbia was the capital of the grain trade. The stuff flowed around them like the waters of the Borysthenes river, even in a summer beset by flooding and war.

Kineas nodded. 'I thought so too,' he said, 'and so I learned a new lesson of war. Listen.' He picked up Leon's scroll. 'Assume that every soldier eats a measure of grain a day, and every horse eats two measures,' he quoted. The old soldiers nodded agreement at the figures. 'That means that our little army will consume five *thousand* measures of grain a day.' He looked up from the scroll. 'Every man can carry ten measures of grain in addition to his equipment. Each horse can carry twenty measures of grain in addition to its equipment. So the army can sally forth with ten days' food.' His eyes raked them. 'It is at least *ten thousand stades* to the roof of the world where the Massagetae await us. At best, if we never slow, we will take sixty days to cross the sea of grass. The Sakje themselves allow fifty days for their fastest men, and ninety days for tribes.'

He began to make marks on the wall of the barracks with a piece of charcoal from the hearth. 'None of us has traversed the land to the east except Prince Lot and, of course, Ataelus. I have only his report, and the contributions of the more adventurous merchants from here and Pantecapaeum. If we go north to follow Srayanka, we risk tangling with Marthax – even if his forces are disbanded. And we'll have to cross great marshes as we go east. Srayanka will follow the great road of the Sakje – the high grassland that runs east into Sogdiana and Bactria and the land of the Massagetae.'

'We'll have to wait for spring,' Coenus said with a happy shrug.

Niceas sneered at him. 'I take it we have another option?' he asked Kineas with the raise of an eyebrow.

Kineas nodded. 'I've sent Eumenes to arrange it – I hope. Merchants cross the high ground between the Euxine and the Kaspian – what some men call the Hyrkanian Sea – by following the course of great rivers and then arranging passage on the Hyrkanian Sea when they arrive. If I can, I'll take the whole army along the Tanais river and across the high ground to the river that the Sakje call the Rha. If we go hard, we'll make the mouth of the Rha before the snows come.' He drew on the wall with the charcoal, indicating the position of Lake Maeotis and the Bay of Salmon, the course of the Tanais and the course of the Rha and the distant salt sea with flicks of his stylus.

Diodorus whistled. 'We're leaving the world we know,' he said.

Looking around, Kineas could see the same thought reflected in every man. He nodded. 'When some of you chose to follow me to Olbia, we left our world behind,' he said. He rubbed his beard and sipped wine. 'When we marched out on to the sea of grass in the spring, we left the world behind. This is farther and farther yet – but the world continues. Petrocolus and Leon and other grain merchants know the Tanais and the Rha well enough, and their factors attest that there is a route across to the Hyrkanian Sea – a route that many men have travelled.' Kineas turned to his sketch on the wall and then turned back. 'Prince Lot has made the journey several times, as has Ataelus.'

Niceas raised a hand. 'And then we cross this Hyrkanian Sea one boatload of horses at a time?'

Kineas made a sign that indicated that it was with the gods. 'Twenty boats at a time. They move caravans, Niceas. They can move us.'

Niceas shook his head. 'Caravans have a hundred horsemen and two hundred horses,' he said. 'And what little kingdom will receive our army without feeling that they have to massacre us?'

Kineas rubbed his beard. 'Yes,' he said. He shrugged. 'Nicomedes traded with a kingdom on the Kaspian Sea.'

Philokles laughed. 'Yes, you've got it taken care of? Or yes, it's a good point?'

Kineas raised an eyebrow, feeling the opportunity to make back some of the ground he had lost the night before. 'It seems to me,' he said with all the effort of a good rhetorician, 'that our company has a fine man, gifted by the gods with the power of making fine speeches, with a tongue that drips honey and a talent for philosophy – the very man to go from here to the far side of the Kaspian Sea with the summer caravans and arrange for a proper welcome and a winter camp in the barbarous country of Hyrkania.'

Philokles glared at him, but the other men laughed.

Niceas grinned. 'If we're sending Philokles,' he said, 'then I'm confident we'll be massacred.'

'Unless he kills them all before we arrive,' Diodorus said.

Kineas looked around. 'Humour aside, that's my intention,' he said. 'Across the high ground and the sea before winter falls, and a winter camp in the thousand kingdoms – that's what it is called.'

'Enchanting,' Philokles said. 'I'll wager it's called the thousand kingdoms because there are a hundred thousand bandits all fighting among themselves.'

'Yes,' said Leon. He smiled. 'Namastae is the most vicious of the lot. That's where we're going.'

They all looked at him. He shrugged. 'We have a factor there,' he said. 'After we lost half a dozen merchants, my master – that is, Nicomedes – sent a mercenary.'

'And?' asked Philokles.

'Now there are a thousand and one kingdoms,' Leon said. 'And Namastae trades with us. Hyrkania has riches.'

Philokles leaned forward, interested despite himself. 'And Hyrkania means ... ?'

Leon grinned. 'The land of the wolves,' he said.

Niceas stretched and rubbed his nose. 'Food?' he asked.

Kineas looked at Leon, and Leon rose to his feet. His voice was shaky as he began – he was not used to speaking to groups of men – and as he went on he spoke faster, and his voice became shrill. 'We'll march with a herd of bullocks and ten days' grain,' he said. 'The Tanais is farmed by the Maeotae and the Sindi as far north as the great lakes, and we will not travel so far on the river.'

Kineas interrupted because he could sense the ignorance of the audience, and because Leon wasn't doing credit to himself. 'Much of the grain traded through this port and through Pantecapaeum comes from the Tanais,' he said.

The soldiers nodded. Leon, emboldened, glanced at Kineas and then continued. 'At the portage we'll leave the Tanais and cross the high ground to the Rha. Merchants do it every year in the summer and autumn.' His voice was getting quieter and his words came more slowly as his confidence improved.

Lycurgus, Memnon's former lieutenant and now their commander of infantry, raised a hand. 'Son,' he said with authority, and he was obviously old enough to be Leon's father, 'are you trying to tell us that we can get grain as we march?'

Leon gave a shaky grin, glanced down at his scrolls, and frowned. 'Yes, sir.'

Lycurgus motioned to a slave for water. 'Then just say so, son.'

Leon stuttered for a moment and then began again. 'It will be harvest time when we march from the Bay of Salmon, or close enough. By the time we run out of our rations, the harvest will be in and we'll have access to the cheapest grain in the circle of the world.'

Kineas stood again. 'I will pay for the grain – at least for this winter.'

Lycurgus grunted. 'That will convince the shirkers,' he said. 'At least until spring.'

Kineas smiled. 'And then it'll be too late to change their minds,' he said.

Memnon laughed. 'It worked for Xenophon,' he said. 'You almost tempt me to come along.'

'What's in it for us?' Lycurgus asked. 'I'm in, however you put it – I followed you this summer and I like the idea. But for the boys in the ranks, what's in it for them?'

'Whatever loot we can get,' Kineas said. 'Was anyone dissatisfied with the booty from the Macedonian camp?'

Diodorus snorted, but Coenus cut him off. 'Are you seriously suggesting that we'll get to loot Alexander's camp?' he asked. 'I'm not sure, but I'd bet that counts as hubris.'

Kineas spread his hands, acknowledging the point. 'I can't say because we're talking about a march of ten thousand stades – at least ten thousand stades. Four hundred parasangs and maybe more. I will say that I expect some pay from the Massagetae.' He tilted his head to give Philokles a private look, and then said, 'If you know your Herodotus, we're marching right into the land of the eastern Sakje – the land of gryphons and gold.'

Lycurgus nodded. 'I can sell that,' he said. 'Especially if they can leave their loot from this campaign here, safe, and march knowing that you'll pay to fill their bellies.'

'Until we run out of money,' Niceas said.

'Then we'll just start taking what we need,' Diodorus said. Some of the younger men looked at him. He met their glances and shrugged. 'Sure, it gets ugly. But that's what armies do.'

'Out on the sea of grass, there's no one to plunder,' Leon said. 'And after the grass, there's desert.' He looked around. 'But chances are any army that you march out there will be the toughest proposition in Hyrkania. There'll be contracts in plenty, if we want to spend the spring fighting for their petty tyrants. I can arrange one before we arrive, if that's what you want.'

Lycurgus shrugged. 'Cross that desert when we come to it,' he said, and they laughed.

After listening to Kineas and Leon and wrangling over half-made plans, they were all tired. Arguments had begun to have a personal edge and the fumes of last night's wine were like poison. It was then that Sappho entered, and Arni, and a dozen of the barracks slaves, with ewers of water and flagons of wine and loaves of bread.

'Best of women!' Diodorus said, and got a real smile from his companion.

Kineas bit into the bread – crusty and excellent – and savoured the olive oil with it. 'Sappho, you are a paragon.'

She lowered her eyes and smiled. 'I crave a boon, Kineas.'

Kineas mopped his beard with his bread. 'Anything,' he said, expecting humour.

'Allow me to accompany the army,' she said.

Kineas flicked a look at Diodorus, but he appeared as surprised as if a bolt from Zeus had fallen among them.

Sappho took his hesitation for an opportunity. 'Every army has followers,' she said. 'I can manage them. I can ride a horse. I am as hard as a rock.'

Kineas, whose hands could remember the muscles in Srayanka's legs, doubted that Sappho was as hard as she thought, but he couldn't ignore the fact that she was correct. Every army had followers. Often, their fortunes affected the morale of the army. Generals and strategoi often ordered them to be abandoned, as if the men who served in the ranks had no feelings for the bodies that warmed their beds or the voices that shared their campfires. They were wrong.

Kineas looked at Diodorus – she was, at least temporarily, his property in many ways. Diodorus smiled his devious smile, and Kineas wondered if the man hadn't known of her request all along. Kineas disliked being managed as much as most men, but he liked Sappho well enough, and he liked the idea of having an 'officer' to deal with the followers.

'You agree to obey my orders?' he asked. 'And if I order you home, you'll go as meek as a lamb?'

She raised her eyes. 'I am always as meek as a lamb, Strategos,' she said.

No one had referred to him as strategos before. He felt himself blushing. Nonetheless, he hardened his tone. 'That is not an answer,' he said.

'Yes,' she said. 'I will agree to obey you – in all things.'

She raised her eyes just a little on the last word, so that he caught a flash of their colour. The glance affected him. He turned his head away and tried to ignore the pulse that shot from his head to his groin. And met Diodorus's eyes – and his raised eyebrow. Kineas looked away in confusion, made an excuse to walk out to relieve himself, counted to a hundred in Sakje. Then he rejoined his company, made jokes and laughed at them, and fell back into the tide of masculine camaraderie.

After they had shared bread and wine, Kineas rose and carried his wine cup to the centre of the room.

'A year ago in this room I asked my officers to swear an oath. If you will accompany me against Alexander, I'll ask you to swear again.' He raised his cup.

Niceas rose and gave him a rare grin. 'Who'd've thought, a year ago, when we had a tyrant to tame and the threat of Macedon stirring, that today we'd be planning to march an army into the east?'

Diodorus, sober, raised his cup. 'Who'd have thought that we would be officers with commands? Or rich men? Or citizens?'

Coenus raised his cup. 'Who would have guessed which among us would have fallen, and which would live to ride again?'

Andronicus raised his wine. 'Give us your oath, Strategos. For me, I long to ride.'

Then Kineas raised his cup. 'Hear us, God who shakes the mountains and whose bolts cause men to fear. Hear us, Goddess of the olive who wears the aegis. Hear us, God whose horses ride the very waves, whose hand raises the storm or stills it. May all the gods hear us. We swear that we will remain loyal to each other and the company until it is dissolved by us all in council.' Kineas spoke the words and they repeated them with gusto, no voice lacking, just as they had a year and more before, and the new voices were no softer than the old.

Despite the late afternoon hour when the meeting broke, Kineas threw on a cloak and went to the palaestra. He needed to feel the daimon of exercise. He was introspective enough to question his own motives in welcoming the Theban woman on the expedition to the east. He suspected that he would regret it even as his unexercised body fantasized about her.

He banished her green eyes on the sand of the palaestra. By the time he had loosened the muscles around his two healing wounds and freed his thighs from ten days of lassitude, the sun was low in the sky, but he was determined to run.

Other men were drawn to him, and his progress across the exercise floor attracted an entourage, and his announcement that he would run brought a chorus of approval. Philokles appeared at his side, and Diodorus as well, and Coenus.

They ran well, without a lot of conversation except some rude banter about the length of Kineas's legs – more banter when he slowed out by Gade's Farm, and then they had only enough air in their lungs to run. Memnon led the pack, his dark skin untouched by frost or the exertion, and he ran with his head up as if he could go all day and all night – which he probably could. Philokles stayed close to him all the way, and the two were just visible to Kineas, a dark back and a pale back in the distance.

Kineas was at the rear of the pack, a stade or more behind the leaders, and he ran on willpower and annoyance, burning off the last of his wine and bad temper and temptation, the air coming out of his mouth in gasps until he got his second wind. With the dolphin gates in sight, his head came up again, and he ran across the agora in fine shape, gaining some lost ground. Memnon was already running a strigil across Philokles in the marble portico of the palaestra, and the steam from the baths was welcome, but Kineas felt like a better man before he ran past the temple of Apollo, and he enjoyed his bath with the devotion of a man who might not see a gymnasium for sixty thousand stades – or ever again.

He was lying in the steam with a slave working carefully around the wound on his bicep when Helladius sat on the next slab.

'It must be nice to be so young,' said the priest. 'I was comforted that I could run at your shoulder, but then, in sight of the gates, a god gifted you with new strength and you ran away from me as if I stood still.'

Kineas laughed and pointed at Philokles, who was waving goodbye – clean, strigilled, massaged and cloaked for the walk home. 'You must be old indeed, to finish behind me,' he said.

'Memnon looks like a statue of Ares,' said Helladius. 'And your friend the Spartan might be Zeus.'

'You are full of flattery today, priest,' Kineas rolled over so that he could look the man in the eye.

'*It is not that the dead require anything from you*,' the priest said suddenly.

Kineas felt his stomach twist as if he'd just seen a corpse.

'*It is rather that they are trying to give you something*,' Helladius continued. His rich and melodious voice was somehow *wrong* for the message he was conveying. As if something else was using his voice to speak.

'What are they trying to give me?' Kineas asked.

'Philokles might be Herakles, or Achilles, come to life,' said the old priest, as if nothing of moment had been said.

'*That is for you to learn*,' said the slave in his accented Persian-Greek. Kineas sat up suddenly and whirled on the slave.

'What do you say?' he demanded.

The slave looked afraid. 'Master?' he asked and backed a step, fearing a blow.

Kineas looked at the priest. 'Didn't you hear him?' Kineas asked.

The priest looked puzzled. 'Do you speak his barbarian tongue? I doubt he speaks much Greek.'

Kineas was slow to place himself back under the slave's hands. 'Didn't you speak to me of my dreams?' he asked, after a long silence.

Helladius summoned another slave who began to massage the older man's legs. 'I questioned the gods, and sought answers in augury, and none was granted me. It is a difficult question.'

Kineas felt the cold sweat of fear despite the steam and the pleasant fatigue of the run.

The fear would not leave him. And it banished all thoughts of Sappho.

98

8

The expedition gathered a momentum of its own, so that by the day the first grain ships raised their sails, Kineas had volunteers from throughout the north shore of the Euxine, many of them men for whom he had little use, and a cheering crowd to see them all off. He stood on the beach with Petrocolus and watched the last chargers embark, and the last soldiers.

'I will miss you, Kineas,' Petrocolus said. 'The city will miss you.'

Kineas embraced the older man, and then embraced his son, Cliomenedes, who would be acting as the city hipparch. The two men, father and son, were now the most powerful political figures in the city, but there were already factions. Nicomedes' nephew, Demosthenes, had taken up much of the rhetoric of Cleomenes the elder, Eumenes' father, who had betrayed the city to Macedon – a fact that was already dwindling in the consciousness of many citizens. Demosthenes had not emerged from his house in a week – but his terror would pass. He had both money and voices in the assembly. He would not be quiet long.

On the other hand, Kineas had arranged – or more properly, Diodorus, Sappho and Philokles had arranged – that the assembly chose Petrocolus as archon. He was one of the city's richest men, he had hundreds of clients and he had earned his own fortune through hard work and quick wit, and his son was a hero of the war. Together, they had the leverage to hold Demosthenes at bay.

Kineas handed the older man the ivory stool with relief and a certain pride. 'Don't sit on it too often,' he said. 'It becomes addictive.'

Petrocolus accepted it and nodded gravely. 'I will keep it for you,' he said, but Kineas shook his head.

'I don't expect to return,' he said. He pointed to

Demosthenes, where he stood glowering with a bodyguard of armed slaves and some followers – most of them men who had once followed Nicomedes.

Kineas thought bitter thoughts about his fellow citizens, and Greeks in general. He had watched his father play the game of democracy, and now he played it himself. Men like Cleomenes the elder and Demosthenes played it without rules or ethics, bending men with money to suit their own tastes, never considering the *eudaimonia* of the city as a whole – or so Kineas saw them. He hated that good men like Anarxes, a rich farm boy who had ridden in the second troop, served loyally all summer and acted as Eumenes' second officer when the older boy was lying wounded, now rose in the assembly to demand that Kineas show his accounts for city money he expended. The man did so at the behest of his new political master, and Kineas was sorry for it – and hurt. And the more eager to leave, before the call for an accounting crippled him. Or before he lost the special regard he had received.

He waved to the crowd and embraced the old man one more time, and then he waded out into the surf and climbed the side of Demostrate's galley. The navarch gave him a hand up the side. 'You could have ruled,' he said by way of greeting.

Kineas liked the ugly man. Demostrate was an effective commander, a retired pirate and a loyal ally. 'Would you, if you had the chance?' he asked.

Demostrate laughed, a roar like Poseidon's. 'Never!' he said. 'Easier to calm the waves in a storm than to ride the tides of public opinion.' He gave a lopsided grin that made him look like a satyr – or more like a satyr. 'Bad enough that I stopped being a pirate.'

Kineas smiled to himself, and said less than he might once have, but went aft to the awning, where Philokles and Diodorus and Niceas waited, and the red ball of the sun rose in the east, licking the waves to ripples of fire, so that they seemed to be sailing into the east on a road of flame.

PART II

HIGH GROUND

9

The same sun burned like a line of fire on the late-summer grass of the prairies beyond the low beach in the Bay of Salmon where a dozen galleys were pulled up on their sterns. Small waves lapped against their armoured beaks, and gulls shrieked and whirled where a crowd of Sindi fishermen hauled a net full of silver fish from their boat to the temporary market, where they would be sold for hard cash.

Beyond the warships, the grain fleet of Athens was anchored out in the Bay of Salmon, well clear of the sloping sand and mud. The great ships were not built to beach like warships – with their size, they required the support of a volume of water or their hulls might split, heavy supporting members breaking under the strain. So they anchored out in the deep water, and local boats and hastily built barges emptied their holds and took their cargoes on to the beach, a reversal of the usual process.

Sauromatae horse-herders drove their spare horses straight over the rails of the great ships so that the horses plunged into the sea. The girls then leaped naked into the sea behind them, tangled their fists in sea-wet manes and swam ashore with their charges.

Philokles, equally naked in the late-summer sun, laughed. 'Poseidon, Lord of Horses and Lord of the Sea, must love you, Athenian,' he said.

Kineas gave the Spartan half a smile. 'All the gods love a man who plans carefully,' he said.

'Not Aphrodite,' Philokles said with a wry smile. 'The goddess born on foam hates a man who plans too much.' He frowned. 'You never mention the Foam-born when you make sacrifice.'

Kineas's eye caught Sappho, cloaked like a matron despite the sun and wearing a large conical straw hat, sitting on a stool further down the beach with Diodorus's not inconsiderable camp furniture. 'Speak to me not of Aphrodite,' he said. 'I ask only that she withhold her hand from me until I see Srayanka.'

'Brother, that is exactly the way in which mortals ask the Foam-born for trouble,' Philokles said. His eyes continued to follow the Sauromatae girls as they rode their horses out of the water. 'Have you ever wondered why Poseidon is Lord of Horses and Lord of the Sea?'

Kineas, his head full of figures and the minutiae of the landing, shook his head. 'I must confess that I have not.'

Philokles ignored the hint. 'I used to think that perhaps our ancestors – those Dorians who came to Sparta and took it in the time after Menelaus and fair Helen – that perhaps they brought a lord of chariots, and the locals had a lord of the ocean, and as the two peoples merged, they merged their gods.'

Kineas was drawn to his friend's lesson despite himself. 'I can never decide whether you should be teaching in the agora as a philosopher or thrown from a tall rock as a blasphemer,' he said with mock concern. But he was listening.

'But just now, watching those girls, I wonder if it is not hidden, like all other lessons, inside the Poet,' Philokles said. 'Wherever the long-haired Achaeans travelled, they took chariots – it is in the *Iliad*.'

'True enough,' Kineas said, amazed that he had never given the matter a thought, though as for most Athenian boys, the *Iliad* had been the centre of his every military fancy since he first heard it performed in his father's tiled garden.

'And the Poet must have seen what we are seeing many times before he lost his sight,' the Spartan added, peering from beneath his hand. 'Perhaps I was too simple. Perhaps the Lord of Horses and the Lord of the Sea have always gone together.'

'Perhaps you've just noticed that the Sauromatae girls are naked, and extraordinarily handsome,' Kineas said.

Philokles released a great sigh. 'Aphrodite is close to you, brother,' he said. He gave a wry grin that made him look ten years younger. 'When women stir my loins, they must be stirring indeed.'

Kineas had no time to consider naked women of any sort, however, because as soon as the bulk of his army had landed he had to put it in a state of defence, had to start the parts of it in motion, had to arrange orders to cover various eventualities, because he was not marching the whole of it together but sending pieces of it across the three thousand stades that separated them from the Kaspian Sea to the east.

Eumenes had done his job. Herds of cattle waited on the beach, already penned together with Sindi shepherds and Sindi sheep. Inland, Ataelus's prodromoi had marked the road with signs used by the Sakje – sticks and bits of fleece, skulls of dead animals, piles of stones. Kineas could read them, and the Sauromatae girls could read them better. Ataelus was gone – long gone, by all accounts – but Eumenes had been waiting for them when the first warships pulled up on the flats, and he and Philokles and Leon were due to head east as soon as the first troops were prepared to travel – the infantry under Lycurgus, because they would be the fastest to ship and the best at defending the camps.

Kineas divided the rest of the army into two groups. Ataelus was gone with the first group – just the elite prodromoi, used to living off the land. They had been off as soon as their horses swam ashore, scouting the route that the army would take across the high ground. Kineas expected daily reports from the scouts – Ataelus had enough riders to send a messenger every morning.

Diodorus commanded the second group, composed of the bulk of the Greek infantry and the Sindi psiloi. They would make their best speed to the coast of the inland sea, where shipping should by then await them, covered by two troops of Olbian cavalry.

Prince Lot would lead the rest: the Sauromatae as well as Heron's troop of cavalry and Eumenes' troop. They were to move across the trail blazed by Ataelus in easy stages, starting last by a week and covering the movement of the other groups because they were the best fitted to living off the steppe.

The Greek infantry marched out of the camp in good order on the second day after their landing, their goods piled on their mules. Every one of them had just completed a summer on campaign. They carried too much baggage, but that was true of soldiers the world over. Their bodies were hard, and they sang as they marched out.

The hoplites set off at a pace that would eat a parasang (thirty stades) in an hour – a pace they and their donkeys could maintain all day if required. Barring disaster, they would have crossed the high ground between Lake Maeotis and the Kaspian Sea in thirty days, swamps, ridges and all, and still have purchased grain to eat while they awaited Leon's boats on the Kaspian.

The whole army marched, and ate, as Greek soldiers had marched for generations. Every man belonged to a mess group – eight or ten men and their women and slaves under a file leader. They marched together, fought together as a file and ate together, buying their food from the daily common market and cooking it by turns over the group's fire when they camped. That fire was often the centre of their lives – home and hearth combined. They had no tents and no blankets but the cloaks they all carried, and rain or snow or beating sun, they could live, and march.

The system was so old and so endemic to Greeks that even the gentry – the cavalry and the officers – followed the same system. At the very top, the strategos was *not* expected to cook – he was too busy. But he could cook, and he did, on occasion. Greek notions of democracy were not limited to politics, and Spartan or Athenian, Olbian or Heraklean, every Hellene soldier knew that his food was his own responsibility.

Kineas was much given to thoughts of food these days. He dreamed of food supply at night when he wasn't fighting against the dreams of the tree, and awake, he pondered how to ship grain ahead of his army, pondered the purchase of additional mules, pondered the possibilities of farming failures and war and the results for his tenuous supply.

'Do as you think best,' Kineas had said to Philokles before they rode away, wrapped in his Spartiates cloak of scarlet, sitting beside Leon in a splendid blue cloak that lacked the wear of a season in the field, a study in contrasts. 'Don't be tied to my plan. Make your judgements on the ground. If we can ride around the north of this Hyrkanian Sea – the Kaspian – or if it seems better to you, or if you cannot hire the shipping, or if it is too late in the season—'

Philokles put his hand on Kineas's shoulder. 'You've already told us every word of your worries,' he said.

Kineas gave a wry smile. 'I will worry until I see you again,' he said, and Leon shifted his weight, embarrassed by their obvious emotion.

Kineas smiled at Leon. 'Don't feel it too keenly when this plan of ours is discarded,' he said. 'We may never make Hyrkania.'

'I won't let you down,' Leon said.

'I'll while away the stades discoursing on your flaws and bring him back cured of hero worship,' Philokles said. He stroked the neck of his heavy charger, a magnificent animal he had preserved throughout the year's campaigns by the simple expedient of fighting on foot. 'I haven't missed you, you brute,' he said. 'My thighs will burn like a river of fire before night.'

He embraced Kineas, and they patted each other's backs for a long minute. Then they parted, and Kineas embraced Leon. 'Do well,' he said, and turned away to hide his tears.

Kineas found it difficult to wave goodbye to Philokles.

An hour later, Kineas stood on a low hill – almost certainly an ancient kurgan like the one that now held the body of Satrax – and watched his infantry with pride. He had climbed the kurgan alone to have time to think, a luxury for a commander, even of a thousand men. He waved at Philokles, who still sat his charger like a sack of grain, and Leon, who rode like a centaur and carried a shield on horseback, one of the few men Kineas had ever seen do such a thing. Neither saw him until the army was already a stade out on the plain, their singing just a chant on the wind, when Leon happened to look at the top of the old mound and Kineas saw him trot his mount alongside Philokles. The Spartan turned in his saddle, looked, put a hand to his eyes and then waved.

Kineas waved back enthusiastically. He found that he was crying again. He waved until he had to strain his eyes to see them, and then he sat in the hollow at the top, resting his shoulders against the stone, and closed his eyes.

'May the gods send that I see you again,' he swore.

'*You will*,' said a deep voice behind him, but when he turned there was no one there but the Sakje child.

'How do you know?' Kineas asked her.

She looked at him with all the puzzlement that children use for adults who don't behave themselves. 'Know what, lord?'

Kineas bit back a retort. The voice had been hers – and yet had not been hers. 'Surely there is someone else for you to haunt, girl,' he said.

'No,' she said simply, and came around him to sit on the sacred stone that capped the kurgan. The sword that should have rested in the stone or in the earth beside it was gone, either long since rusted into the ground or taken for its power by a *yâtavu*, a sorcerer. Ordinary mortals avoided sitting on the kurgan stones, fearing the spirits of the dead. She did not.

'What is your name, girl?' Kineas asked.

'When will you come for your horses, Strategos?' she asked. 'They pine for you – and you ride inferior blood. You are king. I say so. My father says so. It pains him to see you astride some Getae hack when you should be riding a royal horse.'

Kineas sat down on the low bank of grass-covered earth created by the slow collapse of the roof of the kurgan and sighed. 'They are fine horses,' he admitted.

'And my father is cross that you will not climb the tree. He says,' and here she scrunched up her face and squared her shoulders so that her back was straighter, an eerie performance, 'he says that you let your fear guide you instead of your sense as a baqca.'

Kineas sighed again. 'Kam Baqca is dead,' he said.

The little girl shrugged. 'Many people are dead,' she said. 'Should they also be silent?'

Kineas spoke too fast, because he didn't want an argument, and because she was annoying him. 'We don't believe that the dead speak.'

The little girl regarded him from under her straight dark brows. 'That's not true,' she said.

Kineas caught his own mistake, and he laughed at his own inability to defeat a young woman in debate. 'The dead may speak on great occasions,' he said.

'The dead may speak whenever it suits the gods to allow them to speak,' the child said, as if teaching a lesson. 'So you should not lie. The dead speak to Odysseus in the *Odyssey*. If the Poet says a thing, it must be true, don't you think?' She looked at him. He felt the hair on the nape of his neck begin to rise.

'You have read the Poet?' he asked.

'Of course,' she said, her young voice utterly dismissive. 'And in plays – the dead speak all the time in plays. I saw one in Olbia.'

Kineas shook his head. 'Who are you?'

She got up, laughing, for all the world like any other happy twelve-year-old girl. 'Nihmu White Horse of the Royal Sakje,' she said proudly. 'Kam Baqca was my father, and Attalos One-Eye was my grandsire. Arraya Walks-Alone was my mother and Srayanka the Archer was my father's mother.' She rattled off her impressive lineage in the sing-song voice of memorization.

Kineas helped her down from the stone as he would any girl – and he remembered his sisters in the family olive groves, and how they had claimed to be women as soon as they could walk. This child seemed to be every age and no age. 'Where do you camp?' he asked.

'With the prodromoi,' she said.

'The scouts are all gone for the Kaspian,' Kineas said. He was disconcerted again. Thunder rumbled in the distance, late-summer thunder that did not bring rain.

She frowned and shook her head rapidly. 'You'd better hurry,' she said. She took his hand and pulled on it like one of his sisters wanting a honey treat in the agora. 'Hurry!'

'Why?' he asked. Now she seemed far away.

'*Because you'll die!*' came the deeper voice. But the girl looked as startled as he was, and ran off down the hill and into the gathering dark.

*

When Kineas awoke, Niceas was at his shoulder, shaking him. 'I knew you'd slipped off to have a kip,' he said.

Kineas looked around and gradually realized that he was curled up against the kurgan's stone. His body was like ice, and he was scared.

'What's happening to me?' he asked the sky.

Niceas's raillery vanished and was replaced by concern. 'What's the matter?'

Kineas put his head in his hands. 'The veils between the world of dreams and the waking world are tearing,' he said. 'Or I am going mad.'

The next night, Kineas dreamed of his own death, and he dreamed of the tree, and he dreamed of skeletal figures offering him the gift of sand from their mouths – one a Persian archer, another a man he'd bought a cup of wine after the sack of Tyre. Sometimes they were not even recognizable – the worst was a corpse with no head, who vomited sand from the stump of its neck. Dreams like this cost him his rest, and he began to fear to place his head on his cloak. And he could not face the tree dreams. The idea of climbing the tree was like an assault on his Hellenism, and the dreams were worse now that he had left the city behind.

In the morning he rode among the camps. He watched the Sindi farmers and the Maeotae fishermen drying their salmon. He watched the Athenian captains purchase fish sauce by the hundred beakers in the market on the beach and load their cargoes before they weighed anchor and beat slowly out through the grey-green waves of the shallow sea towards the dykes that almost – but not quite – blocked navigation on Lake Maeotis. When their sails vanished over the horizon, the enormity of his commitment to the expedition – his own fortune and his inherited wealth were heavily engaged – began to weigh on him, and that, combined with lack of sleep, made him dangerous.

Kineas knew that Niceas was watching him with growing alarm, perhaps even anger. Niceas did his best to keep his Kineas busy: arranging inspections, riding the beach, throwing a seaside symposium to wish the sailors of Pantecapaeum farewell. None of them served to occupy Kineas fully, and his temper grew shorter and shorter. So did Niceas's.

After a few days of inactivity and more nights of brutal dreams, Diodorus's command marched, carrying most of the remaining grain from the magazine that Eumenes had arranged. The herds of cattle were already down by a third.

'Why don't we ride with Diodorus?' Niceas asked. 'The prince can get himself across the height of land – Ares, he could ride all the way to Marakanda without us.'

'Go with Diodorus if you want,' Kineas said.

Niceas whirled on him. 'Don't be an arsehole, Strategos,' he said. 'You've been a burr under my butt for a week and I don't have to take it. I'm trying to help and you are shutting me out.'

'I can't go to fucking *sleep*,' Kineas said.

Niceas handed him a flagon of wine left from the symposium. 'Philokles told me how to deal with this,' he said. 'Start drinking. I'll tell you when to stop.'

'I'm the commander of this expedition,' Kineas said. 'I can't get drunk.'

Niceas held out the flagon. 'Greek wine for Greek dreams, Philokles says.'

Kineas shook his head. 'I'm sorry, friend, but I'm not as bad as that yet.'

Niceas raised an eyebrow. 'All the gods keep me from the day you are worse.'

Kineas managed a smile. 'You're right. I need to get out of this camp.'

Niceas rubbed his nose. 'About fucking time.'

Kineas smiled back. 'Let's go hunting. We'll catch Diodorus as we go. I'll inform Lot.'

10

The pressure in Kineas's head subsided as soon as he rode away from Lake Maeotis, so that by the time his horse had completed the first of the great curves of the Tanais, he felt nothing but an agonizing fatigue. He allowed Niceas to lead him on for a few parasangs and they camped on a bluff that hung over the great river like a fortress built by nature.

'I just want to sleep,' Kineas said.

Niceas handed him a horn cup of watered wine. 'Drink this first,' he said.

Kineas looked across the river at the farms on the north shore. 'We're in Asia, according to Herodotus.'

Niceas shrugged. 'I've been to Asia before,' he said. 'Tomorrow, if you insist on keeping this up, we'll have to hunt.'

Kineas nodded. Instead of relaxation, he felt only the anxieties of a commander away from his troops. 'I shouldn't have left the army,' he said, and drank the wine. Then he had another cup, and finally he fell asleep.

The tree climbed away above him, an endless profusion of fecundity, with ripe fruit – apples, lemons and richer prizes all dangling in a riot of colour and life. Birds swooped in and out of the tree, plucking food from the tangle of branches. And around the fruit branches, up and up, to a layer of branches and clouds that hid the horizon, there were branches of hardwood and soft-wood, each lush and perfect, without disease, so that the tree was all trees, and it covered the world.

His feet were mired in the mud and the blood of the dead at the base of the tree, and when he moved he could feel the bones breaking under his feet no matter how careful he was. He needed to climb – indeed, he could see a pair of young eagles cradled in one of the branches above him, and they called to him, and he had to go to them. Their needs were greater than his. But as he began to push through the ordure, a corpse rose from the muck to confront him. It rose gracefully, without the stiffness that the dead so often displayed, and the corpse's face was fresh and clean and unmarked despite the wounds on his body.

It was Ajax.

Ajax smiled. It was a smile full of sadness and other things – comradeship, love, loss and longing – but it was a smile. He reached out his hand towards Kineas, and Kineas took the hand.

Around them, other corpses appeared, familiar corpses – the men from his other dreams, a silent clamour of dead and rotting flesh. Kineas shied away from them, but they pushed at him, each with a handful of sand.

Beyond the heartbreaking spectacle of dead companions and friends – men whose deaths in many cases sat on his shoulders, who had died under his orders or at his side – was a dreadful plain of dead, Persians and Getae and others, trailing away to the horizon.

Ajax pulled at him and then pushed him towards the tree, interposing his body between Kineas and the other dead. Kineas seized the trunk and threw himself up to the first branch with all of his dream strength, threw a leg over the first branch and hung there, terrified and sweating, as Ajax vanished in a mêlée of the dead, and Kineas felt that he had abandoned the boy, left him for dead, and he wept. And the weeping was excruciating, raw pain coming from his eyes as if the eyes themselves were threatening to burst from his head, and then grains of sand poured from his eyes into his hands, sand intermixed with blood, and he screamed and screamed and ...

Niceas had his arms and was murmuring in his ear until he calmed. In his fear- and fatigue-swamped thoughts, he knew that Niceas was speaking to him as he would to a scared horse, and that comforted him, and despite his fears, he slipped back into sleep.

It amazed him that he returned to the dream in the same place, with one leg over the rough, oak-tree bark of the tree's lower limbs. He could not see the ground, only the sort of low mist that rolled over the sea of grass in the autumn, and the dead were gone. He was on the tree. He admitted to himself, there in the power of the dream, that he had resisted going to the tree since the day of the battle, and now he welcomed it.

He climbed to the branch where he had seen the young eagles, and they were gone — higher in the tree, he could see now. They leaned out from their branch, their immature and drab brown plumage somehow comic, and watched him with curious eyes, and made raucous calls at him as he hoisted himself to another branch. Each branch at this height was as large as a noble tree in a royal forest in Persia, or in a temple grove in Arcadia, and climbing the main trunk was a matter of careful searching for hand- and footholds in the rough bark. He searched, and climbed, and his head was filled with memories from his youth — memories of sitting in the dust of the agora in Athens and listening to tutors and philosophers, some wiser than others, some brilliant rhetoricians and one unable to speak more than a few phrases without halting and staring blankly at the world around them, often to the hoots of his companions — his own hoots.

Why? Why had he been so derisive? The man was a pupil of Plato, a brilliant mind who studied many things in the circle of the heavens, but his halting speech had earned him nothing but ridicule. And their tutors had done nothing to stop them, until the poor man had fled the agora. Even in dream, Kineas winced at remembering that he had been the first to call an insult, feeling bold, manly, adult.

And why had their tutors not restrained them?

Perhaps because they, mere tutors to the idle rich, enjoyed the discomfiture of one more gifted than they?

It was a deeply painful memory, an ignoble act in which he led others to act badly. And it had been one of the moments that defined his leadership over the other youths — his daring had made him a leader.

The consequence of an evil act had been his own success as a leader. Of course, his leadership of aristocratic youths had caused him to be sent to Alexander, and then exiled. And Moira had sent him from exile to be archon of Olbia, and then to here.

He pondered it all, and climbed higher.

There were other forms of horror than rotting corpses …

He awoke in the morning, better rested than he had been in weeks, to the roar of Niceas's snores. Below the bluff on which they had camped, the Tanais swept by majestically, still swollen by the rain that had lasted a month, as wide as a lake. The sun rose and then leaped into the pink-striped sky as Apollo's winged chariot began its course across the heavens. Kineas listened to the sounds of the forest behind him, watched a herd of deer come to the river beneath the bluff, an easy javelin throw that he passed because he could feel the peace of Zeus on the whole of the Tanais and he had no wish to break the truce. Birds called.

He was confused by his dreams. It was years since he had last thought about tormenting the scholar in the agora, but he now knew the dream to be a true one – indeed, he now remembered the incident, and his secret shame. He felt the shame anew. He nodded at the thought, having learned something. He was tired, but strangely full of new life.

'I should not have stayed away from the tree,' he said quietly.

'*No*,' said the wind and the snores and the birds in the sky. It was terrifying, because the 'no' was not quiet.

Kineas sprang to his feet, but there was no one there but Niceas with his prosaic snores, and the deer, running along the river as if pursued by wolves. Even as he watched, the deer slowed, paused and, with infinite caution, began to drink again.

Kineas sighed and set to work building the fire, hands shaking as they did after he had been in combat. He was patient and thorough, remembering many things – his first hunting expeditions with his father, his first days in the field with Niceas. He split small twigs with his eating knife and broke larger sticks into uniform lengths. From his pack he retrieved a tube of hollowed reed, carefully preserved through ten years of campaigns, and blowing through it softly, he raised the embers into hot coals and then summoned fire on the split twigs he had prepared, building upon those flames one stick at a time until he had a raging fire. He put a small bronze pot on for tea and sat back, temporarily satisfied.

Out in the river, a salmon leaped, and then another. A sea eagle swept in from the right, took a salmon in its great talons and beat away, wings struggling to handle the extra load, so that the great bird swept down the river a few *dactyloi* above the surface of the water.

'Thank you, Lord of the Heavens, Keeper of the Thunderbolt,' Kineas said.

The augury was of the best, and more, the truce of the god was broken by the Lord of the Heavens himself. Grabbing a javelin, Kineas crept carefully down the bluff and then moved from tree to tree along the riverbank. In the distance he could see a series of farms at the next bend of the river, smoke coming from their hearths in the new morning.

The lead buck raised his head and Kineas, downwind, froze. A doe's head came up, and then another's. It was a long throw, and the time Kineas would take to change his stance to make a cast would render it impossible. He waited.

Another head came up – a young buck. He took a step towards Kineas, and turned his head as if trying to see something across the river.

Kineas remained motionless.

The doe's head went down, back to drinking, and then the young buck moved a step and did the same. Kineas took a step, and then another, now almost flat to the ground.

A head came up. Kineas couldn't see as well, having sacrificed line of sight for his own cover. He stopped moving. He was in range now, but awkwardly placed behind a hillock of grass where a great tree had fallen, probably during a spring flood, and then rotted into the loam to leave a miniature ridge.

Above him, just a *plethron* away on the bluff, Niceas rose to his feet and stretched. The heads came up, watching this new movement. Across the river, the eagle, freshly gorged on salmon, let out a raucous screech of contentment. As the herd's heads turned together, Kineas rolled from behind his hillock to his feet. In their panic at his appearance, the young buck fouled one of the does and both stumbled, losing a stride, and his javelin flew, arcing into the heavens before falling to strike the young buck between the shoulder blades. He took one stride and fell, legs splayed, already dead. The doe leaped his corpse and ran.

Kineas opened the buck, giving a prayer to Artemis he had learned as a boy, and gralloched his kill in a nearby tree. He left the buck hanging there and washed in the river before climbing the bluff with a pair of steaks wrapped in oak leaves.

'Somebody's feeling better,' Niceas said. He was huddled in his cloak with a horn cup in his fist.

Kineas laid the steaks on their leaves by the fire. 'Yes,' he said. He wore a grin that split his face like an athlete's crown of honour.

Niceas began cutting green branches from the alder at the top of the bank. 'If you wanted to go hunting, you could just have said,' he joked.

Kineas shrugged, still looking across the river. 'I didn't know what I wanted,' he said.

'Fair enough,' Niceas answered. He speared the deer meat carefully, putting three of the springy sticks into each steak and then putting the sticks deep into the loam around their fire. In the fire pit, he pushed the coals from Kineas's earlier blaze into deep piles, one each under the lattices supporting the meat. The meat began to sizzle almost immediately and Kineas's stomach made a wet noise. They both chuckled.

'It's hot,' Niceas said. He'd boiled water in a copper mess pot and added the herbs he'd learned from the Sakje and some honey. It was a good drink in the morning, and it saved the wine.

Kineas took the cup from his outstretched hand and drank. He smiled. 'We're going to end up becoming Sakje,' he said. 'What's the herb?'

'Something the Sakje call "*garella*",' he said. 'I found some growing here when we made camp.'

'Bitter,' Kineas said. 'Good with honey.'

Niceas shrugged. 'It's warm and wet. Srayanka – your Medea – likes the stuff. That's how I learned about it.'

Kineas nodded and drank more. It tasted better. Or was that his imagination?

'We could go back to Athens,' Niceas said.

Kineas stepped back from the fire as if he had been burned. 'What?' he asked.

'We could go back to Athens. Your exile is lifted – all your estates restored. Right?'

Kineas looked at the other man. 'Where is this coming from?'

Niceas shrugged, pulled the sticks from the ground and flipped one of the pieces of meat. It smelled delicious, and it had very little fat. 'The plains aren't good for you. All these dreams. And war. We've had enough war, haven't we?'

Kineas looked at his hyperetes as if seeing him for the first time. 'Have you had enough war?'

'The first time I saw it, that was enough,' Niceas said. 'But like Memnon, it's the only life I've ever known. I keep waiting – waiting for you to retire, so that I can retire, too.'

Kineas was watching his friend's face. 'I will not be going back to Athens, old friend.'

Niceas shook his head. 'Of course not. Silly of me to mention it, only – only I don't see an end. We ride east. Then what? You find Medea and live happily ever after. What about the rest of the boys? Do we just pick a Sakje bride and settle down, or what? Do we fight Alexander? Do we just go on fighting Alexander? Maybe keep moving east? Come back here and make war on Marthax?' Niceas was growing angrier as he spoke. 'It won't ever end, Kineas. You'll become fucking Alexander, at this rate. What's it for?'

Kineas rubbed his beard, stung. 'I promised Srayanka.'

Niceas nodded. 'You promised her. Did you promise her Eumenes? Diodorus? Antigonus? Coenus? Me?' At each name, his voice rose. 'We'll leave our fucking skulls out east in some Tartarus of wilderness beyond the world, won't we?'

Kineas drained the garella and sat. He pulled his legs up close and put his arms around them. 'Why didn't you say all this back in Olbia?'

Niceas shrugged. 'It didn't really come to me until I saw what this campaign was doing to you. And when I saw the ships sail off. That hurt.'

Kineas turned his face away. 'I have to do this. You don't. I told you all that in Olbia.'

Niceas's voice was gentle instead of angry. 'That's horse

shit, Hipparch. We'll all follow wherever you choose to go. You have trained us to be that way, and now we are. Diodorus won't leave you, I won't leave you. Now Eumenes won't leave you. It's almost funny, because every one of us has our own little following – the damned following the damned following Kineas.'

Kineas thought of the other boys hissing their catcalls after the fleeing philosopher. Instead of an angry retort, he nodded. 'Would it help if I promised that this was the last time?' he asked.

Niceas shook his head. 'No. Because being who you are, it won't be the last time. But it'd help those of us who follow you if you put some planning into the trip home, instead of just the trip out.'

Kineas met his friend's eyes. 'I won't be coming home,' he said.

Niceas met his glance. 'If you say so. Maybe the rest of us will, though.'

Kineas nodded. 'I understand.'

'Good,' said Niceas. 'Because the meat's done.'

An hour later, they were riding across the plains between the oak woods and the river. They passed farms and Maeotae farmers, paler than the Sindi but wearing the same colourful clothes. They were prosperous, and the women wore gold, even when they worked with hoes in their gardens or brought in the harvest. Twice, the mounted pair passed groups of Maeotae in their hundreds reaping a field of wheat. There was grain in every basket and more coming in every apron. Stone barns and turf barns dotted the landscape along the river, each with a small dock and every one bursting with wheat.

Kineas shook his head. 'The golden fleece,' he said.

Niceas nodded. 'Alexander is wasting his time on Persia,' he said. 'These are the richest farms I've ever seen.'

When the sun stood at the top of the sky, Kineas stopped where a group of Maeotae sat in the shade of a great oak tree, eating bread and cheese. He dismounted. The men watched him warily.

'Do any of you speak Greek?' he asked.

The oldest of the farmers stood and approached, but he shook his head.

'Sakje?' Kineas asked.

The farmer smiled, showing more teeth than gaps. They were a handsome people, with hair as golden as their crops in autumn and the stature of those who ate well all through the year. 'Some,' he said.

'You know Olbia?' Kineas asked.

The farmer nodded.

'We are from Olbia. An army is coming this way, up the Tanais. My army. We'll pay for grain.' Kineas found that Sakje forced him to be succinct.

The farmer nodded. 'Soldiers come. Horsemen come,' he said. 'Say same. Pay gold for grain.' He nodded.

Kineas held up a silver owl. 'I'd buy bread and cheese, if I could,' he said.

The farmer shrugged. He went to his wife and returned with a basket full of bread and cheese. 'For nothing,' he said with evident pride. 'For friend.'

Niceas nodded. 'Any farmer would do the same. These are good folk.' He went to his horse and removed a cut of the buck and carried it to the farmer. 'For nothing,' he said in Sakje, and the farmer grinned at him.

They rode on, eating as they went. 'March discipline must be good,' Niceas said, 'or those folk would be pissing themselves at the sight of soldiers.'

'This is Grass Cat land,' Kineas said.

'I don't think those Maeotae would agree,' Niceas said. 'This is no man's land.' He looked at Kineas under his brows. 'You could build something here,' he said.

Kineas looked at him. 'Build something?' he asked.

Niceas grunted, and they rode on.

They stayed the night in a heavy stone house. Kineas got a bed by the hearth – the nights had developed a bite – and he was asleep as soon as his head was on the furs.

The two young eagles were above him again, and they were noisy. He smiled at them and they regarded him with curiosity, and then he began to climb to them. He got one leg well up to a knot in the bole of the great tree and pressed himself close to keep his balance, and wrapped his arms around the trunk ...

Around her waist, and she made to push him away, just the palm of her hand and not very hard. He pushed her chiton up with his free hand until he could feel the warm vellum of her hip under his fingers, and his erection took on a life of its own.

'No, my lord,' she said, but without much force. More weariness than refusal, really. She was pretty, with heavy breasts and a slim waist, and all the young men wanted her. She had smiled at him many times, and today when she came into the stable with two buckets of water he had kissed her, and now he had her under him in the straw.

He ran his hand under the thin wool, over the mound of her belly and on to her breast. The garment bunched around her hips and she moved them in discomfort. 'Stop!' she said, with a little more emphasis. 'Please?' she asked.

He ran his hand over her nipple and it sprang to life under his hand and she moaned. 'No, master. Lord. No,' she said. He kissed her and she responded, slowly at first and then more, until she was tugging at him and he was in her, spending as quickly as he entered her. Then she rose and dusted off the straw and pulled her chiton into shape, wiped her thighs a little and went back to watering horses.

She never smiled at me again, Kineas thought. I raped her. She was a slave and she could no more refuse me than refuse to eat, but let's call an action by its proper name. It was rape.

'Yes,' said Kam Baqca. She was mounted on her great charger, and she towered above him. 'It was not meant with anger, but it was ill done. When a lord forces a slave, where is the crime?'

Kineas thought the question was rhetorical, but the dream lingered, as did the question, and ...

He awoke with the question on his mind, and the sure knowledge that his body thought that Srayanka was too far away.

He rose and drank a honey drink that he enjoyed and ate fresh bread. The farmer spoke to him at length, discoursing about the harvest, apparently, and hoping for the dry spell to continue. Kineas understood one word in five, but he knew that the man meant well.

They rode on in the morning, poorer by a silver owl and their horses loaded with food. The rafters of the house had been packed with produce – drying herbs, cheese, dried meats – and the family had owned four goblets of gold.

'These people are rich!' Niceas said. 'But no slaves!'

Kineas rubbed his beard and rode on. 'A form of riches all its own,' he said, thinking of his dreams.

Niceas nodded thoughtfully. 'What was he on about, there at the end?'

Kineas rubbed his beard again. 'Weather and crops. And something else. I *think* he was warning me about bandits, although it might just as well have been an admonition against *being* bandits.'

Niceas grunted. 'You saw the scorch marks on the stone?' he said.

Kineas had seen them. 'Recent,' he said, and Niceas nodded.

That afternoon they caught up with Diodorus's rearguard. Coenus was surprised to see Kineas, but his men kept good watch, and he was saluted and greeted and cosseted as he and Niceas rode the length of the column. They halted for the night with the cavalry and shared a buck that Coenus killed, intending to ride on in the morning, despite Diodorus's protests.

That night Kineas had another dream of his youth that left him quiet when he woke, a dream in which he and some boys tormented a dog. It had happened. He had forgotten it.

As he mounted after breakfast, Diodorus came up on horseback with Sappho and several of his own staff.

'The strategos should not be haring about alone,' Diodorus said. 'Local people say there are bandits in the hills.'

Niceas grunted.

Kineas raised an eyebrow. 'Should I be afraid?' he asked.

Diodorus shrugged. 'You know what I mean,' he said.

'Ataelus will have scouted the country,' Kineas said.

'This valley is broad enough that Ataelus could put one of

his bare-breasted scouts every stade and not cover it,' Diodorus mocked. 'You just want to have adventures.'

'Yes,' Kineas said. Anything he added would only encourage more teasing.

Over Diodorus's shoulder, Sappho smiled. She was mounted on a cavalry charger, a bigger horse than most women could handle. She rode well.

'Lucky bastard,' Diodorus said. After a pause he said, 'Let me come, too.'

Kineas considered it a moment. He'd like few things better than to have his last two Athenians riding by his side, two of the three men in the world that he loved most. But he shook his head, looking at the column. 'They need you,' he said.

Diodorus grimaced. 'Truer words were never spoke,' he said ruefully. He shrugged. 'They need you, too.'

Sappho pulled her horse up by them. '"Reason, my lord, may dwell within a man,"' she said, quoting Sophokles.

'"And yet abandon him when troubles come,"' Diodorus said, capping her quote with relish. Their eyes met, and they shared a smile that touched the faint lines at the corners of her eyes.

Kineas looked at both of them. 'I take it that means I have your permission to ride on?' he asked.

Diodorus nodded, laughing.

They rode along the river for half a day, and Kineas said nothing beyond comments on the fields and the weather. Finally, as they crested a long ridge to see another in the distance and rising ground all around them, Kineas turned to Niceas. 'Do you ever think on the evil acts you've done?' he asked.

Niceas looked out over the river. 'All the time,' he said.

'And?' Kineas asked.

Niceas looked at him and frowned. 'And what? They're done. I can't undo them. I can only try not to commit them again.'

Kineas rubbed his beard. 'If we ever return to Athens, I'm going to set you up as a philosopher.'

Niceas raised an eyebrow. 'If we ever return to Athens,' he

said, 'you are going to set me up as a brothel keeper. Perhaps I'll teach the boys and girls some philosophy.'

Kineas grinned at the picture and rode on, keeping his thoughts to himself. After dinner, they curled in their cloaks, the fire crackling away, and for the first time in weeks sleep evaded Kineas.

'I missed this,' he said.

Niceas snorted. 'What, four weeks in Olbia and you missed lying on the ground?'

Kineas rolled on his back and stared up at the wheel of heaven. 'Longer than that. Remember the ferryman when we crossed the Tanais?'

'Who thought we'd all be dead when the Getae came? I'll never forget that night. Why?'

Kineas said, 'That night I thought a dozen men and a pair of slaves was a weight of responsibility on my shoulders. I was thinking it was funny that I could forget how much of a burden it was to lead.'

Niceas grunted.

'You?' Kineas asked. 'Why do you remember it?'

Niceas rustled – he was changing position while trying to keep the warmth trapped under his cloak. 'It was the last time I slept by Graccus,' he said. Niceas and Graccus had been friends and lovers for years, and Graccus, of course, had died the next day.

'I'm an idiot,' Kineas said.

Niceas snuggled against his back. 'Yes,' he said. 'Now go to sleep.'

When they mounted their horses the next morning, they could see that the ground rose on either side of them, and the river ran fast through a narrow channel, so that there was no longer any possibility of a ford or a crossing. Kineas killed another buck from horseback, a mounted throw that earned him a grin from Niceas.

'Show-off!' Niceas shook his head. 'You could have lost your best spear!'

Kineas grinned back and they divided the meat and then

bathed in the swift-flowing water to wash off the blood. It felt like ice.

That night was the coldest yet. Kineas was again feeling the weight of his responsibilities, and wondering if he could afford to ride off and leave them, and again he lay awake – still fearing his dreams, with the additional complication that he was sated with sleep. Niceas was already snoring beside him, and it was too cold to get out of his cloak and the heavy wool blanket that covered both of them. As it grew colder, he pushed in closer to Niceas, and then he worried about his army. Most of the hoplites in the vanguard wouldn't have a spare blanket. He thought of Xenophon's soldiers in the *Anabasis*, and he worried, and worrying, he fell asleep.

Ajax pushed him quickly to the tree, and his dead friends were fewer. Kleisthenes was gone. Kineas felt like a coward as he scrambled on to the tree and began to climb. It was easy to climb as high as he had gone before, and then ...

Running through the fields north of his father's farms, legs afire. Rabbit-hunting.

He was among the last men in the field, all the older men and the keener hunters stretched ahead in a long arc after the dogs. He could hear the dogs, their gross baying, their animal eagerness to kill, and it sickened him, and his legs slowed, unwillingness to see the result coinciding with his own fatigue. He fell further behind, so that even the slowest boys passed him.

The cry of the hounds changed, and their baying became a chorus of growls and then a ferocious roar that scared him. It always scared him. He slowed down further, hoping to avoid the end, but he could already smell it – the rich earth-and-copper smell of an animal wrenched apart by a dozen sets of jaws.

'You are an embarrassment,' his father said. 'What did I tell you?'

Kineas cringed. 'You said that I must not be last,' Kineas said. 'I tried!' he whined.

His father's fist caught him on the side of the head and knocked him flat. He could smell the dead rabbit and the sweat on his father and the other men. 'Try harder,' his father said ...

He awoke exhausted, his bladder bursting. It was too early

for the new light of day, and the cold was so deep that it was an effort of will to rise from the warmth of Niceas. The fire had sunk to mere embers, throwing little warmth and no light, and he tripped on their javelins before he found a place in the dark to relieve himself. A lifetime of camp discipline forced him to put the last of the wood on the fire but he couldn't find the woodpile and he stumbled around, cursing the cold.

'Piss for me, while you're up,' Niceas said.

Kineas found the firewood by tripping over it. He gathered it up, blind, and as he found the last decent stick he heard a horse. He put the firewood near the embers and felt for a javelin. He could barely stand with the fatigue of his dream.

'You hear that?' he asked.

'Horse,' Niceas said.

He heard Niceas dropping the blankets as he rose. It was that quiet. Kineas reached into the still-warm blankets and retrieved his sword. He put the baldric over his shoulder and felt for his sandals. He wasn't sure he was awake – he could barely focus his attention.

Niceas bumped into him. 'Two horses,' he whispered, his mouth close.

Alert and ready, the two men crouched back to back. After a few minutes they retrieved their cloaks and donned them.

The sky began to show light – the first touch of the wolf's tail.

'If they're coming, they'll come now,' Kineas said.

They didn't.

When the sun was up, they found hoof prints in the stream bed that ran around the base of their hillside camp. A little further west, Niceas found the print of a shod horse, with a heavy toe iron like a Macedonian horse. He shook his head.

'Could be anything,' he said. 'Might have been one of ours from yesterday. Ataelus, perhaps.'

Kineas couldn't get over the notion that he was being watched. High ridges rose on either side of the river, and anything might be moving in the trees up there.

'As soon as we ride out of the stream bed, we're visible,' he said.

'So?' asked Niceas.

'Fair enough. Let's get out of here.' Kineas went back to their camp and finished the tea, then retied his cloak behind him.

They rode along the stream bed until it rejoined the road (such as it was) a couple of stades downstream, and then they rode quickly along the road, alternating trotting with short canters.

The Tanais was entering a great curve, and the valley broadened and deepened. The river was flowing almost due north. As the ground rose, Kineas watched for the path to fork east.

'There's a sight for sore eyes,' said Niceas.

Kineas, intent on the trail, looked up to find a bare-chested Sauromatae girl sitting on a pony just half a stade away.

Ataelus met them at the top of the pass where the eastern road crossed the ridge before continuing east to the Rha and the Kaspian. He had half a dozen riders with him. Two of them were wounded.

'For making happy!' Ataelus proclaimed, and grasped his arm.

Kineas embraced the Sakje man. Then he pointed at one of the Sauromatae girls who was boiling a human skull in a pot. 'What in Hades is that?'

'Wedding present!' Ataelus said, and laughed, slapping his knee with a calloused hand. He was so pleased with his retort that he translated it into Sakje and repeated it. All of his prodromoi howled.

Kineas shook his head. 'Wedding present?' he asked.

'Sauromatae girl for needing to kill man before wedding,' Ataelus said. 'Clean skull for stinking less, yes?' He grinned.

'Who did she kill?' Kineas asked.

'Bandits,' Ataelus said. 'For finding bandits in hills. Farmers say "bandits kill us steal our grain" and I say "for finding bandits."'

Niceas twisted his mouth and made a noise. 'Macedonian-shod?' he asked.

Ataelus looked at him without comprehending. Ataelus's

Greek was good enough, but it never seemed to get better than 'good enough' no matter how much time he spent with them.

Niceas got down and lifted a hoof of his Macedonian charger. He showed the shoe.

Ataelus nodded enthusiastically. 'And Persian. And Sakje.' He pointed to two small ponies with iron-grey hides and bloodstains.

'What about Philokles?' Kineas asked.

Ataelus shrugged. 'Eight days ahead. More? For riding hard.' Ataelus waved east.

Kineas nodded. 'And Nihmu?' he asked.

'For child?' Ataelus asked. 'Nihmu yâtavu child? For being somewhere! For being under the foot of my pony when I fight, or for dropping rocks on bandits. Who knows where the child is for going?' He grinned. 'Her horses I am for having.' Sure enough, the dozen royal chargers towered over the scout's remounts like a separate genus.

Niceas explained that Diodorus was a day or two behind, and Lot a week behind him.

Ataelus watched the ridges behind them while Niceas spoke. When Niceas finished, Ataelus pulled at his nose and drooped an eyelid. 'Time to find bandits,' he said. 'For taking their horses, bring them fire. When Diodorus for coming, bandits scatter.' He pointed down the other side of the ridge, towards the Kaspian and Hyrkania. 'Bandits thick as rain, for fighting. Out on the high plains. All way to Rha. Lost two men getting Spartan to coast.'

Kineas rubbed his beard. 'How many bandits, Ataelus?'

'Many and many,' Ataelus replied. 'Kill bandits here, for making others feel fear. Yes?'

Kineas could see that Ataelus already had a plan. So he nodded.

Ataelus grinned. He motioned to one of the Sauromatae girls. She slipped off her mare, pulled her saddle blanket off her horse's back and threw a double armful of dew-wet bracken on the fire. Thick grey-blue smoke pulsed into the sky. The Sauromatae girl put her blanket over the fire in one smooth motion, so that the smoke was cut off. Then she whipped it clear and another pulse of smoke shot upward.

She repeated this three times.

Ataelus grunted in satisfaction.

'Neat trick,' Kineas said.

'Have we ever seen them do that before?' Niceas asked.

'No,' Kineas answered.

Already there was a picket galloping up the ridge from the eastern road. He pulled on his reins in the camp and Samahe, Ataelus's wife from the Cruel Hands, barked orders at him. He grinned, dismounted, cut another pony out of the herd, remounted and galloped away.

A pair of Sauromatae girls galloped in from another direction. Before the sun rose three fingers more, there were a dozen riders gathered, and they were riding hard along one of the many stream beds that criss-crossed the wooded ridges. A trickle of water flowed over rocks under their horse's hooves, but the banks were clear of leaves or brush on either side up to the height of their horse's withers, indicating how full these little valleys ran when the rains fell.

Ataelus seemed to know just where he was riding. Kineas was content to ride along.

The shadows stretched away when they stopped. All the Sakje and the Sauromatae dismounted and relieved themselves without letting go of their reins. Kineas and Niceas imitated them.

There was a hint of smoke on the cold wind over the strong smell of urine. A clear-eyed blonde woman handed him a gourd of water and he raised it in acknowledgement before he drank. She looked to be fourteen or perhaps fifteen. She had two skulls on the ornate saddle of her horse.

Kineas grinned at her and she returned the grin.

'We for hitting them at dark,' Ataelus said. 'Understand for hitting?' he smacked his right fist into his left hand.

'I understand,' Kineas said.

'For watching two days, since girls get in fight and Samahe for finding camp.' Ataelus shrugged.

There was something untold, some story that made Samahe

wrinkle her nose and made one of the girls blush and wriggle in her saddle. A story he'd never know, Kineas thought.

'You knew we were coming?' Kineas said, suddenly making the connection.

'Nihmu says for coming, says "protect him king".' Ataelus shrugged. 'Not for needing child for telling for protecting.'

'You watched us last night?' Niceas asked.

'No. For today since sun rose this way.' Ataelus closed one eye and raised a hand, palm flat, just over the horizon.

Niceas shook his head. 'They were on us last night. If they watched us meet ...'

Kineas took a deep breath, suddenly eager to have it over with. 'If they intended to ambush us, they've had all day to do it.'

The shadows lengthened across the meadows below them, and the air grew frostier as the sun's rays fell further away. Niceas and Kineas had to work to curb the impatience of their horses. Kineas's Getae horse was the worst, fretting constantly and jerking his head at any motion, so that Kineas had to dismount and hold his head.

The blonde woman gave him a glance of pity – pity that his horse was so ill-trained.

Twice they heard voices, both times Persian speakers getting water from the Tanais below them. Then, while the sun was just visible, they saw a pair of riders come out of the meadow and ride a short distance up the ridge, from where they had a good view of the eastern road at their feet.

Ataelus grunted in disgust, because by chance or purpose, the new pickets had a much better chance of warning the camp below of his approach than the pair they replaced. He clucked his tongue in his cheek as he watched them, and after a few minutes, he summoned one of the Standing Horse warriors in his band and the two of them rode off down the back of the ridge. Samahe dismounted and lay in the leaf mould, her hand shading her eyes.

Time dragged by. The Sauromatae women were as nervous as kittens, but their horses were calm, munching quietly on anything in reach and otherwise immobile. Niceas drew and resheathed his sword a dozen times. Kineas was busy keeping his under-trained horse from mischief.

He was amazed at their discipline. All over again. He couldn't have kept a dozen Greek troopers so quiet without the hope of massive gain.

Even as he thought it, he wondered if he was making a poor assumption. Perhaps the Greeks could do as well. Perhaps with training, some rides out with Sakje patrols ...

Samahe rose to a crouch and Kineas snapped from his reverie to watch the ground below him. The two mounted pickets were almost invisible, even from above, but little movements in the trees betrayed their position to a careful watcher. But unlike Samahe, Kineas couldn't see Ataelus or his partner, so the first he knew of their movement was a pair of arrows appearing from the rocks to the right and falling silently on the pickets.

'Now!' Samahe said in Sakje, and she vaulted on to her mare and set off down the hillside at a speed that terrified Kineas, who was right behind her and couldn't, for the sake of honour, go any slower. He reached the valley floor at a gallop, already past his fear because the ride had been so bad in itself, and he readied a javelin as the pair of them raced across the meadow. He could see the camp now, and it seemed to be *full* of men and horses – dozens of them. A few had bows. One raised his and loosed, but the arrow flew well over Kineas, who ducked down on his horse's mane and galloped on, straight at the heart of the bandit camp.

Samahe's horse sidestepped some obstruction in the meadow grass, and on her next rise she shot, her arrow licking across the flowers and the sweet grass to drop one of the few bandits to get mounted. Her second arrow was in the air.

The Sauromatae girls weren't shooting. They were screaming with all the gusto of the young warrior, screaming away their terror and their exhilaration, and they bore straight at the bandits by the river.

Kineas went through the camp without touching his reins. No one opposed him and he rode past the huddle of bandits at the riverbank and then up a short rise to a clearing in the riverbank woods, where there was an abandoned farmstead and the bandit horse herd. There were ten men in the clearing and despite the screams from the riverside, they seemed surprised when he appeared in their midst, and two of them were down before any got weapons to hand.

Kineas wheeled his horse and extended his arm, using the momentum of the move to twirl the shaft in his fingers so that he changed grips in a single stride of his mount, and a circle of blood drops flew from the point of his rotating javelin.

He felt like a god, at least for a moment.

One of the men had a bow and shot his horse, who crashed to the ground in another stride, and he fell, getting a leg under him and then rolling, javelin lost. He came up against a tree and he rolled to put the bole between him and the archer.

The archer laughed. 'Try this!' he called, in Persian. He shot. The arrow hit the tree and shattered, and the man laughed again. He had a black beard and kohl-rimmed eyes like a Bactrian nobleman.

Down by the river, men were dying. Blackbeard drew another arrow. 'Get horses,' he called over his shoulder, and two boys sprang to do his bidding.

Kineas pulled his cloak off and whirled it around his arm, moving to his right to a larger tree.

'Try this, Greek!' Blackbeard shot again, and his arrow hit the new tree.

Kineas jumped out and retrieved his javelin, avoiding the slashing hooves of his dying Getae mount and leaping behind another tree just as a third arrow skipped along the bark and slapped into the rolled cloak on his arm.

'Try this, harlot!' Kineas yelled, and threw his javelin. Then he charged, leaping a downed tree as he ran, heedless of the odds. It was better than letting a master archer take his time, and something had gone wrong in the fight by the river.

His javelin hit the man by the archer's side, knocking him flat like the deer. The archer turned and ran, and Kineas ran after him. There were men in the clearing and they set themselves to stop him, but none put the archer's life higher than his own, and Kineas ran through them, downing one with a sword cut as he ran by.

The two boys had grabbed a pair of horses apiece, and Blackbeard took the first he came to, tossed the boy clear of the saddlecloth and vaulted astride, pulling the horse's head around. At the other side of the clearing, Samahe appeared, shooting as she came, and the other boy went down with an arrow in his guts, screaming. Kineas found himself crossing blades with yet another Persian – another nobleman, from the rags of purple on his cloak. The man had a good sword, and he was aggressive.

Blackbeard pulled his horse around and shot. So did Samahe. Neither hit. Both were moving fast, flat to their horse's backs, and then Kineas had no attention to spare.

The Persian leaped in and cut hard at his head. Kineas parried and the blades rang together, and the Persian kicked at his shin under the locked iron. Kineas pushed his hooked blade up and over his opponent's guard and then slipped a foot behind the man's ankle and pushed, hoping for a throw, and the Persian jumped back, cutting high.

He was a swordsman.

Kineas parried and cut back, a short chop at his opponent's hand, but the Persian had seen such a move before, and he made a hand-high parry that turned into an overhand cut to the head – and Kineas just managed a parry, taking a blow that was not quite a cut to the shoulder. His left hand closed on his Sakje whip in the sash at his back, and he pulled it clear and changed his stance to lead with his left foot, the whip out as a shield.

The Persian had a knife in his left hand and he stamped forward, leading with the knife.

Kineas backed away, kicked pine needles and risked a glance over his shoulder. Ataelus was shooting behind him – shooting back the way he had come. Something was *wrong*.

The Persian was smiling. He flicked with the knife – a feint with just enough power to draw blood. Kineas retreated a step and the Persian's smile grew wider. He suddenly changed tempo, pivoting on his front foot and thrusting with his sword and then trying to trap Kineas's sword against his own with the dagger.

Kineas just barely evaded the trap, twisting his body, pulling a muscle in his neck, inwardly cursing. Again he backed away, aware that this fight was taking *too much time*. Ataelus called out in Sakje – something about a wound.

Kineas made a high attack with his sword, scoring just a touch of a cut against his opponent's forearm and drawing the same high counter-attack – but this time, Kineas gave the man's sword hand the full weight of the lash of his riding whip and then cut low with his blade, catching the Persian just on the hip bone and cutting him deeply. The man fell back. He wasn't grinning, but he had the grace to salute with his dagger hand.

Kineas leaped forward, cut hard at the Persian's sabre and knocked it right out of the man's hand – the lash had hurt, as Kineas could see.

'Yield,' he said in Persian.

The Persian glanced over his shoulder, where Samahe had an arrow pointed at his back. He nodded three times, as if some point of philosophy had just come to him, and tossed his dagger on the ground. 'I yield,' he said.

Kineas raised his own blade, stepped well back and looked for Ataelus and Niceas. Ataelus was at the horse herd, calling orders. Niceas was nowhere to be seen.

The swordsman was the only prisoner. His cousin – Blackbeard – hadn't survived the archery duel with both Samahe and Ataelus, and the rest of their troop had been cut down or had fled. Kineas was a little surprised at the savagery of the Sakje – but only a little. He was more worried about Niceas.

Niceas lay out on the meadow of flowers with an arrow in his ribs. He wasn't dead, but he was deeply unconscious from the fall, and the arrow had skidded up his ribs and ripped open his shoulder as well.

'Shit,' Kineas said.

'I'll save him,' said Nihmu.

Kineas whirled. He hadn't seen her approach, hadn't seen

134

her horse. She had a strung bow over her shoulder and her quiver was empty. She turned and ran across the meadow towards the bandit camp, and Kineas was left to make his comrade as comfortable as possible. He rolled Niceas's cloak and put it under his head and cut the remnants of his tunic free from his body.

Nihmu came back with a copper beaker of water, still steaming hot from the bandits' fire. 'It looks worse than it is,' she said with the confidence of an adult. Then, more quietly, 'Sirven died.'

'Sirven?' Kineas asked.

'Lot's daughter older. The blonde girl.' Nihmu shrugged. 'I told her she would die if she fought here. But when she went down, they all fought over her body. Ataelus took a cut.' She pointed at a red-haired girl of fourteen weeping. 'Her sister lost a finger and took an arrow in the leg. They are all angry.' She sounded like the child she was – and like an upset child, at that.

Kineas felt his post-battle fatigue come on him, as the daimon that animated him to fight left his body empty of feelings except sorrow.

Nihmu was washing the wound with hot water, her dark hair hanging in uncombed tangles over her face so that he couldn't see her. 'They are all angry.' She repeated. 'So they killed all the bandits.'

'All?' Kineas asked, turning to look for his prisoner.

'You should stay by him. He will do you a good turn one day, that one. If Ataelus doesn't take his hair.'

Kineas turned and trotted off into the dusk to find his Persian.

The man was burying Blackbeard. Kineas listened to the Sauromatae mourning Sirven and her sister. Mosva, he thought. She's called Mosva. Kineas left his Persian prisoner working and walked down to the river to find Ataelus.

'Stupid girl,' Ataelus said bitterly. 'Stupid Sauromatae barbarian girl.' He had tears in his eyes and a quaver in his voice. 'Fight like wild things, sword to sword with grown men – hard men. And me for fool! Too long fighting stupid Greeks.'

Kineas hugged the little Sakje, and pressed Samahe's hand, and embraced the little red-haired princess, who clung to him and wept until he was embarrassed, and then for a good time beyond, so that he stared into the gathering darkness and patted her hair, thinking bleak thoughts about the quality of right and wrong, good and evil, and about how far he was from being a man of virtue when he couldn't comfort a bereft sister. But eventually she felt his awkwardness and drew back with an apology, and then he punished himself and went to help the Persian bury his cousin. Later, he sat by the fire making barley soup for Niceas, who was deeply unconscious.

'I came to find you,' Nihmu said, kneeling by him. 'I didn't like it when they killed the prisoners. It made me afraid.'

'Killing prisoners is never good. Sometimes it must be done – when they are wounded, and you can't help them. Sometimes it – happens.' He shrugged, the image of the Getae man he had killed a year before rising in his mind, so that he gave a little shiver of revulsion.

'It is time. Are you climbing the tree yet?' she asked.

Kineas nodded. 'Yes,' he said.

'I saw you in the dream world – three nights ago, I think it must have been. You are an eagle.'

Kineas shuddered again with a different disgust. Speaking of the dream world this way was like discussing sex – he knew men who did it, but he didn't himself. Speaking of the dream world with this – this child – was almost impossible. 'Yes,' he said, repressing his feelings as well as he might.

She flicked a smile at him and put some herbs into the barley soup. 'He won't die,' she said, as if Niceas's continued existence were obvious to anyone.

Kineas looked at Niceas and felt tears come to his eyes. His throat threatened to close, and he couldn't speak. He knew that Niceas might die – in any skirmish, on any day – but the reality of his unmoving body was deeply painful.

'You need a horse,' the girl said.

Kineas took a deep breath to deny it and then slumped. 'Yes,' he said.

'I have a horse for you,' the girl said. 'A magnificent beast, who will carry you from now to the day you fall.'

Kineas smiled. 'The way I ride, I may fall later today.'

Nihmu looked back at him with a child's intensity and a child's impatience for adult humour. 'You know what I mean. Take the horse.'

And Kineas agreed.

11

The Persian's name was Darius – every first-born son in his generation was Darius, it seemed. He was tired of war, which had been his life since he was seventeen. He was twenty-three.

He related the tales of his life as he sat beside a small fire, heating water to clean Niceas, who was still unconscious and had no control of his bodily functions. 'I left home six years ago to fight the Great King,' he said. He gave a wry smile. 'The usurper, that is. Darius.' He shrugged. 'Real Persians – the true Persians of the great plain – he was never our king.' He looked into the fire, rolled over to get more firewood and winced as the cut on his hip pained him.

Kineas nodded.

'And your Alexander rode right into our rebellion. He defeated us in the west – were you there?'

Kineas nodded. 'Pinarus river. I was with the Allied Cavalry.'

Darius shook his head. 'I was still a rebel. Then, after Alexander won, it was clear to most noblemen – clear enough to my father – that if we continued to rebel, we were handing our empire to the foreigner. So we marched to the so-called Great King at Ecbatana, and followed him to Gaugamela.' He shrugged. 'You were there?'

Kineas nodded. 'On our left.'

Darius looked surprised. 'Our right? I was there!' He winced again. 'By fire, you cut me deep.'

Kineas began trying to feed soup to Niceas. Beyond the fire, the Sauromatae and the Sakje were mourning the dead woman, singing her songs to her pyre. The smell of horse meat was strong.

'It might have been deeper,' he said.

The Persian nodded. 'So it might. I was at Gaugamela, and we almost broke you.'

'But you didn't,' Kineas said with satisfaction. He might not serve Macedon any more – indeed, he was probably an enemy of Macedon, when sides were counted – but Gaugamela had been the last fight of the Hellenes against the Persians, and he was proud of his role there. He had won the laurel for valour, because his unsung Allied Cavalry had held the line when the Persian cavalry threatened to break Parmenion's flank and bury the taxeis under an avalanche of Persians.

'It was the longest fight I can remember. I lost two horses – and lived.'

Kineas nodded in agreement. In his experience, most field battles were decided fairly quickly, and the other side took the punishment when they broke. At Gaugamela, the decision hung in the balance for an hour, and both sides died.

'After the battle, my father was dead and my household dispersed. My cousin claimed the lordship – he was older and ...' the Persian gave an expressive shrug. 'We never got home. We moved north into Hyrkania, but there were too many wolves there already and we kept going until we came here. We thought to carve out a kingdom, far from the Hellenes.' He gave a self-deprecating smile, the same smile he'd worn when he lost his sword in the fight. 'We ended up as bandits.'

'This might make a good kingdom,' Kineas said. He pointed at Niceas's form. 'He thinks so.' They sat in companionable silence for some time. Eventually, Kineas asked, 'Are you worth a ransom?'

'Somewhere, if my mother lives, I have some small riches,' the man admitted. He shrugged again – he shrugged a lot. 'I doubt it. You Greeks have everything around Ecbatana now, and most of our eastern holdings, too. We had a tower in Bactria – I doubt it even tried to hold your mad king.'

'Not my mad king,' Kineas began. It was his turn, and the young Persian with the perpetual shrugs was a good companion. Kineas intended to win him as a friend and put him in a troop – he was a good sword, too good to waste. But Niceas chose that moment to sputter around a spoonful of soup. His body gave a spasm and he sprayed soup out of his mouth.

His eyes were open.

'What the fuck?' he said.

Kineas felt his eyes fill with tears. 'You stupid cocksucker,' he said with tones of those born to the agora in Athens. 'You fell off your horse!'

Niceas smiled. 'More soup,' he said.

The next day, Diodorus caught up with them. His part of the army camped above them on the heights where the road turned east and went down into the country of the Rha. Diodorus came down the ridge with a dozen troopers, including Coenus and Eumenes.

Diodorus went straight to Niceas, as did Coenus. Afterwards, Diodorus ordered a tent put up for the strategos, and Eumenes went to fetch it. 'I heard the old man was dead,' Diodorus said. His face was still red and blotched from emotion – perhaps from weeping. 'He's saved my life more times than my nanny paddled my behind. I came as fast as I could.'

Kineas nodded. He'd slept through the night once Niceas's sleep had given way to healthy snores, and he felt ten years younger. 'I thought he was gone,' Kineas admitted.

Coenus was feeding the hyperetes more barley soup. 'He still looks like shit,' he said.

Niceas croaked something about feeling better.

Kineas shook his head. 'He took an arrow in the side. We weren't in armour. Bad decision on my part. And the bandits were good – damned good. Tough fight.'

Coenus thrust his chin at the Persian who was tending the soup. 'Prisoner?'

Kineas nodded. 'And recruit. When Eumenes gets back, put him in his troop. He's a swordsman – as good as me. I assume he can ride.'

Coenus laughed. 'He is a Persian.' He coughed. 'You and Ataelus killed all his friends ...'

'I get the feeling he doesn't miss them. If he cuts all our throats, I'll be proven wrong.' Kineas pulled his cloak tighter. 'I'll stay here with Niceas.'

Coenus and Diodorus exchanged glances. 'Nah,' said Coenus. 'You're the strategos. This isn't the only bandit band

– ask Ataelus. The plains are full of them, by all accounts. You go and command. Leave me with my section and I'll bring the old boy along when he's ready.'

Diodorus stepped forward. 'He's right, Kineas.'

Kineas rubbed his beard. 'You are both correct, of course. Very well. Coenus, I'll send your section down the ridge. Diodorus, let's get Ataelus and plan the next set of marches. Lot is five days behind you. Somebody gets to tell him that his daughter is dead.'

Diodorus winced as if cut.

The high plains between the Tanais and the Rha were indeed full of bandits – an endless profusion of masterless Persians and outlawed nomads and Macedonian deserters, so that there wasn't an intact farmstead between the two rivers. Four years of war in Hyrkania and the south had filled the high plains with the human flotsam of war, and like wolves on the verge of a hard winter, they were desperate men. When forced, they fed on each other, band against band. All raided the settlements on the expanding edge of their self-made desert. Ataelus had already lost three men to them before the fight with the bandits on the Tanais, and his prodromoi were eager for revenge.

Kineas and Diodorus assigned the second troop, heavy with the Keltoi, to reinforce Ataelus. Kineas took charge of the column and Diodorus took charge of the extermination of the bandits. He didn't catch as many as he wanted to, but the main body crossed the high plains to the valleys of the Rha without losing a single horse or man, and unknown to them, the Sindi and Maeotae farmers blessed them. Diodorus drove the larger groups across the marshes to the north, and twice he caught bands and the Keltoi and the Sauromatae wrecked them. They brought back a rich haul of horses, some very fine, and enough gold and silver to please the men who did the fighting. Casualties were gratifyingly light – as was to be expected when employing overwhelming force.

Kineas called his new horse 'Thalassa', after days of riding the magnificent silver charger and trying out various temporary names ('Brute' seemed the front runner, as the beast towered over most of the other warhorses by the width of a man's hand). The big horse had the colour of a stormy day at sea. She was sure-footed and had an amazing quality of stillness – not lack of spirit, but something like patience – that suited a commander's horse. And on the day that Sappho insisted that so noble an animal needed a better name than 'Brute', the lead elements of the army crested the last ridge of the Rha's frontier and saw the Kaspian sparkling in the distance, the Bay of the Rha full of ships, and like Xenophon's men seventy years before, they cried out for the sea, and the name was given.

The crossing had not been particularly arduous except for recruits and the men of second troop who'd spent a week fighting bandits, but the army's grain supply was very low – most men had only a day's grain in their packs, or less if they'd been improvident. The sight of fifty small boats in the bay raised everyone's spirits, and the presence of Philokles on the gravel and mud beach drew a roar of acclaim. Kineas embraced him.

'Does this place have a name?' Kineas asked. Philokles smelled *clean*.

'Errymi, the Maeotae call it.' The Spartan gave a wry smile. 'It is *good* to see you, Kineas.'

Kineas embraced him again for an answer. 'Are all those for us?' Kineas asked.

'If we can pay,' Philokles answered. 'Otherwise, I suspect they'll murder me and sail away.'

Kineas watched the mules bearing the army's treasury coming down the last ridge, guarded by the most trustworthy men in the army. 'And wintering over?'

'Northern Hyrkania,' Philokles responded. 'Strategos, your kingdom awaits.'

Kineas shook his head. 'I don't want a kingdom.'

Philokles gave an enigmatic smile. 'How about a woman?' he asked.

Kineas laughed. 'I have a woman. She's ten thousand stades distant, but I'll catch up.'

Philokles gave him an odd look. 'Have you made an offering to Aphrodite, brother?' he asked.

Kineas laughed. 'No!' he said.

Philokles gave a distant smile. 'You should.' He looked over the sea. 'Our winter camp is in a kingdom ruled by a woman, and she – she moved *me*, and I have no tenderness for women. I fear for you.'

Kineas furrowed his brow, stung. 'What reason have I ever given you to fear for my behaviour with a woman?' he asked.

Philokles continued to watch him with the air of a man who has seen the world. 'I would prefer you to cross the Kaspian with your eyes open. This woman desires power, and men with power fascinate her. She lay with Alexander, they say. Now she awaits us.' He glanced around. 'She offers a great deal of treasure for our spring campaign.'

Kineas shrugged. 'I'm of a mind now to push on in spring. The march went well and the bandits in the hills put some gold in our coffers.' He looked at the ships. 'And our ally? Leon's factor?'

'Her late husband. She remains an ally – she paid Leon an enormous backlog of moneys owed without demur – but I doubt her. I wish you to be immune to her.'

Kineas shook his head in mock wonder. 'I am immune,' he said.

Nihmu laughed. 'No man is immune to the yâtavu of Hyrkania,' she said, 'except those who love only men.' She came and went from the command group, red hair like a helmet crest announcing her arrival. She sat on her great white horse amid the mud and the flotsam on the beach. 'If you fail, Strategos, your children will not rule here.'

'What?' Kineas shrugged and turned his back on her. She spoke like an oracle, but she was a stripling, and he was busy. 'Think as you will. This is a foolish conversation. To whom do we speak about paying these ships?' he asked Philokles.

Philokles explained that every captain was an independent operator. The boats were small – half the size of a Greek pentekonter, and some smaller than that, with ten or twelve oars a side. A few were sailing vessels, like large fishing smacks. Kineas cast his eyes across them and shook his head, changing the subject again to calm his temper. 'I don't see transport for two thousand horses,' he said.

Philokles rubbed his forehead, pulled his cloak tighter against the autumn wind and met Kineas's eye. 'Two hundred horses at a time,' he said. 'It was the best I could do.'

Kineas nodded apologetically. 'I didn't mean you haven't done your best,' he said. 'You've done enough that you are here, and with food and so much transport. Let's start shipping them across the sea. How many days?'

'Two days each way, with luck and a friendly wind. It is a very small sea.'

Kineas shaded his eyes with his hand, pushing his straw hat back on his head to keep the flapping brim out of his line of sight. 'We captured quite a few horses on the way here,' he said. 'Let us arrange sacrifices to Poseidon, and some games – horse races such as the Trident-bearer values above all things. Let us celebrate his power tonight. And then let's start loading. The autumn is wearing on, and winter is coming.'

Kineas was among the last of his men to leave for the winter camp in Hyrkania. He stayed on the beach in Errymi to shepherd the men across, to keep morale high on the beach, to prevent incidents with the locals ... and to wait for Niceas.

As the weeks passed, while storms slowed the ferries and the stores of food dwindled and the conditions in the seaside camp worsened, he found that his presence heartened his men and that all his skills as a leader were required to prevent mischief and even murder. He had the cavalrymen dig earthworks, an unheard-of demand that served to raise a barrier against the constant wind and, more importantly, against boredom – at least until the walls were complete.

Prince Lot's knights were even less inclined to dig than Greek aristocrats, but time and the example of Prince Lot himself got most of them to it, and Kineas was too versed in military leadership to believe that every one of the Sauromatae needed to be set to digging. Some hunted – for food and also for bandits. The killing of Lot's elder daughter was a mistake for which the masterless men of the high plains paid for three months, and the aggressive mourning of the Sauromatae would cease only when the last boats were rowed away from the empty marching camp. Kineas didn't intend to burn the huts that had been built, however. Instead, he handed the finished work to a group of Maeotae farmers, dispossessed men whose families had been burned out by the bandits and who had fled to the marshes to eke out a living. With the marching camp as a fortified town, they had every chance of holding their own. A dozen Keltoi, too badly wounded in the fall's fighting to make the crossing, would remain as military settlers.

Kineas discovered that it was Niceas he was hanging on for when he saw the unmistakable width of Coenus's broad shoulders coming down the ridge from the west. Closer up, the dozen Greek troopers were obviously *not* a returning patrol, and closer still, Kineas could see Niceas, swathed in fur robes, riding a big pony.

Kineas sent a boy for his riding horse and went out to meet them, his throat tight. It remained tight while he embraced Niceas, who winced and cursed, and Coenus, and Crax and Sitalkes and Antigonus. Niceas looked twenty years older, and Coenus looked considerably thinner, but the rest of them smiled a great deal and shuffled when Kineas praised them.

Privately, Coenus was less sanguine. 'He's not the same,' Coenus said. Niceas was sitting on the rim of the hearth, visibly soaking up warmth. 'I'm not sure he'll ever fight again. But he's alive, and he's as tough as a slave's sandal.' Coenus drank back his wine – his third cup – and swallowed a handful of olives.

'Was it hard?' Kineas asked.

'Never,' Coenus said. 'Best hunting of my life. Like Xenophon's notion of Elysium. After Lot came, we sent back for grain, and later the farmers came to us. It was never dull, and those are good men you gave me.' His grin had a self-conscious air to it. 'I loved it.' He narrowed his eyes. 'Niceas says we should carve a kingdom out of this land.' Coenus, usually fastidious, had a bushy beard, and he rubbed it with his fingers as if embarrassed by it. 'I want to sign up. I'll put a shrine to Artemis in that valley – I know just the spot. I'll hunt until I'm too old to ride, and then I'll sit around losing my teeth and telling lies.' Then he stopped grinning. 'Watching him was hard,' he said.

Niceas was grey with fatigue and went to bed too soon.

Kineas lay next to Niceas in the tent. Niceas slept more deeply than he had before his wound, and he lay still, as if in death, so that Kineas often listened to him like an anxious parent with a sick child, leaning across the older man's body to hear his soft breathing. Tonight, Kineas had Philokles on his other side – it was a cold, damp night with a threat of freezing rain in the air, and every man in the army pushed close to his tent mates.

Kineas was tired with worry and relief, but sleep would not come, and he lay listening to the sounds made by his night guards, by two thousand horses in the dark, by a few foolish soldiers lingering late by their mess fires. They, too, were relieved to find that boats were waiting for them.

And then, as subtle as the first fall of snow, he was … *standing amidst the bones at the base of the tree, surrounded by the silent combat of dead friends against dead foes. He reached for a limb and drew himself up until the combat beneath him vanished and he looked up. The tree towered over him, reaching into the sky. He noticed that the tree lacked the misty quality of his first dreams – now it was as palpable and as solid as any tree outside the world of dreams.*

The owl shot by and made a showy landing above him, and squawked. Kineas grinned at it.

'I know what I'm here for,' he told the owl. Instead of a slow climb, he reached for a branch overhead, planted his feet and leaped to grab the next major limb.

He just caught it, and he hung for a moment, the strain on his arms as real as anything in the outer world, and it took the concentration of all his years on the floor of various gymnasiums to lever himself up and over, to lie panting for a full minute before he pushed himself up and climbed carefully to his feet …

In the agora of his youth with a sack of scrolls hanging over his arm – fourteen, too young to be a man and old enough to desire to be one. Diodorus and Graccus walked by his side, alert for trouble. Demosthenes had spoken in the assembly against Philip of Macedon, and all of the agora was talking about it. Kineas and his two best friends drifted from group to group, abandoning the safety of their group of rich boys to listen to the conversation of older men.

There was a large circle of men gathered around Apollion, and he walked around them. Apollion – tall, handsome, blond Apollion, who the assembly loved and who fought in the front rank in the phalanx – had made advances, just yesterday, making it clear that he could push Kineas's career as an orator if Kineas would suck his dick for a few years. He'd put it better than that, but Kineas's anger – and fear, for Apollion was a big man, dangerous in combat and in the assembly – blinded him to rational behaviour. He'd struck Apollion, in front of everyone in the gymnasium, and fled.

The man looked up from the crowd he was haranguing and gave Kineas a wolfish grin.

Kineas froze, caught between the desire to defy and the desire to flee.

Diodorus didn't hesitate. 'It's like finding Socrates talking in the agora,' he called out.

Many of the older men laughed aloud. Apollion often liked to quote Socrates – but Socrates had been notoriously ugly. It was a two-edged gibe.

Grinning like the fox he was, Diodorus gave Kineas a shove to get him moving again. 'Don't act like a deer caught in torchlight,' Diodorus hissed. 'He'll think you're pining for him.'

Graccus, who admired Apollion, shook his head. 'I'd have him in a moment.' He grinned – he was given to grins. 'I can't imagine what he sees in you!' He swatted Kineas on the leg.

'He's saving himself for Phocion,' Diodorus said, and Kineas, stung at last, smacked him in the ear. Phocion – Athens's greatest soldier – taught all of them in swordsmanship and in the use of the spear. It set them apart from other rich boys, many of whom disdained military service as something for those too stupid to make money.

Kineas called them idiotai, after Thucydides.

In the dream world, Kineas knew what was coming, and part of his mind flinched from it, even as he experienced it again . . .

They had crossed the agora and were well down the road to the gates, far from their own haunts, still listening to men gossip and discourse. They were in a bad part of Athens, where men went for cheap wine and cheap sex.

'We should get out of here,' Graccus said quietly.

Diodorus looked around. 'Those are brothels!' he said. He sounded interested. 'Some day, I'm going to purchase a hetaira and fuck her every minute of the day.'

'Is this before or after you've sailed beyond the Pillars of Herakles?' Kineas jibed, but a commotion in the doorway of the nearest knocking shop drew their attention.

'I've fucking paid for an hour, and I'll have every fucking grain of sand in the glass,' shouted a man. He sounded like a foreigner – a Corinthian or a Theban. He had a boy by the neck. The boy was short, tough-looking, with heavy dark circles under his eyes. He was naked and there was blood running down his legs.

He wasn't crying. His shoulders were rigid with tension. He suddenly burst into action, breaking free of the foreigner, but the man was too fast. He tripped the boy, and then, as he went down, he kicked him savagely in the stomach, so that the boy heaved up, vomiting. The foreigner stepped back. He turned back to the brothel keeper. 'I'll fuck him in the street if I please,' he said, his voice so devoid of strain or inflection that the hairs rose on Kineas's neck.

'We need to get out of here,' Graccus said.

Kineas felt something inside him – some combination of his own ideas of right, of Apollion's desire to force him to have sex, his anger at having failed to stand up to the man.

The brothel keeper shook his head. 'Respected sir, you must not abuse him – and if he refuses you, you must go.' The brothel keeper was not a small man and he wasn't cowed. He wouldn't have held his place if violence cowed him. 'The boy is not a slave. You are a foreigner. If you make a fuss, I'll have you taken.'

The foreigner moved suddenly, grabbing the brothel keeper's ears and slamming his head against the doorpost of the brothel. Then he raised his knee and smashed it into the brothel keeper's chin. 'Anyone else want some?' he asked the street. He reached down and picked up the boy. Closer up, Kineas could see that the boy wasn't as young as he had thought – he was, in fact, a few years older than Kineas, just scrawny and ill-fed.

Diodorus reached out a hand, but he was too late. Kineas slipped away and stood in front of the foreigner, whose eyes glittered with something Kineas hadn't seen before.

'Put him down,' Kineas said.

The foreigner was a soldier – he had all the marks of wearing armour on him, and a heavy knife at his belt of the kind soldiers wore when they didn't wear swords. 'Or?' the man said. He didn't grin or frown. It was as if his face was dead. Kineas's voice cracked in fear, but he stood his ground.

'Put him down,' Kineas said. 'And don't even think of harming me.' Me came out as a squeak, as the man dropped the boy to fall in the garbage of the street. 'My father is—'

'I don't give a fuck about your father, little arse-cunt,' the man said. He was fast, and he swung hard, punching Kineas in the side of the head before he was ready. Pain exploded in Kineas's head and he stumbled, hit the wall of the brothel and bounced back, almost into the foreigner's arms.

Guided by the gods.

The man wasn't ready for him and as Kineas jostled him, his right hand closed – of its own accord – on the man's knife. The man shoved him, annoyed now, and Kineas stumbled back with the knife in his hand.

'Put that down or I'll rip the flesh off your face,' the man said.

Graccus was no fool, he was screaming for the watch, running back to the agora because the watch didn't come down here.

A stone hit the man in the head. It was well thrown, a jagged bit of mortar from the ill-kept tenements, and it made the sound of a dropped melon when it hit. The man's eyes flicked to Diodorus.

'You're dead,' he said, without changing facial expression. He stepped forward, intent on Kineas.

The boy – the older boy – had one of his legs. The man tripped, stumbled and Kineas blocked a piece of his blow with his left arm and thrust hard with the knife, the whole weight of his stocky body behind the blow. But he struck too high and the knife caught the man's breastbone and skidded up, cutting sinew, slashing all the way across to the point of the shoulder.

The man shrieked and punched, left-right-left, and one of the blows caught Kineas and flung him back, his jaw broken and blood pouring from his nose. Tears burst from his eyes.

He didn't drop the knife or lose sight of his opponent. That much of Phocion's training stuck. He was conscious that this was a fight to the death, and that to lose control to the pain would be the end. But beyond that, his body seemed to be in the fight by itself, with his brain unable to affect the outcome.

And above it, Kineas the dreamer already knew the outcome. And the pain.

The street was filling with people and many were calling for the watch while others wagered on the outcome.

Kineas set himself in his sword stance, left leg forward, left arm out like a shield, knife close to his body. Blood and tears and mucus were running down his face and his whole head hurt.

The foreigner was also hurt. He took the respite to step on the boy lying under him, breaking his ribs with an audible popping sound. The boy screamed in rage, fear, helpless pain.

The man stepped over him and pointed at Diodorus. 'Run,' he said. 'Or I'll kill you next.'

Diodorus hit him with a paving stone. He half-missed his throw, because it was too heavy, and so instead of hitting the man's head, it fell short on the man's right foot.

The man screamed in pain, his right leg collapsing. But even from one knee, he managed to stumble at Diodorus, landing a heavy blow that knocked the red-haired boy unconscious.

Kineas made himself attack. He stepped forward, limbs leaden with fear, and made a half-hearted cut. The man took it on his arm and moved to punch Kineas, but he couldn't put weight on his shattered foot and he fell.

Kineas was on him without thought of chivalry. He fell on the man's back and plunged the dagger into the man's kidneys – not once, but three or four times.

The man flipped him off, rolling and pinning him in one move. He reached back, his fingers searching for Kineas's eyes, for his throat. Kineas stabbed wildly, squirmed, landed a feeble cut that nonetheless invoked the man's flinch reflex and then he was on his feet, slick with the man's blood.

The man was gushing blood. He half rose to his feet. 'Ares,' he complained, as if in a conversation. 'Spear-wielder, I'm being killed by a pair of whores in an alley!'

'I'm no whore, mercenary!' Kineas hissed through split lips and blood and a broken jaw. He felt the balance shift. He was going to win. He stood taller.

The foreigner sat, suddenly. 'You've killed me,' he said, as if in wonder. 'Not a whore, you say?' He tilted his head to one side, like a dog watching a man. 'Got the guts to put me down, boy? Or are you going to stand there and let me bleed out?'

'I'm Kineas, Cleanus's son, a citizen of Athens.' Kineas held the man's glittering eyes, stepped in close despite those arms and plunged his dagger into the man's throat as if he were hitting the paint on the practice stake behind Phocion's house.

And then the watch came, and Diodorus's father, and then his own father. He was wrapped in blankets, in attention and love, even in admiration. There were too many witnesses to the man's brutality – and the brothel keeper was dead. Only later would parents ask why three boys had been standing outside a brothel.

Kineas insisted that his father's slave carry the broken boy – the whore – home. A doctor set his ribs and Kineas sat by him, night after night, day after day. Diodorus came and took his turn, and Graccus. The boy lay still, so still Kineas often thought he was dead, and Kineas would lean across his body to hear him breathe, but gradually the dark stains like bruises faded from under the short boy's eyes, and one day, they opened.

Months later, Kineas asked him one day while the four of them were climbing a crag on one of Kineas's father's farms, looking for bird's eggs. 'Why were you a whore?'

'Not much fucking choice,' Niceas answered. He fingered an amulet at his neck. 'Only good thing I've got – I'm free. Not a fucking slave.' He rubbed his nose in thought. 'Being a free man doesn't feed you.'

'Is it better – being my groom?' Kineas asked.

Niceas shrugged. 'Stupid fucking question,' he said. And then he aimed a mock blow at Kineas, who ducked and . . . awoke.

*

The next day Niceas responded to Kineas with grunts. He never swore. If he didn't want things, he simply turned his head away like a child. The night before they were due to take ship to Hyrkania, he suddenly turned to Kineas.

'I don't want to die like this,' he said.

Kineas hadn't heard so much in his voice in a week. He stopped pouring wine. 'You aren't dying,' he said.

Niceas shrugged, head down, shoulders sagged. 'I am. You can't see it, but I am.'

Further prodding revealed nothing and promises of a physician led only to the turned head.

And then he forgot those worries as they prepared to sail on the Kaspian Sea, and a new set of worries descended on him.

12

A hard winter sun cast the last of its cold light over the icy beach as the pentekonter hove to in the appointed bay in Hyrkania, the anchor stone cast while the rowers backed water against the growing wind, and at last came to rest – a fitful rest, as Poseidon rocked them.

The Land of Wolves lay under a blanket of snow when Kineas finally waded ashore in the bleak twilight, bare-legged and cursing the cold water, wolves howling in the distance. Crax and Sitalkes clambered over the side of the pentekonter carrying Niceas in a litter while Coenus pushed the horses over the rail and into the water to swim ashore on their own. They'd lost one at sea – a slow death of terror for Coenus's favourite mare, a painful, terrible event – and the big man was subdued, but when they were all on the beach he led them in a prayer of thanks to Poseidon and then they sang the hymn to Apollo in the last light of the sun.

The merchants' stalls at the top of the gravel beach were either closed tight or lined in drifted snow. There was no welcoming party. So they rubbed their horses down as best they could, drying them with straw from a mouldering stack Crax found and then headed inland on the only visible track. Kineas sent Crax and Sitalkes out as scouts, made sure that all his men were armed and went back to the beach to pay the last coins of his passage to the captain, a piratical Persian called Cyrus.

'How far to the camp?' he asked as the Persian counted the coins and tested the silver ones with his teeth.

'Three stades. Less.' The man smiled, showing too many teeth. 'Before the waters went down, the town was on the beach.' He shrugged. 'It must be as the gods will it, eh?'

Kineas agreed that it was so.

'You're going to fight Iskander, yes?' the Persian asked. And not for the first time. He had a gold toothpick which flashed around his lips as he talked.

'Yes.'

Cyrus extended a hand. 'Good luck. They say he is a god.'

Kineas nodded. 'He says he's a god.'

'Excellent argument,' the pirate said. 'They say you might throw a garrison into the fort you built at Errymi.'

'I might,' said Kineas, anxious to be gone but unwilling to be rude.

'Good for business. Might get a piece of the grain trade.' Cyrus winked. 'Boats like mine would pay a fee to have a real harbour in the north.'

'I'll think on it,' Kineas said, and they clasped arms again.

The camp was less than three stades inland, east of the beach and south of the town itself, as the scarred man had said, and as they approached, they saw a pair of towers built of wood and rubble, and closer up, earth walls and neat rows of huts. Outside the walls there was a sprawl of cruder huts and leather tents. And emerging from the gate between the two timber towers came a troop of well-mounted Greek cavalry led by Diodorus and Philokles.

The snow in the air accented the smell of burning oak from the hearth fires, and closer to the market they smelled olive oil, something none of them had seen in a month. Niceas raised his head at Kineas's side. 'Smells like home,' he said.

'I think we are home,' Kineas answered.

It took Kineas days to stop marvelling at the quality of the camp – and his praise was appreciated at first and later resented a little because it suggested he hadn't expected as much of them. In fact, Diodorus had plenty of experience in building fortified camps and Philokles had chosen the site well: on a clear running stream, with a broad meadow stretching away to the north for exercise. The town of Namastopolis sat well above them, three more stades to the south, surrounded by tiny subsistence farms. It wasn't a rich place, more like a robber-baron's holding than a town, and the citadel was an ugly fortress of crude stone atop the acropolis, although rumour had it that the inside was as opulent as the outside was prosaic.

Lower down, many of the town's least reputable elements

had picked up and moved to sit at the gate of the military camp, because the soldiers brought money, and the town had the means to take it away. The sprawl at the gate featured a market – almost an agora – where the soldiers bought food and oil for their messes. There were legitimate merchants there, with wine and olive oil, weapons and armour. There were a dozen wine shops, from a newly built tavern with solid walls, its own hearth and prostitutes hanging over the balcony of the *exedra*, to hide tents with a board over a pair of wooden horses and a few amphorae of wine stuck base down in the snow. Followers abounded, from prostitutes of both sexes in the market, to new wives in the snug huts that lined the streets inside the walls with military precision. Kineas's little army numbered almost twelve hundred men and women, at least half the population of the town and citadel above them.

The town and the citadel had its own soldiers, a mix of Greek mercenaries released from Alexander's armies, deserters and survivors of various Persian armies. They put on airs and swaggered, but the Olbians didn't think much of them, and Lot's Sauromatae had killed a couple in brawls – rather to make a point, Diodorus said.

Kineas heard Diodorus's report after he had eaten, slept, steamed and run. He listened to his officers report in turn, rubbing his beard as Leon gave them a report on the army's treasury (a report that made the strategos very thoughtful indeed) and Eumenes spoke on the state of the horses after their long march and short sail (a report that depressed every cavalryman present).

Lycurgus gave a hard smile. 'You'll all be hoplites before more snow falls,' he said.

'We need a lot of fresh horses,' Niceas growled, one of his rare contributions.

'Let's save the ones we have first,' Kineas said. 'Coenus, what shall we do?'

Coenus was reading from a scroll. 'You'd think Xenophon, who fought his whole life from horseback, would have mentioned this problem.' He shook his head. 'Buy more grain. Feed them as if we were fattening them for sacrifice. I'll ride out and find a good winter pasture with some rock under their feet – they're wet to the fetlocks all the time, the poor things.' He looked around. 'We'll need to buy more horses,' he said apologetically.

'We don't have as much money as I would have wished,' Kineas said. 'Even as it is, we'll need to send a convoy back to the Bay of Salmon and get more money. Leon and I will have to sell estates. Ares and Aphrodite, but we spend money like water!'

Philokles pretended to be looking through the cabin's log walls at the citadel. 'I know where there's money,' he said.

'Is this another Spartan solution?' Kineas asked.

'She's a harlot and a brutal ruler. The peasants hate her. She squeezes them for cash and flaunts it.'

There was a knock at the door. Darius, now a section leader in second troop, bowed from the waist. 'There is a messenger from the palace. I held him at the gate as per Niceas's standing orders.'

Niceas nodded. 'Escort him to the guardhouse and get his message. He comes no farther than the guardhouse.'

Kineas shook his head. 'Why are you so adversarial with the palace?' he asked his officers.

Sappho came in through the door and pushed the linen chlamys she wore as a wimple back from her face.

'Have you already had trouble with the queen?' Kineas asked.

His receiving room was larger than all the space he'd had in the barracks at Olbia. Diodorus and Philokles sat in barbarian chairs, Niceas lay on a couch, Coenus reclined with a bucket of scrolls, while Eumenes, Darius and Leon sat at the desk doing accounts. Ataelus sat quietly on another barbarian chair, speaking with Prince Lot and Samahe. Sappho sat in a chair that had obviously been set aside for her.

Kineas wondered why she was present. 'I'm glad you have all made yourself comfortable in my absence,' he said.

Darius returned, a drift of cold entering with him. 'The strategos is invited to attend the queen,' he said in a neutral voice.

Kineas looked around the room, a hint of annoyance in his tone as no one was answering his questions. 'You dislike her? Philokles, has she given you trouble?'

Philokles raised an eyebrow. 'I'm not the sort of man who would have trouble with the queen,' he said. He laughed. 'No, she's given no trouble.'

Eumenes blushed and kept his head down.

'What's all this costing us?' Kineas asked.

'Actually, we're getting a few minae a month profit. We're defending her over the winter, aren't we?' Diodorus gave a wry smile. 'I hadn't realized that salesmanship was part of my duties.'

Kineas nodded. 'Well done.'

'Not all crap. Every one of these petty kingdoms in Hyrkania is out to eat every other one. Our arrival here guaranteed her farmers an uncontested harvest – that's worth a few acres of land for one winter.' Diodorus looked around the room. 'Our troops have put a lot of silver into the locals – one way or another.' He gave his words the intonation of an actor – a comic actor. Diodorus had a new scar on his brow from the fighting in the autumn. It made him look older. There was grey in his red hair that Kineas hadn't noticed before – the price, no doubt, of command. He steepled his hands. 'There'll be Hades to pay in the spring,' he said.

Other men were nodding their heads.

Kineas swirled the wine in his cup and waited.

'She thinks we'll fall into her arms and conquer her neighbours for her,' Diodorus said. He and Sappho exchanged a glance, and Sappho raised a plucked eyebrow before her eyes went back to her scroll.

Leon looked up from his numbers, drew breath for speech and then thought better of it.

Kineas had to smile, despite his best resolve. 'She's a harlot?' he asked.

'She's no harlot,' Philokles said. 'You'll want to see for yourself.' He paused. 'She has wit.'

Diodorus leaned forward. 'She calls herself Banugul. It's a Zoroastrian saint's name. The peasants call her Asalazar. That means the demon of honey.' He gave a lopsided sneer. 'It's not meant as a compliment.'

Heron, silent until then, spoke up. 'They say she's Artabazus's bastard daughter – Barsine's sister. Barsine is still with Alexander. They're rivals in every way. They say she's the lovelier of the pair – and that Alexander preferred her, but needed the satrap's alliance.'

Kineas shook his head. 'So she's been fobbed off with a piece of Hyrkania? She can't be that beautiful, or she'd have got something better. Cappadocia, perhaps?'

They all laughed. Hyrkania was all rock – the farmers among the soldiers couldn't stop commenting on the uselessness of the soil.

'I think you've all been away from civilization too long, and begging Sappho's pardon, you sound like characters in *Lysistrata*. You may all love her more than you love the gods – but when the ground is hard and our horses have their hooves hard and their summer coats, we're riding for Marakanda,' he said. 'Srayanka is waiting, and Alexander's army is growing.'

Diodorus nodded. 'I'd rather be fighting Alexander right now.' Again he and Sappho exchanged glances.

'I must meet this goddess,' Kineas said.

Diodorus cut in, 'She's trying to use us against her father. And she's dangerous.'

Kineas nodded, his mind already moving on to the new logistikon that Leon was compiling. 'Is there enough fodder and grain in this petty kingdom to get us moving in the spring?'

Leon cleared his throat. 'Yes,' he said. Under his dark skin, he was flushed. 'But it will require some work to collect it. There are not enough wagons for us to buy. We'll need more oxen to drag the wagons and some for beef on the hoof.'

Kineas glanced back at Diodorus. 'Why would we fight her father?'

Diodorus shrugged. 'For money?'

Sappho raised her eyes and then lowered them – again.

'I think you're all barking at shadows,' Kineas said.

After a minute of silence, he turned on his heel and walked back into his sleeping quarters to change for his audience.

A slave brought Kineas wine while he rummaged through his baggage. He tried to read a new piece – new to him – by Aristotle. Its release had apparently enraged Alexander, but so far he could make nothing of it. He had just located his best sandals in the leather bag under the bed when he heard a noise behind him. He looked up when the curtain that guarded his sleeping quarters rustled, and he shot to his feet when he saw that it was Sappho.

She smiled enigmatically as she entered. 'Sometimes,' she said, 'it is almost worth three years of forced sex and the loss of my husband and children to be free to enter a man's quarters and speak my own mind.'

Kineas started to reply, but his mind was grappling with what she had said, and all that came out of his mouth was 'I'm sorry.'

She nodded. 'As am I. And pleased to have your full attention.'

Kineas nodded. 'Wine?' he asked to cover his confusion.

She shook her head. 'No, I've had enough. Listen, Strategos. You are a man like my brothers and my father. Like Diodorus. A man who does things – worthy things. I know your type.' Her kohl-rimmed eyes were large and green, and very close to his.

Kineas sat back. 'I'm sorry,' he said, again.

She choked a little. 'I don't think you should meet her alone. I speak for Srayanka, who is not here.'

Kineas narrowed his eyes. 'I like a challenge,' he said.

'That is why you will fall,' Sappho said. 'Your own courage and your sense of challenge will betray you, and you will fall.' She stood again. 'Look at you – and you are only dealing with me. You look into my eyes, you measure my body, you hear that I have been abused – I could have you kissing me just by moving closer and putting my hand like this.' She suited action to the word, fitting her body alongside his and putting one raised hand to the back of his head, and Kineas flinched away, stepping back to hide the immediacy of his arousal and the truth of her assertion.

She laughed.

'Enough,' Kineas said, turning away, disgusted at his weakness and her accuracy. He nodded sharply. 'I appreciate now that you all take this seriously, and I can tell from what you say – and what you don't say – that this woman has caused tensions.' He backed away and selected a chiton, at a loss how to proceed, trying to cover his confusion and his sudden arousal. 'I'm sure you all have my best interests at heart.' He was growing angrier by the moment – angry at them, angry at himself. 'But I dislike that you see me as an overgrown child.'

'You control yourself so much that you are like clay for someone who can control you in turn,' she said. 'Please – call it whatever you like. Make sacrifice to the Foam-born and stay home tonight.' She smiled gently. 'Admit it – you, too, are like a man in *Lysistrata*.'

Kineas shook his head. 'Bah,' he said. 'I am a commander, not a schoolboy.'

Sappho shook her head. 'Athena, I tried,' she said, and retreated through the curtain. Before she withdrew her head she said, 'Philokles volunteered to try to speak to you first. But confronting you before you met her was my idea.'

Kineas nodded dismissively. 'I appreciate your vote of confidence, madam,' he said. Just at that moment, he hated her – her feminine superiority, the ease with which her physicality had taken him in. Then he sat on his bed, considering how far short of his own notions of good conduct he had just fallen.

After a few hundred heartbeats, he dressed quickly.

Antigonus sat on his charger with ten of his Keltoi in their best kit mounted behind him in the street by the gate. Sitalkes handed Kineas the reins of Thalassa, and Kineas swung his leg over the mare's broad back, briefly remembering back to his first attempts to mount a tall horse in the middle of the Pinarus while Persians rained blows on his breast- and back-plate.

His hesitation caused him to push the mare through half a circle before he got his leg up, bringing him to face Coenus, who was standing in the snow with a bag of scrolls over his shoulder like a giant schoolboy on his way to the agora.

'You too?' Kineas asked.

Coenus shrugged. 'Me too what?' he asked. 'Need a hand up?'

Kineas snapped. 'No!' he shot out, and then followed the charger through another half-rotation without getting his leg over.

Coenus was laughing. The escort were doing their best not to laugh. When Kineas's pursuit of the horse went around again, Coenus grabbed her headstall. 'Need a hand up?' he asked again.

'Fuck off,' Kineas said. He made a face. 'Yes.'

Coenus held her bridle while Leon made a step. Kineas sprang on to the mare's back and pulled his cloak around him.

'They aren't fools,' Coenus said, pointing at the open door of the commander's building. 'They all love you, and every one of them wants what is best for you. Damn it – this is what Niceas does.' Coenus gave a lopsided smile. Even on foot, he came up to the middle of Kineas's chest while mounted. 'I'm a pompous aristocrat, not a rhetorician. If Niceas were himself, he'd swear a lot and you'd take it. The queen is dangerous. She writes letters to Alexander. Beware.'

Kineas found he could smile. 'I had gathered that,' he said.

Coenus raised an eyebrow. 'Have a splendid evening at the palace, then.' He gave a salute.

Kineas gave a shake of his head, backed Thalassa a few steps and whirled her around. 'Let's go,' he said to Andronicus, who exchanged an amused glance with Coenus, barked an order and surged into motion.

The ride up the hill was cold and longer than Kineas had expected. He kept his mind carefully blank. The citadel was a grim reminder of what Hyrkania really was. The fortifications were high and strong, old stone courses at the bottom and new stone facing, with a double gate and towers every half a stade. Kineas whistled with professional appreciation as he rode under the gates.

'Tough nut,' he said to Andronicus, who shrugged.

'We could have it in an afternoon. Garrison is crap,' Andronicus said. He spat. 'Walls are no better than the bronze behind them.'

As if to make the Kelt's point, a pair of lazy sentries in green-spotted bronze breastplates greeted them under the inner gate.

'What do you want, sir?' asked the older sentry.

'Invitation from the queen,' Andronicus said.

The man nodded and straightened slightly – not exactly attention, but a better slouch. He held out his hand and Andronicus dropped a coin in it.

'Nice that all these fucking foreigners are so ready with their cash,' the sentry said in Persian to his mate. He was contemptuous.

Andronicus grinned and nodded like a stupid barbarian. He'd served four years in Persia. He refused to let the palace grooms take their horses. Instead, he told off four of his troopers to take the horses to the stables. The other men followed Kineas inside, where slaves took their cloaks and sandals and washed their feet.

The floors were tiled and heated. The interior of the citadel bore no more relation to the outside than the citadel-palace in Olbia. But the tyrant of Olbia hadn't run to heated floors and mosaics. And slaves. Kineas had seldom seen so many slaves devoted to personal service. Most of them were women, and all were pretty, and naked, or next to it. The mosaics were not subtle.

Like a gymnasium, the palace grew warmer as one got further in, and the decorations more costly, more colourful, from beige and white tiles in the outer receiving rooms and barracks to red and purple and glitteringly erotic mosaics in the heart of the castle, a throne room warmer than blood with naked men and women glistening with oil waiting on a dozen courtiers and the queen herself.

She was not naked. She was dressed like a Persian matron, her hair dressed with ropes of pearls and lapis, her limbs and breasts well covered. Amidst a plethora of sensual and aesthetic possibilities, hers was the body that called out to be watched, to be caressed with the eye. Even fully clothed, modest, apparently unadorned, she was beautiful. Her proportions were worthy of a statue – from her delicately arched feet to her intelligent eyes and straight Greek nose.

'Welcome, Kineas of Athens,' she said. 'I am Banugul.'

She had an appraising look, as if he was a horse and she was a Sakje. She crossed her legs and her Median trousers of silk rode up one leg, revealing an ankle and a bangle. 'Your men worship you as a god,' she said. Her intonation suggested that such worship was probably misplaced.

Kineas grinned, although it was the kind of grin he wore when he was fighting. 'They only worship me from afar. In person, there's a great deal of dispute.'

She was smaller than he had thought at first impression. She leaned her chin on a small fist, a man's gesture that suited her. 'Your men give the impression of excellent discipline. What do they dispute?'

'My godhood. We are Greeks, my lady. We worship with a great deal of argument.' He looked around, suggesting with body language that she might offer him a seat.

She sat up straight. Her shoulders were square and her bearing had dignity. 'I know Alexander,' she said. She smiled, and one manicured eyebrow rose a fraction. Her choice of Greek words was perfect, and her facial expression said, *I slept with Alexander and I mean you to know it, but I am not crude – and I was not impressed.* It was an enormous burden of communication for a fractionally raised eyebrow and two Greek words. She handled it easily.

Kineas's opinion of her intellect rose considerably. 'He says he is a god,' Kineas noted with a certain reservation.

'Hmm,' she answered. 'He never claimed to me to be a god. He claimed gods in his ancestors, but we all have gods among our ancestors, do we not?'

Kineas nodded.

'You are not impressed with Alexander?' she asked.

'I served him for some years,' Kineas responded. 'He is

the best general I have ever seen – and yet, a headstrong man capable of error and vice.'

'You rebuke me like a philosopher,' she said. 'And like a sophist, you have not answered my question.'

'Yes,' Kineas said. 'I was impressed.' He paused, and thought, Why not? 'I loved him,' Kineas said.

'But he spurned you, did he not?' Banugul smiled, and the smile informed her face – her smile said that happiness was not the normal state of her being, from her green eyes to her pointed chin. Her smile took the sting from her words – she meant no insult, nor was she drawing a comparison. She, too, had been spurned. 'I understand that he sent all his Greeks away.'

'You are well informed,' Kineas said.

'And now you will make war on him?' she asked.

'Yes,' Kineas answered.

She nodded. 'Would you care to sit down?' she asked. 'I thought you might be the ordinary kind of soldier, who boasts and ogles my girls. I apologize for my poor hospitality.' She waved a hand and a pair of slaves brought a chair.

Kineas sat.

'What could I offer you to fight my father in the spring instead of Alexander?' she asked. She motioned at a slave, a small hand with almond nails, and a silver cup of wine appeared at Kineas's elbow. He sipped it. It was excellent.

'Nothing, my lady, will sway me from my plans for the spring,' Kineas said. 'When the ground is hard, we'll march.'

She nodded.

'What did Alexander give you when he sent you away?' she asked.

'Gold,' Kineas said.

'You had the better bargain,' she said. 'I got a small piece of the Land of Wolves, and no dogs of my own to protect it. What do you think of my guards?'

Kineas sipped wine. 'They are adequate,' he said. He glanced at her captain of the guard, a Thessalian she had not bothered to introduce.

'I have seldom heard anyone damned with such faint

praise,' she said, and laughed, her chin tilted back and her throat dancing in the torchlight. 'Do you read?' she asked.

Kineas was startled. 'Yes,' he answered. He was determined to stop speaking in monosyllables, but she was robbing him of his wits. He felt as if he was wrestling with a master, missing every hold. 'I'm reading the new Aristotle now.' He winced inwardly at the boyishness of the boast.

She leaned forward, a wolf ready to spring. 'You have the new Aristotle?' she asked.

'I had a copy scribed before I left Olbia. It came out on the Athenian grain ships.' He grinned at her eagerness. 'If you have a scribe, I can lend it to you for copying.'

'Hah!' she laughed. 'No work on my taxes this winter!' Her eyes gleamed. 'Do you like singing?' she asked.

'I like conversation that is not all interrogation,' he said carefully.

Her chin went back on her hand. 'I do apologize, but we're a little short of polite company here in Hyrkania. You're from *Athens*! You're only the tenth Athenian I've ever met.' She shrugged. 'Men expect women to ask all the questions and carry the conversation. Especially beautiful women.'

Kineas smiled. 'I like singing. I enjoy reading. I'm an excellent soldier and I will not fight a spring campaign on your behalf.' He rolled his shoulders. 'I will see that your fiefdom is protected all winter, and perhaps we can negotiate a garrison or a few officers to help your levies.'

She nodded. 'Strictly business. Very well.' She sat up. 'You are used to dealing with women, aren't you?' she asked. 'Alexander isn't.'

Kineas shrugged. 'My mother wasn't Olympias,' he said. Alexander's mother was a byword in Greece for cruelty and manipulation. He rose to his feet.

She rose gracefully, despite having taken two cups of wine in less than an hour. 'I look forward to hosting you again. I burn for your copy of Aristotle.'

That made him grin. 'If you want it, you will have to wait while I finish it,' he said, and bowed.

She nodded her head and motioned at a slave to escort him.

'Winter in Hyrkania is long and arduous,' she said. 'You'll have time to read it many times. I hope that I can provide you with some equally worthy amusements.'

The next afternoon, Kineas was sitting with Leon and Eumenes in the smoky tunnel of his wooden *megaron*, reading scrolls by the light of twenty profligate oil lamps, with Niceas reclining, cursing the smoke and muttering advice.

A gentle tapping against the logs of the hall heralded Lycurgus, who came in through the layers of woollen blankets that covered the door. Greek military architecture wasn't ready for the cold of highland Hyrkania.

'Patrols just picked up a soldier,' he said. 'Ten local horsemen as guards. An Athenian gentleman. I expected that you'd want to see him.'

Kineas leaned back so far that his stool creaked. 'Anything to free me from paperwork,' he said. He went over to the hearth, waving a hand in front of his face and trying not to breathe. He started rebuilding the fire, trying to find the combination of wood and draught that would stop the incessant smoke.

'Leosthenes of Athens,' Lycurgus announced, returning.

Kineas had an actual flame going. He brushed off Leon's attempts to take over – the boy reverted to being a house slave too easily – and coaxed the flame, adding twigs. What he wanted was the tube from his campaign kit, but he didn't have it. He leaned forward to blow on the fire. Leon blew on it from the other direction. Then both men started coughing and had to turn away to the cold air beyond the fire. Kineas took a lungful of clean air and snatched a hollow quill from the table. He leaned close enough to the embers to scorch his eyebrows and breathed out. The embers began to make the noise – the low moan of wood on the edge of ignition. Both men redoubled their efforts and suddenly the whole pit sprang into flame, as if by magic. Light drove the winter shadows into the corners of the hall, and a rush of heat forced Kineas to take a step back.

'You don't look as if you eat babies,' said a voice in aristocratic Attic Greek.

'Hard to eat them if you can't cook them,' Niceas said.

Leosthenes and Kineas gripped forearms. Kineas smiled, and the other Athenian beamed. Leosthenes was of middle height, well proportioned, with curly black hair and green eyes like a cat. He sat on a corner of the table without invitation. 'The famous Kineas of Athens,' he said dramatically.

Kineas rubbed his beard, discovered that he had singed it and winced. He shrugged. 'Where in Hades did you come from, child?'

'Three years' service in Alexander's army and you call me a child? But suit yourself – I have to deal with all those years of hero worship.' He turned to the other men. 'Kineas was Phocion's star pupil – the best swordsman, the best officer. We all loved him. But he went off to serve Alexander.' Leosthenes grinned. 'When I was old enough, I followed you.'

'By all the gods, it is good to see you, Leo.' Kineas couldn't get the grin off his face. 'Have you been home?'

'Home?' Leosthenes asked. He shook his head, and flushed. 'I haven't been home. I've been to Parthia and back.'

'Are you rich, then?' Kineas asked.

'You know how Alexander uses mercenaries!' Leosthenes said bitterly. 'Second-line troops. Garrisons. And the fool never really conquers anywhere, so he always leaves it to the garrisons to do all the nasty bits.' The younger man shrugged and Kineas could see that in fact most of his youth was gone. There was a set to his shoulders and hollows in his eyes that Kineas hadn't seen at a glance. 'You remember Arbela?'

Kineas nodded.

'Of course you do!' The younger man turned to the other officers. 'You were a hero, leading the Greek horse. I was with the hoplites in the second line. We never engaged. Then I spent six months chasing tribesmen with Parmenion.'

'How'd you get here?' Niceas asked.

'I was in the garrison at Ecbatana,' Leo said. 'Shit's coming down there. I gathered a few like-minded friends and we ran.'

Kineas looked thoughtful. 'Deserted,' he said flatly.

'It's going to be war between Parmenion and Alexander,' Leo said. 'Not battlefield war – stab-in-the-back war. Parmenion sent me with a message to the king, and I thought I was going to be executed. So – yes. I deserted. With some friends. We took service with one of the Hyrkanian kings – these hills and the lowlands to the south are full of men from Alexander's armies.'

Kineas caught himself rubbing his beard. 'Is this a social visit, Leo?' he asked.

Leosthenes had the grace to look embarrassed. 'No,' he said.

Niceas gave a snort.

Kineas turned to Eumenes. 'Go and get Philokles and Diodorus. Ask Sitalkes to bring us wine.' He turned to Niceas. 'I need to buy a slave,' he said, with irritation. Slaves annoyed him, but he was just too busy to fetch his own wine and get the fire burning.

'Have you met your employer?' Leosthenes asked.

He had to notice the intake of breath throughout the room.

'I get it – you've *all* met her.' He laughed.

'Don't be crude, Leo.' Kineas smiled, but his voice was hard. 'I like her.'

Diodorus pushed through the curtains, followed by Philokles, toting a sack of scrolls. 'We've all met her,' he said wryly. 'Oh, my. Look who it is! The nursery must be emptying into the phalanx.'

Kineas rose. 'Leosthenes, son of Craterus of Athens. An old friend.' Kineas was grinning, which wasn't his normal look these days. 'More of an old student, really,' he said with a glint in his eye.

Leosthenes grinned back. 'I can take you, sword to sword. Any time, old man.'

Kineas shook his head. 'I've a Persian – Darius – you have to best first. He's probably better than me.' He grinned. 'In fact, I'd like to see it.'

Philokles poured himself wine, and then poured wine for the others and distributed it. The local potters made good cups that fitted the hand, shaped like a woman's breast with a nipple instead of a base. The joke was that you couldn't put the cup down – you had to drink your wine. Or at least, that was one of the jokes.

Sitalkes pushed in through the blankets.

'Would you be kind enough to mull us some hot wine, lad?' Kineas asked.

The Getae boy went to work without complaint. It was a matter of months since he'd been freed, and he was still happy to serve – if asked politely.

'So – you've met her,' Leosthenes asked again.

'Yes,' said Kineas, into a silence as thick as the smoke had been.

'And?' the Athenian persisted.

Kineas shrugged. 'She's beautiful. Intelligent. Educated.'

'Evil incarnate,' Leosthenes said in a gentle voice.

Kineas shrugged again. He looked around the room. The smoke had mostly cleared.

'You didn't fuck her, did you?' said Niceas. 'I listened to all that griping and you *didn't* fall for her.'

Kineas shook his head wearily. 'My private life is mine. I am not about to endanger this expedition to satisfy my own lusts.'

Philokles made a face, rose to his feet and bowed. 'I salute you, philosopher! And apologize. I, for one, thought that you would fall straight into her coils.'

'Apology accepted,' Kineas said. 'Yes, I've met her. I wasn't shown any particular sensuality, but I was made to appreciate her intelligence. She wants us to fight a campaign in the spring. She can pay very well. I'm tempted.'

'My employer is the target,' Leosthenes said. 'I'm here to buy you off.'

Kineas stopped himself from rubbing his beard. 'What?'

'She wants southern Hyrkania. Her recent and much-lamented husband held all the land as far as Parthia – she lost a lot of it when she murdered her husband and stayed loyal to Alexander.' Leosthenes shrugged. 'I serve Artabazus – Barsine's father. Alexander's satrap, not that his writ runs here. He's a canny old fox. All he has to do is survive until Parmenion kills off Alexander and he'll be king.'

169

Kineas nodded, aware that Artabazus had been named as the target of the spring campaign and unwilling to give that much away.

'And he's told us a lot about *her*. She's not Greek. She's more like one of the Persian demons – some kind of monster.' Leosthenes leaned forward, pressing his point.

Kineas sat back. 'Child, you put me in mind of the tale of the fox and the grapes.'

Leosthenes laughed aloud, his head back. 'I think you have it right, at that.' He went on laughing. 'Persians never read Aesop. They ought to!' He had to clutch his hands over his stomach.

Kineas stood. 'Stay for dinner, child. But don't press me on this. I keep my bargains, and I wouldn't sit here and banter with your Persian fox were I ten times more a mercenary.' He nodded, glanced at Niceas. 'If it weren't you, I'd be tempted to crucify the messenger to make my point.'

Leosthenes nodded soberly. 'I made much the same point to my employer. Luckily, I am me.'

'This time,' Kineas said. 'Next time, you might be mistaken for someone else.'

After Leosthenes and his ten Hyrkanian nobles had ridden for home in the dark, Kineas tugged on his cloak. Niceas and Philokles were still on their couches.

'I'm for the palace,' Kineas said.

'I thought you weren't smitten,' Philokles said.

'I'm not smitten. But I'll wager that she has excellent sources in this camp, or at least in the agora outside our gate, and she'll know in an hour what's been offered. I want to make sure she got the right message. And double the guards. I don't like anything about this place.' Kineas finished the last wine in his cup and tipped it up on the sideboard. Was he smitten? He certainly had the same urges as any soldier.

Philokles nodded agreement. 'I'd like your permission to try and place someone in the palace,' he said.

'Slave?' Kineas asked.

'Best you not know,' Philokles said. Kineas could see how

uncomfortable this conversation made his friend. He desisted with a grunt.

The ride up the hill in blowing snow and the warmth of the rooms with their hypocaust floors couldn't have been a sharper contrast. Kineas shed his cloak and sandals in the outer rooms and passed, clad only in his tunic, to the inner sanctum, where the queen sat in state surrounded by her slaves and courtiers.

'You had a visitor,' she said cheerfully, as soon as he entered.

'A very old friend,' he said. 'I taught him to swing a sword.'

Banugul rose, took wine from a naked woman whose pubic hair was shaved to resemble the Greek letter alpha, and brought the cup to Kineas with her own hands. The smell of her caught at his breath – the hint of a smell, somewhere in the arch of his nose. A clean, delicate smell, like mint. Her head came to his shoulder, and from his advantage of height, he could see even more of her to admire. He raised his cup to her.

'What did he offer you to betray me?' she asked, very close.

Kineas wondered if there was a killer standing behind him. He was weaponless and her tone belied the clean purity of her scent – she was angry, working herself up for murder. 'I refused to hear his offer,' Kineas said.

'Really?' she asked. For the first time, he had said something that took her by surprise. She returned to her throne and sat. To Kineas, her motions seemed to take a very long time.

'Really,' Kineas answered.

She sighed. 'I would like to trust you,' she said.

Kineas shook his head gently. 'You trust no one,' he said. He looked around. 'May I have a chair?'

She gave him a small smile. 'I can do better than a chair.' She motioned, and a proper couch was brought for him. While he arranged himself on it, another was brought for her. More couches arrived and her courtiers, half a dozen men in a mix of Persian and Greek dress, settled on to them uneasily. She arranged herself on hers with her usual grace, rose on one elbow and toasted Kineas with her gold goblet.

Kineas poured a libation to the gods and then toasted her with a line from Aristophanes that made her smile.

She took a long drink of her wine and then rolled on to her stomach. 'If I have you killed, right now, I can buy your soldiers and fight any campaign I please,' she said.

Kineas's stomach twisted. He was not immune to fear, and his hands betrayed him. He clenched his goblet. She was serious.

'My soldiers would storm this citadel and put everyone in it to the sword,' he said, with the best imitation of calm he could muster. He could hear the fear in the end of his sentence.

Her guard captain revealed himself, standing just out of his line of vision to his right, by snorting his disdain. 'Try, fucking Greek.'

Banugul gave an enigmatic smile and indicated her guard captain with her chin. 'This is Therapon, my strong right arm.'

Kineas took a deep breath. He didn't turn his head, although he noted the alcove where the man was standing. 'Every one of your men is bribable. You have little discipline – so little that even now, the towers on the citadel's north walls are empty because the men don't want to get that cold. No one is watching the north wall.'

'No one can climb the north wall,' the queen said, but her eyes flicked to the guard captain, and he looked away.

'Like Leosthenes, Diodorus, my second, is a childhood friend from Athens. You could never bribe him, lady. Unlike this dog of a Thessalian you keep to bully your guards, my men are soldiers, fresh from a summer of victory.' He was beginning to convince himself, and his words flowed faster. 'If you murder me, all of you will die.'

She met his eye easily, and smiled. It wasn't a smile of seduction, but a smile of pure calculation. She was not young. Nor was she old. She was at the turning point of age, where the lines at the corners of her eyes did not mar her looks but only added to her dignity. 'What was Artabazus's offer?' she asked for the second time.

'I refused to hear it,' Kineas repeated.

Her eyes opened wider for a fraction of a second and then narrowed. 'Why?' she asked.

'I cannot be tempted by something I haven't heard,' Kineas said. 'Do you know the famous soldier Phocion?'

'I know his name and his reputation. His honour is proverbial.' She raised her eyebrows expectantly. She smiled, and Kineas knew that he was not going to die. He thought he had her measure.

'He used to tell us that the best way to avoid temptation,' Kineas felt the tension falling away from him, 'was to avoid temptation.'

She nodded, eyebrows arched. 'I often seek temptation out,' she said. 'But I am a queen.' She looked at the grapes in the bowl next to her. 'Every grape,' she said, taking one, 'has been seeded in my kitchens by slaves. That is the fate that awaits you if I discover that you have received more messengers from Artabazus. Have I made myself clear?'

Kineas held his ground. 'If Leosthenes the Athenian comes to my camp, I will always receive him, Despoina. And I will present myself for examination immediately afterwards.'

'Strange man,' she said. She looked at him for some time, eating grapes. 'Am *I* a temptation?'

'Yes,' Kineas said.

She nodded, her face serious. 'Yet you do not avoid me.'

Kineas rubbed his chin and chewed a grape. 'I concede your point.'

She leaned forward, interested. 'Men do not usually allow women victories in conversation. You concede my point. But? There is a but?'

'You are observant, my lady. But you are my employer, and to avoid you would create misunderstanding. You are a queen, and any temptation you offer will come with enough barbs to hook a Euxine salmon.'

She raised her chin and allowed a slight smile to indicate that his point had merit. 'I grew to womanhood at a Persian court. Both of my uncles were poisoned. My mother was murdered with a sword. My father now seeks to kill me. Do you understand?'

Kineas nodded, hands calming gradually. 'You keep your slaves nude to know if they carry weapons.'

She pulled her legs under her and leaned towards him. 'I disarm my enemies in any way I can,' she said. 'I have few enough weapons. If I were a man, I would be strong. I am a woman. What would you have me do?'

Kineas shook his head. 'I'm a canny fish. I can see the hook and the bait and even the boat.'

She curled a lip. 'What a very safe answer.' She motioned past him, and a man with a lyre sat on a stool and began to sing. He was excellent and his purity commanded silence. Kineas turned his head to find that the singer was fully clothed – not a slave.

'Persian?' he asked after the first performance.

'Lycian,' she answered. 'Or Carian.'

Kineas stroked his chin. 'The words are strange, but the cadence is like Homer.'

Her body faced the singer, but she turned her head to him, stretching her neck and back. Her smile was as beautiful as dawn in the mountains, and as fresh. 'Are all Athenians as well educated as you are?' she asked.

'Yes,' he said. He put a hand over his goblet so that the wine slave backed off. 'Where did you learn Greek?' He looked away, towards the singer. Therapon glared at him steadily. His hate made an emotional counterpoint to Banugul's magnetism, and Kineas steadied himself on it.

'Darius's chief eunuch was a Greek. And my sister and I were prisoners of Alexander for two years.' She smiled as if they were conspirators. 'While you still served him.'

Kineas felt like a fool for missing the obvious connection that they had shared the whole campaign. 'Of course – you were taken with the women after Issus?'

Banugul rolled over, and Kineas was conscious of her body, even across a gap of several feet. 'I remember them cheering your name when you won the prize,' she said. 'We were waiting with the dowager, wondering if you barbarians would rape us.' She managed to make the experience sound light-hearted.

'But you were all too busy slapping each other's backs to mind us much. It was days before Alexander looked at us.'

Kineas had been unconscious for days after Issus, but he somehow doubted that she had heard his name being cheered. He frowned at the attempts at flattery. 'It is odd, that we were in the same camp for so long.'

'Hmm,' she said, conscious that she had stepped wrong, and waved for the singer to perform. 'Not so odd,' she said. 'If the gods willed it so.'

Warm for the first time in days, Kineas rode down the hill to the neat Greek military camp. A pair of sentries stood huddled in every tower and there were twenty men in the guardhouse by the gate. He inspected every one, chatting with the sentries, listening to the boredom of the Sauromatae and the complaints of the Greeks, until he was satisfied that they were alert. He was cold again, cold from a wind that seemed to blow warmth out of the top of his head. He swore that he would abandon Hellenism and get a Sakje cap before he wrapped himself in furs and blankets and shivered. He lay for a while, trying to imagine Srayanka beside him. He had a hard time seeing her face, and it tended to slide into a narrower face with blonde hair that made him shiver.

'I need to leave here,' he said aloud.

The transition from anxious wakefulness to sleep was so sudden that he ... *was taken unawares by the presence of the tree and the pair of young eagles screaming above him. They called and swung out over the endless combat of the dead, pecking at dead foes. Ajax and Graccus and Nicomedes seemed more outnumbered than ever, but he was not to be deterred. He had to find Srayanka. He reached out a hand for the branch above, swung to gather momentum and reached out a leg to hook and roll. In a moment, he was surrounded by brambles and bracken, thorny stuff that tore at his skin and pricked at his hands, his forearms, his eyes ...*

He was climbing a thicket, or crawling through it, blind. He had to reach Srayanka, and she was somewhere on the other side of the brambles and thorns, and he threw himself at the flexible, prickly mass and made no dent on it except to tear his arms and leave ribbons of blood on the trunk of the tree.

He strove and strove, angry, frustrated . . .

He awoke, his cloak wrapped in a tangle around his legs, his heavy Hyrkanian blanket pulled up between his legs, the hairy wool scraping at his flesh. He was cold.

He got up, moving carefully in the darkness, and remade his bed, adding another blanket from his pack roll on the floor. Then he lay in the new warmth of his blankets and waited to fall asleep. Whatever thought he summoned, whatever plan he touched in his mind, the image before his eyes was of Banugul, turning her head to smile at him. He eventually defeated her smile with a tally of the grain wagons his army would require in the spring, and he fell back to sleep, warm and frustrated.

13

Their sport that season was archery. Hyrkania had a crueller winter than the Euxine cities ever saw, with snow in drifts more than once and freezing rain every week, but it was still clement enough to exercise horses and shoot the Sauromatae bows.

Lot and Ataelus started it, setting up straw bundles against the earthen walls of the camp's citadel and shooting for wagers. Kineas knew a good thing when he saw one – a sport that benefited his troops and cost very little, passed the time, maintained discipline – perfect. He offered prizes at a weekly competition, good prizes, and he competed himself.

The first weeks saw Ataelus's prodromoi and all the Sauromatae gathered to laugh at the sight of Greeks shooting the bow. Some were either natural shots or had practised, especially the gentry from the Euxine cities – Heron was a fine shot, as were several of his riders. Eumenes shot with a sort of weary acceptance, as if his Apollo-like skills were a curse and not a gift. But others were not so fortunate. One young man from the phalanx somehow managed to snap his bow while stringing it, the resulting lash of the bowstring drawing blood. Many of the tribesmen thought this the finest jest they'd ever seen, which didn't do much for the daimon of the whole corps and led to two nasty incidents. Other men simply missed the targets, week after week – Diodorus threatened to stop competing on the basis that his exceptional ability to shoot arrows over the top of the straw was undermining his authority.

'Didn't you learn to shoot as an ephebe?' Kineas asked, wickedly. In fact, he could remember taunting Diodorus as the luckless seventeen-year-old failed to hit the target again and again.

Diodorus responded with a grunt, but when they wrestled later in the morning, Kineas noticed that he was being dropped in the icy mud with a certain annoying regularity. Diodorus was angry. Kineas kept his taunts to himself after that.

Six weeks of constant archery meant that the meanest of the hoplites could hit a bale of summer straw, and the best were becoming quite proficient. Kineas placed orders for bows and arrows with the local craftsmen. He knew his *Anabasis* well enough to appeciate that arming all his troops with bows, even if they were merely carried in the baggage, would make them more capable of dealing with the threats they would face in mountain passes and high valleys where the battlefield tactics of the phalanx and the cavalry rhomboid didn't apply.

Some men preferred the sling and Diodorus convinced Kineas that slings were an acceptable distance weapon, so that some dozens of the Euxine Greeks could be seen pounding at the straw bales with long slings and heavy rocks. They lacked the range, but had enough hitting power to drop an ox – a demonstration that Diodorus performed to the applause of all the slingers on the winter feast of Apollo.

The barbarian Sauromatae were far more of a leadership challenge than the Euxine Greeks. They were a long way from home, wintering in a military camp, subject to regulations that they barely understood and seldom respected. But the military successes against the bandits and the willingness of the Greek officers to lead by example and be seen to fail at archery and other contests narrowed the gap.

The greatest difficulty concerned breaches of discipline and how they should be punished. Kineas could remember quarrelling with Srayanka about Greek notions of punishment. She had maintained that she would have to kill a tribesman to enforce Greek discipline, because anything else would lead to blood feud. Memories of Srayanka and a growing understanding of tribal custom made Kineas careful. He couldn't be seen to favour the barbarians, but he had to make his judgments fit their own notions of fairness.

Kineas was never bored.

The army had suffered through two snowstorms and had camped in Hyrkania for eight weeks when Kineas held his second court and various units brought their offenders to him to be judged. Sometimes the local Hyrkanian authority demanded to have the man sent to the citadel – which Kineas always refused. Each refusal required a visit to the citadel.

The Sauromatae, with their arrogance and their lack of interest in the niceties of trade and purchase, were frequently hauled before the court as thieves, an accusation likely to cause even the laconic Lot to lose his temper. Sauromatae gentlemen were only thieves in their own tribes if they stole horses, a 'crime' only when the stolen horse came from one's own tribe. Horse thievery was punishable by immediate exile – or death. The arrest of a Sauromatae nobleman or woman for thievery led to open-air assemblies for fair prosecution and resolution. The Euxine Greeks viewed these open-air assemblies with much the same relish as the Sauromatae viewed archery matches. The entertainment value helped them deal with the snow.

'The merchant says that you stole the value of the girl's bond,' Kineas said in passable Sakje. The Sauromatae trooper – a lord among his own people, dressed in a purple tunic with gold plaques over fine caribou-hide breeches worked in deer hair – stood straight as an arrow. His demeanour was respectful, but proud. His name was Gwair. Kineas thought of him as Gwair Blackhorse, to separate him from the other Sauromatae Gwair, also a lord, who rode a grey horse. Even with a foundation in Sakje, the Sauromatae clan names defeated him.

'No, lord,' the man said, standing tall. His eyes met Kineas's and he smiled. 'I liked her and she liked me.' The man shrugged. 'We fucked. She warmed my bed.' He smiled. 'We please each other, so she can stay with me.'

Kineas sighed. 'She is a slave at this man's brothel,' he said. He indicated the Hyrkanian merchant next to him, a big man in his own right. Beside him stood Banugul's captain of the guard, Therapon.

Gwair grinned. 'He wants to fight me for her?'

Kineas shook his head. 'You know better than that, Gwair.'

Blackhorse grinned again. 'Stupid merchant can't keep a girl like that. Girl like that is for heroes. You know that.'

Therapon rolled his shoulders. 'I'll fight him,' he said. 'And when I kill him, the queen will be satisfied.'

'Not so fast,' Kineas said. The problem was that Kineas knew that among the Sauromatae, slave girls went to those who could hold them – until the women stepped in. Sauromatae women fought with the lance and bow like the men, and were not easily crossed, and the men who married them had to be heroes. Kineas turned to Lot, who was sitting next to him. 'Would you be so kind as to send for some of your noble-women?' Kineas said. 'I think we need their help.' Kineas had to be seen to do everything he could before he ordered a Sauromatae to be punished or to fight a duel that he was unlikely to win. Therapon was a dangerous man and none of the Sauromatae would be his match.

Lot raised an eyebrow and rose to his feet. Kineas's initial impression of a slow, cautious man had turned out to be the product of the language barrier. Lot narrowed his eyes at Kineas, glanced at Therapon as if considering the man's potency and gave one sharp nod. 'Yes,' he said. 'Although, as you must know, I cannot summon them. I must go and ask.'

Kineas nodded. 'Should I go?'

'That would be better,' Lot said.

'This assembly is to wait my pleasure,' Kineas said, and rose.

'Get on with it,' said Therapon. 'Punish the barbarian and move on. I'm cold.'

Kineas ignored the Thessalian and turned to Niceas, who sat on a stool bundled in sheepskins. 'Can you deal with the Greek defaulters while I'm gone?'

Niceas gave a wolfish smile, much more like his old self, and bawled out the name of a pair of hoplites who had started a fight with the local mercenaries. Kineas pulled his cloak about him, walked along the main street of the camp, past his own log megaron and Lot's heavy wagon, to where the Sauromatae yurts lined the streets in Greek military order that made them look out of place, like regimented kittens.

Most of the women lived with their men, but the unmarried noblewomen had a yurt to themselves. Most were between fourteen and twenty, but a handful were older – spear-maidens who chose to remain warriors. Kineas rapped his riding whip against the doorpost and one of the young maidens popped her head out and immediately blushed and bowed her head.

'Lord Kineas!' she said.

Kineas smiled. No Greek called him 'Lord Kineas', and it was ironic that the Sauromatae accounted for most of his discipline problems, because man for man and woman for woman, they worshipped him, a far cry from the views of the average Olbian trooper.

'I would like to see the Lady Bahareh, if she will receive me,' Kineas said.

Bahareh came to the door of the tent, took his hand and led him inside. She was an older warrior, with grey in her braids and a face that was more leather than flower petal. She was also one of the army's finest lancers and her deep female voice carried over any amount of strife. She held no particular rank, but in battle, she rose to command.

Kineas accepted a cup of her tea. 'I wish you to come and help me with the judgment of Gwair Blackhorse,' he said.

She raised an imperious eyebrow. 'He took that heathen girl from the slaver. Is this a crime?'

Kineas nodded. 'The slave is like a horse – a thing of value to the brothel keeper.'

Bahareh frowned. 'So he should buy her.' The Sauromatae women smiled. 'She is quite a piece.'

'The brothel keeper wants her returned. He does not wish to sell the woman.' That's what I tried first, Kineas thought.

Bahareh snapped her fingers and a pair of teenaged girls helped her don her long, fur-lined coat. It weighed almost as much as armour. Unlike a man's, it fitted her figure – a very elegant garment, even for a barbarian. Another girl put her hair up and she pulled on a Sakje cap, extinguishing her sex utterly. She looked like any other well-to-do Sakje. As she rose to her feet, she asked, 'Is the girl pregnant?'

Kineas wanted to slap her on the back.

'I hadn't thought to ask,' Kineas said. 'Let us assume she is pregnant.'

They were walking down the street. Lady Bahareh had longer legs than Kineas and he had to hurry to match her stride.

'Then when she gives birth, if she lives, she is a free woman of the clan. He gives her a few horses as a birth present, and the baby is part of his family. That is the law.'

Kineas grunted. 'I see how to judge this. Listen, lady – I wish you to let it be known that tribesmen who visit the brothels must pay – every time – and that the next man who takes one of these girls to his yurt will suffer as if he stole her from another tribe. If you will do this for me,' he stopped her in the middle of the street because her stride was so long that she was going to walk him back into the assembly before he was ready, 'I will tell a lie and save Gwair Blackhorse.'

Bahareh was tall – almost eye to eye with him. She frowned. 'It is not for you to punish a tribesman, Lord Kineas. That is for our prince to do.'

Kineas held her eye. 'Lady, we will not make it through the winter as friends unless all obey. Surely it is the same in a winter camp of the Sauromatae?'

She toyed with her whip. 'Yes,' she said. 'Fair enough. Save Gwair – he's a fool, but most men are – and I'll whip the men into line.' Her whip made a sharp whisper as it cut the air. 'Lot is right to follow you,' she said.

Kineas spent the better part of the next hour bargaining with the brothel keeper and the town's self-appointed archon over the value of the woman, while Therapon, balked of his fight, stalked off. Kineas used her pregnancy to prise her loose from her owner. He made the whole clan pay her inflated value, putting Gwair neatly in the wrong with his own people. The process took roughly four times the time and money it would have taken him to punish one of his own people.

'This is going to be a long winter,' he said to Niceas.

'That's not good,' Diodorus said, pointing to the gate.

Two horsemen came up in a shower of snow, riding hard. One of their pickets. The riders pressed right through the assembly.

'There's a boat down at the beach,' Sitalkes said. His breath steamed and so did the breath of his horse, whose panting was audible. 'From the fort we built at Errymi. Someone from Olbia.'

'That's not good,' Diodorus repeated.

Kineas sent a patrol with spare horses down to the water, three stades distant, with Sitalkes in command. They came back with Nicanor, a freedman who was now the head of the household that had been Nicomedes'. Kineas had the man taken into the megaron, where he stood by the hearth, soaking up the heat. 'I thought I'd never be warm again,' he said. 'I've been on that boat for three days, cold and wet through.' He sighed. He was fat, over-dressed and very out of place, and the whine in his tone was not something often heard in Kineas's camp.

'Thank you for coming so fast. You have a message for me?' Kineas asked gently.

The man reached inside his tunic and drew out a scroll tube. Even the bone tube hadn't resisted all of the wet, but the vellum inside was clear enough.

Lykeles to Kineas of Athens, greetings.

My friend, I received your request for funds and could not fill it. The city is near a state of war – the factions have twice attempted the murder of Petrocolus and his son. I dare not send wealth out of the city for fear that it will be stolen and used against us. I send Nicanor to you that you will see how hard-pressed I am. If you are not gone too far, please come back. And together we will crush this upstart.

I know that I have failed you in this, but I cannot see another choice.

I enclose a letter that arrived at the Maimakteria from Athens. Surely if our own city expects you to campaign against Amphipolis, your duty must recall you.

Kineas read the letter, and the enclosed letter from Demosthenes of Athens, or one of his faction, with growing alarm. He handed them both on to Philokles, who had been questioning Nicanor. The former slave was reduced to tears already.

'You were very brave, crossing the Kaspian Sea at this time of year,' Kineas said. He flicked a glance at the Spartan, as if to say 'Look what you've done!'

Nicanor shook his head, eyes on the ground. 'I had to come,' he said. 'Master Lykeles said – that I had to reach you – and – and I did.'

Philokles finished the letters and handed them to Diodorus.

'They're not up to ruling the city,' Nicanor said. He was still looking at the ground. 'That's what I came to say. I served Nicomedes for ten years as his chief factor. I know how business is done. Lykeles wants to use direct action – he paid for a killing. I know – I found the money and I paid the killers.'

Kineas nodded. He had seen this coming; he suspected that he already knew. 'Alcaeus?' he asked.

Nicanor started, and his hands twitched. 'You knew? Did you order it?'

Kineas shook his head.

'He will make himself a tyrant. He cannot bargain. And Petrocolus is weak – kind, well-intentioned, but weak. He is lost without my master – that is, Nicomedes – and his friend Cleitus. He vacillates. His allies leave him.'

Kineas took a deep breath. 'This is not good.'

The megaron was filling up with his closest officers. Rumour spread fast in the camp, and they were a small community. Heron was out on patrol and Lot seldom showed interest in the politics of the Greeks, but the rest were there very quickly, slipping in past the blankets over the door.

Leon nodded. 'We need money. Without it, we're going to be in trouble for remounts in the spring. I'm already worried about making the next payment to the hoplites.' He had an arm around Nicanor's shoulders. 'I can't understand why there isn't enough money,' he said uneasily. 'I'm making deals here – I expect my credit here to be backed in Olbia and in Pantecapaeum. If it isn't, we'll have angry creditors when spring comes – and my new business prospects will vanish.'

'Lykeles is trying to bring us back,' Diodorus said. 'I hate to be the one to say it, but someone has got to him. He's trying to withhold your money to get you back.'

'Athens?' Philokles asked.

'Macedon?' asked Sappho. 'It is an open secret that you go to fight Alexander. That woman in the palace still serves him. I'd wager my life on it.'

'Odd, how their interests coincide,' said Philokles. He looked thoughtful. 'If you were to return to Olbia, the army would remain here for the spring, would it not?' He glanced around. 'What do you say, Kineas?'

Kineas sighed. 'If I go back, I'll never leave again. I can feel it in my bones.'

Diodorus shrugged. 'Have you settled with the queen on a spring campaign?' He shrugged. 'Sorry for asking, but it *is* related. If we're making a spring campaign, we have time to send someone back.'

'She wants a great deal more than just a spring campaign,' Kineas said, unintentionally setting them all to smirks.

Niceas spoke out, his voice rough. 'Let Diodorus fight the spring campaign. You'll have the time to ride there, whip everyone into line and come back. We'll be moving by high summer.'

Diodorus grinned. 'I admit, I want to be in command again.' He looked at Niceas. 'I don't think it'll be that easy for Kineas, though. If this is what I think it is, the powers behind the recall will have various devices – all perfectly legal – to hold Kineas at Olbia.'

Kineas nodded and looked at Philokles. The Spartan put his chin on his hand. 'There's sense in what Diodorus says. You might restore order in a matter of days.' He sat up. 'Or not. You might get embroiled in months of debate – a year of accusations.'

Diodorus spoke up again. 'And the cream of the army – the votes that will always back you – will be here.'

Philokles took a deep breath. 'And they might well have you killed.'

Eumenes' voice could be heard like an undercurrent, explaining the politics of the situation to Darius, whose Persian youth left him with no experience of the fickleness of a Greek assembly.

'Yes,' said Coenus. 'Fox, you're right for a change. Lykeles is in over his head, that's for sure.' Coenus grinned. 'I guarantee he's not crooked – Diodorus, you know better than that. He's been with us for ever. But he can be a fool.' Diodorus nodded, acknowledging the truth of both statements. Coenus went on, 'But he's one of my oldest friends. Send me. Not that it's how I want to spend the winter.' Coenus's chosen method of spending the winter was Artemesia, the most beautiful of Banugul's ladies. He shrugged. 'If you go, Kineas, they'll mire you in crap, like Odysseus there claims. If you send me, no one will waste a daric on killing me, but I can sort out Lykeles, get some cash from him and move it by ship. I probably won't be back until late spring – until Lake Maeotis is open to navigation, anyway. But no one will hold me. And,' he shrugged, 'I have a certain name. No one is likely to fuck with me.'

Diodorus glanced at Sappho. 'He's right. I rather fancied the part where I commanded the spring campaign, but he's right.'

Philokles nodded agreement. 'He spent the fall hunting the high passes on the Tanais. He knows the ground – he'll go the fastest.'

Kineas hated giving up any of his closest friends. He glanced at Leon, at Eumenes, but both were associated with city factions and neither could do what needed to be done. 'You're ready for troop command,' Kineas said. 'Do this for me, Coenus, and you'll have it.'

'Bah,' said the aristocrat, 'I don't need a bribe to make the trip. If I don't go, Lykeles will make an ass of himself and we'll all lose by it. Besides, I'm a citizen of Olbia now. It's my duty to the city, don't you know.' He looked around at the command council. 'Swear to me that you'll all stay out of Artemesia's bed. I may wed her.'

Laughing, they all swore.

Coenus sailed north with the ten men he'd led all fall. He sailed on a gentle winter's day with a fair wind for the north. Nicanor stayed to run Kineas's household. He said that he'd rather conquer Asia than cross the Kaspian in winter again. It took him a day to purchase four slaves, and Kineas didn't have to pour his own wine.

Two days later, their third snowstorm came, with the flakes falling like the white feathers of some monstrous bird, just as Herodotus described, and gathering in drifts driven by the north wind.

'Coenus is safe at the mouth of the Rha, drinking hot wine in our old fort,' Philokles said.

Kineas said a prayer to Poseidon and sacrificed a lamb the next day with his own hands. At the citadel, he continued to refuse to fight a spring campaign a day after the spring feast of Persephone, despite the blandishments and the gold that the queen flung at him.

They heard that Antipater, the ruler of Macedon in Alexander's absence, had defeated Sparta decisively.

They heard that Alexander had vanished off the eastern edge of the world – or that he was in Bactria, or perhaps Sogdiana.

They heard a rumour that Parmenion was lining up the satraps of the west to destroy Alexander if he returned. Leosthenes had told them that Artabazus was Parmenion's man, and that their employer, Queen Banugul, was Alexander's, and doomed to fall. And that Athens was prepared to throw off the yoke and go to war with Antipater.

Leon sat in the market, or in the megaron, listening to traders speak of the east – the trade road that led over the mountains and deserts and plains, to a far country they called Kwin. His eyes burned with something like lust. The Hyrkanian traders and the steppe nomads wintering in Hyrkania told Leon that Kwin was the source of silk.

All around them, east and west and south, they heard the stirrings of revolt and war, until the snow came in earnest.

And then the snow settled like soft fortress walls and all the rumours came to an end.

Until spring.

PART III

LAND OF WOLVES

14

Philotas stood easily under Alexander's glare. 'What *exactly* am I supposed to have done, your majesty?' he asked.

'Be respectful when you speak to the king, Philotas!' barked Hephaestion. The king's best friend and sometime lover was dressed simply, his bronze hair unadorned, but he seemed to have grown in stature overnight and the accusation in his tone snapped like a drover's whip.

Philotas turned his head with exaggerated lassitude, as if looking at Hephaestion was too much work for him. 'I am respectful,' he said. He shrugged. 'I'm also busy.' His eyes went back to the king's, and the dismissal of Hephaestion and everything about him was palpable. The two men had always disliked each other. Philotas was Parmenion's son, and the best cavalry officer in the army. His arrogance was the kind the troopers liked – an arrogance born of accomplishment. That he was handsome and well born didn't hurt, but he hadn't risen on his father's name alone. He was brave, calculating and, above all, relentlessly successful. Some of the old guard said that without him, the battle at Arbela might have ended in defeat.

Hephaestion's place rested on his relationship with the king. Keen observers, and the military court that surrounded the king of Macedon was full of such men, noted that whenever commands – fighting commands – were handed out, even the besotted Alexander passed over his friend for Philotas.

So despite two days of whispering throughout the camp, Philotas stood at ease in front of his king. 'I've heard a lot of talk,' Philotas said. 'Am I accused of something, your majesty?'

'You are accused of aiding in a plot to kill the king,' Hephaestion said.

Alexander remained mute.

Philotas continued to look at the king. 'Crap,' he said. 'I'm utterly loyal and everyone knows it.'

'The plotters have betrayed you,' Hephaestion said.

'I don't give a cunt hair for what your torturers dragged out of some peasant,' Philotas said.

'Why didn't you come to me with Cebalinus's accusation?' Alexander asked. His voice sounded tired.

Philotas nodded sharply. 'I knew this was what we were on about. Look, Alexander,' Philotas, as a noble and a Companion, had the right to address the king familiarly, 'you know what a bitchy fool Cebalinus can be. Like any boy-lover,' and here Philotas smiled at Hephaestion in obvious mockery, 'he gets all womanish and he gossips. So he heard something while he was being buggered. I heard him out. It sounded like crap. I ignored it.'

'It wasn't crap,' Alexander said. 'We have full confessions.'

'If I was wrong,' Philotas said, his tone conveying that he thought the whole thing a set up, 'then I make my most profound apology. Your majesty must believe that I would never allow a plot against him to go forward. On the other hand ...' Here he paused, because he realized that his arguments were about to cross on to forbidden ground. *If I reported every plot against you, we wouldn't have an army* didn't seem like a good thing to say.

'You seem to be comfortable with treason yourself,' Hephaestion spat.

'This is a lot of crap,' Philotas said. He was losing patience. It was too *stupid* an accusation to be taken seriously.

'You say in private that you saved the king at Arbela. That you and your father have won every battle – that the king is not competent to lead an army.'

For the first time, Philotas was alarmed and it showed. He raised his chin. Thinking quickly, he decided on utter honesty. 'I may have boasted foolishly, when drunk.' He tried to win a smile from the king. 'It's been known to happen with soldiers.' When no smile was forthcoming, Philotas widened his eyes. 'You can't be serious. I'll apologize to the army if you require it, your majesty – but drunken boasting is *not treason*.'

'Your father has been plotting against me for years,' Alexander said, suddenly. He sounded shrewish.

'What?' Philotas said. He was now alarmed. 'No he hasn't. Ares' balls, Alexander, you wouldn't even be king if it weren't for my father!' No sooner were the words out of his mouth than he saw that Hephaestion had played him like a lyre. He glared at the favourite. Hephaestion glared back.

'Traitor,' he spat.

Philotas stood tall. 'Prove it, minion!'

Hephaestion turned to Alexander. 'He'll confess under torture.'

'You can't torture me!' Philotas spat. 'I'm the commander of the Companions! On the bones of Achilles, the best of the Achaeans, I swear I am no traitor! And you'll never prove it before the assembly!' He stood there, tall and handsome, the very image of the dashing officer.

But the assembly thought differently, two days later, when he was brought before them toothless, with much of his face gone. He looked like a traitor with his hands broken. Hephaestion said that he had confessed his own guilt, and the king said the same. No one could understand Philotas when he spoke.

They executed him.

'Now I can clean house,' Alexander said to Hephaestion. It was a private council, with only a few men – Eumenes and Kleisthenes and Hephaestion.

'You have to kill Parmenion,' Hephaestion urged. 'When he hears—'

'Yes, Patrocles!' Alexander ruffled his bronze hair. 'I know. The father must go, now that the son is proved a traitor.'

Even Kleisthenes, a sophist and a professional propagandist, was cut to the bone to hear the king call Philotas a traitor in private. The king had convinced himself – a dangerous precedent.

Eumenes the Cardian kept his face composed. 'Spitamenes has accepted our suggestions about negotiation,' he said. Eumenes had learned not to use words that the king might take to mean that the Macedonians were suing for peace with a rebel satrap. The truth was that Spitamenes, with the remnants of Bessus's Persian army and the support of the Massagetae and the Dahae, was slowing up their conquest of the north to an unpalatable degree.

The king drank some more wine. 'When Parmenion is dead, the areas to my rear will be secure,' he said. 'I'll have all the time I need to conquer the rest of the world. I don't need Spitamenes. Tell him to fuck off.'

Hephaestion laughed aloud.

Eumenes, who had laboured all winter to get negotiations on the table, took a deep breath. 'Spitamenes is interested in religious issues, your majesty. He does not desire to be King of Kings.' He got the bit between his teeth and spoke the truth. 'As long as he has the Scythian tribes, he can cross the Jaxartes at will. We cannot follow him there.'

Alexander turned his head and his mad, white-rimmed eyes bored into Eumenes' head. 'There is nowhere my army cannot go,' he said.

Eumenes flicked his eyes to Hephaestion, hoping that the indulgent man would remember his own self-interest.

Hephaestion swirled the wine in his cup and then leaned forward. 'If we campaign across the Jaxartes, we'll lose a whole campaign season from India.'

He ought to have been an actor, Eumenes thought. He wiped his brow.

Alexander threw himself back on his couch. 'Fine. Even Achilles listened when Phoenix spoke. But I want an Amazon – better yet, a dozen. Tell Spitamenes to get me a dozen Amazons.'

This was the type of demand that could unseat a negotiation in a moment, but Eumenes knew his master's voice. He nodded.

'Yes, majesty,' he said.

And Kleisthenes shuddered.

15

The first flowers bloomed through the last snow in Hyrkania, and the winds coming across the Kaspian were still cold enough for Hyperboreans and strong enough to discourage even the keenest bowmen.

Kineas felt fat. He'd eaten too well and exercised too little, although they'd built a gymnasium and used it, too. He'd never been so cold in his life as in the dead of winter in Hyrkania, when the snow hit like hard-blown sand and the wolves howled every night. And too often his exercise consisted of climbing the steep hill to the citadel, where the queen entertained him with stories in Greek and Persian, the questionable antics of her slaves and the sensuous pleasure of her heated floors and luxurious baths, as well as the more intellectual pleasures of scrolls and singers and poetry.

After Therapon had presented her with too many coloured versions of Kineas's law court, she asked with a smile to come down the hill and see one – and to see his camp. He had no way to refuse her and so the next day her cavalcade wound its way down from the citadel, a dozen local gentlemen on horseback with some of her guards in hastily polished bronze. She wore a fur-lined cloak over a richly embroidered Scythian jacket and wool trousers tucked into small boots, with a tall Median cap and a veil that covered her eyes without disguising them.

And a sword.

The ground was frozen hard and Kineas's men put on a display on horse and foot. The Olbian cavalry threw javelins, the prodromoi shot their bows, and the hoplites marched and counter-marched and demonstrated a change of front in the Spartan fashion, to her beaming approval. They shot arrows at targets and she insisted on having a turn, shooting competently, although Kineas allowed himself to note that Srayanka would have filled the targets with arrows while riding at a gallop.

She looked into the wine shops and the brothels of the camp's marketplace. 'Am I supplying all the women for your army, Kineas?' she asked.

Kineas looked away. 'We brought a few of our own,' he said.

'Yes, and a hetaira to manage them,' Banugul said. She laughed. 'So well organized. Do the men stand in line waiting their turn when they can't get Hyrkanian farm girls? Or go without?' Then she began to recite:

> Baulked in your amorous delight
> How melancholy is your plight.
> With sympathy your case I view;
> For I am sure it's hard on you.
> What human being could sustain
> This unforeseen domestic strain,
> And not a single trace
> Of willing women in the place!

As she spoke, she deepened her voice because it was the male chorus part in *Lysistrata*, and they all laughed with her.

Therapon glanced at Philokles. 'Perhaps they have no need of women, my lady.'

'If that were the case,' she said with a twinkle, '"Then why do they hide those lances, that stick out under their tunics?"' Her wicked paraphrase of Aristophanes made them all laugh again.

Philokles stepped closer to the queen. Looking up at her, he declaimed, '"She did it all, the harlot, she – with her atrocious harlotry."'

Therapon whirled, his face red, but Banugul reached down from her horse and took the Spartan's hand. 'I love a man of education,' she said. 'You are Philokles the Sophist?'

He laughed, obviously flattered. 'I am Philokles the Spartan, my lady. I can't remember being called a sophist, except by Kineas here.'

She beamed. 'If you can call me a harlot, I can call you a sophist.'

'I will be more careful of my epigrams,' Philokles said, clearly stung.

She blew him a kiss. 'Why do you not come and visit my court, Spartan? All the others come – save Diodorus here, who has ceased to visit me. But you never come.'

'Sophistry takes all my time,' Philokles said, gravely.

Diodorus went so red that he turned away, and even Kineas had to stifle a guffaw, while Banugul blushed a little, but she didn't flinch. 'Implying that harlotry takes all my time?'

'I said nothing of the sort,' Philokles said, drawling the words.

'Pederasty, more like,' said Therapon quietly, but his voice carried.

Kineas stepped between them. 'Philokles, the lady is not a target for your wit.'

'I can protect myself, Kineas,' Banugul said. 'By all the gods, I see now what I missed by staying in my citadel. And I see now why Kineas can parry any little wit I may employ if this is his daily sparring.'

'More than sparring,' Therapon said broadly. 'Perhaps they entertain each other exclusively.' He leered.

Philokles seemed to ignore the Thessalian's jibes until later, when the Olbians were showing the queen and her entourage around their log-built gymnasium. Philokles had the queen's arm and her ear, and he spoke of Greek wrestling and of *pankration*, their unarmed combat sport, until she clapped her hands.

'I would love to see that,' she said. 'I have read so much about it.'

Philokles smiled, and the warrior that lurked under the skin of the philosopher came to the surface. 'I would be pleased to show you, my lady,' he said. 'I'm sure your Therapon would be delighted to fight me chest to chest.'

Therapon was not the kind of man to refuse a challenge, and he stripped. 'I'm not likely to let you behind me,' he mocked. 'I know what naked Greeks do.'

'We fight naked,' Philokles said to the queen, by way of apology.

'My harlotry extends to male nudity,' Banugul replied.

Philokles dropped his heavy cloak and pulled his wool chiton over his head, exposing the body of a statue. Therapon was heavier and had the start of a gut, although his arms were longer and immensely strong. Kineas tried to catch his friend's eye.

Banugul put a hand on Philokles' naked shoulder. 'I would take it amiss if you hurt my captain,' she said. Her nails brushed Philokles' chest as she withdrew her hand. Her smile was a private one, for Philokles alone, and Kineas was appalled to find within himself a tingle of jealousy at their intimacy.

Then the two men were circling on the sand, bent low, intent. They circled long enough for the queen to grow bored and smile self-consciously at her host, when suddenly some shift in posture or intent brought the two contestants together, arms locked high, feet well back as they heaved against each other's strength. Muscles stood out in strain and, despite the cold, a sheen of sweat covered both men.

Banugul leaned forward, her hands on her hips. Kineas watched her as she watched the contestants.

Philokles changed his weight suddenly, as if surrendering to the Thessalian's embrace, but he got his body turned as he stepped in. One arm moved and he struck the Thessalian in the head with his forearm and suddenly Therapon was on his back and Philokles landed on him, driving the air from his lungs.

'He does that to me all the time,' Kineas said ruefully.

Banugul turned to him, eyes alight with mischief. 'The things I could imply,' she said. But she reached out a hand to his chest and shook her head. 'I am too crude for words. I mean no hurt.'

It was the first time she had touched him. The warmth of her palm on his chest seemed to light a small fire there. She withdrew the hand while he was still surprised by its presence.

Philokles swung to his feet and offered Therapon his hand, but the other man didn't take it. Instead, he stood brushing sand off his sweat, glowering. Philokles held his eyes. 'Another throw?' he asked.

'Perhaps another time,' the Thessalian said, and reached for his chiton. Kineas disliked the look the Thessalian gave his friend. It boded ill.

The queen's tour started a new round of visits between camp and citadel, and the new ties between them did not make Kineas entirely happy. The first thing that annoyed him was Darius, whose skill with the bow and willingness to learn had endeared him to the Olbians. Kineas was becoming used to seeing his officers in the corridors of the citadel from time to time – Banugul had made it clear that they were welcome. But Kineas saw Darius too often, almost every day, and Kineas worried, both for the Persian boy and for his loyalties.

'You spend a great deal of time here,' Kineas said, several weeks after the queen's visit to the camp.

Embarrassed, the young Persian shrugged. He smelled of perfume. 'I like to hear Persian spoken sometimes,' he said. 'They are not unlike my people,' he went on in the tone of outraged adolescence. Despite his upright carriage, he had the whine of the young to him when he replied, and it annoyed Kineas still more.

'You are on the duty roster today,' Kineas said.

'Only for the reserve,' Darius said. He shrugged. 'They won't be called out. What, is Alexander coming through the snow?'

Kineas tried to decide whether what he felt was jealousy at the smell of her perfume or annoyance at the tone of bratty innocence and justification. 'Why don't you make your way down to camp and take a spell on the walls while you consider the difference between insolence and disobedience?' Kineas said.

Darius was not a fool. He saluted and left. Later inquiry showed that he had spent the entire shift on the walls. Kineas dismissed the incident.

Four days later, Darius was in the citadel again on his duty day, and Kineas barely restrained his temper. He felt that his orders were being flouted – worse, he suspected that he was himself being unjust. *He* visited the citadel, and he was the commander, the most responsible man of all. A poor example.

However, despite his own transgressions – perhaps because of them – Kineas lost his temper. 'March your arse down to the duty office and wait there!' Kineas barked.

Later that evening, Kineas found Darius sitting in his megaron. 'You are banned from the citadel until further notice,' Kineas said.

'Oh, that's fair,' Darius said with fluent sarcasm.

'One more word and you can shovel snow for the rest of the winter,' Kineas said.

Darius looked as if he wanted to say more – a great deal more. When the Persian marched out, his silence made Kineas feel like a bully, the more so as Darius cast such a look of supplication at Philokles, who was just coming in, that Philokles put his arm around the young man's shoulders and stepped out into the snow to talk to him. When Philokles came back in, he was shaking his head.

'*You* go to the palace, Strategos!' Philokles said.

'I am the commander, and responsible for our relations with the queen.' Kineas offered the Spartan a cup of wine.

'Ares and Aphrodite, and you call *me* a sophist?' Philokles grinned. Then he stopped smiling. 'Listen, I'm here for something serious. Have you watched Leon and Eumenes? Together?'

Kineas made a face and shook his head. 'Should I? What, are they lovers?'

'Ares, you're blind as a bat. No, much the opposite. They're facing each other like armed camps on a plain.' Philokles drained his wine. 'You need to keep them apart.'

'What's it about?' Kineas asked.

Philokles narrowed his eyes and frowned. 'I may spy for you from time to time, or for my homeland. I don't carry tales about my comrades.' He turned the cup upside down and stomped out.

Alerted, Kineas couldn't miss the growing competition between Eumenes and Leon. Kineas didn't know where it had started or what it was about, but it was out of hand. The incident that brought their misdeeds to light for Kineas was a torch-lit horse race on the snow, where the riders competed to bring fire to the altar of Demeter at the spring equinox, a tradition that Olbia shared with Athens. The competitors raced around the circuit of the camp and finished at a gallop down the main street, riding flat out for the building that served as a temple for all their gods. Eumenes lost when his horse, tearing around the corner of one of the soldiers' cabins, slipped and fell. The young man broke a rib and walked with a limp for two weeks, and his horse slid on the ice, limbs flailing, and ended up injuring a dozen bystanders. Kineas saw the turn and saw the rough play between Leon and Eumenes in the moments before the fall.

When Kineas inquired, he received the kind of knowing looks that told him that most of his commanders already knew that something lay between the young men, and weren't going to inform on them. When Kineas confronted the two combatants, they glared at each other like a pair of fighting cocks. When he upbraided them in private, they wore looks of humiliation and apology.

It was a week later, when he saw Leon talking to Lot's surviving daughter, Mosva, that Kineas began to see how the winter wind blew. Because even as he watched Leon, who lost all of his courtly polish in her presence and had the body language of a young dog, shifting, shrugging, rolling and hanging his head, he also saw Eumenes watching the two of them, his face a thundercloud.

Aha! he thought. But it didn't resolve the issue.

It was about the same time that Kineas went up the hill to see Banugul about a matter of logistics and found she was not available to receive him. Darius's pale roan horse was in the citadel stables. Kineas rode back down the hill in a foul temper. He called for Diodorus.

'Have the fucking Persian dismissed. He has disobeyed me for the last time.' Kineas was so angry he spilled wine.

Philokles came in through the multiple blankets that now made the doorway. 'Problems?'

Kineas was silent. Diodorus raised an eyebrow. 'Kineas's

Persian boy has become a little too popular in the palace,' Diodorus said. He made a face.

'Fuck you,' Kineas said. 'I gave him a direct order and he disobeyed. I am ordering him dismissed.'

'You're over-reacting,' Diodorus said. 'He's an excellent horseman and a top-notch fighter. You've said yourself he's a better swordsman than you, and you're the best I know. I'm ready to put him up for phylarch.'

'Dismiss him,' Kineas said, voice hard.

'Don't be an ass,' Diodorus said.

Philokles shook his head. 'Probably better if you dismiss him,' he said after a moment.

Diodorus looked hurt. 'The strategos is thinking with his little head,' he said.

Philokles raised an eyebrow. 'I say that it is for the best.'

'Fine!' Diodorus said. 'I'll obey. I think you're both idiots, though.'

Kineas didn't see the Persian again, but the rumour mill said that the young man had immediately taken service in the citadel, with the queen's guard.

Kineas felt like an idiot, but it didn't cause him to apologize. Winter was taking its toll. And despite his best efforts, he wasn't able to stop his own visits to the citadel. Kineas tried to limit them to matters of business, but he was aware that he stretched those boundaries to fit his needs. As winter howled outside his megaron he admitted to himself that, like a wine-bibber denied his tipple, four days of snow had denied him his addiction and he was growing fractious. He decided to punish himself for the dismissal of Darius by avoiding the citadel. He snapped at Philokles on the fifth day of imposed abstinence from Banugul's charms and the Spartan grinned.

'I can find you a nice clean Hyrkanian girl who'll reduce that swelling in no time,' he quipped.

'Keep a civil tongue,' Kineas barked.

'"The situation swells to greater tension. Something will explode soon,"' Philokles quoted, laughing. 'Aristophanes covers almost every sexual situation, I find.'

'Go fuck yourself, Spartan,' Kineas said.

'The same might be suggested to you, Strategos.' Philokles ducked a blow and slipped out of the door.

Two days later, Leosthenes the Athenian paid another visit and Kineas felt himself excused to climb the hill. It was early evening by the time he was admitted and Banugul was reclining on a couch, alone, with a dozen guests on couches eating a banquet. Darius was nowhere to be seen.

'Dear Kineas,' she said. 'I would have invited you, but I feared your rejection. Please join us.'

She was modestly dressed in an Ionic chiton that left her shoulders visible. The wool was fine and pure white, and her skin stood the comparison. She rolled from a reclining position to sitting and clapped her hands, and a pair of male slaves rushed from the room.

'Sit by me, Strategos,' she said, patting her couch. She waved a languid hand at her guests. 'Do you all know Kineas of Athens?' she asked. 'Sartobases was a loyal officer of my mother's family and has followed me here.' The Persian, obviously uncomfortable on a couch, rose to a sitting position and bowed from the waist. 'Philip serves in the household of my sister Barsine,' she said, indicating a Macedonian just out of boyhood. Alone of the men in the room, he seemed comfortable on his couch.

'I congratulate you on crossing the passes in this weather,' Kineas said.

'I had good guides, sir,' the young man said with enthusiastic courtesy. 'And every reason to reach my goal!'

Kineas smiled at the young man's earnestness. 'Well done,' he said. 'You came from Ecbatana?' he asked, as if uninterested.

'Oh, no,' Philip said. 'The king is at Kandahar, and so is my mistress. Parmenion holds Ecbatana.'

'Kandahar in Sogdiana?' Kineas said.

'Perhaps you could show a little more interest in your hostess and a little less in spying on Alexander,' Banugul said lazily. To Philip, she said, 'My good strategos is taking a small army east to make war on your master.'

Philip looked as if a wasp had stung him. Then his face

relaxed. 'My lady is pleased to make light of my youth. No *Greek* would dare to make war on Alexander.'

The slaves returned with another couch and placed it by the queen's. Kineas didn't notice how close she had been until he was alone on his own couch and the distance seemed like a gulf of stars, but the analytical soldier in his head was already measuring the stades to Kandahar. 'The king has made peace in Sogdiana, then?' Kineas said, drawing a glare from Banugul.

Philip shook his head, making a face to indicate that he was a man of the world. 'The rump of the Persian empire continues to rebel. Spitamenes – a rebel against Darius, and now against my lord – is in league with the Scythian barbarians on the sea of grass. My lord will punish them soon.'

None of the Persian men were pleased by this speech, and Sartobases, who had a strong face and might have played Old Nestor in a tragedy, made the motion of spitting. 'Listen, boy,' he said. 'Your master may have won Syria and Palestine and Egypt by his spear, but the land of the Bactrians and the Medae is not conquered.'

'Hush, uncle,' Banugul said. 'We are all friends here.'

Kineas didn't think so. He looked at Banugul with new understanding. How many plots were in this mosaiced room tonight?

'Do you wish to ask me about Leosthenes?' Kineas said quietly.

'Why, did he visit you again?' she asked, her voice light. 'Wait until we are private.'

They were educated men and they spoke of astrology, at her bidding, of signs that they had seen come to pass, portents and dreams. Kineas admitted to having god-sent dreams and Philip listened with wide eyes as the youngest Persian told a story of intrigue and murder based on predictions drawn from the stars. Then she had her Carian singer perform. He sang in his own language and then, with a bow to Kineas, he sang the Choice of Achilles from the *Iliad*, and Kineas applauded him. And then the Carian sang in Persian, a simple song of forbidden love. Kineas's Persian was good enough to catch the illicit nature of the love but not the details. He was more interested in watching old Sartobases look disapprovingly at Banugul.

It was nothing like a symposium – no ceremony with the wine, which was served by slaves, no contests and no performances by the guests. Philip watched the dark-haired slave girl who poured his wine like a falcon with a piece of meat, and began to stroke her at every opportunity, until his hostess made a sign and she was replaced. Aside, she said to Kineas, 'Do Greek men really allow themselves to be publicly pleasured at parties?'

Kineas felt himself flush. 'Young men – hmm. Yes. Not at nice parties.'

Banugul laughed, her irritation banished by his embarrassment. 'You're blushing! You've done this yourself?' She laughed aloud. 'I can't picture it.'

Kineas sat up.

'Don't be a prude. It's quite a picture.' Banugul shook her head. The other guests were disputing Bessus's right to be King of Kings. 'You are so reserved—'

'I was young. It was all fascinating. And easy. And I was challenged—'

'Is that what you require, Kineas?' she asked, rolling closer to him. 'A challenge?' Her face was a hand's span from his. 'Shall I dare you to pleasure yourself on one of my maids?' she asked, eyes sparkling.

'I am out of practice at this sort of banter,' he replied. He rolled on to his stomach for a variety of reasons.

'I can tell,' she answered, casting him a half-smile of challenge over her shoulder as she turned to address another guest.

She played the hostess perfectly, demure as a Persian maiden, witty as an Athenian hetaira. All things to all men, Kineas thought. He willed himself to make his report and go.

But he did not.

Her guests took themselves off one by one, and Kineas was conscious that he was not leaving and they were – but she had asked him to stay, and the matter of Leosthenes remained between them, or so he told himself.

Sartobases was the last to go, and he raised an elegant Persian eyebrow at Kineas.

'We have unfinished business,' Banugul said, indicating Kineas.

Sartobases shrugged. 'I can well imagine,' he said to her in Persian.

'He speaks Persian,' Banugul said, indicating Kineas.

Sartobases bowed deeply and flushed. 'My apologies, lord.'

Kineas shook his head. 'None required, lord. We are in the Land of Wolves.'

Sartobases nodded, his eyes narrow. Then he was gone, and they were alone, except for twenty slaves clearing away the food.

'Come and lie by me,' she said lightly, as if it were a matter of no importance. She patted her couch.

'I think not,' he said, hating the sound of weak prudery in his voice.

'Who says you rise to a challenge? Then make your report and go back to your barracks.' She sat up.

'I am sorry. I mean only—'

'Don't be weak.' She smiled dismissively.

'I find you ...' he began, hoping to excuse his refusal.

'Now you will make me angry, Kineas. Do as thou wilt, and only as thou wilt. That is the law of kings and queens. If thou wilt not, then so be it – it is not my fault that you have chosen so.' She slipped between formal Persian and Greek in every sentence.

Stung, Kineas sat back down on his own couch. 'There is more to virtue and vice than doing as I will,' he said.

She smiled at him. 'No,' she said. 'All your philosophy is merely to cover the weakness of those who cannot attain all the things they desire, or master them once attained. Your virtue is merely abstinence, and the avoidance of your vice is merely the cowardice of fear of consequence.'

'Fear of consequence?' he asked. She *was* angry. And she was no longer all things to all men.

'Alexander has found the philosophy of kings. I learned it

from him. Perhaps he learned it from your Aristotle? *There is no law.* That is the only law.' She was serious.

'You will not debate me into your arms,' Kineas said, standing up.

'Will I not? I get more response from you like this than with honey.' She stood too, and walked straight to him.

'Your philosophy—'

'To Hades with philosophy, Kineas.' She came up close, and he could see her, backlit by the torchlight from the room's north wall from knee to shoulder through the thin stuff of her chiton. 'I need you to protect my little kingdom in the spring.' She came closer and raised her face, where flecks of gold sparkled in her mascara. Her voice was low, husky and tired, but she smelled like spring. 'In the autumn I was willing to pay the price. Now I am eager to pay it.'

Somewhere beyond her in the torchlight, a slave dropped a heavy silver platter with a noise like a man beating a metal drum, or like a goddess clearing her throat. Kineas stepped back and kissed her hand, his resolve steadied.

'Coward,' she said. 'I can *feel* your desire. And I am no painted harlot.'

He took a breath, and all he breathed was her. 'I am a coward,' he said. He couldn't pull his eyes away from hers. 'You are no painted harlot.'

She shrugged and moved away. 'Go,' she commanded.

Riding down the hill, he felt nothing but shame at his own indecision.

Kineas vowed not to return.

Again.

Because his horses were thin and he needed remounts, because Coenus was due with the bullion, because the passes had been closed by snow and they were all worried by the lack of news – and because the queen had abandoned modesty, Kineas felt the urge to act. So when he saw flowers coming through the snow, Kineas summoned his friends. He served the last of his good Chian wine.

'I want to be ready to march,' he said. He looked around.

Every man met his eye, and the grunts of agreement were clear. At his elbow, Philokles nodded. Niceas, who had grown a bushy beard, scratched at it.

'Fodder,' Niceas said.

Kineas agreed. 'That's the problem. We need fodder. The fodder has to come in from the queen's peasants. They hate her, for starters, and she's none too fond of us right now, because we're marching away and leaving her to Parmenion's vultures.'

'That's one reason,' said Philokles, who missed nothing, when he was sober.

Diodorus rubbed his eyes. Smoke from the hearth was stinging them all, and every eye in camp was constantly red-rimmed. 'Her own mercenaries are ready to sell her to Artabazus. That citadel won't last a feast cycle when we march away. Everyone has their money on Parmenion.'

Kineas motioned to Nicanor, who signed to a slave, who poured wine in Kineas's cup. Kineas stood. 'She's intelligent and resourceful and dangerous as a wolf. I want the guard led by someone in this room until we march. I want to set a date and publicize it. Then we'll march two days early, in combat formation. And I want the prodromoi out as soon as Ataelus is willing to go, covering the route east all the way to the edge of the desert.'

No one disputed his ideas.

Diodorus held out his cup for wine. 'We should be drilling the combat formation for marching. We should do it by sections, so that it's not obvious to anyone watching.'

Kineas frowned. 'That's excellent. Draw up the plan and let's give it to every officer by tomorrow. Nicanor, can you scribe for Diodorus?'

Nicanor nodded.

Heron had grown up again during the winter. Now he spoke out. 'Two things, sir. First, do we need an operational plan in case we need to gather the forage ourselves? And second, if we leave,' he coloured, 'I hesitate to use the term hostile, but if the queen is not our friend when we march away, what becomes of Coenus and the bullion?'

Kineas, who had spent all winter worrying about Coenus,

took a deep breath and released it. 'We send a message to the fort at the top of the Kaspian, telling Coenus not to land here, and send guides to help him follow us.'

Heron jutted out his jaw insistently. 'Easier to seize a town on the coast and hold it for him,' he said. 'With a garrison that can become his escort.'

That silenced the room. Kineas glanced at Philokles. 'I had thought of leaving the infantry behind, or sending them home,' he said.

Lycurgus, who had heard this idea all winter, shook his head. 'We can keep up, if it comes to that. But Hades, Strategos, the boy's plan isn't a bad one. March up the coast and seize one of the wolf towns. It'd take us three or four days – there's nothing up there to stop three hundred hoplites.'

Diodorus cut in. 'I could go beyond that. Leosthenes says Hyrkania is full of Hellenes – deserters from one side or another. I've seen them – there are two groups of men who've sniffed around our camp, looking to be recruited. We could buy them.'

Kineas shook his head. 'My goal is to strike a blow against Alexander with Srayanka. I'm not interested in the conquest of Hyrkania – which, let me tell you, would be a harder nut than you two seem to think.'

Leon shook his head. 'Can't we keep the queen sweet?' Like Heron, Leon had grown over the winter. In his case, he was not just older but also more confident of his status as a free man. He frowned at Kineas. 'I have money tied into this place, now. So do you. If the queen repudiates all the contracts I've made, I've wasted the winter.'

Kineas groaned.

'Listen to me, Kineas,' Leon insisted. 'There's more to the world than Herodotus thought. For two years I've heard rumours – Nicomedes heard them – of a great empire in the east, beyond the sea of grass. The place from which silk comes.' He looked around at all of them, his eyes hot, and Kineas smiled inwardly, because Leon was no longer a slave. 'It's called Kwin, or Qu'in,' he said, voice husky with passion. 'I mean to go there!'

'Good for you, lad,' Niceas said with a smile.

The black man grinned. 'I'm getting carried away. But I'm telling you, if we could open this route – if we could manage even a tithe of the trade across the old trade road – we'd be richer than Croesus.'

Eumenes frowned. 'I think we need to discuss war, not trade. Trade is for merchants.'

Leon raised his chin. 'Your father was a merchant.'

'Shut your mouth!' Eumenes said. He rose to his feet.

'And a traitor,' Leon said, conversationally.

Diodorus didn't need a glance from Kineas to deal with adolescents. He put a hand on each combatant's shoulder. 'You are both rude and your comments have no place in a command conference. Apologize or suffer the consequence,' he said. His words were spoken quietly, but they carried over every whispered side conversation and the room fell silent.

'I apologize,' Leon said. He was blushing so hard that his dark skin seemed to be engorged with blood.

'I apologize for Leon's bad manners as well as my own,' Eumenes said. 'He spent too much time as a slave and can't help himself.' Eumenes spoke rapidly, still enraged, and then looked stricken when he thought about what he had said aloud.

Kineas raised an eyebrow. 'You may go to your quarters, Eumenes. Do not communicate with any other person. I will come and pay you a visit.' He waited a moment, as the stunned young man stood frozen. 'Now, Eumenes.'

Eumenes walked from the smoky hall in a daze.

When he was gone, Kineas found himself stroking his beard and made his fingers stop. He sipped his wine – excellent stuff, with a smell like wild berries, dark as ox blood – and nodded. 'We're not here to open a trade route,' he said. He raised an eyebrow at Heron. 'We're not here to give you a base against Pantecapaeum, either. But if you lads can accomplish your dreams while obeying the orders of this council, I'm not against it.'

Heron's family had provided generations of tyrants to Pantecapaeum, and he was currently in exile. Heron made no secret of his ambitions to be tyrant there – perhaps king of the Bosporus, as well. He gave a careful smile. 'I appreciate your help. When I'm king—'

Niceas laughed. 'Heron the first?'

Philokles laughed. 'Eumeles, I suspect. The melodious one. Won't that be your reigning name?'

Heron gave a wry smile. 'You learn every secret.'

Philokles shook his head. 'Not much of a secret. So we're to be richer than Croesus?'

Niceas laughed. 'Richer than Croesus is good,' he said, giving Leon a smile. He winked at Heron. 'Your parents actually called you Eumeles?'

'They hadn't heard my voice yet,' Heron replied in his usual croak.

Diodorus leaned forward, cutting back to the matter at hand. 'You really think we can live without the infantry?' he asked. His face was burning – he was in the grip of a grand idea.

Kineas answered, 'Yes.' He tried to sound cautious.

Diodorus turned to the rest of them. 'We leave Lycurgus. He starts recruiting tomorrow. He can keep the quality high, get a thousand hoplites and train them to our standard. The queen is saved – no force in Hyrkania can evict a thousand hoplites from this fort and the citadel. We're saved – we have a secure town in our rear. Coenus can come here. Our contracts are safe.'

'Until Artabazus sends the whole levy of the satrapy.' Kineas glanced around and shrugged. 'It's not bad. Lycurgus?'

The old mercenary shrugged. 'Big command. You'd have to leave me another officer.' He shrugged. 'I came out here to follow Kineas, not to garrison some barbarian hill town.' He shrugged again. 'But I obey orders.' He grinned. 'Make her pay through the nose.'

Heron stood. 'I'll stay,' he said. It was clear to all the gentlemen present that Heron saw the town as a springboard to recruit mercenaries and go back to seize Pantecapaeum, just as Kineas had said. But being Heron, he didn't hide his motivations. He just bulled towards them regardless of consequences.

Kineas suspected that he shared Banugul's philosophy. *Do as you will.* A suitable virtue for a tyrant.

Kineas was not slow to realize that many of them were not as keen to march away to fight Alexander as he was. They'd had a winter to hear tales of the eastern deserts and the impassable mountains that ran to the edge of the world.

But Diodorus's plan was sound.

'I'll think on it,' Kineas said.

'Don't forget the fodder,' Niceas said, and coughed. Red sprayed his fist. He tried to hide it, and Diodorus and Kineas exchanged a look of shared concern.

The next day, the sun came up and stayed, and no rain fell on the fields of mud beyond the town and the citadel.

Diodorus, Leon and Nicanor were hard at work behind him, scratching out rows of Greek characters to represent every man in the line of march and to give the officers a manual on which to drill their men. Across the drill square, by the gate, Lycurgus was recruiting and drilling men that he had turned away all winter, wolfish Greeks and nondescript Persians. Beside him, Temerix the smith stood bundled in sheepskins, also recruiting from the brigands who came to the gate as soon as they heard that Kineas was paying silver for service.

He didn't want to go to the palace. They had nothing to say to each other, except as a mercenary and his employer. He glanced around the smoky hall, looking for a man he could send in his stead.

Diodorus was busy, and besides, Sappho would not forgive him for sending her man.

Eumenes was under house arrest, and Kineas meant to let him stew.

Leon might do. Except that he was busy, and sending him would expose Kineas's unwillingness to do what needed to be done.

Do the thing. Men said it when they asked for death, or when they sealed a deal in the Acropolis. He was evading responsibility. Facing the queen was his job.

He knew with the finality of oracular prophesy that if he

climbed the hill again, he would fall into her arms, vulgarity or none. She would think that his offer of service by his infantry was a concession to her charms. And he was not made of wood, or stone.

Cowardice.

A gust of wind picked up dust and dry snow from under the eaves of the huts and brushed it across the parade ground in a long swirl of dirty white, and when it was gone, Nihmu's slight figure could be seen riding across the drill field.

'Do you never appear as other people do?' Kineas asked, by way of greeting.

She laughed and lifted a leg over her horse's head and slid to the ground all in one elastic motion. 'The world is about to change,' she said, her face suddenly serious. 'I rode to tell you.'

Kineas nodded.

'The woman in the palace – the sorceress. She is very dangerous to you – today and tomorrow and tomorrow again after that. Be on your guard.' Nihmu's odd eyes met his square on.

Kineas nodded again. 'I was just thinking the very same thing as you rode up.'

Sometimes, when dealing with Nihmu, it was possible to forget that she was a child. At other times, it was painfully obvious. 'I have not had as much time for you this winter as I ought.'

Nihmu nodded. 'You are often at the palace. All the Sakje fear me. I long to talk to you. And my father orders it.' She looked around. 'I like your Nicanor. He is funny, and he makes good cakes.'

'I'm sure that Nicanor doesn't make cakes himself.' Kineas couldn't imagine the pompous and rather staid Nicanor amusing a child.

Nihmu made a face. 'Fat lot you know, Strategos.' She laughed.

Behind her in the drill square, Lycurgus dismissed the twenty files he was drilling and they broke up into knots of men talking and shouting. Another group, mostly Olbians, were heading out to the brothels of the agora, and they were shouting at a third party that was returning. The noise level swelled.

Suddenly all the voices in the drill square shaped themselves into one voice. '*Your blindness will kill as effectively as your sword*,' it said in the tone of a god.

Kineas fell back a pace. Nihmu's eyes were wide and her face was contorted, not the face of a child but that of a priestess. And then she grabbed at the bridle of her horse and ran away, crying.

He sent for Ataelus when he gathered the tangled skein of his thoughts. Ataelus rode up looking at the sky. 'Sun again tomorrow,' he said. 'For drying earth.'

Kineas nodded. 'I need you and the prodromoi to start making a fodder inventory,' he said.

Ataelus shrugged. 'Huh?' he asked.

Kineas started again. 'I need you and the scouts to go out every day and give me a report on the farms within a day's ride – the number of wagons, the amount of fodder they have in their barns and stores.'

Ataelus grinned. 'For counting wagons *and* for scouting trail to east. Anything else for scouts?'

Kineas spread his hands.

Ataelus leaned down from his horse. 'Temerix for counting barns and wagons. Ataelus for scouting east.'

Ataelus never cut corners and he never feared to argue with his leader, which was welcome, even when the news was bad.

'You are right.'

Ataelus nodded. 'Yes,' he said. 'If sun is for shining, scouts ride tomorrow. Back when moon is full.' He shrugged. 'Unless for dead. Always unless.'

Kineas pointed at the throng of would-be warriors at the gate. 'Anyone worth recruiting for the prodromoi?'

Ataelus didn't turn his head. 'No,' he said.

Having dismissed centuries of Hyrkanian horsemanship in one word, Ataelus grinned. 'Anything else, Strategos?' It was a word Ataelus relished – he trotted it out too often.

'You taking the girl – Lot's daughter? Mosva?'

'When for riding east? No. Stay with father. Last child. Not for scouting.'

Kineas rubbed his beard and then snatched his fingers away. 'I'd rather she went,' he said.

'Oho!' said the Scyth. He nodded and gave a big grin. 'Good. I for talking Lot.'

'Go with the gods, Ataelus.'

'Go with horses. For coming *back* with gods.' Ataelus grinned. Then he wheeled his horse and rode away.

Kineas went to finish some discipline.

He slipped through two layers of hanging cloaks and blankets to enter the hut that Eumenes shared with Andronicus and six other gentlemen-troopers. The hearth was cold and so was the room, and the whitewashed walls served only to make it colder. There was no table and no chairs and no couches, only a rack of beds made by local craftsmen and covered with piles of blankets and furs and sheepskins. At the far end of the dark hut, one of the troopers – a Kelt called Hama – was ploughing a local girl, moving slowly and rhythmically under a tent of blankets. They whispered to each other, moaned and giggled together. Eumenes sat in misery, trying to pretend he was not there.

'Let's walk,' Kineas said to Eumenes.

Eumenes took his cloak from the doorway and followed Kineas into the sunshine.

Kineas walked them up the snowdrifts to the walls. Troopers were punished with snow-clearing duty outside the walls, where a beaten zone was maintained. Inside, the snowdrifts sometimes added to the height of the fort.

'You and Leon are competing for Mosva, Lot's daughter,' he said when they were out of the wind.

Eumenes nodded.

'I have sent her off east with the prodromoi. I suggest you apply yourself to your work as a professional soldier. Buy a girl if you feel the urge. That outburst in the meeting was ill-meant and bad for discipline. And you started it. I hope you understand me.'

Eumenes flushed despite the bite of the cold. 'It's not fair. He called my father a traitor.'

Kineas put his hands on the boy's shoulders. 'What you mean is that it's not fair that your father *was a traitor*. He was. And Leon *was a slave*. And both of you *are* important officers in this company, and we need you to function as adults and not as brainless children.'

'Not fair,' muttered Eumenes. He was weeping.

Kineas embraced the boy, who had suffered so much in the last year and was now weeping for the loss of a girl and some prestige. His embrace obviously comforted the young man, and Kineas thought of Mosva crying in his arms after the fight in the high ground to the west, and how useless he was at comforting anyone.

He did his best.

Without really intending it, Kineas didn't climb the hill to the citadel that day, or the next. Ataelus's twenty riders trotted out over the mud into a sunny morning and vanished into the eastern hills before the sun was a hand high in the sky. The mercenaries – new and old – drilled on the parade under Lycurgus's eye, with Diodorus watching and Leon taking notes. Eumenes had the cavalry out all day, conditioning their horses, walking them up and down, riding for brief stints, and the young man was merciless in working himself and every trooper under him. Temerix's men went out in twos and threes, unarmed, and began the long job of locating fodder. Kineas watched the Kaspian for ships from the north and the mountains to the east for a rider from Ataelus.

Another day passed, and Kineas failed to climb the hill.

Towards evening on the third day, Philokles joined him on the porch of the megaron. It was spring, unseasonably warm, in fact, and three days of sun had caused avalanches on the hillsides and probably opened the hill passes south. Crocuses pushed up through the rubbish and the tree bark that had accumulated along the foundation of the megaron, and Kineas marvelled at their colour as only a man who has survived a long winter can do. Outside the gate, he watched a mounted man gallop past his sentries, straight up the hill to the citadel.

'There is much beauty in the world,' Philokles said.

Kineas grinned. He put a hand on Philokles' shoulder; he loved it when the philosopher ruled and his friend made statements of this sort. 'There is,' Kineas said. And then more soberly, 'And much cowardice.'

Philokles sat on the step of the megaron. He stretched his long legs in front of him and took a sip of wine before handing the cup to Kineas. 'The queen?' he asked. His voice was carefully neutral.

'I lust for her. I marshal a thousand arguments against her – all excellent, I might add. Srayanka. The men. Her own – bah. I lack words to express it. And yet I fly back to her like a moth to an oil lamp. And then I resist.' He shrugged. 'It is like a contest.'

Philokles raised an eyebrow. 'You do love a challenge,' he said.

'It's more than that,' Kineas said.

Philokles rested on an elbow. 'Do you think I might have a sip of the wine I brought out to us? Thanks. Is it? More than a challenge? The camp is full of whores – you could have any one you liked, and no diplomatic incident need follow. You could fuck ten of them and no one would tell Srayanka. Indeed, I wouldn't think it Srayanka's business. But instead of a little helpful penetration of a whore to work off your male humours, you wander off into a game with a queen. The game is being played about dominance and submission. Sex is just a piece on the board. Stop dramatizing. In a few weeks we're riding away – fuck her and leave her, or don't fuck her and leave her. Neither one of you will ever submit.'

Kineas laughed ruefully. 'When you came out with the wine, I was remarking to myself what a pleasure you are when you are in a philosophical frame of mind.' He took the cup and drained it. 'I forgot that your philosophy often kicks like an army mule.' Kineas took the cup back and finished the wine. 'She says all our philosophy is cowardice, and every man should do what he wills.'

Philokles nodded. 'That's the philosophy of a despot – or a woman trying to seduce.'

'She's wrong, though.' Kineas wasn't sure whether that was a question or an answer.

Philokles looked into the empty wine cup and frowned. 'You drank all of my wine.' He looked hurt. 'The good wine that tastes like berries.'

Kineas nodded. 'And now I'm going to ride up the hill and see the queen.'

Philokles nodded. 'I find it very much in keeping with the way the gods drive men to action that I began this winter begging you to avoid her, and tonight I use my tongue as a lash to push you up the hill.' He held out the cup. 'Since you'll go inside to change, bring me out another cup of wine? There's a good fellow.' He waited until Kineas was halfway in the door. 'She's not wrong. Nor right. *This is not about her, but about you.*'

Kineas stopped for a moment and then nodded. When he returned in a fine woollen tunic and cloak with a bronze ewer of wine, Philokles had been joined by Nicanor and Diodorus. Nicanor served wine and took a cup for himself.

'So you're taking the bit between your teeth?' Diodorus said. 'Sappho says to take care.'

Kineas curled one corner of his mouth. 'I will,' he said. He slammed back a second cup of wine, causing his friends to look at each other.

Lycurgus raised an eyebrow. He was leaning against a column, watching the agora. 'Lot of messengers moving around,' he said.

Sitalkes brought his horse, one of the royal stallions that he rode to rest Thalassa. Beyond the gate, the rest of his escort waited. The evening was calm and warm, and curiously quiet except for the messengers. Kineas listened for a moment and diagnosed the problem – it was warm like spring, but there weren't any insects yet.

In the west, the sun slid down towards the cold blue waters of the Kaspian.

Kineas got a leg over his charger, settled himself and turned back to Lycurgus and Diodorus.

'Double the watch and have the quarter guard stand to arms,' he said. 'I'm scared of shadows.' He hated to be like that – in a sentence he'd condemned forty men to lose their evening of rest.

Diodorus shook his head. 'No – I feel it too. All the beggars are gone from the gate. Stay here.'

Lycurgus nodded agreement. 'Something has changed. I don't like it.'

Kineas shrugged. 'After two days of screwing up my courage? To Hades with that.'

Philokles came up beside Diodorus. 'You're both jumping at shadows. You're going to give her *good news*.' He shook his head. 'I'm worried, too. My man in the palace hasn't reported in three days.'

Kineas nodded, but his mind wasn't convinced.

'You should take a sword,' Diodorus shouted, as Kineas turned his horse.

Kineas shook his head and rode for the gate.

The gate to the citadel was heavily guarded. There were eight men on duty and every one of them was in full armour. They seemed surprised that Kineas had come and they sent for the captain of the guard rather than passing Kineas.

First he fumed and then he worried. Behind him, he could hear Sitalkes speaking quietly to his men, all big Keltoi.

'Don't be separated from your weapons,' Kineas said. 'Something is wrong.'

The captain of the guard came out in a polished iron helmet with a scale aventail and a scale shirt. He was armed for war. 'Last person I expected to see,' he said.

'You are awaiting an attack,' Kineas said flatly.

The captain shrugged. 'Not my place to say. The queen will receive you, if you are coming in. Your men must wait in the courtyard, disarmed.'

Kineas shook his head. 'No. I've been in the citadel a dozen times and my men have never been disarmed.'

The captain shrugged. 'Then they wait out in the wind,' he said.

Kineas turned to Sitalkes. 'I'm sorry,' he said. 'It'll be cold. I'll see to it as soon as I speak to her.'

'Never mind us,' Sitalkes said. 'Take Carlus, at least.' Carlus was the tallest man in the army, two hands taller than Kineas. He rode big horses and men got out of his way wherever he went.

Kineas turned back to the captain. 'One bodyguard,' he said. 'Armed.' He handed the man a silver owl.

The captain grunted and took the money. 'Whatever the fuck. One man. It's cold – let's go.'

Kineas gave his horse to Sitalkes, who threw a blanket over her. They waited in the icy wind on the gravel road under the walls and Kineas passed inside, into the sensuous warmth, led by one of her slaves.

Carlus grunted twice – once when the warmth of the floors penetrated his sandals and again when he saw his first oiled slave girl. Other than that he was silent. Kineas left his cloak and his sandals in the outer rooms. Carlus followed him silently.

Kineas could see the tension in every visible ligament on the slaves. He followed the slave into the throne room.

It was much the same as his first visit, except that she was back to wearing the clothes of a Persian matron, and most of her male courtiers were in armour. They fell silent as he entered. There was a man in silvered scale mail standing at her shoulder, who looked like a prince. His face was covered by the nasal on his helmet. He looked familiar.

'You are a fool to come here, Kineas of Athens,' she said.

Kineas agreed. The man at her shoulder was Darius. Kineas felt foolish – he'd seen all the signs that the Persian was changing sides, but he'd ignored them. 'I come with an agreement about the spring campaign,' he said, still thinking to buy her complacence. Perhaps it was just another round in their game. The fear round.

'You are a fool, Kineas,' she said, and this time she sounded sad. 'The spring campaign is already over. I have need of your soldiers. And if I can't have them, no one will.' She looked to be on the verge of tears, but she steadied herself. She motioned at Darius. 'Kill him.'

Carlus gave his third grunt. Kineas whirled to see the giant Kelt with a dagger rammed through his cloak into the armour on his back. He was wearing a heavy cuirass made of layers of linen quilted together, half a finger thick, and the dagger skidded off the armour and ripped across his neck. The Kelt grunted a fourth time and ripped his heavy sword from its scabbard. He killed two men in as many blows and scattered the guardsmen, forcing their captain back as if he was a giant in a riot of children.

Kineas was unarmed and unarmoured, but he knew where the alcove was. He leaped back from the first rush, grabbed a bronze platter and stopped a killing blow from the man concealed there and another from one of the courtiers nearest the throne. Darius was down from the dais and moving towards him.

'Philokles!' the Persian shouted, and ripped a sword from another courtier and threw it at Kineas.

Kineas rammed the edge of the platter into a man's nose. Then he took the man's arm, whirled him and broke it, so that he screamed like a wounded horse. Kineas swept his feet and pushed him flailing into the line of guards, kicked with his bare feet, set his back against the wall and grabbed for the sword as it bounced off the wall. Philokles? he thought, and his right hand closed on the grip of the sword, a back-curved hanger like a small *machaira*, with a heavy guard that completely covered his hand. His left hand had the platter by one of its gryphon-head handles, and he hurled it like a discus at the crowd by the throne. The men facing him fell back a step.

Carlus was bellowing like a bull. There were three men in the blood at his feet and two more clutching wounds and none of the guard would come near him.

Darius dispatched one of the courtiers with a thrust to the chest – no wasted effort. The two survivors by the throne turned to look at him and Sartobases yelled 'traitor!' at him in outraged Persian.

'Philokles!' he shouted again.

Women were screaming and the smell of death and offal

carried across the warm, moist air. He glimpsed Banugul moving away from the throne, one hand pointing at Darius.

Darius cut down another man and joined Kineas at the wall. 'I work for Philokles!' he said as if a battle cry, and the words penetrated Kineas's brain. He laughed and attacked the men in front of him. They scattered and he cut one down in his retreat, but then the front of the hall began to fill with the queen's guard.

'Follow me!' Darius called. He slipped behind a drapery.

Kineas would not so lightly abandon his bodyguard. 'Carlus!' he yelled. 'On me!'

The Kelt swung his sword wide, so that the blade was a blur – back and forth – and then sprang away, the two great swings covering his retreat. He knocked a slave girl flat, smashed his fist into a man's face, scattering teeth, and ran across the slick floor.

A guardsman threw a javelin. His aim was true and it struck Carlus in the back, but it lacked power and the cuirass held it. Still, the giant stumbled a step. The guards gained heart and charged.

Kineas ripped the hanging off the wall – a Persian procession of conquered peoples carrying gifts – and ducked through the concealed door. 'Follow me!' he shouted. He could feel Carlus pushing through the door behind him. They were in a dark corridor. Behind them, Therapon's voice was calling for archers.

They turned sharply right and the corridor climbed a flight of stairs, lit by pitch brands. 'Hold them here,' Kineas said to the big Kelt, who was panting with exertion, fear and pain. 'Never let their archers get a shot at you. Use the curve of the wall. Understand? I'll be back for you!'

Carlus placed his back against the wall. He pushed himself to a full standing position. 'Aye, lord,' he said. He grinned. 'Aye!' His effort to push himself erect left a smear of wet blood on the plaster. The whole stairwell stank of burning pitch and the sweat of fear.

Kineas turned and followed Darius again. 'Where are we going?' he asked.

'Postern gate,' Darius said. 'Been trying to tell you for three days – she means to attack the camp. Tonight.'

'She's insane! We'd kill her!'

Darius sagged against the landing and Kineas could see he was wounded, the flowing blood black in the fitful light. 'You'd have killed her men – except that you came here. And she owns some of your new recruits. Or thinks she does.' The man was pale with fatigue.

'Let's get to this gate!' Kineas said.

They went through a door, into a rich apartment and then down a long curve of steps set into the outer wall. The stairwell was pitch-black and cold as the outer wells of Hades, with a thin cold wind coming in through the arrow slits. Outside, Kineas could hear Greek voices – probably his bodyguard demanding news. The sounds of fighting could be heard right through the walls. Carlus was killing men, roaring his challenge.

They went down, and down again, and through a door.

There were a dozen men waiting for them.

'Fuck!' said Darius in Persian, and his sword flashed as he cut at a man. 'Run, Kineas!'

It was too late to run. Kineas pushed up beside the Persian and killed a man with an overarm thrust. The blade went right over his shield and into his eye – Kineas was using the bend in his own blade to baffle his opponent in the torch-lit dark. The man went down like a sacrifice and Kineas sank to one knee and swept his blade *under* the shield of Darius's opponent. Even with his shorter, lighter blade, the cut severed the man's ligaments just below the knee. He fell backwards, fouling his mates and buying Kineas a few seconds.

Kineas was already stripping the corpse of the man at his feet. He ripped the shield off the man's arm, tearing at the straps, hacking with his blade at the dead man's shield arm – the shield's *porpax* caught on the dead man's wrist and hand, a ring, a bracelet – Kineas pulled, shouting curses – the shield came free. Darius backed a step as an armoured man charged him. Kineas, uncovered, whirled, cutting with his sword, still trying to get the shield over his own arm. He cut low, cut high and met his opponent's shield both times. Desperate, he tried a school dodge – he backed a step, placed a foot on his opponent's shield and pushed.

The man fell back. Not a gymnasium-trained man, or he'd have known the trick. Kineas pushed back through the door. Darius was above him on the stairs. The shield dropped on to his forearm, ripping flesh, and the grip came into his left hand.

'When your Kelt goes down, we're finished,' Darius said. Carlus was three rooms behind them, his bellows audible even through the stone. Kineas heard the tense humour in the Persian's voice. 'I rather enjoy having you on my side, though.'

Kineas had to laugh at that. 'Stay on my shield side and get anyone who tries to pass me,' he said. 'None of them are your match. We'll get through this.' He turned his head and gave the younger man a broad smile.

Darius straightened up. He met Kineas's torch-lit glance. 'I was tempted …' he began.

Kineas grunted and pushed forward through the door, ignoring whatever confession the younger man was considering. 'Guard me!' he called.

The men on the other side didn't expect him to attack. He pushed – shield in the face, cut low, push – and they fell back. His second back cut, luckier or more accurate than the others, cut a dactylos above a guardsman's shield, the point slashing through his eyes and the bridge of his nose so that he fell dead between breaths, never seeing the blow that stole his life.

'Athena!' Kineas roared with the whole weight of his chest.

Confused shouts beyond the wall.

'Athena!' He bellowed again, and cut, pushed, pushed again. Darius was covering his side along the wall, thrusting with reckless energy to force his shielded opponent back.

Kineas flicked his shield out, caught another man's shield with his own rim and pulled. Then his sword licked out, thrusting into the man's chest. He thrust too hard and his borrowed sword fouled, caught on a rib. He kicked, pulled, pushed with his shield as the dying man screamed.

The sword broke at the hilt, leaving Kineas with a hand's-breadth of iron.

Too late to hesitate.

He threw the hilt into his next opponent's face. Then, using a pankration move learned from Phocion, he lunged, throwing his shield leg back, and his empty sword hand grasped the rim of the next man's shield and used it as a lever, ripping the arm in a circle and breaking it. He hammered his shield into the man's undefended face as he fell, grabbed for the man's sword and missed. The man's sword clattered against the cobbles of the floor, vanished in the darkness. A spear punched into his shield, penetrating the bronze surface and embedding in the wood lining. Kineas used his superior leverage to rip the shield free. Again the spear came at him, this time raking his shin because he couldn't see it coming low. He stepped back and the spearman came forward, the point of a three-man wedge that filled the corridor.

Darius was still fighting a man from the last rush. He gave a shout and his opponent screeched as Darius cut off his hand. The man backed away, blood spurting from the stump, and the three spearmen lost several heartbeats as they tried to cover him.

'Sword!' Kineas said. He put his hand back.

Darius slapped his own sword into the open hand.

Just like that.

Kineas stepped forward, took the lead man's spearhead on his shield where he could feel it and *pushed*, fouling the man's weapon. The man set his feet and pushed back, his mates helping him. Kineas felt the strain and tilted his shield, bent his knees and rolled low, passing his shield under the lip of his opponent's, kneeling on the damp flagstone. He cut low, felt an impact and stood up, pushing with his legs as Darius came up to guard his back, and the lead man staggered back, shouting that he was cut, and the rest broke, fleeing as best they could from the terror of the darkness and the blood.

Darius rose next to him, having found the sword of the man whose wrist he'd severed.

'Thanks,' Kineas said. The daimon of combat left him, and his knees began to shake. He was *alive*! He almost fell. His chiton was drenched in sweat.

'Think nothing of it,' Darius said in court Persian. He was grey, but he managed a smile. 'Could I have my sword back, do you think?'

Kineas met his eye. They exchanged swords, and something more.

Between them, with shaking hands, they got the postern open. Instead of fleeing, they admitted Kineas's guardsmen, who, drawn by his shouts, were already tearing at the door from the outside. And then, leaving four men under Sitalkes to hold the gate and sending a mounted man to the camp, Kineas led the rest of them back into the citadel for the Kelt.

They found him alive, cleared the corridor in front of him and retreated from a volley of arrows. Carlus was wounded in more places than Kineas could count in the dark, and he was no longer smiling.

'You come!' he said, six or seven times, before he passed out. He fell a few feet from the postern and no one could carry him, so they pulled him to one side and prepared to hold the corridor, piling tables and trunks against the walls as cover from arrows.

'You should go, sir,' Sitalkes said.

'Yes,' said Darius. He was still bleeding, despite a linen wrap, and his pallor had reached a dangerous level. He spoke as if sleepwalking.

Kineas longed to go, but his own sense of himself as a man wouldn't permit it. 'No,' he said.

They waited for a rush of guardsmen. Twice, men peeked around the far corner of the corridor, bronze glinting in the fitful light of the cressets. The nearest one was burning down, past the pitch to the solid wood that burned faster but gave less light. Pine wood smoke and ordure scents mixed, and smoke began to fill the corridor.

An arrow whispered out of the dark. It glanced off Sitalkes' cavalry breastplate and ripped across another man's bridle hand before embedding itself in an upturned table.

They all crouched low, as much to get their heads out of the smoke as to avoid the arrows.

'Get ready,' Kineas said.

'Listen!' Darius said, and collapsed, his limbs loosening all at once so that he slumped forward and his head rang as it hit a table.

'Shit,' said Sitalkes. He and one of the Keltoi grabbed the Persian under the arms and pulled him out of the line and back to the relative safety of the door.

'I hear it too,' said another man. 'Fighting!'

Now Kineas could hear it. There was fighting somewhere else – *Ares! What in Hades was going on?* He rose to his feet and leaned out of the postern gate. There was movement on the slope below him, a line of shapes climbing the hill. He watched them for a long moment – one of the longest of his life – and then he identified something about the set of the cloak and the particular movements of the lead man.

'Diodorus!' he called.

In moments, the postern was crowded with armoured men – dismounted cavalry. Andronicus took command of all the Keltoi. Diodorus embraced Kineas.

'We heard you were dead!' he said.

'Not dead yet.' A roar shook the rafters. 'What in Hades?'

'Before we got your message, Philokles and Niceas said that something was wrong. They're rushing the main gate.'

'Ares and Aphrodite! They'll be slaughtered!' Kineas looked around wildly, even as Nicanor pushed forward, almost devoid of breath from the exertion of climbing the steepest face of the hill, Kineas's helmet and breastplate clasped against his paunch.

'Right,' said Diodorus. He looked up and down the smoky corridor. 'Andronicus, take your troop and push down that corridor. Eumenes, take your troop with me. Kill everyone.'

Kineas got his head into his breastplate. 'Diodorus—'

Diodorus pushed past him. 'You're done, Strategos. Let us do our jobs. Right, follow me!'

Kineas refused to be set aside. Still wearing his captured shield, he pushed in behind Diodorus. They shoved the makeshift barriers out of the way in one long push.

'Don't be a fool, Kineas,' Diodorus said.

'I know how to get to the gate!' Kineas said.

An arrow came out of the dark.

'Shit,' Diodorus said. 'Charge!' he yelled, and he was off down the corridor.

Kineas struggled to keep up and a flood of men led by Eumenes pushed behind him. At the corner, Eumenes pushed his strategos out of the way and got ahead. Side by side with Diodorus, he cleared the corridor, killing an archer and wounding another before the mass of them broke, screaming in panic.

The Hellenes poured in behind them. More men were coming through the postern, and they followed their appointed leaders blindly into the smoke and the darkness. Leon pushed past Kineas without knowing him and raced down the corridor to Diodorus and Eumenes, who were ten strides ahead, and they went up an undefended flight of stairs. Kineas could barely make his legs push him up behind them. Two more men passed him. The sounds of fighting were closer.

'We're above the gate,' Diodorus said, apparently to Eumenes.

In the distance, '*Apollo! Apollo!*', and the screams of wounded men. That was Philokles' roar. Kineas felt new strength from the gods flood into his legs, and he flew up the rest of the stairs and saw Eumenes' silver-chased breastplate glitter coldly at the end of another passageway and Leon's black legs shining in the torchlight. Kineas ran, his bare feet slapping on stone.

The stupid barbarian archers were running for their friends and leading Diodorus to the gate. Kineas understood that even as he leaped over another dead archer in the semi-darkness. There was more smoke than before – something was on fire.

'Athena!' Diodorus roared – difficult to believe that such a thin man could release such a war cry. '*Apollo!*' Closer.

Kineas was right behind Eumenes and another trooper – Amyntas, one of Heron's gentlemen – and Leon. Eumenes and Leon were shoulder to shoulder, looking like gods in the flickering light. Diodorus hammered his shoulder into a closed door and it gave. As Leon and Eumenes added their weight, the door blew open and all three stumbled. An archer shot. Panicked or not, his arrow flew over Leon's bowed head and punched Amyntas off his feet. Kineas leaped over the falling man and cut the archer down. His own sword felt good in his hand. He raised his shield and took an arrow, and then another, and pushed forward.

A spearhead came past him: Eumenes, covering him. He roared his war cry – it came out thin and high, 'Athena!' – and then he felt resistance against his shield and Eumenes was shoving against his back and he cut low. The resistance gave way and he felt a rush of cold air.

There were stars overhead. He was standing at the entrance to a tower, up on the wall and close to the main gate.

Somehow, Philokles had opened the gate. He stood in the courtyard, killing, with bodies all around him and the whole mass of the garrison trying to evict him and the men with him. 'Apollo!' he roared, and Kineas answered 'Athena!' and the garrison soldiers looked up and saw their doom behind them on the wall.

With the unanimity of despair, they broke, and the Hellenes hunted them through the corridors and killed them where they found them. The citadel was stormed, and too many of the Olbians had fallen in the taking to allow for any human behaviour by the stormers. They were animals, and like animals they roared through the rooms and corridors, destroying, raping, killing.

Kineas made no attempt to stop it. He could not have stopped it had he wished – the law of war was strict and the citadel had been stormed. And he lacked any will to resist. He came down from the wall with an avenging rush and they cleared the courtyard in moments, but the Olbian dead were everywhere, some burned with hot sand and some stabbed with many spears, and between Philokles' wide-spread legs was the body of Niceas.

Kineas threw himself on the body of his boyhood friend. Niceas was burned with sand and had a great gash on his un-helmeted head and a spear in his side, but he still had breath in him.

'He lives!' Kineas proclaimed.

Niceas shook his head gently. 'Saves you the price of a brothel,' he said, and coughed blood.

'No,' Kineas said. 'No – Niceas!'

'Graccus is waiting for me,' Niceas said. He smiled, like a man who sees home at the end of a long journey, and died.

And Kineas held him for a while, until the skin under his forearms started to cool.

'Let's kill every fucker in the castle,' Philokles said. He didn't sound like himself. But Kineas thought it sounded like a fine plan.

Dawn. Smoke from burning sheds and the remnants of fires. Olbians, their faces black with soot, huddled against the wind, their bodies slack from exhaustion and guilt. Beyond sated. No man can survive a storming action and ever forget what he did when he was a beast.

A carpet of bodies from the courtyard to the throne room. The floors were cold.

Leon had saved many of the citadel's slaves. He and Nicanor and Eumenes had pushed them into the queen's bedchamber and held the door. So in the light of dawn, Eumenes brought Banugul to Kineas where he sat on her throne. The blade of his Egyptian sword was clean, because he had wiped it fastidiously on the cloak of Sartobases. Just beyond Sartobases was the corpse of Therapon, who had died in the guards' last stand, cut down by Philokles.

Kineas and Eumenes and Banugul were the only living people in the room. The scenes of orgy and debauchery on the walls were sad and pathetic.

'I found her among the slaves,' Eumenes said.

Kineas nodded.

'I heard that – that Niceas is dead.'

'Niceas is dead,' Kineas said, and tears flowed. Eumenes joined him.

Kineas rose from her throne and walked to them. 'I came to offer you life,' he said. 'You stupid bitch.' The anger in him was great enough to kill her, but her death was not enough.

She met his eye steadily. 'I had no choice,' she said. 'Kill

230

me if you must. Throw my body to your wolves to rape if that sates you.' Her voice shook with terror, and yet through her terror she was in control of herself. 'I did what I had to, and failed. I will not go down to hell with lies.'

Kineas punched her so hard that her head snapped back and she shot off her feet and fell in a heap. 'What could possibly excuse *this*?' Kineas bellowed. She had fallen across the bodies of several of her courtiers, and she was fouled with their blood and worse. She spat blood and rose on one arm.

'Alexander has murdered Parmenion,' she said through a split lip and bruised jaw.

Kineas stumbled back and sat on the throne as if Ares had cut the sinews of his legs. 'Gods,' he said.

'My so-called father will be on me in a month with five thousand men, desperate to wipe me out before he too is attacked by Alexander.' She held her bruised head high. 'I am not a slave, to bow my head. Alexander is my lord, and I will fight.'

Kineas didn't want to look at her. The urge to kill was not sated. Every time he thought of Niceas's corpse in the courtyard, he was ready to send more souls to Hades. But another part of him cried for redemption – the part that had roamed the corridors, exterminating archers who would have surrendered and joined him, perhaps, had his sword let them live. Yet another part accused him of behaving badly – seeking revenge on her for her role in showing him weak.

'I'm sorry that I hit you,' he said.

She said nothing. Her eyes roamed the room, looking at the dead.

'Go to him, then,' he said. 'Take your slaves and go.'

'You were right,' she said, her voice dead.

'Right?' he asked. What did he expect her to say?

'My garrison wasn't worth a crap,' she said coldly. 'I wish you had joined me.'

He shook his head. 'Get you gone before I change my mind,' he said.

In an hour, she was gone. And he was master of a citadel full of corpses.

16

Niceas's funeral games lasted three days, after two weeks of preparations. Slaves and freedmen and farmers cleaned the citadel, and Kineas declared that all taxes and tribute would be remitted in exchange for a tithe on spring fodder and wagons. Nor did he offer any other choice – his soldiers collected the tithe with drawn weapons. It was ugly, like everything about Hyrkania in the aftermath of the escalade.

Eumenes and Leon seemed reconciled by their shared roles as heroes, but their reconciliation lasted only until they wrestled for the prize of the funeral games on the third day, with Mosva watching them. The bout became ugly and all their wounds were ripped open in a single word when Leon said something while his opponent had his head down in a hold, and then they were fighting like dogs.

Leon won.

Ataelus had returned with the rest of the prodromoi on the third day of games, in time to join all the old hands in throwing torches on to Niceas's pyre. He wept with them, and threw his best gold-hilted dagger on to the roaring blaze.

Philokles had barely spoken since the storming. He sat in silence and was drunk most of the time. Only Kineas and Diodorus and Sappho knew that he had tried to kill himself with his sword. Sappho had caught him at it and they had all wrestled the blade away from him, Sappho cut and bleeding, until Philokles screamed, 'Can I do nothing but injure and kill! Let me go!' and subsided into weeping. That was in the first few days after the action, and Philokles wasn't the only man in despair.

At the games, he was silent. He stood alone, and when men went to embrace him, he turned away. Kineas failed to move him. It was Ataelus who pushed past his rudeness. He placed himself in front of the Spartan, hands on hips, weeping unabashedly in the Scythian manner. When he had the silent

232

man's attention, he demanded, 'Niceas for killing enemies?'

Philokles's face was streaked with tears in the firelight. 'Yes.'

'How many in last fight?' Ataelus asked. He didn't seem to know, or care, what Philokles was suffering.

Philokles flinched. 'Two,' he said.

Ataelus nodded. 'Two is good,' he said. 'And you?' He looked at the Spartan curiously. 'For revenge? You were killing?'

'Oh, yes,' said Philokles bitterly. 'I killed quite a few. Six or seven in combat – perhaps twice that in cowering, defenceless men. At least one woman. I am *very proud.*'

Ataelus, immune to his tone, nodded. 'Good. Twenty men – good. And you, Kineax?'

Kineas shrugged. 'The same.'

Ataelus shook his head. 'For thinking my friend goes to hell alone! Long faces and tears! Dies like airyanãm! Kills two, even for being wounded! And friends who love him kill forty mens to serve him in death? For what crying?'

Kineas took his arm. 'We behaved like beasts,' he said. He didn't know how to explain it to the Sakje.

But Ataelus shrugged him off. He looked around the ruddy faces lit by the pyre. 'War is for making all men beasts,' he said. He shrugged. 'Hunt men, kill men, act like beast, hunt like beast. Yes?' He shook his head. 'All war bad. All not-war good. But when for making war, then for fighting like beast. Yes?' He shrugged. 'Love Niceas,' he said, and struck his chest. Then he embraced Philokles, who tried to avoid the embrace and was then trapped by the smaller man.

And one by one, all the old hands, the men who had ridden north from Tomis almost two years before and the men who had followed Alexander from Granicus to Ecbatana and the newer men who had stopped Zopryon on the plains, embraced like brothers, and they all embraced Philokles.

That night, for the first time in months, Kineas dreamed of the tree. And Niceas stood among the tangled roots with Ajax, and both of them offered him hands full of sand. He wept when he awoke, but he began to understand. It scared him.

*

Carlus survived, as did Darius. They each took the better part of the next month to recover, and Kineas had so many wounded from the storming that he couldn't start his little force in motion. As it turned out, the weather, which had promised an early spring, then deteriorated, and it wasn't until a week after Niceas's funeral that they had another sight of the sun. The ground began to dry.

Kineas left Heron and Lycurgus in charge, just as Diodorus had originally planned, with orders to forward some of the bullion and use the rest to pay their garrison and cover Leon's investments. The storming of the citadel had gained them all the queen's treasures – not the richest hoard in the east, but enough to satisfy an army of a thousand men for some months and buy them as many remounts as they could find.

'Are we founding an empire?' Diodorus asked. 'First the settlement on the Rha and now a town on the Kaspian.'

Kineas just looked at him. 'Not exactly,' he said. 'The fort on the Rha is Sakje territory, and this is in the satrapy of Hyrkania. We won't hold either for any time. Just long enough to secure our retreat.'

Diodorus rubbed his beard. They all had them now. Winter had eliminated the last clean-shaven men. 'Another hundred mercenaries came in today,' he said. 'Mostly Greeks.'

Kineas grunted.

'Heron is trying to hire your Leosthenes to command a thousand hoplites,' he said. 'Leosthenes is ready to leave the satrap. Man's doomed.'

'As long as Heron pays with his own money, I told him he was welcome to try for Pantecapaeum,' Kineas said. 'We have no friends there. They exiled Demostrate, too.'

Diodorus whistled. 'Heron will make a dangerous tyrant,' he said.

Nicanor came into the megaron. 'Prince Lot is ready to ride,' he said.

Kineas already had his armour on. He went out into the weak spring sun, mounted Thalassa and rode to the head of the parade, where all of the Sauromatae waited, their goods

loaded on pack mules and six heavy wagons. Lady Bahareh
nodded to him as he rode past and Gwair Blackhorse raised his
lance and gave a *ypp!* of exultation.

Lot rode out to the head of his column. 'I'm glad to be free
of this place,' he confessed, in Sakje.

Kineas wrapped his arms around the other man and they
embraced, breastplate to scale shirt. 'Stay safe. Pick us a good
camp.'

'Hurry along, Kineas. Don't dawdle!' The Sauromatae
prince reared his horse for show and then they were off, riding
through the gates of the camp.

'I wish we were riding with them,' Diodorus said at Kineas's
side.

Kineas shrugged. 'Me, too,' he said. 'Time to do the rotten
job.'

Diodorus turned his horse and fell in beside him. 'Leon?'

Kineas nodded. 'Fetch him for me, will you?'

When the young Numidian arrived, Kineas let him wait on
the porch of the megaron while he completed the day's reports
and a letter to Lykeles at Olbia. Then he had Nicanor bring
the young man.

'You have become a very important officer,' he said coldly.
'But your behaviour at the funeral of Niceas was that of a slave.
Let me be clear. When a gentleman competes at funeral games,
he does so in the memory of the dead man, and for no personal
gain or glory. You dishonoured Niceas with your behaviour.'

Leon's knees trembled, and he stood, blank-faced. He
didn't weep. He took his rebuke as a slave takes it, showing as
little as he could.

The lack of reaction enraged Kineas.

'Don't you care? Niceas was always kind to you – Niceas,
who was a whore in the agora before he was a man – who
would understand you and your life better than Niceas? And
you dishonour him at his games?'

Nothing. Leon's body betrayed his emotion, but his face
gave nothing away at all.

'I am tempted to send you away, or leave you here. Speak.
Tell me why I should do otherwise.'

Leon raised his eyes. 'No reason,' he said in a voice bereft of hope.

'Will you accept any punishment I offer without complaint?' Kineas asked.

'Yes!' Leon said, with more emotion than he had shown until then.

Kineas nodded. 'You will shovel snow with the common soldiers until we leave. You will make a public apology to Eumenes at the head of the parade tomorrow morning and the two of you will clasp hands. Both of you will go to the shrine of Apollo on the mountain – together – and spend the night in observance, offering a sacrifice on behalf of the whole expedition. You will keep vigil. You will make apology to the shade of Niceas. You will not sleep, nor will you wear a cloak or hat. Understood?'

Leon hid his eyes. 'Yes,' he barked.

The two men climbed the mountain together the next day.

'What if only one of them returns?' Sappho asked. She was standing arm in arm with Diodorus, and her face looked young and beautiful in the last of the sun, cheeks red from the cold and wrapped in a heavy wool cloak. Her eyes moved constantly from one to the other of the officers. Since the incident with Philokles, she watched them all carefully.

Philokles took cups of wine from Nicanor and handed them around. It was pleasant to stand on the porch in the warmth of evening – comparative warmth. In minutes it would be too cold to stand outside, and Kineas secretly pitied the two men climbing to the shrine. 'They will both return,' he said.

'Kineas has the right of it,' Sappho said, her hand shading her eyes against the last rays of the sun. 'My heart goes out to Leon.'

Diodorus raised an eyebrow. 'Leon? What he did was disgraceful. Like cheating – in a funeral contest.'

Sappho nodded. 'When you have experienced slavery, write and tell me what you think then.'

Philokles turned and smiled at Sappho. 'Well put,' he said.

Sappho blushed and lowered her eyes. 'Praise from a

236

Spartan?' she said. 'Praise from such a great soldier might go to my head.'

Philokles took a sharp breath. 'Oh, yes,' he said, looking at the lees in his wine cup. 'I'm a great soldier.' Turning to Kineas, he said, 'Speaking of which, your Persian asked me to teach him the ways of the gymnasium today.'

Kineas frowned. 'Why?' he asked.

Philokles drank off a cup of wine in a single draught. Then he wiped his mouth with his hand. 'He was impressed with how you killed all those men,' he said. He pointed his chin at Sappho. 'But he doesn't go to Kineas – no, he comes to me.' He poured himself more wine from Nicanor's ewer, sloshing some on the floor. 'For all the gods,' he slurred.

'I didn't mean it that way, Philokles,' Sappho said, touching his arm lightly. 'In Thebes, no soldier was ever offended—'

He stepped back as if her touch hurt him. 'Nor in Sparta. No, a woman's praise for one's ability to kill always comes before a marriage offer, in Sparta.'

Sappho slipped out of Diodorus's arm and made a sign to Temerix the smith. The two of them closed on the Spartan from both sides. 'Why don't you tell me how Spartan women live, Philokles?' she asked.

Philokles glanced back and forth between the two of them. 'I'm not drunk yet,' he said, watching them as if they were sparring opponents on the sand.

Temerix smiled at the ground, embarrassed. 'Yes, lord,' he said, spreading his arms.

'Don't call me lord,' Philokles said.

Temerix stepped back. 'Yes, lord,' he said.

Sappho caught at his arm. 'Spartan women,' she insisted.

'Too brave for me,' Philokles said. 'Just like you.' He held out his wine cup and Nicanor, after a beseeching look at Kineas, filled it again. Philokles glanced at Kineas, a smile on his face. He slammed the wine back and grinned. 'Wants to be a better killer. Who better to ask than me, eh? And the farther east we go, the better we'll be, until we can kill anyone we want. Maybe each other in the end, eh?' He stumbled back and caught himself, holding his wine cup out again.

Sappho hauled on his arm. 'You are being rude, Spartan. Tell me about the Spartan women.'

Philokles drew himself up. 'You are not a Spartan woman,' he said. 'You are a woman of Thebes, hence it is unseemly for you to be out in public, discoursing with men, hence I do not have to discourse with you, as you should not be here.'

Kineas tried to think of something to say.

'I am no longer a woman of Thebes, just as you are no longer a man of Sparta,' she said. 'We are Olbians, are we not? Or perhaps we are the people of Kineas.'

Philokles laughed. 'The Kineasae! And among the Kineasae, it was customary for women to debate with men in the agora!'

Diodorus stepped up beside the Spartan. 'It quickly became customary for sober women to debate with drunken men. Go to bed, Philokles! You're making men look bad!'

All around them, people laughed – friendly laughter, at a situation diffused. And the next time Philokles stumbled, Temerix was there with an arm around his neck. The smith had no difficulty lifting the Spartan over his shoulder, nor did he flinch when the big man vomited wine and bile over his back.

Later, Kineas heard Philokles speaking of the role of women in a well-ordered polis, and Temerix, whose Greek was about equal to directing a wood-cutting party, grunting agreement while he washed the Spartan. Their voices went on and on, and eventually Kineas fell asleep.

Both young men returned from the shrine the next morning, and Kineas, who had not slept well, shared wine with them and prayed to the gods with them. And then he went back to bed.

When he rose again, it was to the final preparations for leaving. With Leon and Eumenes at his side, he picked the best riders from among the hoplites and put them in the cavalry. The rest were left as a core of Olbians with the mercenary recruits to hold the town. Two dozen men, too badly wounded to march but still expected to recover, were left as military settlers.

The column had food and water for ten days, and better wagons and carts than when they'd started, already staged over the last of the Hyrkanian hills and waiting in a camp at the edge of the steppes. More wagons and all the Sauromatae had already crossed the desert. They were as prepared as Leon could manage.

The same weather that saw Kineas's column prepare to march against Alexander brought the first of the spring traders from Lycia. Just as the spring rains in the mountains washed the stream beds clear and brought old trees down the hillsides, so they washed broken men out of the hills, and mercenaries looking for employment, and desperate men fleeing distant catastrophes. Before the column rode, Kineas heard the rumours of a dozen nations spoken in three languages. A Macedonian deserter bound for home said that old Antipater was paralysed by news of the murder of Parmenion. It was said that he had gathered a Thracian bodyguard and went in fear that Alexander might order his death, too.

A Syrian Jew from Lebanon told Kineas that every satrap west of Media was raising an army.

A Cretan who had almost certainly spent the winter as a brigand said that Alexander had marched north from Kandahar before the snows melted. Rumours said that Bessus was dead and Spitamenes was negotiating for a satrapy. It was said that he had sent Alexander a dozen Amazons as a gift.

And on the final morning, when the main column was mounted and the last men were kissing their Hyrkanian wives one last time, Kineas heard from a horse trader that the queen of the Massagetae was rallying the clans east of Marakanda to fight Alexander. Kineas purchased his whole string of horses.

Diodorus shook his head. 'Remember when we were mercenaries?' he asked wistfully.

A pale sun rose between Kineas's charger's ears. On his left was Diodorus and on his right was Philokles, the worse for wine but steady enough.

'Let's go and find Srayanka,' he said. His heart was higher than it had been in a month.

'And Alexander,' Diodorus said.

PART IV

TREE OF LIFE

17

'Your majesty?' Eumenes the Cardian was careful entering the inner sanctum, where the *Iliad* sat in its golden casket and where the panoplies of Alexander's foes decorated the walls. Alexander was becoming more withdrawn, more alien, with every campaign. Crossing the mountains, he had shown one of his bursts of superhuman activity, even of empathy, rescuing snow-blind soldiers and speaking extempore to every knot of pikemen coming down the pass. But now the godlike energy had passed and what was left was a sullen tyrant sitting amidst his favourite treasures.

He looked up, his mismatched eyes listless. 'What, Eumenes?'

'Spitamenes has delivered Amazons, your majesty.' Eumenes kept his head slightly bowed. 'And Barsine's sister Banugul is here from Hyrkania.'

'Hell to pay in the harem when her sister hears she's with me.' Alexander gave a smile. 'I can't say I'm altogether sorry she's here, but you'll have to hide her from Hephaestion,' Alexander said. 'Why is she here?'

'Her tale is complex, lord. She blames her father, but also some Greek mercenary. Indeed, she hadn't expected to find us here – she came over the mountains from Hyrkania, intending to find us at Kandahar.'

'Greek mercenaries are never to be trusted. I thought she had more wisdom than that. Very well, make a note that I will see her. Keep her from Hephaestion. Anything else?' Alexander was petulant.

'As you say, Barsine will be angry when she hears.' Barsine, like the rest of the women, had been left in Kandahar.

'Barsine means less to me than the lowest whore carrying a bag of millet for the army. Banugul is at least intelligent.' Alexander rubbed his head. 'I'm distempered, Eumenes. Ignore the womanish spite.'

Eumenes shrugged. 'She has a tale of an army, lord, coming from the Euxine.'

Alexander glared at him and the Cardian subsided. 'The Euxine? Foolishness. The Scythians would eat their livers. Now – the Amazons. Let me see them. Are they handsome?'

'Not really, lord.'

'Ares, do they stink?' Alexander rose to his feet, stripped off the Persian tunic he had on and summoned a slave with a better chiton, which he slipped over his head. Eumenes could see that he was thinner, the muscles corded like old rope. The mountains had stolen a little more of the king's youth, just as they had killed the older veterans and aged the rest. The march over the mountains had taken the initiative from the rebels and brought Spitamenes, the most dangerous of the enemy leaders, to the table, but it had killed more Macedonians than any of the king's victories.

Eumenes shrugged. 'They smell like horses, majesty.'

Alexander laughed. 'So do we,' he said. He ran fingers through his hair and shrugged off his slaves. 'Come,' he said imperiously.

Eumenes followed him out of the inner tents to his receiving tent. As he entered, Hephaestion, sensing that something important might happen without him, came through the main door at a rush. To one side, a pair of messengers waited for the king's attention, while to the other side of the main door, three barbarian women in tunics of silk and leather breeches looked about themselves curiously under the eyes of a pair of the king's Companions.

'What news, Achilles?' asked Hephaestion.

Alexander, for once not in the mood to be flattered, shrugged. 'Spitamenes' Amazons,' he said. 'Send for Kleisthenes.'

Hephaestion sent a slave, and then grinned at the huddle of leather-clad women. 'Stinking barbarian women? You plan to send them to brothels, I assume?'

Alexander looked at his friend with something akin to amazement. 'These are free plains-women, Hephaestion. If I mistreat them, the Massagetae and the Sakje and the Dahae will come to know of it, and they will make trouble. What I desire is that they submit, as they did to the Persians. Do you understand?'

Hephaestion, unused to being corrected in public, flushed.

The eldest of the Amazons was heavily pregnant but quite beautiful. She had heavy black brows, the perfect skin of an ivory temple statue and a sense of humour. She gave Alexander half a smile.

'The Massagetae never submitted to the Persae, and they will never submit to you.' She bowed slightly. 'Lord.'

Alexander seated himself on his ivory stool and shook his head. 'You speak Greek!' he said.

'Indeed,' she answered.

'The Massagetae submitted to Cyrus and to Darius,' Alexander said with royal finality.

'You have been misinformed,' the woman said. 'The Massagetae killed Cyrus and avoided Darius.'

Alexander raised an eyebrow.

'That does agree with what Herodotus says, sire,' Kleisthenes, the Greek philosopher, cut in.

'Well!' Alexander looked about him. 'I like that story much better. When I conquer them, I will be first!'

The woman laughed aloud and translated for her companions. They chattered in their barbaric tongue and then laughed with her.

Alexander got up and walked over to them. He put a finger under the pregnant woman's face to lift it and she slapped it away with the swiftness of a lioness.

'You have the face of a goddess. But you are gravid. Whose child is it?' Alexander asked.

'Mine,' she answered. 'And my husband's.'

'A Massagetae warrior?' Alexander asked, examining the youngest of the Amazons – pretty, but muscled like a man.

'Do I look like a Massagetae?' she asked. She laughed again.

'All barbarians look alike to me,' Alexander said.

'I am the Lady Srayanka of the Cruel Hand Sakje. We ride the grass where we please, but our farmers turn the dirt in the valleys north of Olbia.'

Alexander looked at Kleisthenes and then back at the woman. 'Is this true? You have ridden all the way here from the Euxine?' This recalled the Cardian's gossip, but he didn't want to speak of it in front of Hephaestion. 'So the sea of grass *does* run all the way from the Jaxartes to the Tanais!'

She nodded.

Hephaestion came up next to him. 'We have wasted too much time on these barbarians,' he said. He turned his back on the Amazons. 'Pregnant Amazons! Some horse trooper's local trull, I'd say. She couldn't fight a child.'

The pregnant woman narrowed her eyes. 'Give me a sword and I'll cut you, boy.'

Alexander waved at Kleisthenes. 'Read me the bit in the little *Iliad* – about Penthesilea, queen of the Amazons,' he said.

Kleisthenes shook his head, but went back into the main tent looking for the scroll.

Hephaestion, annoyed and used to getting his way, leaned past Alexander and shot a fist at the pregnant woman's face. Heavy as she was, she moved with the blow, taking a piece of it on the crown of her head and then she was under his reach, inside his arms. He grunted and stepped back. She had his sword. He was purple with rage.

'You will never conquer even the Massagetae with soldiers like this,' she said. She held the sword in an easy stance despite her bulk. 'Release us, O King. We have done you no harm, and the traitor Spitamenes kidnapped us from the sea of grass. He is your enemy as well as mine and if you release me, my clans will hunt him like a dog.'

Alexander glanced at his swordless companion with grave disappointment and then turned back to Srayanka. 'When your children are born, they will make excellent hostages,' he said. 'You will live comfortably with my women and when I march into your land in a few years, you can help me.' He turned to Kleisthenes, ignoring Hephaestion. 'The sea of grass is real! We can march to Thrace!'

Kleisthenes was watching Hephaestion. 'She does seem to be a real Amazon, majesty.'

Hephaestion calmed himself. 'I want the young one for myself,' he said.

Srayanka still held the sword. 'She is the lady of the Grass Cats, a war leader and mistress of a thousand horses.'

Hephaestion's humour was restored by Srayanka's reaction. 'She can spread her legs for me as well as any woman,' he said, and a few of the soldiers in the tent laughed. 'Give me back my sword before someone gets hurt,' he said in the voice he used to reason with women and animals.

Srayanka nodded, as if thinking. 'I'm sorry,' she said to Alexander, and she cut Hephaestion across the unarmoured top of his thighs so that blood flowed like water – not a deep cut, but a painful one. Then she tossed the sword on the ground at Alexander's feet as his guards grabbed her. 'I don't imagine you'll spread a lot of legs anytime soon,' she said into the pandemonium.

Alexander regarded her with a mixture of horror and pleasure. 'I shall call you Medea!' he said.

Srayanka shrugged. 'Many men do,' she said. 'Release me, or you will suffer by it.'

Alexander grinned – his first spontaneous grin since his ragtag army had fought its way through the drifts of snow from Kandahar. 'I will never release you, lady,' he said. Behind him, guardsmen and slaves were seeing to Hephaestion.

Srayanka drew herself up, and her pregnancy only added to her dignity. 'We will see,' she said. She flicked a glance at Hephaestion, who was rising with the aid of two other men.

'You will be raped by dogs and the corpses of your unborn children ripped from your womb and fed to them,' Hephaestion shouted. 'I will have you tortured until you have no skin, until—'

Alexander slapped him and he subsided, but his eyes watched Srayanka with feverish hate.

'We will see,' she said.

18

Luck, good fortune, careful planning and the will of the gods got Kineas's force across the desert in the full bloom of spring, with water at every major depression and flowers blossoming among the desolate rocks. Fifteen days after they marched, on the feast of Plynteria in Athens, the army was reunited at the edge of the endless grass that rolled away to every horizon but the one behind them, heat mirage and dust devils and a line of purple mountains in the sunset as the last token of Hyrkania.

'You make good time,' Lot said, clasping Kineas's forearm. 'You have truly become Sakje.'

Kineas flushed at the praise. 'We had perfect weather and water in every hole.'

Lot grinned. In Sakje, he said, 'That's why you cross a desert in the spring. Come – I have a little bad wine and Samahe is reporting on Ataelus's adventures in the east.'

'You seem happy,' Kineas said.

'I'm home!' Prince Lot said. 'I think I never expected to live to get here. And here we are! My messengers are out on the grass, riding for our yurts and our people. We'll make rendez-vous in the Salt Hills, and then we will have such a feast!'

Kineas nodded. 'How far to the Salt Hills?'

Lot led on to his 'tent', merely a square of tough linen staked over a pair of lances. Mosva poured them wine in gold cups. 'The cups are better than the wine,' he said. 'Ten days and we'll be in the hills. Ten hard days, and then you'll have all the fodder you need until you reach Srayanka.' The Sauromatae prince sniffed the air, which was heavy with dust and pollen, like an open bazaar. 'That is the smell of home!'

'Will you leave us?' Kineas asked.

'Never!' Lot said. 'Now you are in my land! I will keep you as safe as you have kept me.' He drank his cup and Kineas finished his. 'Ten days' hard riding and then we feast.'

Kineas turned to Mosva. In a way she was a woman, and then in another way she was just one of his troopers. 'Do you fancy either Leon or Eumenes?' he asked.

She gave the grin of a young woman just discovering her powers. 'Both,' she said, and laughed.

Lot nodded. 'They are both fine young men.' He shrugged. 'Among my people, women choose their own mates. Both are rich, well-connected, brave and foreign.' He grinned again. 'My sister's son inherits my tribes, no matter what road my daughter takes.'

'Your sister's son?' Kineas asked.

'Upazan,' Lot answered, and he frowned, as if the name left a bad taste.

'Ten days' hard riding' was repeated throughout the army as they rode east. The desert vanished behind them and they rode over downs of new grass, green as Persephone's robe, but watercourses were rare and only rain saved them from serious consequences until they came to a great river flowing across their path, burbling brown with spring run-off across rocks.

Kineas was on his Getae hack and he led the horse down to the water, careful not to let the beast over-drink. Diodorus and Leon were doing the same. 'Surely this isn't the Oxus?' Diodorus asked.

Kineas shook his head. 'We must still be twenty days from the Oxus,' he said. He rubbed his beard. 'Or more. Lot!' he shouted.

Prince Lot circled his horse through the drinking animals and splashed up.

'What is this river called?' Kineas asked.

Lot shrugged. 'In Sakje, it is Tanais.'

Leon was pulling his gelding clear of the water, because the horse wanted to keep drinking and Leon had no intention of letting him. From the far bank, he shouted, 'They're all called Tanais! It means "river".'

Lot shrugged. 'No Greek name that I know,' he said.

Leon, who interrogated every merchant and traveller they met, went to his pack and withdrew a scroll whereon he made a few marks. 'This must be the Sarnios,' he said. 'At least, that's what the horse-dealer called it.'

They camped in a bend of the Sarnios. Kineas sacrificed a young calf born on the march to the river goddess and ordered a few of their cattle slaughtered so that all the troops got a ration of meat with their grain. Later, well fed and greasy, they sat under the sky, wrapped in their cloaks against the cold night air, and watched the stars spread above them, backlit by the glow of Temerix's forge in the bed of his wagon. Antigonus and Kineas worked on tack, repairing headstalls. Kineas saw that the charm Kam Baqca had given him so long ago in the winter camp on the Little Borysthenes was fraying, and he sewed it down tight. Antigonus had acquired a bronze chamfron, a piece of horse armour, but he couldn't get it to fit his horse without troubling the animal. Every night it seemed he was making adjustments.

'Wish she could talk,' Antigonus joked. 'Tell me if the cursed thing fits.'

Kineas finished his much smaller project and watched Darius attaching nocks to arrow shafts in the firelight. It was finicky work. 'Wouldn't you do better waiting for daylight?' Kineas asked.

The Persian had all his arrow-making kit spread on a pale blanket. 'Yes,' he said. He swore as his hand slipped and a finished nock went sailing off into the darkness. 'But Temerix bought charcoal from a trader. He has enough to melt bronze and he's casting the heads tonight.'

Kineas grinned. 'You could still put the nocks on in daylight,' he said.

Darius nodded. 'There's never time.' He flicked a glance at Kineas. 'The Sauromatae saw deer tracks today. I won't be caught unprepared!'

Kineas laughed. 'You had all winter to make arrows.'

Darius ignored his commander and concentrated on his task.

'Uuggh!' said Philokles, arriving with a bowl and a slab of meat. 'What's that smell?'

'Glue,' Darius said. He had another nock ready and was

fitting it on a neat dovetail into the butt of the arrow's shaft, where the string would catch it. He rolled the nock in glue and slid it home, wiping the excess with his thumb. Then he took three carefully prepared fletchings, all cut from heron feathers, and glued them in place on the shaft. He set the arrow point-first in the ground and went on to the next shaft, methodically placing and gluing the nock.

'Hmm,' said Philokles, interested despite himself. 'Why not set the feathers straight on? What purpose do they serve?'

Darius dropped a fletching in the grass by the fire and swore again. By the time he recovered it, there was glue on the feather itself and Darius threw it in the fire in disgust and began to cut another.

'It looks like a great deal more work than my spear,' Philokles said.

Kineas didn't want to speak. It was the first time Philokles had shown interest in anything – much less humour.

Darius fitted a new fletching and put the shaft into the ground with the other six he'd made. 'Hunting arrows are the hardest,' he said.

'Why?' Kineas asked, to keep him talking, and to keep Philokles interested.

Darius shrugged the shrug of the young. 'War arrows you never get back,' he said. 'I don't even put nocks on them – I just cut a notch into the shaft and wrap a little cord around the base of the notch. But hunting arrows – you hope to get them back. And you shoot them farther, at harder targets. They need to be well made. My father always told us to make our own and not trust other men's arrows.'

Philokles nodded. 'Why the feathers, though?'

Darius shook his head. 'You Greeks always ask why,' he said. 'Ask a real fletcher. I just do as my father taught me.'

Kineas laughed. Philokles looked at him and raised an eyebrow. Kineas shook his head. 'There's something profound there,' he said. 'But I'm too full of beef to get my tongue around it.'

Philokles laughed and punched his shoulder.

*

Across the Sarnios, flowers bloomed, and the Sauromatae girls made themselves wreaths and wore them as they rode, Mosva looking like Artemis. The hunters shot deer in the folds of the hills, and men, when they had water, sang songs to Demeter and her swift-footed daughter returned from exile. Darius shot a deer on the first day of hunting and was insufferably proud.

Despite Lot's prediction, it took them a further ten days from the Sarnios, and it was one of those happy times that soldiers remember when they are old – seldom the boredom or the cold or the heat, but the beautiful spring on the plains and the Sauromatae girls riding along the flanks in fields of flowers. Meat was plentiful and horses that had been near death suddenly grew strong.

A month after leaving Hyrkania, the hills of Dahia were visible through the heat shimmer on the eastern horizon. Men grumbled and openly wondered about their wages, and they ogled the Sauromatae girls when they stripped their tunics to ride bare-chested in the spring sun.

Diodorus pulled his horse up next to Kineas. 'The troops are better,' he said. 'Ares, it's good to be clear of cursed Hyrkania!'

Kineas nodded and looked at his friend, recalled from a daydream of worry about Srayanka.

Diodorus glanced at Philokles, who was riding alone, lost in thought. 'Is he better?' Diodorus asked.

Kineas nodded. 'I think so. Are you?'

Diodorus shrugged. 'I'm a soldier. I've seen a sack before. I—' he began, and fell silent.

Seeing them together, Philokles pushed his heavy stallion into a trot and the horse brought him up level with the other two. Philokles would never be a natural rider, but two years in the saddle had improved him.

'You two look earnest,' he said.

'We're talking about the troops,' Diodorus said. 'And morale.'

Philokles nodded. 'They're back to grumbling,' the Spartan said. 'Always a good sign.'

'You're better?' Kineas asked.

Philokles shrugged. 'I'm different,' he said.

Kineas watched his cavalry riding by. 'They're all different,' he said. 'I'm different too.'

'You let her live,' Philokles said. 'I have no moment of mercy to serve as a sop to my conscience. I just killed men until my arm was too tired to kill any more.'

'I let her live for pretty much the same reason,' Kineas said. 'There was more fatigue in it than mercy.'

'This is my last campaign,' Philokles said. 'I love you, but I cannot be a beast for ever.'

Kineas nodded slowly. 'It was to have been Niceas's last campaign,' he said. 'He asked me to buy him a brothel in Athens.'

'Perhaps I'll be the next to die, then,' Philokles said, and laughed bitterly. 'I don't want a brothel, though.' He looked over the plain. 'It was merciful, but letting her live will cost us in the end. She can tell Alexander—'

Kineas shook his head. 'You and I have both been spies, brother. The world is so full of spies,' he gave Philokles half a smile, 'that one more won't be a ruffle on the grass.' He looked out over the plains, the sea of grass, almost the same as the sea where he had met Srayanka except for the brush of purple brown on the far horizon that betokened a great range of mountains. Wind whispered in the new blades, rippling the green between pale and dark like the footprints of giants racing across the steppe.

'Somewhere out on the sea of grass, Alexander is waiting,' he said.

Diodorus shook his head. 'Whatever he's doing, he's not waiting.'

Kineas nodded. If I don't find Srayanka, I won't care, he thought.

Two days on, and they met the outriders of the Sauromatae host, pickets at the edge of the green hills who watched their approach and cheered their lord, home from the wars. Lot rode at the front of the column and his young women rode along the flanks, bragging of their exploits and showing the heads of the men they'd killed. The column crested the first ridge and was able to look down into the caldera of an ancient volcano, with rich soil to the far wall several stades distant and a camp of yurts and tents that filled the plain on the far side of a small lake.

Then they feasted for a day, resting their horses, and listened to news of the world. Truce had failed. Alexander was at war with Spitamenes, and Spitamenes was laying siege to Marakanda, while Alexander tried to relieve his hard-pressed garrisons in the north along the Jaxartes. All the tribes had been called to gather on the Jaxartes to resist him if he tried to force a crossing, with mid-summer named for the muster.

And the 'westerners', Srayanka's Sakje, were camped four days' travel away, at a bend of the Oxus.

It was all Kineas could do to remain patient. In his mind, he could see the shape of the campaign – the Sauromatae chieftains sketched him the lie of the land, the hills and the desert and the two great rivers that flowed through the high plains.

Lot and his chiefs drew their world in the soft loam of the caldera floor, carefully building the Sogdian mountains to the east and the Bactrian highlands to the south, so that the mountains formed something like a curling wave design, or a cupped hand seen in profile. At the base of the palm was Merv, an ancient trade city that lay on the Margus river at the edge of the southern mountain range. Alexander had a garrison at Merv. At the tip of the curling wave lay Marakanda – the greatest city of the plains, also on the edge of mountains. Marakanda lay on the Polytimeros, a river that flowed out of the Sogdian mountains.

Between Merv and Marakanda flowed the mighty Oxus, the greatest river of the east. The valley of the Oxus passed between two ranges of mountains, rising far to the east in the highlands of Bactria, and it emptied into the Lake of the Sea of Grass, a distant body of water in the far north that Lot had seen and of which Leon had only heard rumours.

The far eastern border of the Sakje lay at the Jaxartes, which ran a complex course like a writhing snake, rising in the eastern Sogdian mountains and also emptying into the Lake of the Sea of Grass, roughly parallel to the Oxus, on a diagonal course from south-east to north-west. The land between the two great rivers was the land of the Massagetae, and the queen was rallying her army north of Marakanda on the Jaxartes, so rumour had it.

Kineas found their descriptions of the terrain bewildering, even with Leon to help him chart it and sort out the complexities. The two great rivers – the Oxus and the Jaxartes – seemed to rise close to each other and empty into the same body of water, yet they ran hundreds, sometimes thousands, of stades apart. He found it difficult to get some notion of distance out of the Sauromatae. This was their home, and the vast reach of grass – here green and deep, there patchy like the wool on a sick sheep – defined their world. They had ten alien words for the quality of grass and none for swimming.

Greek soldiers and Sindi clansmen wrestled and rode and ran and shot bows against their hosts. Kineas gave rich prizes from Banugul's hoard, and Lot did as well. Temerix, the best bowman on foot, received a heavy bow with minute scales of gold under a glaze or varnish that somehow did nothing to reduce the flexibility of the weapon. His victory brought dark looks from Lot's heir, his sister's son Upazan, a handsome blond man who seemed to feel that his uncle had already lived too long and that any contest he lost must have been unfair. Upazan had many beautiful things – a gold helmet, magnificent scale armour, a red enamelled bow and a shield covered in silver that shone like a mirror and had a curling dragon as an emblem picked out in red and solid gold. He showed it all to Kineas with pride, and clearly desired more of the same.

Lot said that Upazan's bow, and the one he gave as a prize, were spoils of raids far to the east, where he claimed there lived an empire mightier than all of Persia, with soldiers in bronze armour. Leon listened with rapt attention. Lot, sensing the Numidian's interest, showed them another bow, this one fitted with a shoulder stock and a bronze trigger mechanism. Kineas shot it for sport and it carried well and punched a bolt through a Sakje shield with ease. Leon listened carefully, drew a picture of the weapon on his scroll and added notes. He was so distracted that Mosva showed her hurt by flirting with her cousin Upazan, whose desire for her was obvious and drew disapproval from the elders.

Kineas watched Upazan. Upazan was bitter at having missed the campaign in the west, more bitter still that his uncle was now a hero, and bitter again to be eclipsed in contests by foreigners. When he and Leon threw javelins and Leon bested him, striking a hide shield five times out of five at the gallop, Upazan responded by riding up behind the black man and striking him with a spear, sweeping him from his mount with the haft.

In a heartbeat every Olbian was on his feet. Leon was well liked. Eumenes, no friend of the Numidian, ran to his side and helped him to his feet. Upazan laughed. 'It is just play such as men play,' he said. 'Too rough for you westerners?'

Lot shook his head and demanded that the young sub-chief apologize, which he refused to do. He stood in front of them without flinching and laughed again. 'Does the black boy need so many mothers?' he asked. 'If he seeks redress, we can fight! I will kill him and then I will own the prize. It should have been mine. You are all fools.'

Under Kineas's direct order, Leon turned and walked away. Upazan laughed at the Greeks, and Kineas let him laugh.

Later that day, Kineas met Lot's queen, Monae, who had held his tribes together while he fought in the west, a campaign that already had the status of legend among the Sauromatae. He saw how she looked at Upazan – with distaste bordering on hate. 'Lot's sister was everything to him and she died giving birth. Lot has never put reins on that horse.' She pointed her chin at Upazan. 'He is more trouble than all the rest of the young men and women together – and many of them worship him, or at least fear him. With the young, the two are often the same.'

Kineas was too old to let one angry young man spoil his pleasure, and he was too desperate to see Srayanka to mind the young man's passions too much. He accepted Lot's apologies in place of the truculent Upazan's.

Later, around a council fire, sitting on the beautiful Sauromatae rugs of coloured wool under the canopy of stars, Kineas listened to Lot talk about the politics of the tribes. Monae was with them, along with Diodorus, Philokles, Ataelus – and Upazan. There was no avoiding the young man – he was, after all, Lot's heir.

'Pharmenax, the king paramount of all the Sauromatae, has made a separate peace with Alexander – has ridden to meet him,' Lot said.

Kineas was startled. 'So your war is over,' he said.

Lot looked at his Monae, who smiled like a wolf. 'No one followed him. Being king of the Sauromatae is not very different from being king of the Sakje, Kineax. He has the title, but he has made a decision that is unpopular, and few of us care to follow him. Now, if this Alexander wins great victories, and if Spitamenes the Persian and Queen Zarina of the Massagetae are defeated? Hmm. Then, perhaps you will see us join King Pharmenax.'

'We should be riding to Alexander now,' said Upazan. 'He is strongest. He will conquer.'

'Spitamenes?' Kineas asked, ignoring the boy. 'I heard talk of him in Hyrkania. Refresh my memory?'

'One of the lords of Bactria. He has given Alexander the former usurper – Bessus. Handed him over – for impiety, so it is said. Bessus is a good man and a poor general.' Monae shook her head sadly. 'It has been quite a year, husband.'

Upazan leaned forward. 'This is not women's talk, Monae. I spoke and I expect to be answered. We should go to Alexander.'

Kineas looked at the boy but said nothing.

Lot put up a hand. 'Upazan, your time as a hostage with the Medae has left you rude. Women may share in any council.'

'Pah – women warm beds and make babies. We are fools to allow them anything else. When I am king, we will have done with spear-maidens.' He spoke with the malicious enjoyment every adolescent experiences in stating a view that he knows his elders will hate. It was hard to tell if he actually believed any of it.

257

'Bessus was the satrap? Bessus?' Kineas asked.

'Satrap? He called himself King of Kings.' Monae shook her head. 'He will die badly, with his nose slit. This Alexander has been fast as a snake to adopt the ways of the Medae.'

'I feel as if I have come out of the oil pot and fallen into the fire,' Kineas said.

'Nothing about barbarian life is simple,' Lot said. He laughed, but there were lines on his face, and his glance strayed to Upazan.

'Who is Queen Zarina?' Kineas asked.

'A spear-maiden who made herself queen,' Monae said. She put a hand to her throat and coughed, and then laughed easily – the world was a humorous place for her, and she showed all her teeth. 'She loves war. She does not love Spitamenes, but she wants to defeat Alexander. She has called a muster of all the Scythians – from the Euxine to the great mountains. Sakje, Dahae and Sauromatae and Massagetae and Kandae and all their kin. There has never been such a muster since the days of the great wars against the Persae.' She smiled. 'And they were once one of our tribes, as well. The Persae. Clan mothers remember.' She shook her head. 'Zarina sees herself as queen of all the people. Will we have her? Will we obey?' She laughed. 'But we will all go – even your Srayanka. If only to see how many horse tails the people can muster, and show this Alexander what power is.'

Kineas caught his breath and then released it slowly.

Lot glanced around and then leaned forward. 'What do you intend, lord?'

'Why do you call him lord?' Upazan asked. 'He is some foreigner, not our lord.'

'You have never seen him run a battle, nephew,' Lot said, reasonably.

'Foolishness.' Upazan had opinions for every subject and no hesitation about showing them. He got up and left the fire. Rising, he managed to kick sand at Kineas. Kineas continued to ignore the boy.

When Upazan was gone, Kineas leaned forward. 'First, I

plan to meet with Srayanka. I understand she's at Chatracharta, on the Oxus.'

Lot and his wife exchanged glances. 'That's where we expect to find the Sakje,' he said carefully.

Kineas nodded. 'If I understand it correctly, we can move north along the Oxus to the Polytimeros, and then – well, then I'm not too clear on the terrain.' He shrugged. 'But we'll go to the muster on the Jaxartes.'

Lot leaned forward and sketched the wave and the two rivers in the dirt. 'All the valley of the Oxus is held by Iskander,' he said. 'And he has forts along the Polytimeros and the Jaxartes. That is his frontier. You'll have to ride around him to get to the muster. That's the word on the plains – stay north of the forks of the Polytimeros, and ride well clear of the Sogdian mountains.'

Kineas shook his head. 'Srayanka will understand this better than me,' he said.

Again he watched his hosts exchange a look that worried him, but he was too close to finding Srayanka to worry about the campaign.

That night, well fed, half-drunk on Persian wine, his head buzzing with the gossip of the east, Kineas threw himself on his old cloak and went to sleep without effort.

He stood on the field of Issus in the dark, a flood of spectral Persians coming at him from over the river, and he relived his last moments at Arbela, his horse carrying him deep into the Median nobles, his helmet torn away, fighting from habit because he had only moments to live, at the Ford of the River God, and his body shifted uncomfortably as he slept. And then he found himself at the base of the tree. Ajax waited there with Nicomedes, and Niceas had his arms around Graccus and the two stood like men who have celebrated a great festival and now help each other home. The four of them watched him steadily as he approached.

'Not long now,' Ajax said. 'Are you ready to join us?'

Niceas grunted. 'Best find that filly of yours and ride her a few times, because there's none of that here!'

The others laughed grimly.

'You know what we've been trying to tell you?' Ajax asked.

'I think so,' said Kineas. It was the first time he could remember being able to converse with the dead. Seeing them – speaking with them – made him absurdly happy.

'Finish it,' Graccus said. He was serious, dignified – just like himself. 'We can hold them until you climb to the top.'

Nicomedes nodded. 'Alexander must be stopped. You will stop him.'

And he set himself to climb. Above him, a pair of eagles shrieked . . .

Kineas awoke to the feel of rough bark under his arms and thighs, and a leaden fatigue in his limbs.

On the third night in the caldera, Kineas sat under a rough shelter, with a scrap of animal parchment on which he'd rendered a rough map of the ground from the caldera to the distant Jaxartes. Philokles lay beside him, and Diodorus sat on the ground with Sappho at his shoulder on a stool. Eumenes and Andronicus sat back to back, both of them mending bridles. Leon was off questioning traders – or following Mosva.

They all looked at the map and made plans: a quick trip across the dry ground to the edge of the sea where Srayanka's Sakje were camped, a grand reunion, and then some hard decisions.

'If the pay doesn't catch up with us, and even if it does, I have to wonder at whether we keep the boys together,' he said.

Eumenes, hitherto silent, leaned into the discussion. 'The men complain that they are too far from home. And many complain that we are not keeping the festival calendar and that the gods will not be pleased.'

Diodorus nodded. 'There's a lot of complaining, Eumenes. But I see it as a sign that the boys are recovering from the march here and the storming of the citadel. Never worry your head about a little bitching.' But to Kineas he said, 'I don't see what we can accomplish here. The Massagetae, all the Sauromatae, the Dahae – they've got more horsemen than the gods. They can bury Alexander in a tide of horseflesh. What can we do with our four hundred?'

'We have discipline they lack, and we've faced Macedon before,' Kineas said. 'But I take your point.' He looked out at the rim of the caldera and the deep blue sky beyond. 'The world is larger than I ever imagined.'

Diodorus nodded. 'I'd like to find my tutors and bring them here,' he said.

Kineas went on as if his friend hadn't spoken. 'But Alexander is still the monster. However great the world is, he seems to bestride it. I will go where he goes.'

Diodorus shook his head. 'Then I guess we'll follow you there,' he said. He watched the sun for a moment. 'Then what happens? I mean, when we fight Alexander. Then what?'

Kineas laughed. 'When we beat Alexander, I will try to persuade Srayanka to ride home.' He shrugged. 'If I'm alive.'

Philokles shook his head. 'Always that old tune. What we're telling you, Strategos, is that if you want your men to follow you to the end of the world to fight the finest army to stride the earth since the long-haired Achaeans sailed to windy Ilium, you had better have a plan for what we do when we win.'

'Or lose,' said Diodorus, cheerily.

On the next morning, the hyperetes of each troop got the men into column. They grumbled and groaned and cursed their sore muscles and their hard lot as they mounted, but they did it. Kineas watched Leon embrace Mosva, and watched Eumenes' face darken almost to purple, and Upazan's match it, but he did not interfere. Leon made a gesture at the Sauromatae chief with his hand – a small gesture of two fingers. Upazan reacted immediately, running at Leon, but Leon was mounted. Smiling, he tripped the Sauromatae with his spear and danced his horse away. An ugly muttering spread among the younger Sauromatae.

Kineas thought of interfering. But he didn't.

Before the sun was a hand's-breadth in the ether, their borrowed Sauromatae scouts were over the lip of the caldera and the great lake of the steppes gleamed like a flat sapphire on the horizon. It vanished as they descended the caldera's side, but the next day it came into sight again. They made good time on the steppe, the scouts found water and they slept in rough camps with heavy curtains of sentries.

Kineas drove them hard.

By the festival of Skirophoria they were watering their horses in the Oxus, and across the river they could see horses and men washing shirts. The Olbians and the Sakje fell on each other like long-lost friends and battle brothers (and sisters), so that discipline dissolved as they entered the Sakje camp. Kineas rode straight for the circle of wagons at the centre, his heart slamming in his chest and his tongue thick in his mouth. *Why had she not come out to meet him? Her scouts must have seen him a day ago!*

He dismounted, with Ataelus beside him. Parshtaevalt stood to receive him, and the younger man looked tired.

Kineas embraced Srayanka's tanist, who all but sighed with relief. 'Where is she?' he blurted out.

Parshtaevalt hugged him harder. 'Taken,' he whispered. 'She is prisoner of Alexander. And we have been betrayed.'

19

Srayanka's absence was like a black storm cloud, threatening to swallow Kineas and sweep him away. He couldn't think of anything but the void she left, and twice on the first evening in the Assagatje camp he wept without cause.

Even in his despair, he could tell that Parshtaevalt needed him. The war leader was out of his depth as Srayanka's tanist, and he hovered near Kineas and spoke twice – haltingly – of summoning the council of chiefs, until Kineas nodded to be rid of him.

Spitamenes' betrayal was not the only news waiting in the camp of the Assagatje. When Parshtaevalt summoned the clan leaders to council, and all were seated in the fire circle before Srayanka's wagon, Kineas saw a stranger dressed in silk. He beckoned to Parshtaevalt. 'Who is that?' he asked.

Parshtaevalt had the look of a drowning man who has been offered an oar to grab. 'That is Qares, one of Zarina's lords from the east. He came expecting to lead us to the muster.'

Kineas rubbed his beard. His eyes felt full and sore, and he didn't want to trouble himself with the leadership of the Assagatje. Indeed, for a day he had shunned his own men.

Parshtaevalt threw his hands in the air. 'What could I do? I am not the lord of the Assagatje!' he said. 'Kineax! Take this burden from me. I can command a raid. But where are we to winter? Shall we ride to this muster? How can we rescue our lady?' He was distraught, his arms raised to heaven as if imploring the gods. 'I am not a king!' he said.

Kineas shook his head despondently. 'Nor am I,' he said. 'But you summoned the council for me when you chose not to do it yourself.'

The Sakje chief scratched his head and sighed. 'I am a war leader,' he said. 'Peace councils leave me confused. I was – waiting. And look, you came!'

'I am not the king of the Assagatje,' Kineas said.

'You are her consort,' Parshtaevalt said. 'That is enough.'

And so it proved. The council made it clear from their respectful silence that they wished Kineas to take command. Kineas had enough experience with Sakje to listen to what they left unsaid. He rose, angered at their hesitation and their silent insistence.

'I am not your king. Why do you sit awaiting my orders?' he asked.

None of the chiefs said anything. Several of them glanced at Parshtaevalt, as if waiting for him to speak. Finally, Bain, the most aggressive of the war leaders, rose. 'Lord, you are the Lady's consort, and you led us all through the campaigns last year. Even if Srayanka were here, she would share her authority with you. Lead us!'

Kineas took a deep breath. 'I want to rescue Srayanka,' he said. 'Is it even possible? We need to know what has happened in the world. I have heard rumour of betrayal, and I have heard that she is a hostage.' Even as he spoke the words, he felt a tide of despair rise in his heart. For a moment the pain was so intense that he stopped speaking and stood in the midst of the Assagatje, head hanging.

Kineas had been following Srayanka for months, and here, in the middle of the sea of grass, he had lost her again. It was too much.

A strong hand clenched his shoulder, warm in the chill of evening. 'Courage, brother,' Philokles said. 'We'll find her.' The Spartan was sober, which he rarely was in the evening since the storming of the citadel. 'Come on, Athenian. Head up. These people are depending on you.'

Kineas swallowed. His chin came up. 'Right,' he said. 'Let's hear from those who know something of what has passed.'

Despite Alexander's best efforts, there was a constant exchange of men and information between the tribesmen serving Spitamenes and their cousins serving the Macedonian king, so that rumours crossed the lines in a matter of days and each side knew what the other intended and what each had done, and the camp of the Assagatje had a dozen warriors who knew what passed on the Oxus and in the valley of the Jaxartes that

264

summer. One by one they rose in council or were sent for by their chiefs.

There were three armies. Spitamenes laid siege to Marakanda, fabled city of the trade route, and his army was the last Persian army in the field against Alexander, with veteran Iranian cavalrymen and hardbitten Sogdian noblemen, exiles in their own land, who had been fighting Alexander for three and sometimes four years. Alexander had a garrison in Marakanda, fighting carefully and looking east towards the king's army for relief. It was in the east that Alexander had his field army, still bent on rescuing the seven garrisons he had left on the Jaxartes and on keeping the third army under observation. The third army was the Scythian horde, led by the queen of the Massagetae. Her force was small, just a few thousand riders, but she had sent out the call for the full muster, and the very grass itself seemed to be moving across the steppe towards the appointed rendezvous.

When her force had been described by one of Bain's horsemen, Qares rose, and when he was recognized, he stepped forward into the council. 'I am Qares, of the Iron Hills Massagetae,' he said, and his voice had the sing-song quality that Ataelus had when he spoke. 'I come from Queen Zarina to your queen. I see a good force here, a force that the Massagetae need and greater than we had dared hope.' His voice was strong. His hair was in a dozen braids, each tied with a gold bell, and he was a handsome man. 'I, too, mourn the loss of your queen. But all the Sakje must ride together to face Iskander. Queen Zarina has a fair host, and she will have more with every week. But when Iskander relieves Marakanda and defeats Spitamenes, for whom we have no trust, then he will turn east. We must be ready. Make haste!'

Kineas nodded and the man fell silent.

'Lord Qares,' Kineas raised his whip. 'How far is it from here to the camp of your queen?'

'Twenty days' riding without haste,' Qares replied.

'Is there water?' Parshtaevalt asked.

Qares shrugged. 'More now than there will be in a month,' he said.

The council came to no decision that night, and Kineas was bitter when he drank wine with his own officers. 'If I had wanted to be archon, I could have stayed in Olbia,' Kineas said.

Philokles was deep in his cups. The Assagatje had a store of Persian wine and Philokles had determined to get to the bottom of it. 'Be a man,' he said, slurring his words. 'These people need you.'

'Go to bed,' Kineas said.

'He's drunk,' Diodorus said. But when Temerix and Sappho had taken Philokles away, Diodorus said, 'He's right. These people need you.'

Kineas took a deep breath. He thought of saying that all he wanted was Srayanka, and he thought of cursing, but he thought better of it and released the breath unused.

Kineas was silent in the morning, having slept in her wagon and having wakened to her smell on the blankets. He lay awake in the dawn watching the heavy felt dragons, gryphons and running deer on her wall hangings move gently in the morning breeze. And when he couldn't lie there any longer, he rose and took Thalassa and rode away on the plains. He rode alone, galloping out on to the long grass until Thalassa was as tired as he was. Then he slipped from her back and wove her a garland of late roses while she breathed heavily and then cropped the green grass that still lay under the summer-scorched grass that stood in golden waves on the plain. Her silver-grey coat was streaked with sweat in black patterns. He rubbed the sweat off her neck.

He placed the garland on her head and she sidled at the prickles, but then steadied, and he sang a hymn to Poseidon. He stood alone under the bowl of the sky and watched, and finally a lone bird rose from the east on his right and turned long circles in the sky. It was an eagle, and after the sun moved towards the west, a second eagle joined it and the two danced in the sky above him and then flew away to the west.

Kineas mounted Thalassa and rode slowly across the plains towards their camp.

That night, he summoned the council in his own name, and a third of all the people came, so that the night was filled with the murmur of their voices. The Sakje sat in a circle with the Olbians, as they had the year before. Kineas rose.

'Will you have me as your leader until Srayanka is returned to us?' Kineas asked.

Parshtaevalt shot to his feet. 'We will!' he said.

'Very well,' said Kineas. He looked around. He invited all the chiefs to speak, and one by one they rose to demand Srayanka's rescue, and to speak about fodder and grass, about infractions of the law, about the dangers of wintering on the sea of grass.

Then Kineas rose with the whip that Srayanka had given him in his fist. First, he sketched with words what he knew of the great war in the south. Then, as best he could, he described how Srayanka must have been betrayed. He stressed that Alexander had no reason to harm any of the hostages – neither Srayanka of the Cruel Hands, nor her young friend Urvara of the Grass Cats, nor Hirene her trumpeter.

Young men and women who had ridden abroad rose to tell of what they had heard at the great camp at Marakanda and from traders on the trade road. They spoke too long, as the young often do, but despite this, the excitement of the circle grew.

And then Diodorus stood. His Sakje wasn't good, and he called on Eumenes to translate for him. 'They don't know us here,' he said. He turned to Qares. 'The Massagetae do not spurn Spitamenes for his treachery, because they do not know Srayanka and how far she has come.' He turned to Darius. 'Spitamenes does not know the campaign we waged last year.' Finally he turned to Kineas. 'Alexander does not know us.' He looked at the circle – Sakje faces, ruddy with firelight, their hair sparkling with gold ornaments, and Greek faces, their beards long and often shot with grey, and Keltoi with their bronze and gold beards. Kineas watched them all – even without Srayanka, he felt as if he had returned home. These were the comrades of his last campaign, and here among them he might have been a few stades from Olbia on a different arm of the sea of grass.

Diodorus paused, and allowed the pause to lengthen. 'It is too bad they do not know us, because if they did, none of them would have allowed this to come about.' He waited for Eumenes to finish his translation. 'A year ago, I heard Satrax say this when Macedon drew near.' He paused again, and in good Sakje, he said, 'Let them feel the weight of our hooves.'

Around the fire, Olbian and Sindi and Sakje shrilled their war cries together. Diodorus turned to Kineas. 'Lead us against the foe,' he said.

Kineas rose. 'I propose that we rescue Srayanka,' he said. Forty voices bellowed agreement. Kineas raised his hands for silence. 'It will require patience and discipline, like the campaign against the Getae, and luck, like all war.'

The circle of forty bellowed approval.

Kineas turned to Qares, the queen of the Massagetae's messenger. 'We will come to the muster. Srayanka has given oath to it, as has Prince Lot of the Sauromatae. But first we must do what we can to rescue our lady.'

Qares shook his head. 'You may be too late, and come only to see the crows feast.'

Kineas nodded. 'It may be as you say. But without Srayanka, we would never have come east. Tell your queen that we come, and the Sauromatae come — after we have tried our best to rescue Srayanka.'

Qares looked around the circle and chose to be silent.

'I want to send scouts south,' Kineas said. He pointed to Ataelus. 'Ataelus will go east to the Massagetae with Qares.' He nodded to Philokles with his chin. 'Philokles will take a patrol south to Alexander,' he said, and their eyes met. In his friend's face, Kineas read distaste — and acceptance. With his Spartan education and his looks, Philokles could walk right into any mercenary unit in Alexander's army and be accepted.

'And I will ask Darius to ride to Spitamenes,' he said.

Darius raised his eyes and looked first at Philokles and then at Kineas. He nodded, but his nod was hesitant.

Kineas's eyes went back to the circle. 'We will move south into the valley of the Oxus, staying concealed from everyone except the Sauromatae to the best of our ability. Ataelus assures me that this can be done. There we will await the reports of our scouts. One of the three will get us news of Srayanka. Only then will we act. Until then, there will be no raids, no private acts of revenge.' His eyes left the Greeks and went to Parshtaevalt and the Sakje clan leaders. Young Bain, the wildest of the chiefs, met his eye.

'I mean you, Bain,' Kineas said. 'If you raid without permission, you will be cast out.'

Bain glared. 'Will we have revenge?' he asked.

Kineas nodded. 'I promise it,' he said.

Bain rose to his feet. 'I, Bain, the Bow of the West, swear not to raise my hand until the scouts return.'

The other chiefs, men and women, nodded approval.

The next morning, Ataelus, Philokles and Darius all rode forth from the riverside camp with retinues of tribesmen, guides and strings of horses. Kineas was left to sit beside the river, drilling his cavalry and gnawing his cheek with worry by day and dreaming of war and disaster and death by night.

After a week, Lot's outriders came into camp and the two groups merged. The grass was too far gone where the Sakje had camped and both tribes moved north and west along the river. Their scouts found swathes of trampled grass and the passage of thousands of hooves on the main trade road, which crossed the Oxus just north of the Polytimeros.

The Sakje were moving east.

Kineas pressed on east for five days and then rested his Sakje and his Olbians, with Lot a day's march away, closer to the bank of the Oxus. Their horse herds were too large to allow them to camp together easily when the grass was sparse, although there was a constant traffic both ways, a traffic in which Leon and Mosva played a role. The war and the trek had made for intermarriage and friendship bonds, and Kineas had seen that the tribes were not so much racial as customary, and when a family preferred one chief over another, they moved their horses to his herd and joined it.

The next night, the whole force was united on the banks of the Oxus. Where their horse herds mingled, brown water flowed in a watercourse three times as wide as the early summer stream, which divided and then reunited in twenty channels, creating thousands of islands, some covered in grass, others in trees. The smell of honeysuckle and briar rose flooded the senses, and the sound of ten thousand horses cropping the rich grass of the riverside meadows drowned out all other noise. At night, tamarisk fires smelled like cedar of Lebanon. All the water tasted of mud.

He used his new-found authority with the Sakje to select the best warriors from among all the clans and tribes that had followed Srayanka. He placed them together in a company of two hundred under Bain. Bain was a superb warrior and that made him a Sakje leader. Kineas would rather have had Parshtaevalt to command the picked men, but he was the chosen leader of the Cruel Hands and Kineas needed him there.

Bain did not take naturally to drill, but he did take to command, and Diodorus, who had worked with both adolescents and barbarians, quickly let the young knight know that his position of command rested on his ability to keep his riders interested in the Greek drills.

'They'll never be very pretty,' Andronicus said. He was working into Niceas's role as the command hyperetes. Every time Kineas heard his Gaulish Greek at his elbow, he missed Niceas, but Andronicus had the skills to do the job. 'But they already use the wedge, and they can rally on the trumpet call, and those two skills will win battles.'

Diodorus had grander plans, as he showed Kineas the next afternoon. Two troops of the Olbians formed up with Bain's Sakje in line behind them. At a trumpet signal, the Sakje began to fire arrows *over* the Olbians, who lunged forward into a charge, supported by the volleys of arrows coming over their heads.

Diodorus rode back to Kineas and pulled off his helmet. 'What do you think?' he asked. 'Like the *hippotoxotai* in our father's time.'

Kineas had noted that Barzes, a Hyrkanian they had picked up at Namastopolis, had lost his horse to a friendly arrow. He pointed this out. 'If the Sakje get a surprise – if you slam into an unexpected obstacle, or your charge falls short – you get to eat a lot of your own arrows.'

'Don't be a stick,' Diodorus said. 'It'll change cavalry warfare.'

Kineas shrugged. 'You're wily Odysseus,' he said. Then he grinned. 'Looks good to me.'

Diodorus smiled. 'If I'm Odysseus,' he said, 'I suppose you're Agamemnon.'

Kineas made a face. 'Ouch,' he said.

With Lot's picked men and his own cavalry, he had almost eight hundred veterans of last year's campaign. He drilled them, amusing the Sakje and boring the Sauromatae, teaching them a few simple trumpet commands, wedge and rhomboid, how to charge and how to rally quickly, until they were all on the verge of revolt, and then he gave them two days of feast and squandered the remaining grain on feeding the chargers.

Samahe came in with word that Lot's western scouts had made contact with Coenus. He was far away beyond the Salt Hills, but he was across the desert and he already had an escort of Sauromatae. Word of his approach did more for the Olbians than a hundred speeches, because he brought gold for their pay and wine, as well as news of home.

Samahe was covered with dust and the smell of horse sweat preceded her into Srayanka's wagon by several heartbeats. Kineas gave her a cup of wine, which she consumed with the satisfaction of a connoisseur.

'Summer on the plains,' she said. 'Stink-fucking desert.' She tossed off the rest of the wine. 'Not like home, where grass stays for summer. High grass is *gone*.'

'Ataelus will be back soon,' Kineas said, and she smiled.

'I stink like dog,' she said. 'Bath in roses for him!'

Her pleasure at the imminence of her mate made Kineas feel as if his heart was opening inside his chest. He smiled at her, but his mind called out *Srayanka!*

He worked to prepare to rescue her. But he didn't believe in it.

*

Kineas sacrificed to the gods and prayed, and on the eighth day he was standing in the brutal sun, wearing a straw hat as wide as his shoulders and grooming his horse with a Sakje brush, a marvellous tool woven like rope from horse tail with bristles of a mysterious animal that apparently lived in the far north. He had groomed four horses for thousands of stades and the brush remained as stiff and fresh as the day Urvara had given it to him, in the hours before the great battle at the ford. He treasured it. Now he was thinking of her and Srayanka when he heard voices calling from the main camp. He saw a rider coming out of the sun, with pickets calling for him on either hand, and he ran up the riverbank to his camp, still holding his brush.

Nihmu rode out of the sun. She was exhausted, her eyes set deep in her head with dark smudges under them as if she'd been struck. She was as thin as a stick of tamarisk, and when she dismounted by Kineas she drank all the water he could give her. The water seemed to make her grow a little, and suddenly she grinned like the sun bursting forth from a sky of clouds. 'Ready your horses, King! Ataelus says, and Philokles says, that they have found a way to rescue the lady.'

Kineas felt his heart begin to pound in his chest, its pressure so great that it might not have beaten for days or even weeks before that moment. 'How?' he asked, seizing her hands.

Nihmu flicked the hair from her eyes. Her braids had decayed in hard riding and she had a halo of bronze hair around her face. She gave a weary shake of her head. 'Not for telling me. Gods, I sound like Ataelus.' She smiled. 'Haven't thought in Greek for many days, lord. I was told that you should bring the people along as quickly as you can to the forks of the Polytimeros. That's all I know. And I am to tell you that Iskander is in the field, that Craterus is on the Polytimeros, that Spitamenes lays siege to Marakanda.' She repeated these last in her sing-song voice of rote memorization.

'Go to bed, girl,' Kineas ordered. He turned to Diodorus. 'Send Eumenes to Lot with the news. Tell him we'll ride in the morning.'

Diodorus nodded. 'Where exactly are the forks of the Polytimeros?' he asked quietly.

Kineas rubbed his chin. 'Best get some guides from Lot, too.'

Then he lay down in his cloak, out under the stars instead of in her wagon, and he waited for the veil of sleep to come over him.

He laughed, because no spray of colour, no cacophony of unreal sounds, no bestiary of dream monsters, could move him as his dreams had once moved him. In fact, he was angry.

Kam Baqca settled on the branch opposite him, her skeletal back nestled against the bark of the tree's main trunk. 'You are almost there,' she said.

Kineas sat with his legs dangling down. Above him, a pair of eagles flew in growing circles around his head and cried. Kineas shouted, 'You – the gods – have made me into an arrow and shot me from your bow. Any day now I will strike the target and shatter, and my day is over. For you, the arrow will have done its work. For me, there is only Srayanka and life. The honeysuckle is sweet. The briar rose smells like love and the Sakje women roll in the petals and sweet grass to prepare themselves for love, and I will be dead without seeing her again.'

Kam Baqca raised her head, so that he could see that most of the skin had flaked away from her face, leaving the skull. She was hideous, yet somehow comforting. Another part of his mind wondered why Ajax looked uncorrupted by death, while Kam Baqca, who died the same day, had rotted. 'Are you a boy, to whine to me of how unfair it all is?' she asked with arch contempt. 'I am already dead. No lover will take me in his arms.' She looked at her own arms – bone and withered sinew. 'How lovely I am! If I roll in rose petals, will it cover the stink of corruption?'

He glared at her. 'You chose your path.'

She smiled, her jaws hideous. 'You chose your path too, King. Archon. Hipparch. You came east. Now finish your task like a craftsman. Go and fight the monster ...'

He awoke to the sound of ten thousand strong jaws cropping grass. He lay in the grass and despair rose around him like early morning mist, and settled on him until he choked and wept. But when he fell asleep again, he ... *passed his dead friends and jumped into the tree again and climbed without much interest. He saw the top above him and marvelled at how far he had come. He looked down and saw a plain below him, stretching away to mountains that rose like a wall and went on for ever, and he knew awe. And then he stretched forth his hand to climb ...*

'If you can't control yourself better than that,' Phocion said, 'I will not bother to teach you any more.'

Kineas was standing in the sand of the practice ring, his arm numb and his eyes stinging with tears. 'It's not fair!' he whimpered.

Phocion's wooden sword slapped him on the side of the head. 'Beasts fight with rage,' he said. 'Greeks fight with science. Any barbarian can out-rage you, boy.'

'I am not a boy!' Kineas bellowed. He meant it as a bellow. It came out as more of a squeak. The other young men waiting their turns tittered and giggled, or stood in embarrassed silence.

Kineas's crime had been to state as a matter of fact that he was the best of Phocion's pupils. Phocion had responded by disarming him – repeatedly – and beating him with soul-destroying ease, not once but ten times running. He used the same simple move over and over again, moving with lazy elegance, and Kineas's responses grew more and more foolish with each engagement, until Kineas burst into tears.

Phocion stepped back. 'If you are a man, then pick up that sword and use your brain.'

Kineas walked across the sand to his fallen sword and retrieved it, his mind hot with the desire for revenge. But he thought of Niceas, and Graccus, and the fight in the alley, and the pain and the blood. And how much he owed Phocion. He stood straight despite ten new bruises. He pushed his brain to consider Phocion's attack – something subtle in the feint. He decided on a simple solution.

'I am ready,' he said, settling into his stance, shield forward, sword back. He moved out cautiously and Phocion danced around him, but this time Kineas didn't offer his sword. He stayed behind his shield, accepted a light blow on his hip and a stinging cut that drew blood from his shield-side knee. Phocion made a back cut and Kineas exerted the full force of his will to avoid the response he had been taught – a cut at the opponent's wrist. Instead, he

274

simply stepped back and blocked with his shield. It was dull, and the weight of the shield pulled at his arm, and after some minutes Phocion feinted low and thumped him on the head and he fell. Phocion extended a hand and drew him to his feet.

'You are a man,' he said. He grinned. 'I suspected as much.'

Kineas nodded. His head hurt.

Phocion smiled at him. 'What is my new feint, Kineas?' he asked.

Kineas rubbed his head. 'No idea, master. It starts with a faked sloppy back cut.' He smiled wryly. 'It only took me ten tries to establish that.'

Phocion nodded. 'And how do you defeat it?' he asked.

Kineas shook his head. 'No idea, master.'

Phocion grinned, looking much younger. 'You may yet be the best of my students, young blowhard. Go and oil yourself and get a rub.'

Graccus shook his head. 'I don't understand, master,' he said.

Phocion shrugged. 'You will,' he said.

Kineas smiled at Phocion. 'I understand,' he said.

And then he was on a branch of the tree, higher than he had ever been.

And then he dreamed that he was a god – Zeus incarnate – and that in his hand he held the thunderbolt, which gleamed with white fire and jumped in his hand, and yet seemed to be composed of men and horses …

And he awoke with the taste of hubris in his mouth.

In an hour, the whole column was moving. They rode north and west along the Oxus, with Mosva's brothers, Hektor and Artu, as well as Gwair Blackhorse all out front guiding the column. They had ten thousand horses and the combined force was four stades long from Kineas at the front to the last Sauromatae maidens, wreathed in scarves, who rode in the dust clouds at the rear, herding the cattle.

Twice they saw distant figures on horseback. Kineas ordered the scouts not to pursue, but he put more Sauromatae out as a screen. He didn't want every tribal chief within a thousand stades to know the make-up of his column.

Now they were at the Macedonian frontier. The Polytimeros was the edge of Alexander's lines.

Late in the second morning since Nihmu's return, scouts reported that the forks of the Polytimeros were ahead, and an hour later, as they ate their cold porridge while their horses cropped grass, Ataelus returned. He kissed Samahe, the two entwined like two trees on a wind-blasted island in the Aegean, and then Ataelus wrenched himself from her and turned to Kineas. He grinned.

'Philokles say "Come now!"' he said. 'Luck for standing at shoulder. More stuff like Philokles for saying.' Ataelus shrugged, grinning.

Kineas gestured at the column. 'Here we are,' he said.

'Come now!' said Ataelus.

'I told you,' said Nihmu. Ataelus ruffled her hair and she grinned.

'How far?' Kineas asked.

'Two days, for riding like Sakje.' Ataelus emphasized this with his fist. 'Like Sakje.' He grinned again. 'Come for rescue Lady Srayanka. Strike blow against Iskander.' His fist smacked into his open hand with a noise like a breaking gourd. 'Hurry! Philokles says for ...' the chief of the prodromoi scrunched up his face, remembering, '*utmost* hurry. Yes?' He looked around at his friends. 'Ride like Sakje!'

Kineas turned to Diodorus. 'Water the horses. Every man to have his remount handy.'

Diodorus saluted. 'Ride like Sakje!' he said with relish.

20

Philokles met them in a grove of willows four hundred stades further east, on the banks of the Polytimeros, which swelled there to be more than a stade wide and flowed just dactyloi deep. The willows were ancient and there were three different altars arrayed beneath the canopy. Darius was asleep under an awning of cloaks held on spears.

Kineas dismounted in the cool shade and they embraced.

'I have seen her,' Philokles said.

Kineas felt the slow flame of hope rekindle in his heart.

'Get your column under cover of the trees and let's talk,' he said. He looked thinner, and beneath his eyes were circles of darkness like a mask of despair.

Eight hundred warriors with ten thousand horses are difficult to hide, but Diodorus and Andronicus and Bain did their best while Kineas drank water and Darius roused himself from sleep. He looked as wrecked as Philokles.

When he was seated, Philokles began.

'We were lucky,' he said. 'And I disobeyed you. I convinced Ataelus to stay with me and let the queen's messenger find his own way home. I took Darius to Alexander's camp. Alexander has so many stragglers since the massacres on the Jaxartes that I walked straight through the sentries without a question.' He shrugged. 'I won't make an epic of it. Darius found the women by posing as a slave. I learned – almost without effort, I must concede – that a column of mercenaries was to march to the relief of Marakanda.'

Darius nodded. 'I learned that Alexander ordered the Amazons to Kandahar. One of them is pregnant and Alexander wants her to deliver among his women. She is to be escorted by the relief column for Marakanda.' He gave Philokles a smile. 'It was as if the gods intended us to know – the Amazons are a three-day wonder in the camp, and there is no security. Tribesmen come and go. Alexander is recruiting

Sogdians, and any barbarian with a bow can ride in through the gates.'

Kineas shook his head. 'This is so much like a miracle that it seems like a trap. How many in the column?'

'Two thousand men. Greek mercenary infantry, and a more polyglot crew of scum you can't imagine. I'd have been decarch in another day. I had to leave before they placed me in command of the whole expedition.' He gave a tired smile. 'Four hundred mercenary cavalry under an officer I don't know.' He shook his head. 'Listen, Kineas, Alexander is mad. Worse, the distrust and the politics of that camp are as bad as anything I've ever seen. It is not so much an army as a collection of factions. The death of Parmenion has cut them hard.'

Kineas nodded. 'He did a lot of the work,' he admitted.

'And a handful of *Hetairoi*, with some mounted Macedonian infantry as prodromoi and a hundred Macedonian cavalry under Andromachus,' Darius said, completing the report. He jerked a thumb at the men in column picketing their horses. 'We can take them.'

Kineas winced. 'Companions?' he asked. His tone reminded them of what a tough proposition a few hundred Companions on wretched played-out horses had been a year before.

Philokles rubbed his beard. 'You are right to be cautious. The Macedonians are dangerous – every one of them is as good as a Spartiate. They've been out here so long that war is the only life they know.' His tone was frankly admiring.

'So much for the philosophy of peace,' Kineas said mockingly.

'I was born a Spartan,' Philokles said with slow dignity. 'Philosophy was learned later.'

'Yet you think we can take them.' Kineas started to ease himself out of his breastplate.

Philokles stood. 'Right here,' he said. 'They'll be here in two days. I sat in the command tent and listened to Cleitus tell Pharnuches, their commander, his march route. I sent Ataelus north and waited until the column marched. There's not another crossing this easy for a hundred stades.'

Darius chuckled. 'We even marched with the column,'

he said. 'The Amazons have a cavalry escort – a dozen of Hephaestion's own Companions.'

'He commands the Companions now,' Philokles put in, as Diodorus came up with the other officers.

'Who does?' Diodorus asked. His armour was off, and he took a helmet full of muddy water from Ataelus and poured it over his head. 'Damn, that's good.'

Ataelus grinned. 'For sick making – too much water,' he said.

'Hephaestion commands the Companions,' Philokles said.

'Fucking catamite,' Diodorus said. 'Alexander must be hard up for cavalrymen.'

Philokles shrugged, and Darius flushed. Diodorus raised his hands to mollify them. 'Well, he is a catamite. He manipulates Alexander – always has. Hephaestion couldn't command a squadron of cavalry in a religious parade.'

Philokles raised an eyebrow at Diodorus. The two men fell silent and something passed between them. Philokles rolled his shoulders, as if he had been carrying weights and they had finally been put aside. 'Have it as you will – you two know these people better than I. But the troopers guarding Srayanka are the best of the best. They're right in the centre of the column.'

Kineas nodded. 'Then that's where the blow needs to fall,' he said.

He put out pickets, a few of the Sakje riding as much as fifty stades south and east, and then he and his selected officers rode the banks of the river for twenty stades north and south, but Philokles' ambush site was the best. To the north of the island of willows was another island covered in poplar, and to the south was a third island covered in rose bushes and tamarisk. More tamarisk grew in a shield-shaped tangle to the north and east along the bank and spreading away south, blocking the line of sight of the approaching force.

That night, he gathered all the officers down to the lowliest file leader and drew a map in the sand. He oriented them on the island of willows where they stood.

'Here is the river,' he said, showing the course of the

Polytimeros. 'Here is the trade road they will come up. The trees from the spring banks shade the road and offer cover.' He allowed the tip of his stick to follow the road. 'Just south of here is a stand – really a thicket – of tamarisk and poplar. The road winds between the trees and the river.' Kineas indicated the riverbank and the current river bed. 'The battlefield will be shaped like a diamond. They enter the diamond here, when they begin to pass between the woods and the river. Their scouts will not find Temerix in the tamarisk trees,' (a ripple of laughter for the pun), 'and will pass down the road. If any of them are really professional, they'll ride right around the trees to the south. If so, we can forget them. The bulk of the column will enter the defile here,' he indicated the top of the diamond, 'and march along the road. There will be eight hundred of them in the front division and they'll cover two stades of road. When the head of the column is ready to cross the Polytimeros *here*,' and he indicated the island of willows where they stood, 'the middle of the column will be passing Temerix. Understand?' He received a chorus of nods and grunts. 'I'll show you in the morning, in any case. Unless some hothead screws it up, the column will keep marching across the Polytimeros. The infantry in the first division will either cross and keep marching, if they're idiots, or they'll cross and form in battle order to cover the second division, if they're acting like soldiers.'

Eumenes, translating at his side, paused. Kineas understood him to be explaining to the Sakje why the Greek mercenaries would form a battle line on the other side. Kineas waited for him to finish. The Sakje nodded and pursed their lips in approval of such a professional move – the assumption that every river crossing was an ambush impressed them.

'The Sakje squadron will be behind the island of poplars here,' he said. They'd be well down the river bed, hidden by the next island to the north and by the habit of scouts to get across watercourses as quickly as possible. The notion that the watercourse was itself a highway *might* not occur to them. Even if it did, few of them would ride two stades off the line of march to check out an island.

He hoped.

'When the signal is given, the Sakje show themselves and attack the rear of the first division. Harass them, shower them with arrows, but do not close. All I require is that the first division be unable to fall back to support the second division.'

Bain agreed, but the gleam in his eye told another story. Kineas resolved to send Eumenes to keep him in check.

'The Olbian cavalry will be here.' Kineas indicated the base of the woods, just a stade from the crossing. 'The woods will screen us until it is too late. If they see us early,' Kineas shrugged, 'we fight it out. But if they don't see us, we charge straight for the prisoner escort. If they run back along the road, they're meat for Temerix. If they flee into the river, we'll hunt them down. Remember that Srayanka and Urvara are waiting. Pray for some luck.' He paused. 'At the same time, Temerix starts punching arrows into the second division. They either counter-attack into the thorns or they flee down the sides of the watercourse into the stream bed.' Kineas pointed at the far side of the diamond. 'The Sauromatae knights are here, behind the island of roses. If the Macedonians come down into the river, the Sauromatae deal with them. Again,' and here Kineas turned to Lot, 'we are *not* here to fight a battle. We are here to get Srayanka and Urvara. Kill some Macedonians if you can, but listen for the second trumpet.' He looked around them, Sakje and Olbians and swarthy Temerix, again in the position of maximum danger. 'When the second trumpet sounds, you break like a cloud of swallows fleeing a hawk on the plains and vanish like morning mist. We rally at the last camp on the Oxus. Unless we fuck up massively, there will be no pursuit because they don't have the horses to follow us across the plain. Right?'

Nods and grunts.

'Sounds beautiful,' said Diodorus. He was grinning. 'What do you think will really happen?'

Kineas couldn't help but grin back, because the dream of the thunderbolt was still with him, and because the power to see Srayanka and hold her in his arms again lay in his own hands, and he was not a boy. 'It will all go to shit and we'll fight our way through it,' he said. 'Look, friends. If all else fails, cut your way to the middle of the column and get the girls. Unless the gods are against us, they'll get free of the escort on their own.'

Philokles leaned in. 'Srayanka is heavily pregnant,' he said. He looked around with the embarrassment most men kept for discussions of sex and women's matters. 'I may have forgotten to mention this.'

A thunderbolt. Kineas looked at his friend with his mouth gaping like a landed fish.

Philokles cocked his head to one side. 'I did forget to mention it,' he said. 'She told Darius that if she weren't so heavy, they'd all have ridden free weeks ago. They may not be able to escape on their own.'

Kineas took a deep breath – he had known, in a vague way, that she was pregnant. This was more real. He felt a blow in his gut and the sudden pierce of anxiety like an arrow in his side. But he thought of Phocion and refused to bow to fate.

'Cut your way to the middle of their column. Get the women. And then run like fire on the plain.' He pointed at Temerix. 'As soon as they try for you, you run down the trails you've cut and out of the back of the woods – right past us and on to your ponies. Understand?'

Temerix never smiled. He gave a curt nod, like a man given unnecessary and patronizing instructions.

'Hey!' Ataelus said. He rattled off some rapid Sakje to the chiefs, and they all grinned together. He turned back to Kineas. 'If the wind for us, give them fire in the faces.'

Kineas pursed his lips and nodded. 'Yes,' he agreed.

In the morning, he led them on a ride around the invisible boundaries of his diamond until every man understood his orders. At nightfall, Samahe came to tell him that the Macedonian column was camped eighty stades up the Polytimeros.

That night, he dreamed again of the thunderbolt in his hand and Ataelus awakened him before the sun with a report from the outer pickets. The Macedonians were moving.

*

It was difficult to hide eight hundred men. Teams of Sindi brushed the main road clear of tracks while the little army set itself in its positions. Men hurried unnecessarily and were injured. A horse fell down the spring bank of the river and had to be killed, and the process of butchering and disposing of the horse took so long that Kineas was close to screaming with frustration.

Even after a hundred helmets full of water, the place where the horse had died was a mass of blood and flies.

Kineas clamped down. 'Leave it,' he said, his teeth clenched, glaring at the miserable Sakje rider who had caused the disaster. 'To your places.'

Kineas was mounted on Thalassa. It was the mare's first time in combat, and she stood tall and firm as Kineas mounted. She snorted, raised her head and then settled herself.

'You are quite a horse,' Kineas said. He clucked his mare into motion and played with the catch on his breastplate. A fine piece of work last spring, the piece of armour had taken so many blows that it was misshapen, and the shoulder catch no longer seated firmly in the back plate. When it popped, the two moving plates rubbed his shoulder raw. He determined to get a new one.

Where in Hades would he find a new Greek breastplate here, on the edge of the world? *On the corpse of a Macedonian, of course.* Except that he couldn't see this fight leaving him time to strip a corpse.

Thalassa fidgeted. Diodorus had all the Olbian cavalry in place behind the thickets, and four of Temerix's Sindi were sweeping their back trail. One of them had a wicker case strapped to his back. They'd caught a young hawk and they'd release her to signal that the enemy was in sight – an old Sindi trick, so he was told.

In the river bed, clouds of flies plundered the rocks where the horse had been butchered and the sound carried up and down the river bed like a manifestation of some evil god. Otherwise, there was silence, punctuated by horse noises – bits on teeth, cropping grass, reins creaking or snapping, gentle whickers and snuffles – and horse smells. The gelding behind Kineas defecated and the clod fell to earth with a heavy plop.

Kineas had waited in a few cavalry ambushes. This one was too large. The sheer number of men and horses involved raised the likelihood of discovery. He tried to decide what he would do when they were discovered. Sweat ran down his face and neck and down the hollow of his back where armour and tunic didn't quite meet.

To be so close to Srayanka without saving her – he banished that thought.

But when he glanced over his shoulder, he couldn't make himself think of sacrificing his friends to rescue his wife.

He farted, long and low, and the men around him laughed. His hands clenched and unclenched on his reins, and he began to tap his whip against his thigh.

Diodorus came up beside him. 'We should dismount,' he said quietly. 'We'll tire our horses.'

Kineas bit back a retort. 'Yes,' he said, and suited the action to the word. Thalassa grunted as he slipped off her back. Philokles tied his horse to a flowering bush with shiny leaves and lay down, as if to sleep.

Kineas hated him for the ease with which he went to sleep.

Dismounted, he could see nothing but three hundred horses and their riders and a wall of poplar trees. I should have arranged my position with a clear view of the enemy's approach, he thought. His knees were weak. He looked at the sun, which hadn't moved a finger's span against the branch he had chosen as a marker.

He glanced around at Diodorus. He was flushed and fingering the edge of his machaira. When their eyes met, Diodorus walked his horse to where Kineas stood.

'I feel like a virgin looking at his first girl,' Diodorus said.

Philokles stood up from his nap. 'The Olympic Games will be next year,' he said, as if this was news. 'I imagine the athletes have already left their homes for the games at Eleusis.'

Kineas looked around, mystified. 'That was two weeks ago,' he said.

'Hmm.' Philokles looked around, as if noticing all of the cavalry for the first time. 'They go to win immortal glory in the striving of peace. All we're going to do is rescue some barbarian woman from Alexander. Why are you two on edge?' He grinned. 'You have chosen an excellent site for an ambush and arranged your troops. All else is with the gods.'

Diodorus put his sword back in its sheath. 'Sure. Fucking Spartan.'

Kineas took a steadying breath. 'We take a great risk here,' he began, and Philokles smiled.

'Friends,' he said, holding up his hand – and the hand shook. 'I merely hide my fears better,' he said.

Kineas performed a quick calculation. 'I am in the grip of blind fear,' he said. 'We must have at least an hour. I am as stupid as the boy who let his horse roll down the riverbank. I should go and see to my men.' He dusted his hands.

Then he went from man to man throughout the Olbians, clasping hands with every man and saying a few words. He teased, he mocked, he complimented, and behind him, three hundred Greeks and Keltoi and assorted professional cavalrymen breathed easier and smiled. As he moved among them, a breeze came up like the caress of a friendly goddess.

Kineas too breathed easier. It took him an hour to circle his troops, constantly on the lookout for the appearance of Ataelus or the sight of a bird rising over the woods in front of him. It kept him busy and he only thought of Srayanka fifty times.

When he came back, Philokles was making water against a stone and Diodorus was staring at the line of tamarisk trees as if he could bore a hole through them with his eyes. Kineas made a show of fastidiously avoiding the Spartan's rock, and then he lay down in the shade of a silver-leafed poplar and pulled his broad straw hat over his eyes.

His stomach roiled and he could feel all of his stress pushing at his colon. His feet felt as if worms were crawling over them and his hands shook.

'He's over it,' Diodorus said with irritation. 'Now he'll take a nap.'

Kineas smiled under his straw hat. Over it, he thought. Despite the growing heat, he was chilled to the bone. *Over it.*

Ambushes are different. In a field action, the commander – and the trooper – can watch the enemy deploy, can track the enemy's countless errors and take comfort, can lose himself in preparation, giving orders or taking them.

In an ambush, he can only wait and the only two options are victory or disaster. No one will stay safely in reserve. No one is likely to escape from the grip of war.

Sakje and Olbian and Sauromatae, most of them were in the grip of fear and panic, and the trees and bushes moved with the quivering of men.

Still, all things considered, they were better off than the Macedonian column.

It was closer to noon than to morning when the hawk burst into the air over the thorn wood to their front, her flight so loud in all the silence that men who had achieved some sort of uneasy sleep were startled awake, all their fears returned.

'Drink water, and mount!' Kineas said in a fierce whisper. The whisper was passed back. Horses whickered despite the best efforts of their riders, and for a minute, the Olbians made as much noise as a bacchanal. Kineas glared at them, a vein throbbing at his temple, but it couldn't be helped.

'We're fucking doomed,' he said to Philokles.

The Spartan shrugged and drank water from a gourd. 'Marching men hear nothing,' he said. 'And "We're fucking doomed" is not a statement to inspire confidence in a commander.'

'Teach that in Sparta, do they?' Diodorus asked. 'Oh, for the benefits of your education, Philokles.'

'Shut up, both of you.' Kineas pushed forward to the very edge of the trees. He handed Philokles his reins and waved at Diodorus. 'Let's go.'

'You know how to hold a horse, right?' Diodorus asked the Spartan.

'If I forget, I'll just run in circles flapping my arms and

286

screaming at the top of my voice until you Athenians come and rescue me,' he replied in a harsh whisper.

Kineas belly-crawled forward under the branches of the poplar, his forearms abraded by rose stems. He pushed forward until he could just see over a low ridge of earth. His line of sight was limited to the ford, the island of willows and the far side of the spring banks.

'Philokles is better,' Diodorus said, and Kineas glared him to silence.

The damned hawk was now circling the tamarisk wood, screaming her head off. 'Remind me of this the next time the Sindi have an old trick,' Kineas said.

Diodorus gave him a sharp nudge. The head of the Macedonian column was emerging from the gap between the spring bank and the tamarisk wood. Either they were moving very fast or the thrice-cursed bird had been released late.

There was an advance guard of Macedonian infantrymen mounted on nags. They had javelins instead of their pikes, but their corslets and short, guardless helmets marked them. Their horses were moving carefully, clearly tired. Even as he watched, the scouts' horses became restless with the discovery that there was water and they began to neigh.

A man rode up the gentle slope from the ford towards the Olbian ambush. He was humming to himself and looking at the ground with professional curiosity. Another flanker joined him. Behind the two scouts, the rest of the advance guard passed, riding quickly, and turned due north to cross the ford, heading for Marakanda. Men fought to keep their horses from drinking and suddenly the advance guard was thrown into confusion. Orders were shouted and any man who stopped lost control of his horse as it started to drink.

'More fucking Dahae?' asked the first scout. He was pointing at something in the dust.

'Somebody butchered a horse in the stream bed,' said the other scout. 'I don't like it. If they passed that close to us, we should see their dust.' He looked up, his eyes searching the very ground where Kineas and Diodorus lay. 'Fu-uck,' he said, his thick Macedonian accent and his Illyrian hill drawl exaggerated by fear. 'Unless they're right here!'

The first man struck him lightly. 'Get a grip,' he said.

The second man shook his head. 'Fuck yourself, whoreson puppy. Look at those prints – erased. No dust cloud. Dead horse.'

Behind them, the last of the advance guard turned and headed across the ford, the horses complaining. The last of their horses splashed into the shallow brown water and the smell of mud carried back to the two men lying in the briars.

'Pharnuches is a useless fucking cunt,' the first scout said. His voice had a hard edge of fear now, too. 'Even if you're right—'

The second rider turned and dashed for the trade road. Behind him, a full squadron of mercenary cavalry rode down the defile, two by two, moving fast. The men had their helmets on and their armour and they were looking to the left and to the right. Their horses were just as eager for water as the last unit's.

'Cavalry is in *front*,' Diodorus whispered.

Kineas grunted in reply, his voice now covered by the trotting cavalry. That meant that the infantry would be in the second division – almost immune to Temerix's arrows, if they had their armour on.

Nothing he could do about it now.

A large group of riders halted in a tangle at the edge of the ford with the two scouts shouting at them.

'Hetairoi,' Kineas said. He began pushing himself backwards as fast as he could.

Five Royal Companions in dun-coloured cloaks and white tunics with heavy armour, a richly dressed man in a purple and yellow cloak and a breastplate, and another in a red cloak. Three women in Sakje dress on good horses, one bent over her saddle, face grey with effort – Srayanka – and another, clearly Urvara, flirting with the Royal Companions. Diodorus crawled backwards.

'Doesn't matter!' Kineas said. He was, in his nerves, answering his own question, unvoiced. It no longer mattered if the ambush was discovered.

As if on cue, he heard the shrieking cry of Bain's elite Sakje, and the ground shook with their hooves. Kineas threw himself up on to his tall charger. He glanced back. They were all there.

'Walk!' he ordered, and they started forward without Andronicus's trumpet. They were in a tight column of fours – that's what they had cut a path to fit, the path that the scouts had no doubt noticed. He had traded rapid deployment for perfect concealment. As soon as his horse emerged from the gap into the clear ground just south of the ford, he called, 'Form front!' and the column began to knit itself into a rhomboid behind him as the head continued to ride forward at a walk.

He turned his head in time to see Bain's Sakje loose a flight of arrows into the mercenary cavalry. They were caught facing the wrong way, with many of their horses head-down in the water, drinking deeply, and their horses suffered terribly in the first volley, their unarmoured rumps feathered like hedgehogs. Two dozen horses went down and the Mercenary cavalry behind dissolved into chaos as the Sakje galloped past along the river bed. Now every warrior shot for himself and some rode ridiculously close. Bain himself, wearing the transverse plume of a long-dead Macedonian officer, leaned so close to an armoured officer waving a sickle-bladed *kopis* that it seemed that his arrowhead brushed the man's cloak before he loosed with a whoop that sounded across two stades and hundreds of men.

Kineas took in Bain's attack in a glance. He pulled his helmet's cheek plates down on his head and fastened the chinstrap. The enemy's command group was now cut off from their cavalry. The thing could be done.

The command group and the Hetairoi had not failed to note that hundreds of well-trained cavalry were emerging from their flank. Their commander in the purple cloak gesticulated, turned and yelled.

Kineas's men were less than a stade away. Srayanka appeared injured – he could see something terribly wrong in her body language. He raised his right fist holding a javelin. 'Trot!' he shouted.

Urvara ripped a Macedonian kopis from the scabbard of one of the Royal Companions. She removed one of his hands on the back cut and reared her horse. Behind her, a second Hetairoi trooper drew his sword and moved to execute Srayanka. Hirene, Srayanka's trumpeter, her grey braids flying, tackled the Macedonian, wrapping her arms around him to pin them. They fell to the ground together and vanished in the rising dust.

Srayanka, free, cut at a third Royal Companion with her riding whip, whirled her horse and rode for the willow trees on the island. The command group was in turmoil – Urvara cut at a second man, her blow sheering through the layers of leather on his corslet and drawing blood.

Macedonian contempt for women was costing them heavily.

'Charge!' Kineas roared. His horse flew like Pegasus over the gravel and sand.

The general's bodyguards were both brave and skilled. They formed well, even as Urvara's brilliant riding and frenzied sword cuts were bringing chaos to their rear ranks, and they launched themselves – all fifty of them – in a counter-charge. But the front rank had only ten strides to gain momentum and Kineas's Olbians had the whole gentle slope behind them and half a stade at the gallop, and they threw the bodyguard flat at the impact, their horses smashing chest to chest with the Macedonian chargers like warships using their rams, bearing them over. Kineas didn't throw his javelin – he used it to parry the *xyston* of a Companion and got himself a painful thrust at his badly protected left shoulder from a lance as he closed, but Thalassa did the work and his first two opponents didn't stay upright to face him. Only when the mare's momentum was spent climbing the shale on to the willow island did he have to fight hand to hand. A Royal Companion, his helmet gone, stood his ground on a heavy gelding and struck out hard with his long xyston, rising and thrusting two-handed. Kineas parried and got his helmet under the point and let his charger carry him in. Close up, belly to belly, the two horses reared, their hooves milling. Kineas caught his own spear up in two hands, left hand near the head and right hand on the butt, and thrust, his point ripping at the man's arms, cutting his reins, punching in over the top of his bronze breastplate and into his throat.

And then another man, with a red cloak. Kineas tried to sweep him out of the saddle with the haft of his spear and the man cut the shaft in two with a powerful sword cut. Kineas leaned out to avoid the man's back swing and Thalassa backed away. Kineas got his Egyptian machaira clear of the scabbard in the pause and then the two men closed, their horses whirling around each other like fighting dogs. Red Cloak was no master swordsman, but he was strong as an ox, heavy, tough, well armoured, and even when Kineas landed a heavy blow on the point of his shoulder, the man only grunted. He had a short dagger in his off hand now, and he leaned in close and punched the dagger at Kineas's midriff, but Kineas's bronze corslet turned the stroke. Kineas cut again, a high feint that he turned into an attack, using the man's strong parry against him and reversing his cut so that the Egyptian sword went in under the man's sword arm, but Red Cloak's corslet held. Thalassa was backing away, Kineas's eyes were full of sweat and he ducked his head and launched a flurry of blows. Red Cloak took a cut high on his arm and then cut back hard, and Kineas's parry wasn't strong enough to stop the blow from shearing his plume and ripping the helmet free against the chinstrap, snapping Kineas's head back. He saw white, and again Thalassa saved his life. He felt his mount rise up and thrust with her legs. As the horse fell forward on to its front feet, Kineas's vision cleared and he parried high, and the two blades locked, the hard edge of the Egyptian sword biting into the soft iron of the Macedonian kopis's forte, and the two riders came together. The bigger man tried to grapple with his dagger coming in at Kineas's thighs, and Kineas ripped his whip from his sash and slashed the man's reaching arm left-handed and was rewarded with a grunt of pain, and then both horses tumbled together and righted themselves with scrambles and kicks that pushed them apart. Kineas was past Red Cloak, free of the mêlée. He looked back and Diodorus was thrusting at the big man repeatedly with a javelin, keeping him at arm's length. Red Cloak was yelling in Macedonian Greek for some help.

Kineas turned Thalassa with just his knees, intending to finish Red Cloak. He wiped at his eyes with the back of his unarmoured arm, feeling the pain in his left shoulder for the first time, and came face to face with Purple Cloak, who had only a short sword and was fully engaged with Urvara. She threw Kineas a look – exasperation or desperation – and Kineas rode into the enemy general's flank, tipping him to the ground without a blow, where Carlus finished him with a spear thrust. Legs locked on Thalassa's barrel, Kineas found himself in a knot of desperate Macedonians in dust-coloured cloaks, probably Purple Cloak's bodyguard. He cut right and left, took another blow on his left shoulder that cut the leather straps on his armour and kneed his charger into a run, bursting through the enemy and into the clear, blind with pain. He grabbed for his lost reins, missed them, but Thalassa turned under him like an equine acrobat, wheeling so sharply that Kineas almost lost his seat. The three bodyguards were locked with Carlus and Sitalkes. Kineas could see the blue plume on Diodorus's helmet beyond Carlus's giant form. He leaned forward on his mare's neck, gasped a gulp of air and glanced at his left shoulder, which appeared uninjured despite the pain. Then he tapped Thalassa's barrel with his heels and the horse responded with another powerful lunge forward, so that he crashed full into Sitalkes' opponent, knocking the man's horse back and losing the enemy rider his seat. Sitalkes put the man down with brutal economy while Kineas engaged his other opponent, trapping his sword in a high parry, cutting his bridle hand with a circular overhead feint and then killing him with a blow to the neck.

He had been riding for almost a minute with only his knees, his charger responding magnificently, but now Kineas reached again for the dangling reins, looking right and left, exhausted by the intensity and the exertion. His breath came in wracking heaves and his knees threatened to lose their grip on his mount. His right wrist barely responded.

Diodorus smacked Red Cloak in the side of his helmeted head with the full swing of his cornel-wood javelin, and the man went down, unconscious or dead. Diodorus immediately began bellowing for the Olbians to rally. Eumenes met Kineas's eyes – he'd downed his man and was also looking around. In the river bed, the big Keltoi on their heavy chargers had blasted the rest of the bodyguard to shreds and were cleaning up. Carlus was already off his horse, stripping the corpses of his victims. Sitalkes gave Kineas a satisfied smile – not bloodlust, but pleasure at being alive.

The shattering noise of the mêlée died suddenly to horse sounds and human agony.

Diodorus was everywhere, rallying his men and watching the battle. Kineas let him do it. He was riding for Srayanka.

To the north, Bain's riders were pressing closer to the beleaguered mercenaries and the Macedonian mounted infantry, firing as they went. The whole fight had become a dust cloud and a cacophony of noise. Horses were dying with screams of anguish. To the south, something had happened – Kineas couldn't see any fighting at all, but neither was there any sign of the mercenary infantry. To the east there was a battle haze rising – someone was engaged with the Sauromatae in the river bed.

All of it could wait while he greeted her. She was off her horse, standing against one of the ancient altars.

'Srayanka,' he said.

She shook her head. 'I feel as if I'm going to die,' she said, so very much herself that Kineas had to smile despite her words. He started to dismount, leaving Thalassa to crop grass in the middle of a battle.

'Fight your battle!' she said through gritted teeth. And then she gave a cry, somewhere between grunt and scream.

'You—' he said, and took her in his arms.

'Bah,' she murmured into his cloak. 'You're covered in blood.' But she smiled.

Behind him, Andronicus called to him. He turned to see Andronicus and beyond him he saw Ataelus coming from the west, riding flat out.

'Look!' yelled Eumenes. He was pointing west, beyond Ataelus. Kineas turned.

There was a dust cloud – a huge cloud that rose like an avenging god over the plains. It was large enough to be another army, and that army was close.

'Athena guard us!' Kineas prayed, reaching for his helmet and finding it gone. A random arrow fell close. 'Rally the Olbians!'

Diodorus had the task in hand. Philokles ran up leading his horse. He, too, began to call for the Olbians to rally. Antigonus surfaced from a knot of Keltoi and began to beat them into column.

'Rhomboid!' Kineas yelled to Diodorus.

Ataelus rode down into the ford and his horse's hooves raised a crystal spray from the red-brown water. His face was a mask of panic. Time slowed. Kineas had time to release Srayanka so that she slumped by the altar.

Urvara seized his hand and broke the spell. 'She's *karsanth*!' The Sakje woman wheeled her horse and pointed at Srayanka. '*Karsanth!* Do you understand?'

Kineas didn't understand, and Ataelus was there, and time was speeding along. 'Big column – ten and ten, a hundred times – more! For coming here!' He gesticulated wildly.

Kineas took a deep breath, the scent of honeysuckle and copper blood mixing like a drug in his nose. Karsanth? Poisoned? 'Who?' he asked Ataelus. 'Macedonian?'

Ataelus shook his head. 'Big and fast,' he said. 'For waiting too long,' he said with bitter self-recrimination.

'What is karsanth?' Kineas asked Ataelus and Eumenes.

They looked at each other while Urvara shook her head. '*Karsanth! Karsanth! How stupid are you?*' She was as frustrated with herself as with him.

Bain's Sakje were out of the river bed now, up on the bank of the river in the sand and gravel, riding in a tight ring around the crumbling wreck of two hundred Macedonians and mercenary cavalry. Even as he watched, Bain waved his bow and his trumpeter blew a long, complex call, almost like a paean, and the Sakje turned inward as one and fell on the Macedonians hidden in the dust cloud. Except that the Macedonians weren't considered the best cavalry in the world for nothing, and even shot to pieces by archery they couldn't answer, they hadn't lost their will to fight. In the few heartbeats Kineas watched, he saw Bain die on a lance.

'Giving birth!' Eumenes shouted. 'She's giving birth! She's in labour!' The young man wheeled his horse and looked at her. She was crouched by the altar, unable to move, her face a rictus of pain.

Kineas looked back at the dust cloud, and over at his love, and before he even knew what he was going to say, his arm came up. He turned to Diodorus. 'Take the Olbians – straight up the side and over the Companions. Wipe them out. Take the casualties – we need a *clear retreat*. You have to build the road. Do you understand?'

Diodorus slammed his sword hand into his breastplate in salute. His face was set. 'I absolutely understand, Strategos.'

'Carry on!' Kineas turned to Andronicus. 'As soon as you hit the Macedonians,' he said, 'sound the retreat. Sound it over and over. Understand?'

The big Gaul nodded.

Finally, Kineas rode to Srayanka. She had her forehead on the altar, and her whole body spasmed. Urvara rode up next to him and her look at Kineas begged him to *do* something.

Kineas reached down as Srayanka began to recover from her contraction. Their eyes met, and then their hands, and he reached to pull her across his saddle.

'Do *not* mistake me for some weakling!' she said. 'I will ride! I am the Lady Srayanka, not some Greek camp follower!'

'We must ride,' he said patiently. Behind him, his ambush was coming apart, and men were dying.

She bit her lip and narrowed her eyes. 'So be it,' she said. With bitter practicality, she said, 'Get me on my horse.'

Kineas and Urvara managed it. She was not light, but they were strong, and behind them, the battle exploded into life.

Two hundred paces distant, the Olbian rhomboid crashed into the fight between the Sakje and the Companions. The Macedonians were brave and skilled, but they had neither the weight nor the numbers to stop the Olbians. The crash of the Olbian onset was like a hundred maniac cooks beating on copper cauldrons and it carried over the whole battlefield.

Srayanka had a Macedonian horse – a beauty, but not heavy enough for war. Kineas reached for her reins and she stopped him with a look.

'I have not come all this way to lose you in a cavalry fight,' he said.

'I have not lived all my life on the back of a horse just to fall off when I'm pregnant,' she answered. She smiled at him, but the edges of her lips were white.

Thalassa bore fatigue without any apparent change of gait. She went up the steep side of the ford in two bounds, and then Urvara was beside him, with Srayanka a stride behind. Andronicus's trumpet rang out, three clear notes, and then again – the retreat.

Kineas reined in at the edge of the battle haze and risked a glance back. The new dust cloud was closer. To the south and east, Temerix's men were already mounted on their ponies, jogging steadily across the last flat ground to the ford.

From the vantage point of a tall horse at the top of the riverbank, Kineas could now see the Sauromatae. Their bronze scale armour glinted in another battle cloud, half a stade east along the river bed. Somehow, the Greek infantry, the mercenaries, had moved into the stream bed.

Kineas shook his head, because this was all taking time and time was something he didn't think they had, but even as he watched, Lot rode clear of the war haze, looking for the sound of the trumpet. Kineas made a sweeping gesture with his arm, pointing north and west. Lot pulled his helmet off and waved it, then gave a broad nod to signal assent. He was still refastening his helmet when he went back into the cloud.

An arrow whistled out of the trees on the far bank and plucked one of Temerix's psiloi from his pony. The man screamed and then Temerix dismounted, waving his men into formation on the surer footing of the island. He already had the golden bow in his fist, and he nocked and drew in one smooth motion. His first arrow brought an answering scream of pain from the poplar trees along the far bank.

Kineas turned to Eumenes and Urvara. 'Gather up the Sakje. Rally them and cover the flight of the Sindi.' He looked down at Philokles. 'Are you walking for a reason?'

'I fell off,' the Spartan said.

Kineas might have grinned, except for the situation. 'Then run back to Temerix and tell him to stop playing rearguard and get his arse across. And then come back. No heroics – we are *not lingering*.'

Philokles saluted – the first time Kineas had ever seen him salute.

Srayanka reached out and took his hand in hers. Her nails dug into his bare forearms and she grunted. Sweat was pouring off her. Kineas tried to steady her.

Ataelus was watching the fight in the ford. 'Spitamenes,' he said, as if he was pronouncing a sentence of death. 'For fucking Persians.'

Kineas looked over his shoulder. Temerix had his Sindi formed in an open line and they raised their bows together and loosed a volley that rose high and fell beyond the brush at the edge of the spring bank. Screams erupted and then a group of Iranian cavalry came through the trees and straight down the bank, riding like Sakje.

'Athena stand with us,' Kineas said. There were a hundred or more Medes. More like two hundred.

Kineas looked behind him. Eumenes had maybe twenty Sakje in a clump. If the Persians came up the bank and into the rear of the Olbians, it would be over. The Olbians would never recover.

Bad luck. He was so close to pulling this off.

Temerix called another order, and his archers formed closer, a pitifully small wall at the edge of the island, but they had a three-foot-high bank to defend. They loosed again and their arrows slammed into the front of the Median charge, and wounded horses reared, tangling the charge in their fall, while others baulked the jump to the island. Philokles arrived, running hard, and he roared at Temerix, who ignored him. The Sindi chief slung his bow and took up his axe.

Eumenes had thirty riders and Urvara had another ten.

'I'm sorry, my love,' Kineas said. He was the only voice they would all obey, and there was no one with whom he could leave her. He reached up to pull his cheek plate down and again found it gone.

'Sakje! Come and feast!' Srayanka sang at his side, and her clear voice carried where a man's voice might have been lost. She reached out and pulled his long knife from the scabbard at his waist.

More riders emerged from the battle haze behind her. She sang again, and every Sakje in earshot was grinning.

Kineas filled his lungs, judging the time as one more rider joined Urvara. 'Follow me!' he shouted. He pointed his sword down the riverbank, and they started to move up behind him. He turned his head and saw Sitalkes, Darius and Carlus range themselves around Srayanka.

The Persian charge slammed into the Sindi. Axes swung against Persian swords, and Philokles bellowed and his heavy spear went through a Persian's breastplate, tearing the man from his horse. His war cry sounded over the cacophony of battle like the cry of a hunting cat over the burble of a stream, and it froze the blood of more than one enemy.

The Sakje counter-charge seemed small and badly organized, but the Sakje weren't Greeks – they didn't require serried ranks to fight effectively. Instead of charging the Persian cavalry, the two groups slipped off to the left and right, every man and maid bent low, shooting hard. The Medes flinched away, fearing for their flanks, and suddenly robbed of their attempt to wrap around the Sindi, they halted and began to shoot. It was a natural decision for Asiatic cavalry, but it cost them the action.

Kineas felt like an idiot for risking himself – and Srayanka. Ataelus, at his shoulder, was rising and shooting, rising again, methodically pumping arrows into the Persians who were tangled with Temerix's men. It was too late to halt, too late to swerve, so Kineas allowed Thalassa to push up the bank on to the island of willows. He was sword to javelin with a Persian veteran. He parried the spearhead and the man tried to use the haft to sweep him off his horse's back. Kineas dropped the reins again, grabbed the haft and cut repeatedly at the man's fingers, but his head burst in a spray of bone and blood and worse as Carlus struck him with a long-handled axe from the other side. An arrow hit Kineas in his breastplate like the kick of a mule on his right side, and he saw Srayanka's face, streaked with pain and battle joy, red and white with exertion. She shrieked something that was lost in the battle, and the Medes answered a trumpet signal and flowed away – not broken, just not interested in further losses. The Sindi rose to their feet – aside from a handful, most had simply lain flat and waited for the Medes to ride away – and scrambled for the ponies who were dispersed over half a stade of island.

'What are you doing here?' Philokles roared at Kineas. Simultaneously, a tight knot of Medes, lost or desperate, punched through the Sindi and came at Kineas.

The great royal charger leaped from a dead halt to a gallop in three strides, her heavy hooves crashing against the rocky island. Kineas had his last opponent's spear and he whirled it end over end and thrust hard at the first rider, a man with a copper beard, and in a moment of fear-induced clarity Kineas wondered if he had fought this man before, at Issus or at Arbela. And then his spear went over the man's parry and under his burnoose and the man flipped back over the rump of his horse, all his sinews loosed, and Thalassa went right through the knot of Medes as two weak blows rang on Kineas's back plate. And then young Darius was there, yelling insults in Persian, his sword dripping blood on to his hand when he raised it over his head, and Philokles was standing over a dead Mede and the survivors rode across the island and vanished west. One of the men fleeing was tall with an excellent horse and gold embroidery on his scarlet cloak, and he was clutching his side.

Srayanka sat on her horse. She had his knife in her right hand, and there was blood on it, and she waved it at the retreating Medes. 'Come back and fight, Spitamenes!' she screeched. She was laughing, with tears streaming from her face, and then her arms dropped and she screamed like a dying mare, a war cry or a scream of pain – or both.

'Ares and Aphrodite,' Kineas said, for the first time in his life praying to both instead of cursing. 'Now, run!'

Temerix's men needed no second urging, regardless of the death wish of their captain. On the north bank, the Medes were forming again, wary now, and pointing downstream where the Sauromatae were vanishing into their own dust cloud.

On the south bank, Diodorus and Andronicus had the Olbians in hand, or close to it, and the bank was lined with horsemen as the Sindi scrambled back. Side by side with Temerix and Philokles, Kineas and Srayanka crested the south bank together.

Diodorus was in front of the reordered Olbians. The rear ranks were sketchy and their horses were blown, but the Olbians were ready to charge again.

'You're an idiot!' Diodorus said cheerily. 'Khaire, Srayanka.'

'You hold here until the Sauromatae are away. Then you. Sakje last under Eumenes and Urvara.' Kineas thought they were going to live – he could feel the loosening in his bowels and the daimon of combat winging away, leaving only bone-ache and heart-ache. But he'd seen the Medes flee – they weren't interested in taking casualties to beat up his rearguard.

'I will command the Sakje,' Srayanka said, her chin high. 'Eumenes and Urvara may assist me.'

Kineas saluted her with a bloody javelin. 'Welcome back, Lady of the Cruel Hands,' he said in Sakje. They were cheering her, Olbian and Sakje together, a roar that must have sounded like a taunt to the Medes across the river. Srayanka raised her knife and the shouts came again.

Kineas felt the wind in his hair as he looked around for Ataelus. The man was stripping Bain's corpse, taking his arrows. Everywhere, Sakje and Sauromatae were stripping the corpses of the fallen.

'Ataelus! Light the fires!' Kineas called.

Ataelus nodded and one of his scouts galloped off into the dust.

Samahe came up from the stream bed, her *gorytos* empty. She reined in next to Thalassa and handed Kineas his helmet, the blue plume of horsehair severed and the plume-box that held it smashed flat.

'Thanks!' he said, slapping her back. She grinned wordlessly and turned away. Kineas wrestled with his helmet, which was deformed and wouldn't go over his head. He tried to bend it between his hands while he watched the Persians, but the bronze was too tough and he couldn't get it back into shape. He tied the chinstrap and slipped it over his sword hilt.

'They're getting ready to have a go at us,' Darius said at his side. The Persian had a cut on his face that had bled over his whole front and the linen burnoose he wore over his helmet was cut and flapped like a pair of wings.

But the Medes showed no further interest in them. While the first flames flickered in the grass and the Olbians re-formed a column of fours and retired, Spitamenes and his Bactrians and Medes began to press the Greek mercenaries to the east.

'Poor bastards,' Eumenes said.

Lot grimaced. 'We did all the work,' he said in his own tongue.

Behind them, the slaughter of the mercenaries began.

Srayanka's spasms came closer and closer.

Ten stades north and west of the battlefield, the column halted where they had left their remounts. Every man changed horses and drank water. Behind them, they could still hear the fighting, and see the dust.

Urvara wept with no explanation. Eumenes held her shoulders. And Srayanka, between contractions that were sharper and closer now, asked for Hirene. Kineas was bent over her, holding her bloody sword hand.

'I saw her fall,' he said.

Srayanka cried out. When she was done, she said, 'She was my spear-maiden, my *mentor*.' The Greek word made her lips curl.

'I will see that we recover her corpse,' Kineas said. He cursed his inability to soften his words, but he was still on the battlefield in his mind, and Srayanka was grey and plastered in

301

sweat, her beautiful hair lank and glued to her face. She was dying.

She lay on a horse blanket, her only privacy the backs of Kineas's friends – Philokles and Eumenes and Andronicus, Ataelus and Samahe and Lot and Antigonus clutching at a wounded arm and murmuring charms, and the young Nihmu as the midwife. Srayanka groaned patiently and then screamed, drank water, and the men's faces reflected a kind of fear and exhaustion that the battlefield hadn't wrought. Nihmu laughed at them.

'Come, my queen!' she said. 'Push! The eagles are pecking at their shells!'

Srayanka screamed one more time, as Kineas chewed his lip and watched his rearguard pickets and hated his life and every decision he had made as his love lay dying in the sand soaked with her own blood. She writhed and sweated and he knew she was going.

Nihmu's eyes, calm and clear, met his. 'Trust me,' she said.

He prayed.

'Sing!' screamed Srayanka.

'Sing!' shouted Nihmu.

Kineas's eyes met Diodorus's, and together they began the paean of Athena. Voices took it up, the circle of his friends and then beyond, and to its martial cry his daughter was born.

And a minute later, he had a son.

He took them in his arms while Nihmu did what had to be done and the women washed Srayanka. The boy howled and the girl looked at him with enormous blue eyes full of questions, unmoved even when her cord was cut and tied off, unmoved when she was washed. Then she reached a hand and grabbed for his beard and burbled, apparently pleased with the world she saw. In his right hand, his son screamed and screamed when his cord was cut and then settled against his father's armour, waving his arms, blinking at the light.

They were so small. He had never held anything so small in all his life. And when Nihmu reached out to take them, he hesitated. But the moment the two of them lay on their mother's breast their faces changed, and the girl's calm became the boy's, and they settled.

Men pounded his back and women kissed his cheek. He had two children, and a wife, and he was alive.

And an hour later they were riding across the sand, free. Behind him, Samahe carried their daughter, and Nihmu carried their son, and Kineas offered a prayer to Nike.

21

'That went as well as could be expected,' Diodorus said that night, when they were gathered around a fire of tamarisk. They were passing a Spartan cup of water, because that was all they had.

Kineas was busy sewing at the straps on his breastplate, punching holes with Niceas's awl and thinking of the man, while Srayanka slept with her head on his lap. Their children slept in a hastily woven basket that was near enough the fire to keep them warm. 'Which part of my plan did you like best?' Kineas asked.

Philokles was lying on his cloak. He intercepted the cup. 'I liked how few of us died,' he said.

Indeed, if it hadn't been for the loss of Bain and half a dozen Sakje when they pressed too close to the unbeaten Macedonians, the action might have cost them nothing. Even with the attack of the Persians and Bain's error, the ambush had emptied very few saddles.

'Someday I intend to plan a battle and have it work,' Kineas said.

Philokles nodded. 'That's when you'll realize you are in the Elysian Fields,' he answered. 'Pah, there's nothing in this cup but water!'

Eumenes took the cup, sipped the water and raised an eyebrow. 'Polytimeros?' he said, rolling the water gently in the cup. 'Day before yesterday? Nice silt, muddy aftertaste—'

He had to duck as Leon swung his water skin. The two young men smiled at each other.

As Philokles vanished into the dark, Urvara came up beside Eumenes, took the cup, finished the contents and raised two heavy eyebrows. 'Aren't you Greeks tired enough? By all the gods! Go to sleep!'

Kineas could have sworn she was addressing Eumenes.

'After a battle, Greek men like to gather and tell each other that they're alive,' Diodorus said. He turned to Ataelus, who sat back to back with his wife. Both of them were sewing, he making a repair to a bridle while his wife repaired her moccasins. Diodorus asked, 'What do the Sakje do after battle?'

Ataelus narrowed his eyes so that they sparkled with reflected firelight. 'For lying about how many enemies killed,' he said.

Urvara sat on the ground as if her knees had betrayed her. 'How is Srayanka?'

Kineas grinned. He couldn't help it – the grins seemed to roll out of him despite the fatigue. He never wanted to go to sleep – he wanted to stay like this for ever, triumphant, exhausted, drunk on joy, with her head across his lap. 'She's asleep. Tough as a ten-year-old sandal.'

Urvara looked at the children. 'I thought we would die,' she said. 'Hah! I'm alive!'

Eumenes, usually so silent, gave her an approving grin. 'I think you've got it exactly,' he said.

She crossed her legs and put her hand on her chin. 'Not the battle, fool of a Greek. Any idiot can survive a battle. You did.'

Diodorus glanced around with a *why me* expression.

'The capture! Always, Srayanka is for saying that we should ride free and leave her, and always we are for telling her that we will stay by her. But I think in my head "I must ride or die!" And Hirene ...' and here she looked into the fire for a moment.

Samahe spoke. 'Hirene died a warrior death. She was a spear-maiden.'

Urvara acknowledged Samahe's statement with a nod. 'But still for dead, yes? But Hirene says "Go, Urvara! The Bronze One lusts to hurt you!" And I feared him, and I feared for Srayanka.' She shrugged. 'I cannot tell it. Much of it was women's fear and no interest to men – Srayanka's belly, the Bronze One's lusts, no exercise, and for treating us like grass priestesses.'

Eumenes, who hung on her every word, asked, 'What is a grass priestess?' When Urvara raised her eyes and shrugged,

Eumenes went on, 'My nurse used to talk about them as if they were – hmm – prostitutes.'

Urvara watched him. 'What is prostitute?' she asked.

'A man or woman who takes money for fucking,' Eumenes said in Sakje, using the coarsest of Sakje words for the act. Even in firelight, he could be seen to be blushing.

Kineas finished his armour strap. He really needed a new breastplate, but the strap would hold for another action. He was laughing quietly at his young cavalry commander's confusion.

Urvara laughed aloud. 'Grass priestess is girl who worships grass with her back,' she laughed. 'Not for taking money. For taking nothing!' When she saw that they weren't laughing, she shrugged. 'Macedonians treat us as if we are for fucking.' She shook her head. 'Never for seeing us for warriors.'

Kineas found that his free hand was stroking Srayanka's neck. Urvara was not telling her whole story – she was making light of something that pained her deeply, and Kineas, who knew both warriors and Sakje, could read her anger and her pain. But he couldn't think of anything to say, and the moment passed. Urvara wiped a hand across her eyes and departed the circle.

Within seconds, Philokles emerged from the dark. 'Admit it, I'm the best man in this army,' he said, and produced a skin of wine. The resulting cheer might have been heard in Marakanda. After the first cup had been poured into the thirsty sand for the gods, Philokles filled the cup and passed it.

Leon sat, and Sitalkes, and Darius, and then the others, and they drank together. And Nihmu appeared by Kineas. She looked down at him, her eyes dancing. She bent and kissed Srayanka's sleeping brow, and then she touched his cheek. 'This is how they'll remember you,' she said.

'Thank you,' Kineas said. 'For delivering the children.'

She smiled. 'I have been trained,' she said.

'You did well. You are growing up.' He took one of Srayanka's golden plaques from her dress – she had a dozen of them around the neck – and Kineas cut one away carefully and gave it to Nihmu.

She beamed at his praise. 'Thank you, lord.' She took the plaque, gave him a shy grin from under lowered eyes and slipped away.

Eumenes drank from the cup and chatted with Philokles, then left the circle in his turn. He returned a little later with Urvara in tow, and they shared the wine cup, hands lingering. Kineas watched them with a smile, but he didn't smile as Philokles methodically finished the wine skin, silently drinking for oblivion.

The Olbians, Lot's Sauromatae and the Sakje made camp together at a great bend in the Oxus after moving fast for a thousand stades to avoid retribution from Alexander. They went to a site Lot knew on the northern Oxus where the river ran deep along the inner bank and shallow on the outside of the curve, and there was grazing for ten thousand horses in the belly of the bow – grazing already used by other passing tribes, but not nibbled flat. A thousand lodges, yurts and wagons were set up along the deepest water, and parties went to get firewood and red deer as far as twenty stades away. In this site they were closer to Coenus, when he came, and ready to cross the river and head east to the rendezvous on the Jaxartes when their wounded had recovered.

Eumenes and Urvara took a party of mixed Olbians and Sakje back to the site of the ambush. They returned with more plunder and Hirene's corpse as well as Bain's. The two of them were given a kurgan on the outer bank of the Oxus. Srayanka declined to officiate, and Kineas, urged by Nihmu, took the part of both king and priest. Diodorus laughed at him and called him a superstitious peasant, and there was a barb to his words, but they all brought their squares of turf and the ceremony and the feast helped to settle something intangible.

'We'll all be Sakje in a few years, at this rate,' Diodorus said, like a man scratching a scar.

'Kineas likes being a Sakje,' Philokles said.

Kineas started to react angrily, but he bit down on his first reply and thought for a moment instead.

'I like their freedom,' Kineas said.

Philokles nodded. 'Yes,' he said. 'And the way they worship you like a god.'

'What are we doing?' Diodorus asked. 'I've bitten my tongue long enough. You're a brilliant strategos, Kineas – I, for one, would follow you anywhere. That last was your best work. We routed twice our weight – in Macedonians – and slipped away from another army. By Ares! I love to follow you.' He looked at the ground between his feet, and then slowly raised his head again. 'But there's too much, Kineas. Most of our troopers have fought four heavy actions in two summers. You need to tell them when they can go home.'

Philokles nodded. 'It's true, my friend. We saved Srayanka and we struck a blow against Macedon. As far as most of your Olbians are concerned, the war is over and it is time to ride home and tell a lot of lies. These aren't Spartans. They aren't even Macedonian peasants to whom we've promised the world. These are men with lives, and they'd like to go home.'

Kineas sighed. 'I know. I see the same fatigue in the Keltoi that I see in Eumenes.'

Diodorus went back to watching the ground between his sandals. 'What's next?'

Kineas shrugged. 'When Srayanka is ready, we ride east.' He frowned. 'The Sakje are in much the same state as our Olbians, but they have nowhere to go. And they have come all this way. We have all come. What's one more desert to cross?'

Diodorus looked up, his head to one side like an alert puppy. 'It's not the desert. It's the battle afterwards,' he said. 'And then the road home. Some of our wounded won't recover in time for another action. Some of the troopers are getting – what can I call it? If we had more wine, Philokles wouldn't be the only one drinking all day.'

Philokles looked at Diodorus in surprise. 'I drink no more than any other man,' he said.

Diodorus shrugged. 'Whatever you say, Spartan. So – the desert, the battle and afterwards. What's the story?'

'It is my problem,' Kineas said. He sighed. 'And my doom awaits me in the east.'

Philokles rolled his eyes. 'Oh, really!' he barked. 'Are you some superstitious barbarian or a man of Athens? Doom, my arse. You are what you are, and I accuse you of making your dreams an excuse to follow Alexander to the end of the world.'

Kineas snapped to attention, stung by this rebuke. 'Like Hades, Spartan!' he spat. 'You've wanted this war against Alexander from the first. It suits Sparta. It suits Athens. And now you want to call it off? Here, in the middle of the sea of grass? Very much in the Panhellenic spirit – we'll just ride home.'

Philokles pointed both hands unsteadily at Kineas. 'Keep us out here for your own glory if you must. Ask us to fight to avenge Hirene – she was well liked, for all her fish-eating ways. But spare us your *doom*. You are a Greek, not some taboo-ridden savage. Their slavish respect goes to your head – Baqca.'

Kineas found himself facing the Spartan with his hands sealed into fists. 'I *know* my dreams. I do not lie about them.'

Philokles leaned in close, threateningly close. 'When I met you, you were the sort of man to laugh at such dreams. Now, you are ruled by them.' The Spartan was breathing hard. 'Are you a barbarian, or a man?'

Kineas stood his ground. He could smell Philokles' breath and feel his spittle when he shouted. 'Fuck you!' he said. 'Since when is Moira not Greek? What price your precious Panhellenism now, Spartan?'

'Brilliantly reasoned, Athenian!' Philokles spat back. 'Is that the best your schools can produce? Any Spartan can do as well—'

'You are going to wake the babies,' Srayanka said. She emerged from her wagon with a shawl around her. 'Are you two going to *fight*? Many Sakje will pay good wagers to watch – I will fetch them. But move away from the wagons and do not wake my children.'

Kineas felt himself straightening up. Philokles gave a drunken smile and waved his open hands.

'Oh,' Srayanka said, with mock disappointment. 'So you only ...' she was at a loss for the word and she did a credible imitation of a stallion rearing, 'like horses, eh? But not fight.' She smiled a half-smile, and then her humour turned to anger and she was livid. 'Listen to me, King of the Sakje and Spartan. The Sakje go to the muster on the Jaxartes. Greeks are free. No man of Olbia owes me service,' and here she glared at Kineas, 'but *my people* will go to the muster because we said we would be there. Six moons we ride the sea of grass and still we *will be there.*'

Then she deflated like a tent with the poles removed. 'And you are right, Spartan,' she said. 'We have nowhere else to go.'

Kineas took her shoulders. Rather than spurning him, as he feared, she leaned back into his embrace. 'They only called me king while you were missing,' he said.

She whirled out of his arms and her eyes searched his face as if she'd just discovered a hidden flaw in a pot. 'No. You are king. Nihmu's horses and my womb make you king. And yet you owe us nothing.' She frowned. 'Satrax warned me of this moment. I am barbarian and you are Greek.'

Diodorus had gone back to staring at the ground between his sandals, but now he looked up again. 'Be fair, Srayanka. The Sakje have had their fair share from this army.'

'We are barbarians to you,' she said. 'Just like we are to Alexander.' She spat. In accurate mockery, imitating Diodorus, she said, 'We'll all be Sakje in a few years at this rate.' She hugged her belly. '*No fate could be more cruel,*' she mocked.

Diodorus winced. 'Listen, lady,' he said with his hands on his hips. 'I've been at war for years. I'm tired of it. I want to settle somewhere and have a wife and a future. The Sakje are like brothers to me – but I crave the world of the palaestra and the agora. How happy would you be if we made you live away from the grass?'

Srayanka hung her head.

Kineas cut in, 'Srayanka, they can go home if they want – but they won't. They'll posture and get drunk.' He glared at Philokles. 'But ...' He looked down into her eyes, their startling blue almost black in the firelight. 'But you do have other choices. You can go back, and when this is over ...' The bit in his teeth, he went on, 'The high ground between the Tanais and the Rha – whose tribal land is that?'

Srayanka used a hand to pull her hair back from her face. 'Maeotae land, and no man's land these last ten years and more.'

Kineas nodded. 'Leave the farmers to their own,' he said. 'The high ground is wolf land – worse than Hyrkania. We cleared the road and made some peace – drove the worst of the wolves off. There's rich pasture there – enough for ten thousand horses. And as soon as you were there to protect it, the Maeotae farmers and the Sindi would return to their farms on the lower Rha.'

Diodorus pursed his lips and looked at Kineas with a different kind of respect. 'You're smarter than you look,' he said.

Philokles raised an eyebrow and looked like a comic satyr. 'So you *have* been thinking of other endings,' he said.

Kineas nodded. 'I had all winter to listen to what was said in Hyrkania – and to Leon's views on eastern trade,' he said. 'Many of the Olbians will go home – but if we declared that we were founding a city, many would stay.'

Philokles beamed. 'You have said nothing of this!' he proclaimed. 'This is brilliant!'

Diodorus grinned too. 'A city of mercenaries and Sakje,' he said. 'I imagine we'll have a fair number of curious travellers.'

Srayanka's eyes went from one to another. 'The Sakje go east to the muster of the tribes,' she said. 'King or no king.' But her look at Kineas was happier. 'But the high ground between the Rha and the Tanais is a good dream, and a dream can keep the people alive.' She shrugged, a curiously Greek gesture on her. 'Who knows? Perhaps it will even come to pass.'

Kineas looked down at her. 'Perhaps we should be married?' he asked her.

'Husband, we have been married since first we played stallion and mare,' she said. 'Sakje people do not worry about the fanfare when we can grasp the trumpet. But,' she smirked, 'I like a good party. And all our men and women need something to hold in their minds that is not fear and death.'

In the wagon, there was a stirring, a distant *thump* and a hearty wail.

'Oh *goddess*,' Srayanka swore, and she raced Kineas for the wagon bed.

22

By Kineas's calculations, the feast to mark their wedding and their victory would fall on the Panathenaia, a festival that celebrated both Athena and Eros. He calculated the date with an eye to the grass on the plains and the speed with which his wife – and his wounded – could recover.

'Nothing could be more fitting,' said Diodorus, with a twinkle in his eye. He and Philokles could be seen plotting in all corners of the camp.

Coenus's arrival made the celebrations possible. Scouts foretold him, and then Samahe located him and brought his column into their camp, cheered by Sakje and Sauromatae and Olbians alike.

Coenus's column arrived with twenty fresh troopers to replace losses, a hundred heavy chargers from the plains of southern Hyrkania, forty talents of gold, his new bride Artemesia and news.

And wine.

Wine flowed for a week as if they were sitting on the plains of Arcadia and not those of Sogdiana. Olbians paid Sauromatae maidens to weave garlands of the shiny leaves that looked most like laurel, and they celebrated the mid-summer feast of Aphrodite a few days late, and no man or woman was altogether sober.

Coenus's lady sat with Sappho, modestly dressed. The two of them had been sewing and embroidering for two days without cease, washing their hands frequently, and hiding their work from all comers.

'You've shared the plan with the gentlemen, I take it?' Coenus asked.

Kineas nodded, chewing on some unleavened bread made from proper wheat. 'I proposed it to Srayanka and Diodorus as well.'

Philokles waved his bread at them. 'Me, too,' he said with his mouth full.

Coenus waved his arms at the west. 'It's becoming a reality already,' he said. 'Heron put a hundred men into the fort on the Rha under Crax and then sent his troop of horse to clear my way. Crax is the lord of all the Rha's mouth, and he has recruited men in your name.' Coenus gave a wry smile. 'I also recruited some men in Olbia and Pantecapaeum, and I added mine to his rather than ship them across the Kaspian. Many of them had already guessed how much bullion I had.' He shrugged.

'And Lykeles?' Kineas asked.

'Not a complete fool,' Coenus said fondly. 'He had no idea of how he was being used. I set him straight. But mark my words – there will be war in the cities before next summer. Heraclea, the strongest city on the Euxine, is making noise of grabbing at the east-coast cities, and neither Olbia nor Pantecapaeum are ready.'

'Heron?'

'Heron is slowly gathering and training an army of the trash of Hyrkania, with Leosthenes as his captain and Lycurgus as the governor of Namastopolis.' Coenus smiled. 'He's not hurting anyone, and his gold is keeping the best men for us. The rest have already gone south over the mountains to Parthia. The knives are out there, and everywhere that Alexander's writ runs. He's a fool to stay in the east. His western lands are going to desert him.' Coenus shook his head. 'And on top of all that, he's recruiting Greeks himself.'

Kineas shook his head. 'I'm not one of Alexander's worshippers,' he said, 'but a year ago, the tyrant of Olbia was telling me that Parmenion would bury him. Now Parmenion is dead. Alexander may be mad, he may leak hubris as most men bleed, but he is canny when it comes to ruling men.' He paused. 'He needs those Greeks. He's bled a lot of men.'

Diodorus gave a hard smile. 'We helped.'

Coenus nodded. 'I won't argue with you. Antipater walks in fear. Olympias is a force to be reckoned with, or so they say.' He drank wine. 'Ares, but that all seems so distant here.'

Diodorus gave a foxy grin. 'The politics may be distant, but the God-King himself is just a thousand stades that way.' He motioned to the east. 'Probably less.'

Coenus sat up as if stung by a wasp. 'That's less than the distance from Athens to Sparta!'

'Just so.' Diodorus reached past his friend and poured wine into his cup. 'His patrols and ours are already on the same ground. If he weren't so focused on Spitamenes, he'd be after us already.'

'So Crax is in the fort at Errymi,' Kineas interrupted.

Coenus rubbed his beard. 'He's a good lord, and the Maeotae like him. His patrols keep them safe. There are already new farms on the Rha. I rode over the divide to the Tanais – there and back, if you know what I mean. I talked to the farmers on the Tanais. They know we cleared the bandits. Unless we over-tax them, they'll be satisfied to have a lord – and a town.'

Kineas shook his head again. 'I haven't sworn to it yet.'

Coenus drank off the dregs of his wine. 'Nonsense. The thing is as good as done.'

Sappho smiled, and so did Artemesia, and Srayanka laughed, all three of them watching the two babies.

Philokles slapped Kineas on the back. 'Will you be a king?' he asked.

Kineas was still laughing when Upazan rode by and something in the set of the man's shoulders killed his laughter. 'I would rather found a city with an assembly.'

Srayanka shrugged. 'We have assemblies, too. But we have lords for war. If we do this thing, I think we should have a king.'

Nihmu reached into the circle of adults and took a warm round of bread. 'The time of kings is coming,' she said. She smiled apologetically, either for her words or for her theft of bread. 'The time of assemblies is almost past.' She smiled timidly. 'That is what the priests said in Olbia.'

Philokles looked at her and frowned. He was bleary with wine. 'Why must it be a time of kings, child? Sparta has kings, and this is scarcely her finest hour,' he said. 'And why must you play the barbarian seeress all the time?'

Sappho shook her head. 'The girl speaks only the truth,

Philokles. And wasn't Cassandra a Greek woman, and no barbarian?'

Kineas nodded. 'Nihmu, your priests are aristocrats to a man and they desire a time of kings. Bad prophets predict futures that they desire. Good prophets speak only what the gods send.'

'Oh, aristocrats are at fault, are they?' Philokles asked.

'Go to bed,' Sappho said. 'You are arguing, not debating.' She sent Nihmu away with a whisper, and Kineas knew that she had sent the girl for Temerix.

Philokles resented her tone. He drew himself up. 'I'm sorry if my wit is not up to your standards, madam,' he said, and walked off into the night.

Sappho, after a worried look, took Diodorus's hand and led him off.

Srayanka put her daughter to her breast. 'If that girl is Kam Baqca's daughter,' she asked, 'who was her mother?'

Kineas drank wine and shook his head. 'She told me. I can't remember. Some lady with your name was her grandmother.'

'Really?' Srayanka asked. 'Srayanka the archer? That would make us cousins. Why don't I know her?'

'No idea, my dear. I didn't grow up here.' Kineas stroked her hair, and then took his daughter and held her, marvelling again at the tiny hands and feet – and how it all worked. And how holding a child made him feel.

'She frightens me,' Srayanka said. 'And if Kam Baqca ever lay with a woman, I would expect to know.'

Kineas raised an eyebrow. 'I like her. Even when she's a Cassandra.'

Srayanka took her daughter and put her back to the breast. 'Greedy beast,' she murmured. 'I may be wrong, love. Kam Baqca was the oddest of beings, and he sacrificed his man-hood, hmmm, seven years ago, or perhaps eight. So the thing is possible.'

Kineas could understand many things of the Sakje, but Kam Baqca's exchange of gender made his stomach turn and he changed the subject. 'You are ready for this wedding?' he asked.

She switched breasts, while Samahe came and took the boy from his basket and began to change him. 'We are already wed, husband. But it will be good for your Greek men to see the ceremony performed, and all our people want to drink wine.' She smiled and changed the subject herself. 'I like Lot's wife.'

Kineas allowed his eyes to follow Upazan. 'I wish she would bear him a son,' he said.

Srayanka made a chucking sound with her tongue. 'Stop thinking like a Greek. His son will not be his heir. That is not the Sauromatae way, or the Sakje way or the Massagetae way.'

'His son *might* be his heir,' Kineas said.

She nodded. 'Less likely with the eastern clans than the western, but possible. But Upazan is his heir, and no child of Monae's will change that. But they are young yet, and Lot is in the full flower of his warrior life. What concerns you?'

'Upazan wants him dead. Upazan hates us, for whatever reason.'

'No reason but the folly of youth.' She smiled. 'Lot should have brought him west.'

Samahe got up, her sewing rolled away in a sheet of linen. 'That's enough milk for any child,' she said. She reached out and took the girl, who cried and had to be shushed by Kineas. Kineas played with her while his son latched on to Srayanka's nipple in moments.

'When will we name them?' he asked, holding his daughter.

'We will name them at the ceremony. They will be a month old, and that is a good age.'

'Greek names or Sakje names?' Kineas asked, trying to sound light.

'Both, I think,' she answered. 'Satyrus – Satrax – for our son. And Melissa – Melitta to Kineas – for our daughter.'

Kineas bowed. 'Well chosen,' he said. 'Just as well I wasn't involved.' He smiled at his daughter and gently touched her cheek. 'Little honey bee,' he said.

The baby's eyes snapped open, and her tiny hand grabbed his finger.

'She has you already,' Srayanka laughed. 'And what would

you know of choosing Sakje names?' she asked him. But her eyes danced. They kissed.

'Your gown is almost finished,' Samahe said.

Srayanka laughed. She loved looking fine, and she was delighted by the idea of a silk gown. 'I can't wait,' she said. 'I'll have to bind my breasts or they'll leak.'

Kineas handed his daughter to Samahe. 'Some things are better for a man not to hear,' he said.

All the world, it seemed, attended their feast. Sauromatae and Sakje, Olbians, Persian traders and even a western Kwin, the purveyor of the silk that made Srayanka's cream Persian gown, embroidered around the hem and all the seams with Greek and Scythian animals and designs depending on which woman had been available to put her hand to the work. She wore the heavy gold collar of her rank and the high headdress of a priestess, with the green-hilted sword of Cyrus in a gold scabbard at her side. To Kineas, she looked like one of the ancient goddesses he had seen in Ecbatana.

Kineas awoke on his feast day to find that he, too, had a magnificent gift – first, a wool tunic of the finest Sogdian work, made from a pair of matched shawls and decorated more fancifully than an Athenian gentleman would think quite right for everyday wear. His Greek friends had refurbished his red sandals and produced a gold laurel wreath for him to wear in his hair.

But the most magnificent gift sat in front of their wagon on an armour stand for all to view: a Sauromatae-style scale hauberk, the scales in alternating rows of silvered bronze and gilt and blue enamel, carefully fitted with dozens of different-sized scales to cover his torso and shoulders perfectly, the scales sewn to a new leather *thorax*. The resulting cuirass was heavy, but no heavier than his damaged Athenian breast- and back-plates, and it glowed in the summer sun with gilded Greek leg armour and a matching bridle gauntlet produced by Temerix in secret. His helmet, refurbished, had a new blue plume.

Diodorus fondled the gauntlet as if it was a woman's arm. 'They wear them in Italia,' he said.

'Craterus had one at Arbela,' Kineas said. 'We all admired it.' He laughed. 'I don't suppose it would do to wear armour for my wedding.'

'Soon enough,' Nihmu said, doing a handstand nearby.

There were games – Sakje games and Greek games, with horse races and wrestling and shooting bows for distance and accuracy, but once the wine and fermented mare's milk began to flow, the contests ran their courses and the contestants hurried to get their share of the drink. Kineas and Srayanka gave prizes to the winners, sitting together hand in hand on a pile of skins in the red sunset, their children in baskets at their feet.

'Do you remember?' Kineas asked. 'On the sea of grass, riding to see Satrax?'

She laughed with him. 'I didn't have ten words of Greek,' she said. 'But oh, how I wanted you.' She looked at him under her lashes, a look that was the more beautiful for its rarity, because she was more frequently the cavalry commander than the lover. 'We held hands, I think.'

They danced and ate and drank wine until the sun set, and then they danced and sang and drank more, strong red wine from Chios that was like berries in the mouth, and they ate venison seasoned with pepper, which was too strong for some of the Greeks but delighted others. They had bread – rich, strong Greek bread, because Coenus had brought Olbian flour all the way across the sea of grass. And the Olbians had strong Maeotian fish sauce, three deep amphorae, to season their bread, and olive oil for the first time in three months, while the Sauromatae and the Sakje tried the Greek foods and passed around their own rich and heavily spiced mutton and foal with flatbreads and honey.

'I brought cider,' Coenus said, 'but it was already turning by the time I reached Crax on the return trip, and we drank it to save it.' He grinned and spoke slowly, the perfect aristocrat even staggering drunk. 'We toasted the two of you, of course.'

They had built a bonfire that towered to the height of three tall men, tamarisk and willow and poplar on top, and the fire took with a rush after it had been blessed by a Persian fire priest who had come with the traders, and roared to life so that you could feel it on your back ten horse-lengths away. The burning cedar smell of the tamarisk mixed with the late honeysuckle and the briar roses that bloomed over every thicket in the river valley.

They were toasted and gifted, and they named their children in the last light of the sun at the top of Hirene and Bain's kurgan, so that the swords of the two dead heroes caught the light and seemed to anoint the heads of the two infants.

Unmoved by all this spiritual glory, the babies roared against their hard fates in being kept up late, and received the plaudits of the crowd despite their ill manners. They were, after all, only a month old.

And then many of the Greek men appeared, drunk, singing obscene songs that Srayanka could only guess the meaning of – not that the guessing was hard, as most of them wore giant erect phalluses strapped to their groins, and they had convinced several young Sakje girls to be lewd. Battering pans and kettles, slobbering well-meant kisses, this raucous crew escorted them to their wagon. The serenade went on until Srayanka said they were waking the children.

'Don't hear that every day at a wedding in Athens!' Diodorus called, and then they were gone.

'There will be more wine than milk in these breasts,' Srayanka said when finally they were alone.

'No reason they shouldn't share the feast,' Kineas said. 'At home, you would have a wet nurse.'

'At home in Greece? A wet nurse, and slaves, and a life in a few rooms.' She frowned. 'I'm afraid you are wed to a barbarian.'

'Well, Barbarian Queen? What will you have as a wedding present?' he asked, kissing the side of her neck.

'Hmm,' she said. 'Mmm?' she whispered. She laughed at him and pushed him away. 'Remember what happened the last time?'

'Killers coming through the side of the wagon? By Zeus,

that seems a long time ago.' He laughed and snuggled next to her.

'Even then, what I wanted was to take my people to war with Alexander,' she said. 'That is still what I want. And when we have fought him – win or lose – *then* we can return to the high ground by the Tanais. We will be king and queen of a united people. Our children will rule after us.' She kissed his hand. 'I want you to bring your people to the muster, King Kineas. That is what I want.'

Kineas knew what keeping that promise would mean. He dreamed of the tree and the river almost every night. But he looked into her eyes and thought that some fates were not as bad as they might seem. 'To Alexander, then,' he said.

PART V

ACHILLES' CHOICE

23

'Am I surrounded by fools?' Alexander asked the assembled officers.

Silence.

'This country is not subdued,' Alexander said carefully. 'We are at war with every rock and tree. There is no room for weakness or doubt, or slovenly soldiering.'

The Macedonian officers were red with fury and embarrassment. The cadre of Persian and Sogdian officers who were present deepened their humiliation.

Alexander had little time for Panhellenism, but it had its uses. 'Two thousand Hellenes *died* at the hands of barbarians. They were not even outnumbered. They were merely careless.'

Craterus, a Companion officer, and Ptolemy, the youngest of the phalanx commanders, exchanged glances. Alexander watched them. They looked as if they might voice some dissent. He was prepared to crush them. But after one exchanged glance, they subsided.

Alexander raised an arm. 'If you gentlemen will turn your attention to the stream bed . . .'

Just to the north, a tributary ran down out of the Sogdian hills into the Jaxartes. The stream bed was nearly dry with midsummer, and forage parties had cleared every stick of burnable brush and every leaf of green forage, so that the stream bed looked like an open mine. Packed into the gully were six thousand blank-eyed prisoners leashed by short ropes to stakes driven deep into the sandy soil. Lining the sides of the gully were soldiers – some Macedonian veterans, and some of the more recent Sogdian recruits. The Sogdians, most of them, were related to the men in the gully.

Alexander gave a sign and all the men, Macedonian and Bactrian, set to work in the mass slaughter of six thousand prisoners. For the most part, the victims waited fatalistically, although here and there men struggled, either panicked into a last resistance or too stubborn to go down without a fight. Their executioners approached with dripping swords and dispatched them. Those who struggled took the longest to die, and those who bowed their heads to the blade went fast.

Alexander watched for as long as it took a thousand men to die.

'I don't want any more mistakes,' he said. 'Nor do I wish to see any softness.' The evening air stank of blood, as if the army was butchering oxen for meat. 'You will all watch until these rebels are dead. Then you may dismiss.'

He turned on his heel and walked away, followed by Hephaestion and Craterus. Neither man walked with his accustomed swagger.

Alexander turned before he had gone ten steps. 'Eumenes!' he called, and the lone Greek on his command staff came quickly.

In his tent, he snapped his fingers for wine.

'I worry that we are teaching the rebels not to surrender,' Eumenes said.

Alexander sat heavily on his couch and swirled the wine in his cup. 'I worry about the same thing, but I had to make an example.'

'For Spitamenes?' Hephaestion asked, and Alexander shook his head while he narrowed his eyes.

'No,' he said. 'For this Scythian queen, Zarina. And for my own Macedonians.' He turned to Eumenes. 'You have all the survivors from Pharnuches' column isolated?'

'Yes, majesty.' Eumenes could feel the lion's rage from across the room, like the heat from a bonfire.

'I considered having them executed with the rebels,' Alexander said. 'But that seemed to send the wrong message. I'm still thinking about it. Tell them from me that if I hear a word of this disaster from the army, I will have one man in every file killed. If I hear more, I'll kill them all.' He took a deep breath. 'Understand me?' he said after a moment. 'I command it.' He looked at Eumenes. 'And we lost our Amazons. Spitamenes must be having quite a laugh at us.'

Eumenes avoided his eyes. 'I do not think it was Spitamenes who ambushed Pharnuches.'

Hephaestion spluttered on his wine. 'What?' he asked. 'Don't be foolish. I interrogated some of the survivors myself.'

Eumenes was tired to death of Hephaestion, so he wasn't as careful as he ought to have been. 'Really? And did any of them mention the enemy had Greek cavalry?'

'What's this?' Alexander asked, his voice harsh as an executioner's sword.

Hephaestion shrugged. 'Diomedes, the surviving Companion, said he fought a Greek. I think the man's deranged.'

Eumenes shook his head. Hephaestion glared at him. Eumenes ignored the favourite and looked at the king. 'Diomedes says that the whole thing was a rescue of the Amazons, and it was done by Dahae and Greeks.' Daring, he added, 'I asked Kleisthenes to help me with the questioning. He thinks that the best-armoured of the enemy cavalry were Sauromatae, who we haven't encountered before.'

'By my father's thunder,' Alexander cursed. 'The king of the Sauromatae sits in my camp and eats my food and his warriors serve Spitamenes! Send for Pharasmenes!' To Eumenes he said, 'I curse the loss of the Amazons. They were something a man could hold in his hand. Some visible proof of our conquests, like elephants. Something to *show*.'

Hephaestion flushed.

Alexander gave a half-smile. 'I want them back. Or replaced with others as fine. If I have to take the army across the Jaxartes, I will.'

'Not, I think, the best use of our assets,' Eumenes murmured.

'You are not indispensable, Greek. I command here. I have crushed the rebels and retaken all our forts.' Alexander looked off into the distance. 'When I break this Queen Zarina, there will be Amazons for every man in the army.'

Eumenes knew the storm was coming. He raised his head and met it square on. 'You will find it almost impossible to raise more mercenaries,' he said.

'Greek soldiers are like snow in the mountains,' Alexander said contemptuously.

Eumenes wouldn't back down. 'Every satrap is raising an army. The lesson of Parmenion has not been lost. And we are a long way from Greece, *majesty*. We don't pay the most, and we kill them like cattle. A thousand with Pharnuches, two thousand in the Jaxartes forts – and those are just our most recent losses.'

'The Thessalians are on the verge of mutiny,' Craterus put in. 'Thankless bastards.' Bitterly, he said, 'And young Ptolemy says the phalanxes aren't much better.'

Eumenes looked around. 'Thankless? They were our very best cavalry.'

'But they loved Parmenion better than they loved me,' Alexander said. 'Best to send them home.'

'And replace them with what?' Craterus said. 'More Persians?'

'Bactrians. Sogdians. These are not soft-handed Persians. These are men of war, like our Macedonians. Mountain men, like us.' Alexander used much the same voice he would use in gentling a child.

Craterus raised his voice. 'Ares' balls, Alexander! Don't fool yourself. They're fucking Persians! Orientals! They're counting the hours until they stab us all in our sleep!'

Eumenes fought back a smile. Craterus was speaking his lines as if they had been written for him, and he, not Eumenes, would now suffer the wrath of the king.

But Alexander surprised them all by remaining calm. 'I understand your concern, Craterus – and yours, Eumenes. But I must have cavalry for this war, and to leave the Sogdians unemployed would be to invite them to join my enemies.' He put his leg up. He'd received an arrow through the leg – a clean wound, but it kept weeping pus and yesterday a bone fragment had emerged. It made the king feel mortal and fallible.

Eumenes exhaled slowly. 'May we at least secure Marakanda behind us before we cross the Jaxartes?' he asked.

Alexander nodded. 'I'll take a flying column myself.' He glanced at Hephaestion, seemed on the edge of saying something and then shook his head. 'No, it will have to be me – another disaster like the one on the Oxus and the whole fabric will start to unweave. I'll be gone two weeks. Spitamenes hasn't the stomach to make a stand – he'll break the siege. If I am fast enough, I'll catch him. If not, I'll come back and we'll try to wrong-foot the barbarians and have a go at the Massagetae.' He gave them a smile that was meant to be re-assuring. 'She'll have Amazons.'

24

The next morning brought Kineas news of another side to his wedding feast. Words had been spoken and blows exchanged, and there was anger in the air – sidelong glances, trouble on the horse lines, voices raised.

Kineas listened to the story from Ataelus, who had a bad cut on his arm, and watched the men and women behind Ataelus spreading the gossip with their eyes. The prodromoi were a tight-knit group who saw themselves as the elite of the whole force. Ataelus was turning them into a clan of his own – a process about which Srayanka had warned him. Kineas had learned enough about Scythian politics to know that weak leaders lost followers to strong leaders, and that even when a clan had a great leader, some men and women would drift away to greener pastures.

'Garait – for kissing this woman,' Ataelus said. 'Derva of the Sauromatae? You know her?'

Kineas shook his head, caught in ignorance of his troops. 'No,' he said.

Ataelus shook his head in turn. 'Derva was *paradâtãm* to Aurvañt of the Sauromatae. But she was kissing Garait.' He shrugged and winced, as the wound in his shoulder hurt him. 'So Aurvañt is for going to Upazan, who is his chief.'

Srayanka came up behind her husband and put her hands on her hips. 'Not a good story, Ataelus,' she said in Sakje.

He bowed his head, but said, 'These young people are *my* people. Derva has denied her paradâtãm for the required number of days.'

'And then what happened?' Kineas asked.

Ataelus frowned. 'Upazan and Garait for shouting,' he said in Greek. He met Kineas's eye. 'Upazan hits Garait, and Leon hits Upazan. Upazan draws a sword. Cuts at Garait. I step in to stop foolish boy-talk and get this.' He gestured with shame at his wound. His bow arm was in a sling.

'What does Leon have to do with this?' Kineas asked, his temper fraying.

Srayanka's eyes narrowed fractionally and she shook her head. 'Leon loves Mosva of the Sauromatae.'

'I know that!' Kineas said.

'So does Upazan,' Srayanka said, as she would speak to a not-very-bright child. 'What do you want, Ataelus?'

'I ask for killing Upazan,' Ataelus said formally at the end of his testimony. 'Man to man and horse to horse.'

Kineas looked at Srayanka, who simply shook her head. 'Am I your queen, Ataelus?' she asked.

Ataelus looked back and forth between Kineas and Srayanka. He had always made a point of his status as a Massagetae, not a Sakje. A visitor, not a subject. But he was thoroughly Kineas's man – Kineas had made him. This, too, was Scythian politics.

The day was hot, but there was an edge of something on the wind and lightning flashed out over the desert. Kineas leaned forward to speak, but Srayanka put a hand on his shoulder to stay him.

Ataelus made a mute appeal to Kineas, and getting no response, he said, 'Yes.'

'Really? You are Sakje?' She was relentless.

'Yes,' said Ataelus.

Srayanka flashed a smile at Kineas. 'As he has declared himself to us, he is subject to our justice.' She nodded. 'It would be bad manners to allow you to fight Lot's sister's son. Bring me this Garait.'

Garait was brought forward, his braids carefully plaited, in his best tunic.

'How many horses do you have, Garait?' Srayanka asked.

'I have twenty horses of my own,' he answered in Sakje, but his pride was audible to every person in the tent. Twenty was an excellent score for a man so young, but of course he had had two years of war to collect them. 'No ponies. No horses-for-meat. Twelve Thessalians, tall and strong. Four Getae ponies fit for any work. Four of our own horses for riding.'

Srayanka nodded. 'And what is Derva's bride price?'

Garait shrugged. 'I do not know,' he said.

Srayanka looked at Kineas. 'You trust me to handle this?' she asked him in Greek.

'You do know the customs better than I,' Kineas said.

'I will speak to Prince Lot. In the meantime,' she turned back to Garait, 'you are forbidden to be within twenty horse-lengths of her. You may not speak to Upazan, nor accept or deliver a challenge. In every case, you will refer him to me.'

'Yes, lady.' Garait nodded, the equivalent of a deep bow among Persians. Then she summoned Leon, who was suspiciously close by, and also very clean and in his best tunic. He looked as if he had a major bruise forming around his left eye, his dark skin almost purple in the sun.

'Do you intend to wed Mosva?' she asked.

The black man nodded gravely. 'If she'll have me,' he said.

'Arrange a bride price and pay it,' she said. 'And be quick about it. Your flirtation is hurting us, Leon.'

Leon smiled. 'I'm not usually slow to close a deal,' he said. 'I had only thought to wait until the campaign was over.'

'Listen, Numidian, if I were to offer you advice, I'd say this. Learn her bride price tonight. Make talk with Lot – ask obliquely. Buy the horses you need and picket them with his herd, and steal Mosva from her tent and put her in yours. Do it now.'

Leon bowed. 'I live to serve you, lady,' he said.

But Srayanka looked troubled.

When they were gone, Kineas turned to Diodorus. 'This is what comes of too much time idle. I want more patrols, south towards Alexander and east along our march route. And a scout – not Ataelus, he's hurt – east, looking for waterholes and fodder. We need to move.'

Diodorus scratched under his beard – a beard that was showing a surprising number of grey hairs. 'You know that we bumped into some of Alexander's scouts three days back, down by the Oxus.'

Kineas had heard as much in the last rush of feast prepara-tions. The encounter had been two days' ride to the south – not close enough to threaten his camp, but close enough to get his attention. 'I know. Get the scouts out. Most of our wounded are able to ride. I'd like to be out of this camp in two days.'

Diodorus nodded. 'Can't be too soon.'

Diodorus and Parshtaevalt organized a string of running patrols well to the south, covering a crescent of possible approaches between the Macedonians, the Persians and their camp. With the help of Lot's Sauromatae, they had plenty of warriors to cover the patrols and the rotation helped relieve the punishing toll of ten thousand horses on the local grass, as well as the boredom. Kineas and Lot and Srayanka had much to arrange before they could make the final push over the Sogdian desert to join the Scythian muster.

The next day, Diodorus and Ataelus pushed the eastern patrols out farther, clearing their route to their next fixed camp. They needed grass and water and a path free of enemies. It took a great deal of scouting.

On the second day after the feast, Kineas summoned the officers and clan leaders to council in the cool of the afternoon. Then he sat with Leon, calculating supplies and fodder, and getting answers he did not like.

Diodorus arrived in camp at midday, well before he was expected. He had a patrol of Olbians – his own troop, with twenty iron-faced Keltoi surrounding a group of dusty riders who appeared at first to be prisoners. Kineas began to approach and Diodorus waved him off, so Kineas went to the shade of the felt awning projecting from the rear of Srayanka's wagon and poured himself a little wine. He poured more for Diodorus as he came in.

'This will cut the dust,' Kineas said.

'I'm bringing trouble,' Diodorus said. 'Did you see who I brought in?'

'Upazan?' Kineas said.

'The very same. Riding south with a war party. Not in our scout rotation. And frankly, he needs a hiding. He's a bully and he's bad for the discipline we've built among the Sakje.'

Kineas shrugged. 'Bring him.'

He sent Samahe for Srayanka. She came with both children

and Sappho, and they all took seats on the carpets of the tent. By the time they were settled, Upazan was brought in.

He stood straight. His face had the natural sullenness of the adolescent, more out of place on an adult. He wore a magnificent coat of bronze scales plated in gold, and wore a golden boar atop his gold-covered bronze helmet.

Kineas nodded. 'I greet you, Upazan. May I serve you wine?'

'I want no wine,' Upazan said. 'I want to ride free. Blood will flow for this insult.'

Kineas nodded and turned to Leon. 'Send Sitalkes for Prince Lot, with my respectful wish that he will come and help me deal with Upazan.'

Leon nodded and left.

Turning to Upazan, Kineas shrugged. 'You spurn my courtesy, so I will waste no more time on it. You left camp without permission—'

'I am Upazan of the Sauromatae, and I *need no permission*, Greek. I may ride where I please, raid where I please. Release me, or there will be blood.'

Kineas sipped his own wine and then walked up close to the young man. Upazan was a finger's-width taller, but they were of a size. Kineas stepped in close. 'Whose blood, yearling? You cannot mean to threaten to bleed on me.'

The roar of laughter did nothing to quench Upazan's temper. Even his own followers laughed.

Srayanka handed Lita to Sappho and rose. 'Upazan, it is agreed by all the people who follow Kineas that they will accept his guidance on matters of war. Prince Lot has accepted. I have accepted.'

Upazan shook his head. 'I have not accepted. I have not seen any of his great skills.' He spat and smiled, uncowed by Kineas's nearness. 'I will fight you, old man. Then perhaps I will take your horses. I need horses to buy the love of a grass priestess.'

'She does not want you, Upazan,' Srayanka said as Lot pushed in under the canopy.

'It is of little matter to me. I will have her.' Upazan raised his chin.

Srayanka spoke slowly and clearly. 'The woman you are speaking of is your mother's sister's daughter. She is not for you. She will go to be Leon's wife.'

Lot interrupted. 'Your time with the Medes has made you forgetful of our ways, boy. No woman goes anywhere against her will.' Lot gave a grim smile. 'She might hurt you.'

Upazan looked around. 'You are all against me. Very well.' He crossed his arms. He had dignity for a man so young and with so much anger. 'Will you fight me, foreigner?'

Leon shot to his feet. 'I will fight you.'

Kineas handed his wine cup to Leon. 'This is a matter of discipline, not of revenge,' he said to Leon. And then to Upazan, 'Are you ready? The stakes are that when I win, you will swear to honour my orders. If you win, you will still follow my orders.'

Upazan spat. 'If I win, I will be king of the Sakje,' he said.

Kineas shook his head. 'It doesn't work that way, boy. Are you ready?'

'Are you ready to be a widow?' Upazan asked Srayanka.

Kineas laughed. 'No one is going to die, boy. Ready?'

For the first time, Upazan hesitated – a tiny crack in his façade. 'Ready?' he asked.

'The time is now.' Kineas took off his baldric and handed it to Leon, stripped his tunic over his head and stood naked.

Upazan stepped back. 'I have no weapons!' he said.

Kineas grinned. 'You challenged me. Among Greeks – and Sakje – that gives me the choice of weapons. And I warned you, boy, that the next time you crossed me, I would beat you like a child. Now, are you ready?'

Upazan narrowed his eyes while the women tittered at Kineas's nudity. Samahe demanded that Upazan strip, too. 'There are things Mosva needs to know!' she called in a voice of brass.

'This is not the fight I want!' Upazan said. 'This is the demeaning squabble of slaves!'

Kineas nodded. 'It is not the fight you want – I agree. So you may apologize and retract your challenge, or fight.'

Upazan looked around for counsel – for the support of the men who had ridden with him. A few of them had come up, watched by the Keltoi, but their faces were carefully blank. Upazan opened his tunic and dropped it to the rugs. He had thick cords of muscles – even by Greek standards, he had a good physique.

He raised his arms. 'I am ready,' he said.

Upazan didn't lack courage, and he was strong. But he was a poor wrestler and he had never even seen boxing.

Kineas had almost finished before Philokles, a late arrival, finished his wine. Kineas took his time, trying to teach the boy how powerless he was – a life lesson the boy clearly needed. He took a blow – powerful but untrained – on the muscle of his arm and then locked the Sauromatae in a hold around his neck, turned his body so that the younger man had no purchase and then hit him once with his fist on the temple. Upazan fell unconscious from his arms.

The Sakje and the Sauromatae joined in their applause, and Kineas was human enough to enjoy their praise while he strigilled with Philokles' help, enjoying the clean smell of olive oil on his flesh. Srayanka watched him thoughtfully.

'You are quite handsome,' she said with a half-smile. 'And the oil is strangely attractive.' Her eyebrows drew together as she frowned. 'But you would have done better to kill him.'

Kineas shrugged. 'I can't kill him and keep the Sauromatae as allies.'

Srayanka raised an eyebrow. 'You can't keep them anyway, my husband. And now – now he will be like a serpent.' She frowned, her eyebrows a single line over her nose. 'We had this conversation before. I was right then and I am still right.'

Kineas shrugged. 'Sometimes, you are like a Greek wife,' he said.

Philokles' strigil found the bruise on his arm where Upazan had landed a blow, and he winced.

Nihmu watched with ill-concealed glee. 'Your mercy is wasted on him, lord,' she said. 'He has none for others!'

'All the more reason for the strategos to show some mercy to him,' Philokles said.

The council gathered as the sun began to go down in the west. The air was almost cool and the dust of the day had settled. Kineas had Nicanor build a big fire in the clear ground behind Srayanka's wagon and he arranged as many stools as he could find. The tribal leaders came in little knots, gossiping about the feast and about Upazan. Kineas noted that Parshtaevalt came with Ataelus and Leon, while Lot stood apart with Monae, his wife. Upazan did not attend. The Olbian officers were all there.

Kineas rose after Nicanor had poured wine for them all. He made a libation, pouring the whole cup of good wine into the fire, so that a cloud of fragrant steam rose around him in the dark. 'I begin to sing of Pallas Athena, the glorious goddess,' he said, 'bright-eyed, inventive, unbending of heart, pure virgin, saviour of cities, courageous, *Tritogeneia*. Wise Zeus himself bore her from his manful head, already armed in bronze and gold, and awe seized all the gods as they looked at her. But Athena stood before Zeus who holds the aegis, shaking a bright iron spear. Olympus shook at the warlike ardour of the bright grey eyes, and the earth all around the mountain cried fearfully, and the sea rolled and spat dark waves and foam in sudden torment, until the maiden Athena stripped the glorious bronze from her lovely shoulders. And wise Zeus was glad.

'And so hail to you, daughter of Zeus who holds the aegis! Now we will remember you.'

Then he turned to his council. 'It is time for us to go and fight Alexander,' he said. 'We are here to discuss who will go, and how we will go.'

'We're best off where we are,' Lot said. 'There's no grazing east of here, and I've heard that the Massagetae camp and all the Scythians fill the vale of the Jaxartes, eating all the grass. Let us wait here until she summons us again.'

'We wouldn't even know if a battle took place,' Srayanka shot back. 'Zarina and the Jaxartes are ten days' ride from here.'

'Or more,' said Ataelus.

'We're running out of grass already,' Parshtaevalt said. He had aged quickly during Srayanka's captivity, and unlike Upazan, he had never had any interest in rulership beyond his own concept of duty. 'Already the herds are twenty stades from the camp.' He gave a bitter smile. 'I send my daughters to fetch my mounts every morning.'

Srayanka nodded. 'The grass is not of the best.'

Lot glanced at his wife. 'We are thinking of leaving our young and old with a guard and sending them back to our summer pasture,' he said. He sounded apologetic.

Srayanka surprised her husband by agreeing immediately. 'We should do the same. We should transform ourselves into a great war host and not a movement of all the people.'

'The warriors left behind will be bitter,' Parshtaevalt said. 'They will miss the great battle.'

Srayanka shook her head. 'Let every warrior left behind be one who served at the Ford of the River God,' she said. 'And let them console themselves with remaining alive.'

Kineas approved, but he leaned over to her and whispered, 'So we leave our veterans? And take only the young?'

She shook her head. 'We take our best, and then leave a tithe of our best as guards. It is the way. Those who stay behind are chosen by chance from those who are picked to go. Do you understand?' She looked at him gravely. 'And if we are badly defeated, the people will yet have an army of proven warriors.'

Kineas nodded. 'A very good system. Yes, I understand.' He smiled. 'I understand that I have much to learn if I am to act as the king!'

Srayanka shrugged. 'No more than any man,' she said. 'Or woman!'

Lot rubbed his beard. 'I fear we cannot host you on our summer grazing,' he said. 'I am sorry. There is hard feeling because of the boy – Upazan, despite his hot head, has many friends. But more, we have many horses – more than I can ever remember.' He rocked his head back and forth in self-mockery. 'I must be a good prince.'

338

Srayanka looked at Kineas. Kineas took a sip of wine – it was almost gone – and nodded. 'I think our own people should start west,' Kineas said.

There was murmuring from all around the fire.

Srayanka looked surprised. 'Now?' she asked.

Kineas nodded. 'Now. If they go soon, and stay on the move, they'll have no fodder problem. Three months will see them at the fort on the Rha. Messengers can tell Crax to buy grain against the winter, and the high plains will have abundant grass in the spring.' He looked at Lot. 'I think we should travel separately – not because of your foolish nephew, but because that's the way we've crossed the bad ground to get here. I want to talk about the route.'

Lot nodded.

Kineas went on, 'As I see it, there are two routes and two sets of risk. If we go straight east, we cross the desert – and crossing in mid-summer will be very different from crossing in spring. Together we have ten thousand horses. Perhaps after we send our people to their winter grass, we'll have four thousand horses.' He shrugged. 'That's a lot of water.'

All around the fire, men and women nodded, picturing the desert crossing.

'If we ride south for two days, we'll be back at the forks of the Polytimeros. As I understand it, we can follow the Polytimeros into the valley of Marakanda, and then go north through the Sogdian gap to the Jaxartes, and never spend a night without water.'

'There is Alexander,' Diodorus said.

'Both routes have risk,' Kineas said. 'Alexander will have outposts on the Polytimeros. The closer we go to Marakanda, the more dangerous it will be. But if we move like Sakje, we could be with Queen Zarina and the Massagetae in a fortnight.'

'If Alexander catches us in the valley of the Polytimeros, we'll be in a lot of trouble.'

'We scout carefully and move fast.' Kineas looked around. 'We've left it late, friends. If we are agreed that we're going to Zarina – that we'll help her stop Alexander this summer – then we must go *now* and we must go *fast*.'

People were nodding.

Kineas continued. 'I have one more argument to make. There's no point in riding to the Jaxartes only to arrive on blown horses who need a month on the grass to fight. The desert is certain – we will take losses. The Polytimeros requires that Athena – and Tyche – smile on us.'

Lot rose to his feet. 'You are persuasive,' he said. 'And I will follow you in battle. But in this thing, I must go my own way. The desert is the surest way. Beasts will die, but unless we're unlucky, no man or woman will die. The Sauromatae will cross the desert.'

Srayanka rose in turn. 'The Sakje will ride the Polytimeros, if the Olbians will go that way.'

Diodorus looked at Kineas. 'Do I actually get a vote?'

Kineas nodded.

Diodorus scratched at his beard. 'If we have to fight, I'd rather fight in the condition we're in right now. I'm with Kineas. I think we can brush the Macedonian outposts aside and move three hundred stades a day. Unless they have a force prepared, we'll be past their outposts before they can catch us.'

Kineas looked around. He saw no outrage, and sensed that enough had been said. 'Then let us divide those who will go to Zarina from those who will go to the winter grass. Say your farewells. Because I mean us to ride the day after tomorrow.'

To Diodorus and Philokles, Kineas made another argument, ladling mutton stew at the mess fire later that night. 'We're going to the muster of the Scythians,' Kineas said. 'Our Greek cavalry will be out of place, and in action they might be mistaken for foes.'

Nihmu, not a member of their mess and not an invited guest, plopped down with her riding blanket, smelling of honeysuckle and horse sweat, and neatly intercepted the bowl of stew. 'Thanks, Strategos,' she said. 'I dreamed you were to cook, and so I came.'

Kineas glared at her and the other men laughed.

Philokles laughed with the others, mopping the bottom of

his wooden bowl with flatbread. After he laughed, he looked thoughtful, his blond beard seeming alive in the firelight. Nihmu put her back against his while she ate.

Diodorus shook his head. 'They don't look like the boys who rode out of Olbia, Kineas. Look at them on parade in the morning. You're not the only man in Sakje armour. We have Greek helmets – so do most of the Sakje. Eh? Hard to find a man who doesn't have a grass wife to sew for him – leather tunics on most, and some in barbarian leggings.'

'They still look Greek to me,' Philokles said. He raised his bowl to Kineas. 'Good mutton,' he said.

'On his grave stele, we can put "Kineas – Strategos and Cook".' Diodorus laughed.

'Even the Keltoi?' Kineas asked, trying to get back to the subject at hand. He'd meant it as a joke, but it made the other two thoughtful.

'No,' Philokles said. 'No, the Keltoi don't look Greek. It is a way of sitting – or perhaps it is the tattoos.'

Diodorus gave a wry smile and held out his bowl for more. 'I long to see your Carlus recline at a symposium. Hah! He'd break the couch!'

Kineas smiled. 'I suggest we send the Olbians back to Hyrkania under Eumenes, with orders to take command from Lycurgus and Heron. Or,' and here he found that his voice faltered, 'or under one of you.'

Diodorus narrowed his eyes, making him look even more like a fox than usual. 'This is your revenge for all my carping? No. I won't miss the battle.'

Kineas shook his head. 'There may not *be* a battle.'

Philokles shook his head in turn. 'Where you go, I go, if only to keep you from your wife's foolish superstitions.' He strained to see Nihmu. 'And yours.'

'Eumenes?' Kineas looked at them.

'He'll obey,' Diodorus said.

'It will depend on what course Urvara takes,' Philokles said. 'He loves her.'

Kineas realized that, as usual, Philokles was awake to signs that he, Kineas, should have noted. 'Of course,' he said. 'And that's why he and Leon are friends now.' He laughed.

Diodorus rubbed his beard. 'I suspect the barbarian lottery is less fair than it appears,' he said. 'Shall I fix it?'

Kineas nodded. 'Excellent idea, but let Srayanka do it.'

Diodorus nodded.

'Let Srayanka do what?' she asked, walking out of the darkness and into the firelight.

Kineas pointed at Philokles. 'He says Eumenes and Urvara are – together.'

Srayanka pretended to inspect Philokles' empty bowl by firelight. 'Not too foul. May I have some of this mutton?' She held out her bowl to her husband. Then she said, 'They are not *together* – yet.' She grinned.

Kineas handed her a full bowl from the bronze kettle at his feet. It was wearing out, the two cast gryphons that held the bucket's bail needed new rivets, and if his cauldron needed a bronze smithy, then every cauldron in the army was in the same shape. One of thousands of things they needed.

His eyes met hers, and they shared something about food and cooking – quarter-smiles that agreed that there was nothing remarkable about a wife returning from setting night patrols to be fed by her husband, the general. 'The children?'

'Surprisingly asleep,' Kineas said. 'They were so quiet I had to look at them twice to be sure all was well.'

Srayanka walked away with her mutton, heading for the wagon. To see for herself.

'So we're settled?' Kineas said. 'We send some Olbians home as insurance for the Sakje. The Keltoi and the mercenaries and any volunteers from the former hoplites may stay under Diodorus and Andronicus. The men who stay get the pick of the horses and are to do their best to trade for barbarian armour.'

Philokles raised an eyebrow. 'What of Temerix?'

Kineas winced. 'Easy man to forget when he's not in combat. I assume he'll come with us to the east.'

Diodorus nodded. He pursed his lips and then said, 'All of those Sindi can ride like centaurs. Let's get them all decent horses – we have the stock. Not much use for psiloi out on the plains.'

Kineas ate his own mutton and drank an infusion of herbs in water rather than wine, which was in short supply. Philokles chewed bread and Diodorus looked at the stars, until Srayanka returned. Nihmu sang a little song to herself and then fell asleep, her head in Philokles' lap.

'They are fine,' Srayanka said, returning.

'We'd like to mount the Sindi on Sakje remounts,' Kineas said.

Srayanka nodded. 'How many? Two per man?' she asked.

'At least,' Diodorus answered. Like all the Greek officers, Diodorus had become addicted to the Sakje system of having three or four remounts for every rider. It made the army virtually tireless.

'Two hundred horses. I have as many,' she said. 'And more. I will ask certain Sakje to give a horse – many have been served by the dirt people, and this should be a reward.'

Diodorus nodded. 'Thank you, Srayanka. They deserve it.' He sat back. 'Since – Niceas died – Temerix has not received the consideration due him. I'm trying to fill the gap.'

'I'm embarrassed to be so reminded,' Kineas said.

And the twins woke with one voice, and all conversation was at an end.

25

'Craterus is at the Forks of the Polytimeros,' Coenus reported.

The sun was rising on a new day, and Kineas was already hot and sticky. He wore only his tunic, pulled on hastily when he heard that there was a scout coming in. Coenus was covered in dust, his usual foppishness ruined, his face a comic mask where runnels of sweat had carved lines across the coating of grey-brown grit.

He had insisted on leading a patrol because he was, he felt, 'out of practice'.

Kineas sent Nicanor for all the leaders. 'You saw him?'

'In person.' Coenus gave a dusty grin. 'He's not somebody you soon forget! A thousand cavalry – perhaps some mounted infantry as well. I didn't stay to scout the whole column. Mosva had just come in with another Sauromatae girl to tell us that Spitamenes was moving north – they found his camp – and the next thing I knew my outriders were shooting arrows at his outriders. He came up in person while I was still trying to guess their numbers.'

Kineas rubbed his beard. 'He'll block our way.'

Diodorus came running up with Philokles and Eumenes close behind. 'He'll be in among our wagons in a day. What the hell is he doing here?'

Coenus shook his head. 'He's fast. But I'll wager a daric to an owl that he's after Spitamenes – trying to cut him off from the sea of grass.'

Diodorus started buckling his cuirass. 'You are ready to command armies, Coenus. The problem is that he must have taken your scouts for Spitamenes'.'

Kineas found that Nicanor was bringing him his armour. He stuck his arms up while Nicanor lowered the linen and scale cuirass over his head. As soon as the shoulder flaps were fastened to the breastplate, he started drawing lines in the dust.

'If you were Craterus, in pursuit of Spitamenes—' he said.

'I'd have wine,' Coenus said, hefting an empty amphora. Nicanor brought him a towel and a clay bottle of water. Nicanor enjoyed serving Coenus because Coenus had the kind of standards that Nicanor liked to live up to – unlike Kineas, who didn't feel the need to dress to Athenian fashion in the midst of the sea of grass. He wiped the dust from his face and started to towel his hair. 'If I were Craterus, I'd break off and go home. If I hit resistance on the Oxus, I would think that Spitamenes was ahead of me.'

'Or I'd press the pursuit, hoping to hurt his rearguard,' Diodorus said. 'Let's face it, that's more like Craterus. He's a terrier – once he gets his jaws on something, he never lets go. When have you ever known him *not* to press a pursuit until his horse fell?'

'You all know this Macedonian?' Philokles asked.

'He's older now,' Kineas said, by way of an answer. 'Alexander's left fist, we used to call him.'

'He doesn't have Parmenion to hold his hand, either,' Diodorus shot back.

'So it could go either way. He could turn back, or he could be on us in, what, four hours?' Kineas looked at Coenus.

Ataelus came in, his bow arm still bound in a sling. The wound had infected and bled pus constantly. Ataelus looked like a man with a fever and he walked unsteadily.

'You're not fit to ride, Ataelus. Get back to your pallet and your wife.' Kineas saw Samahe behind her husband. 'Take him away!'

'Alexander is coming, and you for sending me to bed?' Ataelus stumbled and caught himself on the tent's central pole. 'Need scouts. Need for seeing over hills. Prodromoi go!' Ataelus struck his chest. 'Samahe go, Ataelus go.'

Coenus, who had always got on well with the Scythian, shook his head. 'We did do a certain amount of scouting before you came on the scene, brother.'

Ataelus grinned. 'No little cut for keeping me from this. Alexander comes.'

Coenus, cleaner now, tossed his towel to Nicanor. 'It's

not Alexander, Ataelus. It's just Craterus. We can handle him without you.'

Diodorus was looking at Kineas's marks in the dust. 'Where's Spitamenes?' he asked.

'Ares, let's not make that mistake again,' Kineas said.

Diodorus picked up a stick. He threw a glance at Ataelus, who stood by his shoulder to correct him if he went wrong.

'I think I understand. Let's say this anthill is Marakanda. Let's say this line is the Polytimeros and this is the Oxus,' Diodorus drew a line from the anthill that represented Marakanda, and then a second at right angles to represent the Oxus. 'If Alexander has raised the siege at Marakanda – that's my guess – then Craterus is pursuing Spitamenes west – right at us.' Diodorus moved the stick along the line of the Polytimeros and stopped at the Oxus – the cross of the T. 'If Spitamenes went straight across, he'd vanish into the sea of grass – south of us, but not by much. If the girls saw the camp right, the Persians are *west* and *south* of us.' He drew another line. 'If Craterus is at the forks of the Polytimeros,' he went on, stick pointing at the place where the Polytimeros met the Oxus, 'then we're three points in an equilateral triangle: we're at this end of the T, Spitamenes at the other end of the crossbar and Craterus down here on the base. And if Spitamenes chooses to try to link up with Queen Zarina,' he continued his line, 'he'll go right through here, following the crossbar. With Craterus right behind him.'

'And he can't miss us,' Coenus said. 'And if Craterus mistook our Sakje for Spitamenes' Sogdians, he's already on his way. And then he's between Spitamenes and us.'

Srayanka rubbed the bridge of her nose. 'We have to fight.'

Lot came in, flanked by two of his knights. 'Alexander is here?' he asked.

'He may be less than a day's march away.' Kineas recapitulated the crisis. 'It is Alexander's general Craterus. The king himself is at Marakanda.' Kineas shrugged. 'Or so we think.'

'Our people must march north,' Lot said. 'Most of us are packed. The wagons of the Sakje will slow us.'

'Without them, many will die this winter,' Srayanka shot back.

Kineas looked around, catching their eyes. 'Get the pro-dromoi out. We'll make a stand here. Perhaps even try a little negotiation.'

Diodorus raised a red eyebrow, but then he hurried out. Philokles stood by. 'Which one would you negotiate with?' he asked.

Kineas shook his head, staring at his map in the dust. 'Alexander is the enemy we came to fight,' he said. 'Spitamenes sold Srayanka to Macedon.'

Philokles stroked his beard. 'I'm tired of war,' he said. 'Neither of them seems so very bad to me. Alexander is a tyrant, but a Hellene. Spitamenes is a Mede, but a patriot.' He shrugged. 'Who is the enemy?'

Kineas looked at his map. 'Craterus will be here first, if he's coming,' he said. 'If we held him, and sent a messenger to Spitamenes – we could defeat him here.' Kineas looked around.

Philokles waved a hand dismissively. 'Do we need to fight?'

Kineas nodded. 'The wagons will roll in two hours,' he said. 'We need to hold here at least until darkness, or we could have Craterus's outriders in among the columns.'

Scythians travelled the sea of grass in two or three parallel columns of wagons, with the herds penned between them and watched by a vanguard and a rearguard of young riders. The columns raised so much dust on the summer plains that they could be seen for fifteen stades and the rearguard was often blind owing to the dust raised.

'He'll push his men after the columns of dust,' Coenus added. 'May I speak frankly, friend?'

Kineas was surprised by his tone. 'Of course!'

Coenus finished his water. 'Do you really want to ambush Craterus? To what purpose?'

Philokles nodded as if in agreement, but after a pause of shocked silence, he said, 'For the liberation of Greece.' He stood up like an orator. 'Any defeat Alexander suffers weakens his choke hold on Greece. If he is beaten out here, all the states of Greece will rise up and be free. Sparta – Athens – Megara.'

Coenus laughed. 'Don't you believe it, Philokles. They'll find a way to fuck it up, trust me. They'll fight among themselves.' He shook his head sadly. 'I'm not much interested in liberating Greece. I'm a gentleman of Olbia now.'

Srayanka licked her lips, and then smiled. 'We should defeat Alexander because he is dangerous,' she said. 'Because he is like a wild dog, and if he is not killed, he will savage our flocks.'

'Craterus is the enemy. Spitamenes is a possible ally – otherwise, just an interruption. Spitamenes poses no threat to Olbia.' Kineas looked around and got nods of agreement. 'Glad that's settled,' Kineas said. He was armoured – so were most of the men he could see. 'Let's move.'

The columns rolled off before the sun crested the sky. The Sauromatae led the way, although Lot and his best warriors were left behind with Kineas's force holding the high ground just west of the Oxus. The Sauromatae held the right of the line, hidden in a fold of ground behind a low ridge that ran parallel to the track of the trade road. Kineas placed the trained Greek horse in the centre under Diodorus, with the Olbians on the right under Eumenes and Antigonus and the Keltoi on the left under Coenus and Andronicus. On the right, Srayanka led the Sakje with Parshtaevalt and Urvara. Kineas kept a reserve of mixed Sakje and Greek cavalry – men and women who had trained together for a month – under his own command in the rear. The total force was a little less than eight hundred, because more than a third of their strength was guarding the columns and herding the animals.

Darius was off to find Spitamenes and, if he could, persuade the partisan to alliance or at least tolerance, over Srayanka's objections.

Ataelus and his prodromoi, with Coenus and his picked men, were out in the trough of the Oxus valley and farther south and east.

It was noon before the battlefield was prepared and all the men in place. Kineas sat atop the ridge with Leon, Philokles,

Diodorus and a handful of Sakje maidens as messengers. There was no shade and the sun painted them in fire; not a breath of wind stirred the dust. Anywhere that the casual exercise of riding caused bare skin to contact armour – all too common – left a line of pain. Kineas used his cloak to cover his armour and then sweltered in the gritty heat of a wool cloak.

His mouth was so full of dust that even after he rinsed and spat, his molars ground together as if he was chewing pottery.

Leon watched the wooded ground in the valley with all the stress of a lover worried for his friend. Which he was. Mosva was down there with Ataelus instead of back behind the ridge with her father.

An hour passed, and then a second hour.

A third hour.

A fourth hour.

The sun was sinking appreciably. The day was cooler. The horses were restless, eager for the water they could smell in the bed of the Oxus, signalling their displeasure with shrill calls and a great deal of stomping and rein-chewing.

Kineas watched it all in an agony of indecision and doubt. *If I water the horses, and he comes – if Spitamenes refuses to cooperate – if Spitamenes comes first – if Craterus comes from the east on this side of the Oxus – if the horses require water – now? – now? – now? Where is he? Where is he?*

Where is Craterus?

They saw the dust cloud before they got a report. The cloud looked to be forty stades distant, or more, but distances could be misleading on the plains. While all his friends debated its meaning, Samahe rode in, the cloud towering over her shoulder like a thunderhead. Her red leather tunic was almost brown with dust, but her chain of gold plaques glinted in the sun.

'Craterus comes,' she said. 'For killing one enemy I shot.' She mimed her draw and release. 'Ataelus for saying "Ride and tell Kineas – he comes!" and Ataelus say word. Say "Iskander deploys!"' She pointed. 'And for dirt-eating Sogdii! Fight for Iskander, fight for Spitamenes. Same.'

Kineas leaned forward. 'Samahe, are you *sure* these are Craterus's men? Not Spitamenes' Sogdae?'

'Greek men in bronze with cloaks like yours,' she said, nodding. She pointed.

Kineas looked around. 'Time for the army to water their horses?' he asked.

'Easy,' she answered. 'Hour. Maybe more.'

Kineas nodded. 'Water the horses,' he said. 'Craterus is on to us. We have about half an hour. Bring the whole army down; give the beasts a good drink and then straight back to your places. Push the prodromoi right across to cover the watering. Tell Eumenes to have a section ready to reinforce the picket line at need.' And he watched in agony, waiting for the Macedonians to come and crash into his horses as they drank.

No Macedonians appeared, but there was someone out in the tamarisk scrub on the far side of the Oxus, and there was more and more dust above the flood line, and glints of colour, flashes of steel, movement. After half an hour, Ataelus's prodromoi were under constant, if inaccurate, arrow fire from the high ground of the opposite spring bank. Nihmu came back, walking her royal stallion, which was calling loudly in pain with an arrow in his withers. Nihmu was bleeding from her shoulder. She was pale, but she came up to Kineas. 'Ataelus asks that you send him some force. We are hard-pressed.'

Kineas nodded. 'Get that wound looked after,' he said. The girl was at most thirteen years old – to Kineas, too young to be in battle. But as he watched, she was taking the arrow out of her horse's rump, crooning to the beast while she used a tiny knife to slip the barbed head free. He never kicked. When she was done, the work of a moment, she vaulted into the saddle.

'Ride down to the river and tell Eumenes to take his sortie across,' Kineas said. The watering was taking too long, and sending Olbians to clear the Sogdae would only slow it further.

Eumenes took almost half his troop across the Oxus. Kineas watched them trot across at the main ford and turn south in the tamarisk scrub in the valley, spreading out in a skirmish line. Every man had his javelin in his fist, ready to throw. They swept south and east, and suddenly there was a swirl of dust and a keening yell and Kineas's guts clenched. There were Sogdae riding out of the brush, at least forty of them.

He couldn't hear Eumenes and he couldn't see what was happening and his imagination was worse than the reality as the dust swirled and thickened. He clenched his reins and worried, riding back and forth on his ridge. He watched the people watering their horses and tried to urge them to go faster, to cut through the crowds on the riverbank, to get back in battle order.

'Eumenes can handle a fight with barbarians,' Philokles said.

'Not if he's badly outnumbered.' Kineas shook his head. 'Athena, be with us in our hour of need.' Kineas turned to Diodorus. 'Should we send him reinforcements?'

Diodorus shook his head. 'Let's wait for his report. Ares, I'm getting sick of this.'

Just when Kineas was preparing to order Diodorus into the scrub, Eumenes returned, riding across the ford with six empty saddles. He was injured, blood all down one booted leg, and his face was pinched with anger and pain. 'The scrub is full of them,' he said. 'Hundreds of them. Sogdians, I think – I don't know whether they're Craterus's or Spitamenes' – who in Hades can tell?' He shook his head. 'We rode into an ambush. I'm sorry. It is my fault.'

Kineas watched. 'Samahe says they're from Craterus.' The Sakje, their mounts watered, were already clearing the Oxus and returning to their positions. The Olbians were slower, and the heavily armoured Sauromatae were used to having maiden archers to do this sort of thing while they baked like ovens. They were *slow*. Kineas cursed the bad luck of it all – and the loss of the remounts and manpower that the horse herds and the wagon columns had taken. Then he reached out and clasped Eumenes' hand. 'In war, we lose men. We carry the responsibility.' In his head, his words sounded unbearably pompous. 'You did the job I sent you to do. Did you hurt them?'

Eumenes shook his head, at the edge of a sob. 'I walked into the ambush,' he said. 'They were waiting in the scrub. I should know better.' Sullenly, he said, 'I hurt them. I pushed them out of the scrub and back up the bank, but they'll be back.' He looked across the river, where the dust of the skirmish hung in the still air, and wiped his brow. He'd lost the brow band that held his hair.

Philokles reached into his shoulder pack and produced another. 'Let me tie your hair, lad,' he said kindly.

Eumenes continued to slouch, looking at the ground in misery. 'I should have done better,' he said again.

Kineas rubbed his chin. 'Sit straight and suck it up,' he said.

Stung, Eumenes sat straight.

'That's better,' Kineas said. He nodded. 'Let Philokles look at your wound, and then back to your troop and get the rest of the horses watered. Mourn the dead later. Help me win this thing now.'

Eumenes saluted. He dismounted and let Philokles tie his hair and look at the cut on his thigh. Before he could ride away, Srayanka rode up.

'Let me send Parshtaevalt,' she said. 'We need to clear it before the fucking Sogdae make attacks on our Sauromatae.'

Kineas started to refuse. Then he looked at Philokles and Diodorus. 'I dislike breaking up my force,' he said.

Eumenes pulled his helmet off, his face red with exertion. He spoke cautiously, conscious of his defeat. 'I took casualties trying to rattle them,' he said. 'I think that ...' He hesitated, and then drove on. 'I think Srayanka is right.'

Diodorus nodded. 'It wouldn't take many of their arrows falling on the Sauromatae to cause trouble,' he said. 'There's something going on with them that I don't like.'

Kineas waited another moment, thoughts racing like a galloping horse, and then exhaled. 'Go!' Kineas said to Srayanka. She turned and waved to Parshtaevalt, who raised his bow and pointed one end of it at certain horsemen, and they were away – a hundred riders vanishing into the tamarisk scrub in the Oxus valley. They seemed to ride impossibly fast for the broken ground, passing through Ataelus's prodromoi in their picket line. Samahe, visible in her red and gold, raised her bow in salute as the Sakje rode by, and Parshtaevalt whooped.

A flight of birds burst from the foliage on the far side of the river and then ten Sakje were up the bank. They were hunkered down on their horse's necks, and they were fast, flowing over the ground more like running cats than men and women on horses.

What if the scrub was *full* of Sogdae? Where was Craterus? Was he already scouting another ford on the Oxus? Indecision or, to call the cat by its true name, *fear* moved through Kineas's guts like the flux. Sweat from his helmet dripped down his brow and then down his face like tears, and he could *smell* the dirt on his chinstrap, which stank like old cheese. He prayed for wind. He prayed that he had guessed well. He peered into the gathering dust. The light was going as the afternoon grew old.

A chorus of thin shouts on the afternoon breeze, and riders swept out of the farthest foliage two stades away across the muddy river, firing as they came, ripping shots at the Sakje, who turned and fled as if their horses had neither momentum nor bones – they fled like a school of Aegean fish before the onrush of a predator, a porpoise or a shark. The leaders of the Sogdae pressed the handful of Sakje hard, and one man mounted on a big roan rode flat out for Parshtaevalt, visible because his horse harness was studded with gold. The Sakje chief turned his body an impossible three-quarters rotation and shot straight back over the rump of his horse into his pursuer, catching him in the belly and robbing him of life. Parshtaevalt then slowed his horse and caught the dead man's reins, shouting his war cry. He brandished his bow while a dozen Sogdians bore down on him and another handful shot at him. He grinned, waved his bow and rode off, again shrieking his war cry so that it rang off the sides of the Oxus valley while arrows fell around him and all the ridges rang with cheers.

The Sogdians, angry now, pounded after the handful of Sakje, more and more riders emerging from the brush to avenge their fallen warrior. They were close on the tails of the

Scythian horses when the other seventy Sakje appeared out of the river bed and fired a single volley of arrows and charged home under their own lethal rain, emptying a dozen saddles in as many heartbeats.

Shattered, the Sogdians broke and ran. The Sakje pursued them hard, right up the bank, and dust rose around them as their hooves pounded the dry earth. After a few breaths, they came back, whooping and waving their bows and spears. Parshtaevalt rode back to where he'd dropped his man and, heedless of the stray shafts of the remaining Sogdians, slipped from his horse and cut the hair and neck skin from his downed enemy before leaping on to his pony. He collected his riders with a wave and then they were back among the officers in the river bed.

Parshtaevalt's hands were bloody to the elbow, and rivulets of blood had run all the way down his torso where he had raised his arms in the air to show his trophies. 'Too long have I been the nursemaid!' he said in his excellent Greek. 'Aiyeee!'

Srayanka kissed him, and most of the rest of the Sakje pressed forward to touch him.

Kineas was grinning. 'Was that Achilles?' he asked.

Philokles met his grin with one of his own. 'I have seldom seen anything so beautiful,' Philokles said. He wiped his eyes with the back of his hand. 'Praise to Ares that I was allowed to see so brave an act. Ah!' He sang:

Ares, exceeding in strength, chariot-rider, golden-helmed,
Doughty in heart, shield-bearer, saviour of cities, harnessed
    in bronze,
Strong of arm, unwearying, mighty with the spear,
O defence of Olympus, father of warlike Victory,
Ally of Themis, stern governor of the rebellious,
Leader of righteous men, sceptred king of manliness,
Who whirl your fiery sphere among the planets
In their sevenfold courses through the aether
Wherein your blazing steeds ever bear you
Above the third firmament of heaven;
Hear me, helper of men, giver of dauntless youth!

Shed down a kindly ray from above upon my life,
And strength of war, that I may be able to drive
Away bitter cowardice from my head
And crush down the deceitful impulses of my soul.
Restrain also the keen fury of my heart
Which provokes me to tread the ways of blood-curdling
    strife.
Rather, O blessed one, give me boldness to abide
Within the harmless laws of peace, avoiding strife
And hatred and the violent fiends of death.

The Greeks took it up, and the Olbians had good voices. They sang, roaring the lines as if every man of them was a champion, and the sound carried over the cropped, dry grass and the sand to the Sogdae, who were gathered on their bank, no longer willing to push down into the flood plain and the tamarisk scrub, just visible in the rising column of dust and sand from the fight. Their horses were fidgeting and calling for water.

When the song was done, the Greek horse gathered their mounts and dragged them from the water and up the bank to their ridge. Concealment was now purposeless, but Kineas sent them back over the ridge anyway – easier than giving them new positions, and some shade to protect them. The shadows were long, but the sun still had power out on the plains.

The Sauromatae were still watering their horses. Kineas rode over in time to hear Lot cursing at some men who were still in the stream. One of them waved his golden helmet, and all fifteen of the men in the stream mounted. The man in the golden helmet turned his horse in a spray of water. He had his horse at the gallop in just a few strides, and he rode straight for Mosva, who was watering her father's horse. She looked up and grinned, clearly thinking it a game. She called something, and she died with that smile on her face, as Upazan cut her head from her body in one swing of his long-handled axe. Then he turned and rode at Lot.

'Now fight me, you old coward!' he crowed, riding at the prince.

Leon, at Kineas's side, put his head down and pressed his

heels to his mount. He had a small mare with a deep chest and a small head, a pretty horse that Leon doted on. She fairly flew across the water, her hooves appearing to skim the surface. Too late to save Mosva, Leon rode in. Upazan, his whole charge aimed at Lot, pushed for his target and ignored the Numidian, but the smaller mare rammed the bigger Sauromatae gelding in the rump, forcing the horse to stumble and sidestep, almost throwing his rider.

Upazan took a cut at Leon with the axe. Leon's mare danced back, and the axe missed, and Leon's spear licked out, pricking Upazan in the side. Kineas, still stunned to see two of his own men fighting, had time to be reminded of Nicomedes' fastidious fighting style. The Numidian used his mare to avoid every cut and he landed two more blows that drew blood.

Upazan's companions were milling in confusion and then one of them left the others and rode at Leon.

Lot was frozen in disbelief. 'Bastard!' he called, pressing forward.

Another of Upazan's men drew a bow and shot. The arrow passed between Philokles and Kineas. A second arrow rattled off Lot's armour.

Upazan stood up, knees clenched on the barrel of his horse, and leaned out, whirling his axe on the wrist thong for more reach. It caught Leon on the bull's-hide shield he wore strapped to his left shoulder in the Sakje manner and skidded up, ringing off the Numidian's helmet. At the same moment, Leon's spear licked out again, this time passing under the bronze brow of the Sauromatae's heavy helm and entering the man's face. Blood flowered from under his helmet and Upazan folded.

Leon fell into the river and Philokles and Kineas raced to reach him, while Upazan's friends dragged him free of his horse and bolted for the far side of the stream.

'Arse-cunts!' bellowed Philokles, struggling with his horse and trying to get an arm under Leon. 'Traitors!'

Lot was still cursing. The ranks of the Sauromatae were moving like a corpse full of maggots.

'I must calm my people,' he said. His voice was dull. He

looked like a man who had taken a wound. His daughter's headless corpse lay at the far edge of the river and the water was a sickly red-brown where her blood mingled with the silt.

Several of Ataelus's scouts surrounded her. Others rushed to surround Leon. Philokles and Eumenes supported Leon out of the water. Kineas laid him on the bank and cut his chinstrap. The base of his skull showed blood and his neck was cut so deep that the cords of his neck muscles could be seen. There was blood everywhere.

'He killed her, didn't he?' Leon asked in a dull voice.

Philokles was off his horse and there. 'Concussion,' he said. 'Give him to me. You command your army.'

Kineas handed over that responsibility with thanks and remounted. He swept his horse in a circle, another ugly feeling in his gut.

Upazan's companions had crossed the river straight south and then ridden east along the water. The Sakje, confused, had not loosed an arrow. Even the prodromoi let them go.

Two stades away to the south and east, a man in a dust-coloured cloak with wide purple bands at the edges reined in at the far edge of the Oxus. Behind him was a dense column of purple-blue cloaks and dirty brown cloaks – Macedonian cavalry and a handful of Royal Hetairoi. Trumpets sounded and the blond man waved a dozen troopers forward to intercept Upazan's friends. And then the dust cloud of the column settled over everything.

Kineas turned to Diodorus. 'That is what we call a bad omen,' he said. He couldn't take his eyes off the blood in the water. When he did, all he could see were the Sauromatae, trickling back over the ridge.

Diodorus made a sign of aversion. 'If Spitamenes comes now and decides to take our side?' he said.

Kineas rode back up the face of the ridge that concealed his cavalry. He stopped at the top. The Sauromatae were spread in groups over several stades of the rough ground, and all could be seen to be arguing. Kineas rode down into the valley beyond, looking for Lot. When he found him, in the middle of a dozen furious warriors, he rode straight in.

'Will you hold?' Kineas asked. 'Or do I have to retreat?'

Stung, Lot drew himself up. 'We'll hold,' he said.

Kineas looked around at the Sauromatae warriors, who met his gaze steadily. Kineas pointed up the hill with his sword. 'Two summers, we have covered each other's backs,' he said. 'No *boy*, no *kin-slayer*, is going to rob us of victory.'

Grunts and nods. 'Wait for my signal,' Kineas said, and rode back up the ridge to Diodorus, feeling far less confidence than he had just expressed.

'We're fucked,' Kineas said, showing Diodorus what he saw. 'If even a third of them decide to support Upazan and attack the rest, Craterus can cross at will.'

Diodorus nodded. 'Ares' throbbing *cock*,' he said bitterly. 'We *have* him. Craterus is too late to push us and we're already outfighting his Sogdae. Look at them!' Diodorus pointed at the far bank. The sullen unwillingness of the Sogdae troopers there was conveyed through posture and movement, but to a pair of cavalrymen, it was like a shout.

Kineas waved for Srayanka and cantered down over the ridge, invisible from Craterus's position. Once out of sight, he began to use his hands. 'See that,' he shouted at Srayanka as she rode up.

She pulled off her helmet and her black braids fell free from their coils. 'See it? Husband, my eyes have seen nothing else for an hour. Was that Mosva?' she asked.

'Yes,' Kineas spat in disgust. 'I'm betting that they hold, but I want you to be ready to cover our retreat. If Craterus wants to cross, I intend to make him pay.' He hesitated for a moment. 'I may even attack him.' He pointed across. 'If we leave him here, that's the end of our dream of moving on the Polytimeros.'

She nodded.

Kineas turned to Ataelus, who had just brought the prodromoi back across the Oxus and was now awaiting orders.

'Go north, behind Srayanka, and then back into the scrub. Cover my left flank.'

Ataelus was pale, his shoulder and arm stiff with bandages, but his eyes gleamed. 'Sure,' he said. He turned his horse and waved his whip, and the prodromoi, all on fresh horses, trotted north.

Kineas pointed over his shoulder. 'Our wagons are only an hour's steady ride north,' he said – a silly thing to say, as she would know as well as he. 'We have to fight.' He kissed her and rode back to the Olbians in the centre.

'What the fuck is going on with the boiler-ovens?' Eumenes asked, pointing at the Sauromatae and giving them the Greek name for fully armoured men.

'Upazan made a stab at being king,' Kineas said. 'He killed Mosva and probably intended to kill Lot as well.'

'He loved her,' Eumenes said. He swallowed. 'I was – quite fond …' His attempt to remain laconic failed and he sobbed.

Kineas gave him a hug. 'Not where the troops can see you, my boy,' he said, hiding the younger man with his cloak. 'Choke on it. There – are you ready?'

'Yes,' Eumenes said. He took a deep breath.

'Don't let Urvara see you sobbing for that girl,' Diodorus said.

Kineas glared at him. 'Diodorus!' Kineas said. 'I seem to remember…' he began, and Diodorus gave him a rueful smile.

'I remember too,' he said.

Together, they rode back over the crest of the ridge. A handful of Craterus's Sogdians were crossing the Oxus in a spray of water well to the west. 'Too far west to threaten us very soon,' Kineas said.

Diodorus unslung a water skin. 'Mmm,' he said. 'Muddy *and* warm. Faint smell of goat, too.' He grinned appreciatively. 'By now, Craterus has heard we have problems from that dickless arse-cunt Upazan, so he's going to put pressure on the weakness and then come right across into our faces.' He smiled. 'Of course, by now he sees all the dust Lot is raising. He has no real idea of how many we are and he still doesn't know where Spitamenes is.' He pulled off his helmet and hung it on his sword hilt. 'Even the Dog will take his time. Since we're not Spitamenes, he probably doesn't need to fight.' Diodorus looked up and down. 'But knowing Craterus, he hasn't figured out that we're not his prey. And he's ignoring the fact that his Sogdians are already afraid of us.'

Kineas nodded. 'And he hasn't watered his horses,' he said.

Diodorus scratched his chin. 'Have to admit I thought you were mad to try it, but it surely does give us an edge now.'

Kineas sat still. Thalassa stood between his knees, back unmoving, head up as if it were a cool spring morning and she was eager for a run. He'd never had such a horse. He patted her neck affectionately. 'Have the hyperetes sound "advance by squadrons",' he said.

'We're attacking?' Diodorus asked.

'We're looking confident. The afternoon is bleeding away and we need nightfall.' Kineas pointed with his Sakje whip. 'Look – it's the Farm Boy.'

They had all had an affectionate nickname for the man – a royal Macedonian bastard named Ptolemy. Unlike Craterus the Dog, who'd been hated and feared, the Farm Boy had many friends. 'Commanding Companions.'

'No, he's with the Sogdians,' Kineas said. 'Poor bastard.'

Behind Kineas, Andronicus blew the trumpet call. The Olbian squadrons surged forward across the ridge. Their line was neat and the afternoon sun turned the bronze of their armour to fire.

'Sound "halt". Let's see what they do.' Kineas watched.

A minute later, and there were messengers flying among the Macedonians on the other side of the river. 'They only have, what, eight hundred horse?' Kineas asked.

Eumenes was looking up and down. 'Twice that, surely!'

Diodorus laughed. 'Youth is wasted on the young,' he said. 'Kineas is right. And half of them are Sogdians.'

Kineas looked up and down the riverbank. A stade from the river on both sides, the ground was like desert, with sun-scorched grass and gravel. But the valley itself was two stades wide and it was green – sometimes marshy, sometimes meadows of grass with stands of tamarisk and rose brush. On the far side, there were two distinct groups of Sogdian cavalry, and on Kineas's far left, a pair of tight-knit squadrons of Macedonian professionals. The whole line moved, because the enemy horses were restless. They were moving so much that they were raising a new dust cloud, making it hard to see them.

'I'm going to go for him,' Kineas said, suddenly decisive. He felt better immediately, his guts settling. He *saw* it. 'We've little to gain, sitting in the sun. His horses are tired and mine aren't. If we get beaten, we retire into the sunset. He's a thousand stades from his camp. Sound good to you?'

Diodorus responded by taking his helmet, which hung by the chinstrap from his sword hilt, and putting it on. He was smiling as he tied his chinstrap.

Kineas looked around for a messenger. His eyes fixed on Leon, who had blood on the white leather of his corslet and a heavy bandage under his wide-brimmed Boeotian helmet.

'Leon, ride all the way to Ataelus. You listening, lad? You fit?'

The Numidian nodded fiercely.

'All the way to Ataelus. Tell him to get across and harass the far left of the enemy line. Understand? Say it back.'

Leon pulled off his helmet to listen better. 'All the way to Ataelus. Harass the enemy left flank.'

'Go!' said Kineas. He looked around for another messenger. He found Hama, the chieftain of the Keltoi. 'Hama, go to Srayanka and tell her to move forward into bow range and start plucking at the Macedonian cavalry – those right there. See?'

Hama nodded.

'Tell her to support Ataelus on her left. You understand?'

Hama nodded and gave the smile of a man who'd captained a few fights. 'Tell your wife to harass the horsemen in front and help Ataelus turn their flank,' he said.

'You've got it. Go!' said Kineas. He rode over the ridge and waved his arm at the Sauromatae until Lot noticed him. Then he waved towards the eastern bank. Lot waved back.

Kineas rode back to the top of his ridge, took one more look at the Macedonian positions and pulled his cheek plates down. 'Ready?' he called. 'Slow and steady over the rough ground. Keep your line and look tough and the Sogdians will vanish. Be ready to wheel left by squadron. I'm going to get us up the bank and turn north into the flank of their real cavalry. Got it?' He looked back over his shoulder and the Sauromatae were moving, Lot's helmet gleaming as the Sauromatae started down the tail of the ridge on Kineas's right. Water flashed under the hooves of the lead horses. On the far bank, the rightmost Sogdian group began to mill in confusion.

'Sound "advance",' Kineas yelled.

The Olbian line moved forward at a walk, picked their way down the spring riverbank, slipping and sliding on the sand, and then re-formed neatly on the broad meadow in the river valley. Kineas took the point of the leftmost Olbian rhomboid, with Carlus and Diodorus behind him.

As soon as they entered the green valley, Kineas lost his lofty view of the battlefield. He gripped his first javelin and rolled his hips as Thalassa felt her way across the rough meadow, avoiding the clumps of scrub. The Olbians, old hands at rough riding, flowed around the scrub and re-formed automatically, without orders.

'Ready?' Kineas called. They had the green valley to themselves – the Sogdians weren't coming down off the spring bank.

They came to the river itself and Thalassa splashed across. The spray from her hooves felt good. He gathered his reins. 'Straight up the bank. Spread out. Go up that bank as fast as you can.' He waved his arms. 'Spread out! Double intervals!'

No trumpet call for that, but he was obeyed and the other two troops followed suit. A stand of tamarisk hid the Sauromatae. Too late to worry. 'Trot!'

He put the knees to his horse and wound the throwing strap on his his first javelin.

Antigonus sounded the call and they started up the slope. Thalassa was up in two bounds, and arrows flew by him – one hit his helmet. He leaned forward, and she was up, hindquarters surging, and he pressed his heels into her sides, rose higher in his seat and roared 'Charge!'

A single enemy rider met him. His back was to Kineas, and he was bellowing at the Sogdians to *stand, stand fast*. The man was an officer with a white sash around some Bactrian garment worn over his breastplate. He had a shawl over his head, but Kineas knew him. The Farm Boy.

Kineas grinned and swung his heavy *lonche* javelin like a two-handed axe, blindsiding him and knocking the Macedonian from his saddle. Then he shouted at his hyperetes, already reining his mount. 'Rally!' he called, and the trumpet rang out.

Kineas nodded at Antigonus as troopers fell in behind. 'Stay together!' he ordered. 'Let's go!'

The trumpet sounded again. Somewhere in the dust, Ataelus would hear it and so would Lot and Srayanka.

Kineas headed into the cloud, following the fleeing enemy.

The grey-brown cloud was suddenly full of horsemen. Kineas was shocked to see how many. Bactrians, he thought, from the heads of the horses and the colourful saddle cloths. And then he was on them.

They didn't stand, seemed confused, unaware until the last seconds that they were in danger. Kineas didn't trouble to throw his javelin, but simply unhorsed men to the left and the right with the haft. Behind him, the broadening point of the rhomboid blew through their line and it unravelled like a moth-eaten garment. Men and horses boiled away from Kineas and his escort to vanish underfoot or away into the dust.

'Rally! Rally!' Kineas called, and again the trumpet call rang out.

'Change face – left!' Kineas called to Antigonus. The Gaul raised the trumpet and the call rang out. Kineas couldn't see past the next two files, because now the sand and dust moved like a heavy fog full of spirits, but he pivoted his own horse and went from being the point of the formation to being its rightmost flank.

Trust your men. If the manoeuvre had been carried out, his rhomboid now faced directly along the Macedonian flank. In the dust, he couldn't see anything.

'Charge!' Kineas called.

Antigonus sounded the trumpet. The formation moved, gathering speed, and Kineas began to encounter opponents

– confused men whirling their horses in the battle haze. The path of the charge and the enemy formation – or lack thereof – left Kineas and his flank without opposition. They rode slowly, maintaining contact with the centre of the formation, which was doing all the fighting.

Samahe knew exactly where to find him, reading his mind as neatly as a shaman, probably riding to the trumpet sound. 'Heh! Kineas!' she called as she came out of the dust.

Kineas called out. 'Samahe! On me!'

'For fucking like gods!' Ataelus' grin was so wide that it split his round face in two as he cantered out of the dust behind his wife. 'Hah! I own them all!' He waved his uninjured arm. 'I ride all the way around their flank. Craterus is for retreat. Yes?'

Kineas had to grin at that. 'I'm going to the north,' he shouted.

Ataelus shouted 'Yes!' and rode back into the dust.

'Halt!' Kineas called to Antigonus, and waited while the trumpet sang. 'Face to the right!' Kineas said, and again the trumpet's brazen voice carried above the dust. He couldn't hear very well and he couldn't see ten horse-lengths. He had only his last glance at the battlefield and his guess to go by.

He was again the point of the rhomboid – if there was a formation at all. 'Trot!' he called, putting his knees to Thalassa. She was calm as ever and she carried him easily. He put a knee in the middle of her back and sat up for a moment but could see nothing and almost lost his seat as she flowed over an obstruction.

When he felt that enough time had passed, he began to angle towards the west, leading the formation – if he had any formation – into a gradual wheel along the river, but a stade north, sweeping for the Macedonian cavalry.

The dust began to clear. In as many strides of his horse, he could see his hands on the reins, see a clump of grass in his path, and then he was clear and could see the dust cloud and the squadron of Sogdian horse waiting with obvious indecision just clear of the rising column of dust. The dust of the battle haze was so thick that it rose into the air as if the grass itself were afire.

Kineas unwrapped the sweat scarf from his throat where he wore it to keep his cuirass from chafing against his neck, and wrapped it again, sweat stinging his face, around his mouth.

He kept angling west. He looked back.

The rhomboid was still there. Carlus and Antigonus and Diodorus emerged from the wall of sand behind him, and then Hama, Dercorix and Tasda, and behind them four more. The spacings were far from perfect and there seemed to be a whole wing missing – perhaps ten men – but after two blind facings and a charge, it was like a miracle.

The other two troops were nowhere to be seen.

The Sogdians to their left front had only just seen them. They were moving – the subtle movement of men and horse like a wind through tall grass that betokens indecision and fear.

Kineas whirled, keeping his seat. 'Straight through them!' he yelled.

His men gave a weary shout. They gathered speed.

Out of the dust to their left, a single rider on a black horse emerged like a dark thunderbolt. Kineas knew it was Leon from the moment he saw the bull's-hide shield on the man's arm.

Leon shot straight at the Sogdians. Their leader, a big man with a grey beard, wheeled his horse at the last moment, as if he hadn't expected the Numidian's charge to go straight home – and he was too late. Leon's thrown javelin hit him low in the gut and knocked him to the earth, and Leon's big gelding crashed past the other horse and right into the front of the Sogdian formation.

The local men were as stunned as if a real thunderbolt had levelled their chieftain. Leon vanished into them. Their standard-bearer, another big man on a grey horse with a bronze bull's head on a pole, shouted shrill orders and the Sogdians began to close their ranks. Arrows leaped out of their formation and fell towards Kineas.

Ten strides away, Kineas cocked his light javelin back.

Five strides out, he threw, and just as his horse's head passed over the corpse of the chieftain, he lowered the point of his heavy spear to unhorse the man with the bull's-head standard. Thalassa knocked the man's horse flailing into the sand and sprang over, and Kineas lost his javelin in the man's corpse.

The fleeting moments of clear sight were gone, and again they were deep in the haze of Ares. Kineas reached for his Egyptian sword, gripped it and it wouldn't budge from the scabbard. He raised his bridle gauntlet to block a blow and took it in the side. Pain, like rage, exploded. Thalassa whirled under him.

Another blow against the scales of his corslet and then he was free in the swirling grit. His side hurt, but the daimon of combat was on him and he pinned his scabbard between his bridle arm and his side and ripped the sword free, almost losing his seat in the desperation of his efforts.

He was alone. He turned Thalassa's head in the direction he thought was right and urged her forward.

Carlus emerged from the dust, his heavy spear dripping gore. 'Hah!' he grunted in greeting.

Behind him, Hama pressed forward. 'This way, lord,' Hama called.

The three of them rode into the veil of swirling sand.

A man with a cloth wound around his domed helmet crashed his horse into Thalassa, and Kineas was back in the mêlée. He cut and parried, ever more conscious of the pain in his side and the rising tide of sound. This was a stand-up fight, not a rout. The Sogdians were no longer giving ground.

The Olbians weren't winning. He could hear their calls and the growing shouts of the Sogdians.

He pushed Thalassa straight into his opponent's horse and cut three times, sacrificing finesse for brute force and speed. One of his blows got through and the man reeled, his hands across his face as his horse twisted, all four legs plunging for balance. Kineas was past him.

'Apollo!' he shouted.

All around him in the battle haze, he heard the shout taken up, and ahead of him: 'Apollo!'

He could see the horsehair crests on some of his men off to the right – just a glimpse as a fitful breeze whipped the flying dust. He bellowed 'Apollo!' again and pressed Thalassa with his knees. She responded with another surge of strength, bulling over another rider without Kineas landing a blow. Then a small man who seemed to be covered in gold landed a spear thrust straight into Kineas's chest. The scales of his mail turned the thrust – the man had over-reached. Kineas cut at the shaft, failing to break it but swinging the head wide, so Kineas was in close. He grabbed the haft with his bridle hand and pounded the Medea head of his pommel into the man's face and their horses engaged, so that the two men were pressed breast to breast as their mounts whirled like fighting dogs, biting and kicking. Kineas reached his bridle hand around the man's back – he was heavily armoured. Kineas's left hand closed on the man's sword belt and he wrenched the blade of his own sword up from where it was pinned between their chests – up and up again with each heave of their mounts. Thalassa rose on her hindquarters, biting savagely at the other horse's rump and striking with her front hooves, and Kineas turned his wrist so that the Egyptian blade came up under the other man's jaw ...

A spray of blood, and the gold man fell away, dead weight that almost carried him off Thalassa, and a blow against his helmet ...

Carlus roaring like a mad bull at his side, propping him up. *Apollo!* Hama on his other side and Leon's shield coming out of the suffocating haze. He sat up, pain ebbing, muttered unheard thanks to Carlus and Hama.

He'd lost the sword. He loved that sword – the sword Satrax had given him.

Stupid reason to die, though. Antigonus was pressing through the haze.

'Rally! Sound "rally"!' Kineas said. His voice sounded odd. He'd lost his helmet.

He glanced down, hoping to see the glint of Medea's face on the golden grass at his feet. Instead he saw the blood running over his thigh from somewhere under his corslet.

The world became a tunnel. At the far end, Antigonus – *or was it Niceas?* – was shouting *'Rally! Rally!'*

Niceas turned around as if the world had slid sideways and the ground rose to meet him. Then there was a skull, speaking from a wall of sand.

'Listen, Strategos. We will turn the monster south, away from the sea of grass. Let him play with the bones of other men! Your eagles will rule here, and the life of the people will be preserved. That is my purpose, and your purpose, too.'

Kineas shook himself. 'I am no man's servant.'

'By the crooked-minded son of Cronus, boy! You could die. Pointlessly, in someone else's fight – a street brawl, defending a tyrant who despises you. Or from a barbarian arrow in the dark. It's not Homer, Ajax. It's dirty, sleepless, full of scum and bugs. And on the day of battle, you are one faceless man under your helmet – no Achilles, no Hektor, just an oarsman rowing the phalanx towards the enemy.'

He heard himself – a younger and far more feckless man – speak the words.

The skull spoke with the voice of Kam Baqca, as if they sat together in the sun-dappled contentment of Calchus's paddock. 'That would have been your fate – face down in the slime of a street brawl, the tool of vicious men. And you are better.*'*

Kineas found himself stitching away at a headstall – dear gods, he thought, I seem to have spent my entire adult life repairing horse-leathers. He was facing one of the commonest annoyances of a man sewing leather – he was just three stitches from completion and he was out of thread. Almost out of thread. He would have to stitch very carefully, taking the needle off the thread at every stitch to get it in again at the end. Even then, he wouldn't make it – he could see that.

The handsome warrior leaned over and pulled at the dangling thread, and it lengthened – just a fraction. 'You were a mercenary, and you chose to be something better. Go and die a king . . .'

It was dark. He was Kineas. The babes were crying and Srayanka's hand was on his hand.

'Oh, my love,' she said in Sakje. She pressed his hand hard, so hard that the pain in his bones almost matched the pain in his left side.

'I gather we won?' Kineas asked.

She kissed him again. 'I almost lost you,' she said.

'But we won the victory?' he asked urgently.

'Eumenes rallied the Olbians and came into the fight on your flank, breaking the last resistance. My Sakje harried the Macedonians for thirty stades. Some of my warriors are still riding.'

Well satisfied, Kineas slumped back into sleep – sleep free of skulls or any dreams.

And the next morning, so stiff that he could scarcely mount and needed Philokles to get on Thalassa, he rode to say goodbye to many friends as the two columns parted, and their women and children and many warriors turned east or west.

Even without his wounds, the partings would have been painful, and there were a few – Diodorus and Philokles – who tried to argue that he should go west with the column. But the wound in his side was mostly just cracked ribs – the new armour had held. He had cuts on his thigh and cuts on his arms, but so did every man who had been in the action. And every muscle in his body hurt.

The same was true of every trooper. Kineas was not of a mind to turn west.

Rosy-fingered dawn brushed every gold trapping and made them kindle. Silver and steel were stained the delicate pink of new flowers and the grass itself wavered like new-forged bronze. The wagons of the Sakje were already rolling, their dust stained the same smoked pink as the sky and the farther clouds. Above and to the right, an eagle of good omen circled, searching for prey in the first light.

At the edge of the last watercourse before the Polytimeros, Kineas stood by Thalassa, surrounded by his friends – Srayanka and Philokles on either side of him, supporting him: Diodorus with Sappho mounted at his side; Coenus and soft-handed Artemesia with Eumenes and Urvara resplendent in her gold gorytos and a necklace of gold and lapis; Antigonus and Andronicus standing silently, their gold torcs like bands of lava at their necks; Sitalkes in his Getae cloak, Ataelus and Samahe supporting him; and Parshtaevalt, resplendent in a captured Macedonian breastplate of muscled bronze; Leon quiet and still in an Olbian cloak; Nicanor weeping openly. Nihmu watched them with a stillness that belied her youth, as if her young eyes could record every moment like a scribe's wax tablet. Temerix stood a little apart, braiding leather with his fingers even as he accepted the farewells of Sappho. The Sindi smith had been her ally in helping Philokles.

Only Darius was missing of all of Kineas's closest companions, still out somewhere on the sea of grass, looking for Spitamenes.

One by one those who were going west kissed those who were riding east. Coenus would command. Eumenes would lead the Olbians and Urvara the Sakje, with a tithe of the best warriors. With them would go Nicanor and Sappho, and Artemesia and Andronicus would go as Eumenes' hyperetes.

Coenus embraced Srayanka. Then he came face to face with Kineas. 'My heart tells me that I will not see you again,' he said.

Kineas wiped hurriedly at his tears. 'No, my friend. If what I have seen in the gates of horn is true, we will not hunt together this side of the Elysian Fields.'

Coenus was an aristocrat and a Megaran. He stood straight, his face unmarked by tears. He even managed a grin. He took both of Kineas's hands.

'I honour the gods, Kineas, but after them I honour you. May Moira see fit to leave the thread of your life uncut that we may hunt the valleys of the Tanais together. I will dedicate a temple to Artemis, and I will never cease to think of you. And if the thread of your life must be cut, let it be a worthy end.'

Diodorus spoke as though he was choking. 'At times like this, I miss Agis the most,' he said. To the others, who had not known the gentle Theban, he said, 'Agis was our priest. He died at the River God's Ford.' He took one of Coenus's hands. 'We've ridden together for years,' he said. 'I find it hard to imagine a life without all of you.'

Philokles cleared his throat. 'I lack the god-given touch of gentle Agis,' he said, 'but I will attempt his part.'

At length as the Morning Star was beginning to herald
The light which saffron-mantled Dawn was soon to suffuse
    over the sea,
The flames fell and the fire began to die.
The winds then went home beyond the Thracian Sea
Which roared and boiled as they swept over it.
The son of Peleus now turned away from the pyre and lay
    down,
Overcome with toil, till he fell into a sweet slumber.
Presently they who were about the son of Atreus drew near
    in a body,
And roused him with the noise and tramp of their coming.
He sat upright and said, 'Son of Atreus, and all other princes
    of the Achaeans,
First pour red wine everywhere upon the fire and quench it;
Let us then gather the bones of Patroclus son of Menoitios,
Singling them out with care; they are easily found,
For they lie in the middle of the pyre, while all else, both
    men and horses,
Has been thrown in a heap and burned at the outer edge.
We will lay the bones in a golden urn, in two layers of fat,
Against the time when I shall myself go down into the house
    of Hades.
As for the barrow, labour not to raise a great one now,
But such as is reasonable. Afterwards, let those Achaeans
    who may be left at the ships
When I am gone, build it both broad and high.'

When he was done, they were silent for the space a few heartbeats. Then Sappho embraced Diodorus once more, and Eumenes clasped Kineas's hand. 'We will build your kingdom,' he said.

'Your city,' Kineas said. 'Never my kingdom.'

And then Coenus mounted his horse, gathered his companions and rode into the sunrise.

371

26

Kineas's ribs hurt too much for him to ride, so he travelled in a litter between two horses for three days as they raced north and east along the Polytimeros. Srayanka commanded. He never lost consciousness and there was no fever, but he passed the days in a haze of pain. By the fourth day he could ride, although the pain when his mount mis-stepped was remarkable – if brief.

'Cracked ribs,' Philokles said for the fourth time, pulling the bandages tight.

'A bronze corslet would have turned that point without a bruise,' Kineas said. 'But the Sakje scale is easier to wear all day and covers better. Each people has its own ways.'

'Thank you, Socrates.' Philokles smiled.

As soon as Kineas was mounted, Srayanka called a 'moving council'. All the leaders, Greek and tribal, rode to the head of the column.

Leon handed Kineas the Egyptian sword. 'I thought you'd want this,' he said. 'We held the field.'

Diodorus slapped the Numidian on the back. 'Leon sent one of Temerix's men for me. I brought the rest of the Olbians and Parshtaevalt here.' His smug smile shattered into a brilliant grin. 'Your wife crossed into their flank. Eumenes rode in on the other side. We wrecked 'em.'

'They didn't even stand to fight Lot,' Philokles said. 'A very poor showing for Macedon.'

Kineas shook his head. 'That wasn't Macedon,' he said. 'That was a handful of Macedonian officers with a lot of local auxiliaries. Alexander must be stretched thin.' He coughed and his ribs hurt.

Antigonus gave a very Niceas-like grunt. 'And we took some spoil. Gold. Horses. And prisoners.'

Kineas looked around, unsure whether he was delighted at

the victory or a little peevish that they'd won it without him. 'How many prisoners?' he asked.

'A dozen,' Philokles said. 'Just troopers, except one officer. He's not talkative.' Philokles gave a wry grin. 'I like him.'

Diodorus pushed his horse in close. 'Macedonian bastard.'

All the officers were smiling at some private joke. Kineas ignored them and dismissed the issue of a prisoner until later. 'I take it there were quite a few more of them than we thought,' Kineas said.

'No,' Diodorus said. 'Two squadrons – twice your numbers, if you toss in Ataelus's scouts. You rode rings around them.' He looked around at all the other officers. Parshtaevalt met his eye and both men gave crooked smiles, as if some new understanding had been reached while Kineas was wounded. 'We just showed up and pounded the survivors flat.'

'And now?' Kineas asked.

Ataelus spoke up. 'Iskander holds all the south bank of Polytimeros. Patrols all day, but cautious.' He gave a nod. 'For pissing themselves yellow after fight, I think.'

Kineas nodded. He could see mountains in the distance – closer now. Achievable instead of impossible. 'Polytimeros flows out of those?'

'Yes,' Ataelus and Temerix said together. 'And Macedonian forts – close as teeth in your mouth. Six forts and a camp.' Temerix nodded. 'I scouted them. Myself.'

Kineas looked at his wife and at Diodorus. 'Well?'

Srayanka said, 'We decided yesterday – today we camp early, water up and leave the Polytimeros. Out on to the sea of grass. North and east around the Sogdian mountains and into the desert. We must.'

Diodorus agreed. 'He's got to have another cut at us, Kineas. And we're putting our heads in a noose – the farther upstream we go, the closer we are to his army. His main army.' He shook his head. 'Look, we barely hurt him and we see his scouts every day. This isn't going to work. We have to cut across the desert.'

Kineas rubbed his jaw. He felt terrible – every bone hurt, his muscles were sore and breathing caused a steady pulse of pain in his chest. His head was surprisingly clear. 'Craterus is still on the Polytimeros,' Kineas said. 'But Alexander is moving east. That's what I'd do. He's trying to fight the queen of the Massagetae before she joins with Spitamenes.'

Diodorus narrowed his eyes. 'Heh?'

Kineas swept his arm out to the southern bank. 'We're not even a pimple on Alexander's arse,' he said. When the comment was translated, the Sakje chiefs grinned or laughed aloud. 'Alexander is marching east. He's contained the problem at Marakanda and now he's going to concentrate against Queen Zarina. The plains are dust and dried grass, and forage is brutal – poor and thin. Right?'

Ataelus nodded. They all jogged along for a few strides.

'Alexander won't be able to concentrate long. Not enough food. And Zarina has the whole plain north of the Jaxartes to feed her army. And you Sakje are *much* better at living off these plains than the Macedonians.'

Diodorus nodded. 'I see it. He *can't* turn back to hit us without upsetting his schedule.'

'We're racing him,' Kineas said. 'My guess is that he's due south – not a hundred stades distant – moving east behind a screen of patrols. A day's ride away.'

Srayanka shrugged. 'And? Does this change anything we have settled?'

'No,' he said. 'Not in the least. It means you were right. We must move fast if we are to reach Zarina before Alexander launches his attack. He must mean to cross the Jaxartes and make a late-summer campaign against the Massagetae.'

Srayanka squinted and batted at her braids. 'Then he's a fool. There is no water on the plains in summer.'

'Alexander is not a fool, my dear. He can command man and beast to their limits and beyond. He took his army over the height of the mountains – yes? Even the Sakje speak of it. If he wants them to march out on to the high plains, they will.' He looked around at them. 'After all, isn't this *exactly* what we intend to do?'

'We are a few hundred,' Srayanka shot back. 'Are you

satisfied that we should turn north? Or should we discuss the flight of geese and the movement of the deer on the plains?'

Kineas raised an eyebrow at her. 'Yes,' he said. 'We turn north.'

When the command group had broken up, Kineas pulled his wife close. 'I wish you would speak your mind in council,' he said. 'I hate the way you stand silent, fearing to interrupt me.'

'Which side hurts the most?' she asked, aiming a mock blow at his left.

After the next halt, Srayanka sent the prodromoi off north, leaving Parshtaevalt to screen them from the south. They made camp early at a bend in the Polytimeros, where the ruins of a mud-walled village on the south bank spoke an epic about the years of war this area had already seen. Kineas rejoined his mess group and sat with his back against a sun-warmed rock. Srayanka leaned her shoulder against him and handed him Lita. The rock was the sign of a change in terrain. The ground was rising to the east. They had arrived at the foothills of the Sogdian.

Darius squatted on his heels, drinking captured wine. He was clothed from head to foot like a Mede and seemed embarrassed by the nudity of the many Olbians bathing in the bend of the Polytimeros.

'Welcome back. You found Spitamenes?'

Darius nodded. Kineas put an arm around him. 'I gather Spitamenes has sworn to stay clear of us,' he said, ignoring Darius's clothes.

'He is mortified that he has incurred your enmity,' Darius said. He flicked a glance at Srayanka and then looked away as if Artemis had blinded his eyes. 'He claims that he had no idea of what Alexander intended with the Amazons – he was led to believe that the king desired only to meet some.' He drew himself up. 'He feels his honour is besmirched by what has befallen and he promises any remedy you and your lady require.'

Srayanka was well within earshot. She handed Satyrus to Kineas. 'That is, as you Greeks say, the stinking manure of a dog. However,' she smiled, 'it suits all of us if we pretend to believe him.'

Darius looked shocked. 'He swore on his honour!'

Kineas was surprised at the young man's naivety. 'You liked him!'

'He will make a great king,' Darius said seriously.

'He will end with his head on a spike – or worse.' Srayanka settled her daughter on her lap. 'I will not forget that he gave me to Iskander – but I have a long memory and time is short.' To her daughter, she said, 'You may have my dislike of this Persian with your milk, little sausage.'

Darius was wearing a fine sword, a straight-bladed *xiphos* decorated in gold like a Sakje sword. Kineas reached out for it. 'A gift?' he asked.

'Yes. He was amazed – and pleased – to find that one of my blood lived. He treasures his remaining nobles. Many men I once knew ride in his cavalry.' He smiled at Philokles, who approached from the tamarisk trees on the bluff above them. 'Spitamenes sent wine!'

Philokles grinned and shouted something that was lost in the sounds of eight hundred horses drinking.

Kineas nodded. 'Darius – you may go to him, if it pleases you. You have served me well and you owe me no ransom. I killed your cousin – it is always between us. But I will never forget how you held my side in the castle of Namastopolis.'

Darius stood silent. 'Am I dismissed?' he asked.

'Never,' Kineas said. 'But I understand the ties of common blood and custom. Spitamenes is a lord of your own people. If you desire to ride with him, go with my friendship.'

'And mine,' Srayanka said.

Darius couldn't meet Srayanka's eyes, but his glance slid to Philokles' form walking down the last of the slope and he blushed and bowed and took Kineas's hand. 'I think I will ride with you a while longer,' he said. Then, after an uncomfortable pause, he pointed to the ruins of the town. 'Bessus revolted against Darius four – five years ago. There's been no peace on this frontier ever since. Whichever side holds the upper hand, the other side pays the Dahae and the Massagetae to raid. Now Spitamenes continues where Bessus trod.'

'You rode with Bessus?'

'My father did,' Darius said. 'I rode with the King of Kings.' He gave a narrow smile that didn't touch his eyes. 'It is the way among the Bactrian nobles – one son to each army, or perhaps two – no matter which side wins, the clan remains strong.'

Diodorus and Philokles came up with a bearded man in a dirty red linen robe over a Macedonian breastplate, the star of the royal house engraved across his chest. The man had a hooked nose and a broad forehead. He looked to be forty, or perhaps older, but well built, with an athlete's muscles.

'Look who the dogs caught,' Diodorus said. He was grinning. 'Remember this cocksure bastard?'

Kineas eyed the man. 'Ptolemy!' he said, smoothing his daughter's head. He didn't get up, but he gave the prisoner a smile. 'Farm Boy!'

The Macedonian inclined his head. 'I remember you, Kineas of Athens,' he said. 'Favourite of the gods.' He inclined his head in mock salutation.

'You didn't used to believe in gods,' Diodorus said, poking him.

Ptolemy rubbed his chin and quoted Aristophanes. '"If there weren't gods, I wouldn't be so god-forsaken,"' he said, and they all laughed.

Philokles gave him a bowl of food. 'Mutton?' he asked.

'Horse,' said Kineas. 'I'm sorry about the fight, Ptolemy. I didn't know you in that get-up.'

Ptolemy looked down at the linen robe he wore over his cuirass. Then he glanced pointedly around the fire. 'You don't look much like Athenian hippeis yourselves,' he said. 'Where are the flowing locks of yesteryear? The fancy cloaks?'

Kineas smiled. '"If peace come again, and we from toil may be released, don't grudge us our flowing locks, and skin so nicely greased."'

Ptolemy clapped his hands. 'Well quoted. Not that there's a flowing lock in the place.'

Diodorus poked him again. 'The Spartan here has locks enough for all of us!'

'Last time I saw you, you were modelling a silver-chased breastplate you'd bought from a looter at Ecbatana,' Kineas said. 'We're not the only ones fallen on hard times.'

Ptolemy shook his head. 'Fucking Sogdiana,' he said. 'It's brutal.'

'Still in the Hetairoi?' Kineas asked.

'I served with Philip Kontos before he went back west.' The man shrugged in the firelight. 'After he killed Artemis, I left him for the phalanx.'

Kineas moved as if his side had pained him. 'She is dead, then?'

The Macedonian shovelled food with his fingers. After he chewed he looked up. 'She was our luck, just as she was yours. Kontos killed her when she chose to stay with us, the fucker. She wouldn't go west with him.'

Diodorus had known Artemis, as had Antigonus, but the big Gaul was at his own fire. Diodorus snorted to cover his sorrow. Artemis had led the camp followers when they were in Alexander's army. She had been Kineas's woman from Issus to Ecbatana. 'No,' he said, glancing at Kineas. 'No, she wouldn't.' He raised his cup. 'Here is to her memory.'

Ptolemy accepted the cup, poured a little for her shade. 'Aye.'

Kineas slopped some from his own bowl and drank. 'I put Kontos in the earth,' he said.

The fireside fell silent.

'Small world,' the Macedonian said. 'Surely the gods must have willed it so – that you, whom she loved best, avenged her.'

'I doubt that she loved me best,' Kineas said, pleased despite his own words. 'I dreamed that she was dead,' he added. 'You may go in the morning. Take a horse. Philokles here will see you clear of our pickets.'

Ptolemy stretched his legs out towards the fire. The nights were surprisingly cool, despite the blast of heat every day at noon. 'I praise Ares that I was taken by Greeks,' he said.

378

'Perhaps there is some point in praying to the gods, after all. I would have expected to have my balls pulled off by now by barbarians. You won't ask for ransom?'

Kineas looked up at Diodorus and Philokles. They both shook their heads. 'No. You may ride clear. We took half a dozen troopers as well. You can take them with you.'

Ptolemy nodded. He looked around. 'Alexander would forgive you like a shot, Kineas. And hire your whole command. Sakje? With Greeks? Name your price.'

'I am not for sale,' Kineas said. 'And I have done nothing that needs to be forgiven, Macedonian.'

'Is this some misbegotten Athenian plot? Don't be a fool.' Ptolemy pressed close. 'Let me use this god-given opportunity. Listen! We knew somebody was beating up our pickets. Ever since early summer, we've had reports of mercenary Greek horse on the Oxus. Now that I've found you, come with me! Whatever Spitamenes is paying you, the king will beat it!'

Around the fire, Kineas's friends laughed.

'Spitamenes has no friends here,' Srayanka said. Her Greek was excellent now.

'You're the Amazon!' Ptolemy said. He was typical of Macedonians – Kineas could see that, having ascertained that she was a woman, and a suckling woman, he had dismissed her as being of less importance than the saddle blanket on which he sat. 'The pregnant Amazon!' He looked from her to Kineas and back. 'Your girl?'

'My wife, the Lady Srayanka, Queen of the Assagatje.' Kineas gestured towards her.

She chuckled, even as she adjusted her son on her nipple and put a hand under her breast to support him.

Ptolemy looked at her more carefully. Then he looked at Kineas, as if seeing him for the first time. 'If you killed Kontos, then you defeated Zopryon, didn't you?'

Kineas smiled slowly and wickedly. 'I didn't do it by myself,' he said.

Ptolemy was pale, even in the ruddy firelight. 'So...' he said. All friendliness was gone from his voice. 'Fucking ingrate. Alexander *made* you.'

Kineas felt the blood in his face. Nonetheless, he struggled to remain calm – if only because his calm would infuriate the Macedonian all the more. 'I am an Athenian.'

'You are a fucking *Hellene* fighting for *barbarians.*' Ptolemy was livid and, like most fighting men, heedless of consequence.

Kineas had no trouble meeting his gaze, even when the Macedonian stumbled to his feet, fists closed and twitching.

'You are a barbarian, fighting for barbarians,' Kineas said. He sat up from his reclining position. 'I owe Alexander nothing. I was dismissed by him – and exiled for serving him. My city has commanded my service against him.'

'Athens has sent an army into this haunted desert?' Ptolemy slumped. 'That's not *possible!*'

'My city is Olbia,' Kineas said with pride. 'I am the hipparch of Olbia. Every man at this fire is a citizen of Olbia. The cities of the Euxine united with the Sakje – the Assagatje – to destroy Zopryon. He would have enslaved every man and woman on the Euxine, Ptolemy. He wanted it all.' Kineas stood up, handing his daughter to Darius, and spat in the fire. 'We lost hundreds of riders. Not one Macedonian boy lived to see his mother on a farm near Pella. Not one horse trotted across the grass to his pasture in the high hills.'

Srayanka's voice was angry and arrogant. She didn't rise. 'Tell your king that if he comes on to the plains, we will give him the same. The sea of grass is not for Macedon. My father died teaching Philip that lesson – and none of us are afraid to school the son.'

'Olbia?' Ptolemy asked. His anger was quenched. 'Where the fuck is Olbia?'

That made all the veterans around the fire laugh, because just two years before, most of them would have said the same.

Kineas gave half a grin. 'The richest city of the Euxine.' Even as he spoke, he could see the city as if he stood on the bluff by the Borysthenes, looking down at the Temple of Apollo and the golden dolphins. 'With Pantecapaeum, richer than all the cities of Greece combined.'

Ptolemy controlled his anger, aware that he was one

captured Macedonian. 'That's not saying much,' he said. 'I've seen Persepolis and Ecbatana. Greece is *poor*.'

'Rich enough, with their Sakje allies, to stop Macedon *for ever*.' Kineas sat again.

Ptolemy's long and thoughtful face took on an intense look. 'You may speak your sophistry as you will – the king will never forgive you. We aren't even allowed to mention Zopryon's name. The survivors of the fight on the Polytimeros were threatened with decimation – one in ten to be executed. He actually carried out half a dozen before he ordered them stopped. Did you know that? And we were sworn to eternal silence on the defeat.'

Philokles nodded. 'He guards his myth of invulnerability,' he said. And then, looking closely at the Macedonian's face, he said, 'You hate him.'

Stung, Ptolemy stumbled away from Philokles. Antigonus, arriving out of the darkness with a skin of captured wine, caught his shoulders and steadied him. 'Careful, laddy,' Antigonus said in his heavily accented Greek.

Ptolemy looked around and slumped again. He sighed. 'We all love him and we hate him. He is half god and half monster.' He raised his head. 'Like many men, I would like to go home. I would like to stop playing the endless game of betrayal and politics and advantage for power and influence in the army. I would like to build something. Something real.'

Philokles raised an eyebrow, frowned and nodded. 'So stop?'

Ptolemy shook his head. 'I can't.'

'Why not?' Philokles asked.

'Because if Ptolemy stops playing, somebody under him will have him killed and move up,' Kineas said, and Diodorus nodded agreement. 'We never played the Macedonian game – we're just Greeks. But we watched.' Kineas looked at Ptolemy's face and thought about how often Philokles had asked him questions like this with the same intensity. It was interesting to see him do it to another man, to see the effect, the confusion, the sudden self-doubt.

'Best join us,' Diodorus said. 'We've Numidians and Kelts

and Megarans and Spartans. There's a Babylonian Jew in second troop – or so he claims. We've a couple of Persians. Why not a Macedonian?'

Ptolemy laughed. 'You are—' He looked around the firelight. 'Hah!' he laughed, shaking his head. 'You will actually let me go?'

Kineas nodded. 'Be my guest.'

Ptolemy stood at attention. 'I am honour-bound to report everything I have seen and heard,' he said.

Philokles spoke up again. 'But will you?' he asked.

Ptolemy suddenly looked younger and more vulnerable than he had throughout his time by the fire. 'I – I must,' he said.

Philokles shrugged. 'Except that if you tell the king everything, you will never see home. First, because tyrants always blame the messenger. Is that not true, Kineas?'

'Are you asking me because I know so many tyrants, or because I have been one?' Kineas asked. 'But yes.'

'Which you well know, yes?' Philokles, in his turn, rose to his feet. 'And because if you tell Alexander all you know, you will change his campaign. His Amazon – his prize! – is right here. And so is the man who defeated Zopryon.' Philokles had never looked more like a philosopher, despite his stained tunic and dirty legs, than at that moment, gleaming and golden in the firelight, leaning forward like a statue of an orator. 'If you tell him, he will drop everything to fight us – out on the grass. And you will never see home.' Philokles' eyes were sparkling. 'And you know it.'

Diodorus, still reclining, said, 'There is a god at your shoulder, Philokles.'

The others were silent. Some slurping and gurgling from Lita broke the solemnity of the moment.

Ptolemy was gone in the morning with the other prisoners. Philokles rode with him to the south, accompanied by Ataelus, and returned alone at midday, when the whole column was so far out on the sea of grass that the trees of the Polytimeros valley were lost in the haze. Only the mountains to the east marred the perfect bowl of the earth.

It was not until evening that the desert nature of the ground began to take its toll. The scouts had found waterholes, and their camps were based on those, but no single place gave sufficient water for eight hundred horses. Kineas had to fragment his command into four groups, based more on horse strength than on manpower. Srayanka and the Sakje were at another waterhole. He lay awake listening to the restless, under-watered horses. He was unused to sleeping alone, already missing his children. He awoke with a dry mouth. He drank water from the spring after the horses were clear, and there was more silt than refreshment.

By noon his mouth was like parchment, his tongue had taken on a presence in his mouth it had never had before and his clay water bottle, sized for Greece where dozen of streams crossed the plains, was almost dry. He had travelled through deserts before, in Persia and Media and west, by Hyrkania, so he knew to put a pebble under his tongue and to ration his water skin and pottery canteen carefully. He made sure that Antigonus and the under-officers checked the Greek and Keltoi troopers constantly, made them drink, watched them for signs of sickness.

Even with a host of water problems, they *flew*. Released from the rough ground at the foot of the Sogdian mountains, the four small columns moved at a pace that could only be maintained when every man had at least two mounts. Their second camp on the sea of grass came after what seemed like three hundred stades of travel – an incredible march for one day. The prodromoi rode back and forth between the columns, reporting on the water ahead and the distance that each troop had left to reach their camp, but soon enough the horses smelled the water and then they saw a stream rushing out of the hills – hills that had shifted from the eastern horizon towards the south, and were closer. The stream was still cool and the horses trumpeted when they smelled it and could barely be controlled.

'For worrying,' Ataelus confessed, as they watched the horses charge into the stream. 'For one day on Great Grass.' He pointed mutely at the chaotic drinking. 'Next time, four days. And one night – no water.' He shrugged. His shrugs were so Greek now that he could have sat on a wall in the agora of Athens.

'We'll survive,' Kineas said.

Ataelus gave him a look that suggested that no amount of command optimism was going to cure a night without water.

They all camped together, because of the stream. Kineas snuggled up to Srayanka, and she snuggled back. 'I missed you,' she said. 'I know I will lose you – so I resent being parted. I will yet be a silly girl.'

'No,' Kineas said, smelling the sweet grass and woodsmoke and horse smell of her. 'How were the children?'

She rocked her hips, pushing back against him. 'They were like babies. When their mouths get dry, they cry. Worry more when they *don't* cry.' She rolled her head back to him. 'Most of the women who have borne children are gone – the only other women are spear-maidens. I wish I had someone to ask—'

'Ask what?' Kineas said.

'Lita doesn't – move – as much as I am for liking.' She kissed him. 'I am being a mother. Pay me no heed.'

Kineas lay still for a little while.

Srayanka rolled on to her back. 'What are you for thinking?'

Kineas watched her in the starlight. 'I'm thinking how many things there are to worry about. Babies and water, horses and water. Alexander. Death.'

Srayanka put her hand behind his head. 'I can think of something we can do to stop worrying,' she said, her right hand already playful. 'But you must be quiet!'

Kineas chuckled into her lips. He started to say something witty and then he wasn't thinking about much of anything.

About two minutes later, something hit Kineas's rump. 'Keep it down!' Diodorus called, and forty men and two women laughed.

'Told you to be quiet,' Srayanka said. But her chuckles didn't last long.

PART VI

THE BEACON

27

'So this party of mixed Greeks and Scythians just *let you go*.'
Hephaestion was beginning to see Ptolemy as a competitor, and in his creed competitors needed to be destroyed.

Ptolemy was struggling not to lose his nerve or his temper. In his detached, commander's brain, he wondered that a man could be afraid and enraged at the same time. The Poet always said that one drove out the other.

The Poet had never been to Sogdiana. 'The Greeks made sure of it,' he said. 'There was a Spartan mercenary. He rode me clear of their lines.'

Alexander, far from being angry, seemed pleased. 'So the Sakje barbarians have some Greek allies,' he said. He rubbed the stubble on his chin. 'That makes it more of a fight, don't you think?'

Hephaestion wasn't through yet. 'It might, if you believed this half-arsed story.'

Alexander looked at his closest companion with a certain scepticism. He raised an eyebrow. 'Do Sogdians take prisoners?'

'No,' said Hephaestion. 'Of course not.'

'Dahae? Sakje? Massagetae?' Alexander was just like his tutor when he bored in on an argument. He was at his most annoyingly superior, but since the focus of his superiority was on Hephaestion and not him, Ptolemy was prepared to watch.

'No,' said Hephaestion, now surly as he understood the point being made.

'Exactly. If his story was false, *he wouldn't be here*. So Craterus lost, what, seventy Sogdians?' Alexander snapped his fingers and received a cup of wine. Another cup was offered to Ptolemy, while Alexander shared his with Hephaestion.

Ptolemy nodded. 'More like a hundred, lord.'

Alexander rolled the wine in his cup before he raised his eyes. 'Craterus needs to be replaced.'

Ptolemy shook his head. 'Who could have expected a trained commander in this wilderness? Or an enemy who could make three direction changes inside a few stades?'

Alexander's steady and mismatched gaze didn't waver.

So much for Craterus, Ptolemy thought.

'Will you take command of the Sogdian cavalry?' Alexander asked.

'No,' Ptolemy said, without a moment's thought. 'I would like to go back to commanding my taxeis.'

'Very well,' Alexander said. His annoyance was plain – blood rushed to his face. 'Go back to foot-slogging with my compliments on your report.' He made a hand motion that indicated dismissal. Ptolemy gave a brief bow – a sketchy compromise between a Macedonian head nod and a Persian bow – and withdrew.

As he left, Alexander turned to Hephaestion. 'This Greek mercenary has hurt us several times. I can't believe he's a Spartan – they have no head for cavalry. Agesilaus was the exception, not the rule.'

Hephaestion was pouting. 'Xenophon was a Spartan,' he said.

Alexander laughed. 'What did you do while I went to my tutor?' he asked. 'Xenophon was an Athenian.'

Hephaestion knocked back his wine and shrugged. 'Fine,' he said. 'I want to command the Sogdians.'

Alexander looked at him fondly. 'You command my Companions,' he said.

'You need a soldier of proven worth to lead the Sogdians and stop the defeats we've taken in the little fights along the Oxus.' Hephaestion raised his head.

Alexander met his eyes, put a hand on his head and ruffled his bronze curls. 'It is not a job worthy of you,' he said.

Hephaestion shrugged off his hand. 'I want it.'

Alexander shrugged and turned his back. 'No,' he said.

'I want—' Hephaestion began.

'No,' Alexander said, in a tone of command. 'Fetch Eumenes for me, please.'

Hephaestion stomped out of the tent and Eumenes came in alone. 'Great King?' he asked after an obeisance.

'I need a cavalry commander to cover the movement on the Jaxartes. Who is it to be?'

Eumenes shrugged. 'I thought Craterus had that job?' he asked.

Alexander's eyes bored into the Cardian's, but Eumenes held his ground, not giving a hint that he already knew what had happened. After a moment, Alexander shook his head. 'Craterus got beaten,' he said.

'I'll do it,' Eumenes said. His tone suggested that he didn't want to do it.

'Set a Greek to catch a Greek?' Alexander said. 'My thought exactly. There's a Greek mercenary operating with Spitamenes. Take the Sogdians, a squadron of the mercenary horse and whatever foot you think will help and get him. He seems to have about four hundred horse. Perhaps twice that.'

Eumenes nodded. 'Where is he now?'

Alexander had a rough sketch of Sogdiana on his camp table, although it showed nothing but towns, rivers and mountains. And even then, most of the distances were guesswork, even after a year's campaigning. 'Up where the Polytimeros meets the Sogdian mountains. He'll be on the north bank of the Polytimeros, shadowing us.'

Eumenes looked at the map. 'If he's on the Polytimeros, we'll catch him against the northern wall of the valley.'

'Exactly,' Alexander said. He glanced out of the door of his tent – checking for Hephaestion, no doubt. 'If he was smart enough to beat Craterus, he'll be smart enough to avoid getting trapped.'

'If he's not on the Polytimeros?' Eumenes asked.

'Track him. But mostly, keep him – and Spitamenes – off me while I manoeuvre. I have thirty thousand men to concentrate on the Jaxartes, and if one of these bandits gets into my rear—' He shrugged. Morale among the Macedonians was low. They weren't likely to desert or fight poorly, but mutiny was always possible when they felt hard done by. Both men knew it. They would march for ever without wine or oil – when they were happy.

'So you're going to the Jaxartes?' Eumenes asked. He'd heard rumours, but armies were full of rumours.

'Now. I've already started some of the troops in motion. I need to beat the Massagetae before they join hands with Spitamenes and make themselves a nuisance.'

Eumenes nodded. 'The Massagetae have made no move to attack us,' he said.

'Except to send their men to harass our outposts and loaning horsemen to Spitamenes.' Alexander's tone was commanding. 'When I beat them, Spitamenes will fold.'

Eumenes hadn't risen to power with the king by cowardice. 'I disagree, lord. Spitamenes will fold anyway. We have no need to fight the Massagetae. In fact, a message acknowledging their ownership of the sea of grass would probably end their campaign.'

'Should I offer to pay them tribute, too?' Alexander asked. His voice was very quiet.

Eumenes nodded slowly. 'Very well, lord,' he said. 'Your mind is set.'

'It is. Go and punish this Greek. Recruit the survivors and rejoin me. I won't move to fight this Zarina for twenty days.'

'Hephaestion wants this command,' Eumenes said – not because he had any love of the king's companion, but because he absolutely did *not* want to go chasing a wily Greek with Sakje allies on the sea of grass.

Alexander nodded. 'I love Hephaestion with all my soul,' he said, 'but he is not suited for independent command. And if I ever hear that you repeated those words ...'

Eumenes cast his eyes down to hide the gleam that must be there. Ahh! he thought. Now the game is worth playing. 'I'll catch this Greek, then,' Eumenes said. 'Perhaps I'll bring you an Amazon, as well.'

Alexander sighed. 'I liked the one I had,' he said. 'Even gravid, she had a presence. And her eyes!' Alexander laughed. 'Why do I tell you these things, Eumenes?'

Because you can't tell Hephaestion, Eumenes thought with satisfaction.

Alexander stopped him at the door of his tent. 'Take the savage. What's his name? Urgargar?'

'Upazan, lord?'

'That one. He knows the country and he has a good hate in him. Let him focus it in our service.' The king sat back and drank a little more wine.

28

'There's cavalry behind us,' Diodorus said as soon as he rode up. It was four days since they had left the Polytimeros to ride north, the hills of the Abii on their right and the Sogdian mountains a smudge to the south. Diodorus was so covered with dust that his cloak and his face and his tunic were all the same shade. His wide straw hat had frayed around the edges. '*Phewf* – riding through our drag is enough to discourage any thoughts of glory.'

'How many?' asked Kineas. He looked back, although there was nothing to see but the tower of dust. They were a day and a night north of the last stream, and despite the heaviest load of water they could carry, the dash across the waterless plains had already brought equine casualties.

'Eight hundred? A thousand? No remounts, according to Ataelus.' Diodorus used the shawl over his head to wipe his face. 'They were gaining on us, but Ataelus gave them a sting when they were watering.'

The last water was almost a hundred stades behind them. 'They'll never catch us,' Kineas said.

Diodorus smiled. 'That's what Ataelus said,' he said, and coughed. 'And that's before he lifted fifty of their horses.'

Philokles pulled the shawl off his nose to speak. 'Don't dismiss them. They crossed mountains and deserts to get here.' He nodded. 'If we get into water trouble – we can't go back.'

Kineas nodded. 'I needed more to worry about,' he said.

'That's why you're the strategos,' Diodorus said. 'I used to command a couple of squadrons of cavalry, but now I'm a patrol leader.' He laughed. 'At this rate, another few weeks will see me where I started – as a gentleman trooper.'

Kineas wound his own shawl back over his face. 'Was it so bad?' he asked.

'Nope,' Diodorus said.

*

That night there was water – enough to madden the horses, but not enough to fill them. There was trouble, even with precautions. People became surly, mounts injured themselves and Greek notions of discipline clashed with Sakje ideas of horse care.

Kineas tried calm authority, and when that failed, he punched a Keltoi who was losing his head and then yelled himself hoarse. Angry with himself and with his command, he went to his cooking fire and sat holding his children while Srayanka checked her pickets with Diodorus. The one sandy hole in the stream bed emitted enough water to please one horse every few minutes – which mostly threatened to keep everyone awake all night.

Srayanka came back after the moon went down. She sighed and sank against his back, and together they watched the stars. 'They slept?' she asked.

'Yes,' Kineas said. He had kept his water bottle for them all day and given them the whole contents before they went down. They'd left enough in the bottle to make an attractive sloshing sound. He handed it to his wife and she took a sip, rolled it around her mouth and swallowed. 'You take the rest,' she said.

It tasted like ambrosia.

And then they were all asleep.

He was standing at the base of the tree, and Ajax and Niceas stood before him. 'Are you ready?' Niceas asked.

'No,' Kineas said.

Niceas nodded. 'Get ready,' he said. Beyond him, on the plain, stood thousands of corpses – some rotting, some dismembered. Close to Ajax stood a Getae warrior with a hand gone and a neat puncture wound in his abdomen. 'Do the thing!' he said in Greek. Those had been his last words. But they had a certain urgency. He cut at a Sakje warrior in a fine suit of scale – Satrax, of course. But the king broke him with a single swing.

Behind the Getae were more men, mostly Persians. Darius's half-brother was trying to push past Graccus.

'These are all the men I have killed,' Kineas said. He began to be afraid, even in the dream. The men he had killed were so

many. And for what? As he stood to lose his own life, he found that he had never valued it more. And every one of them had valued his life the same.

Now they were trying to push past other shades, the rage of combat still fresh on them.

Niceas took his hand and pushed him to the tree. His hands were bony. 'Go!' he said. 'Climb!' He looked desperate. 'Don't let this be for nothing!' he shouted.

And then Kineas was on the tree, looking down at where a circle of dead friends stood fast against a rising tide of corpses. He tore his eyes from the sight and climbed higher, swinging from branch to branch at a rate that wouldn't have been possible in the waking world, but feeling fatigue as well. His mouth was dry. He was high enough that the tree itself, despite its immensity, had a motion to it, so that the top seemed to sway like a ship's mast – or had his thoughts of a ship's mast imparted the motion?

The climb became much harder as he neared the top, the immensity of the darkening sky filling his head. Lightning played on every hand and the top moved like a wild animal under him.

Directly in his way, the thin branches of the top intertwined like an old olive tree, making a barrier like a wicker wall over his head, and he paused, trying to push through. The branches seemed to push back, the twigs whipping in the wind and cutting at his face and hands.

He pushed, using the dream strength against the branches, and as he pushed they seemed to consume him – he no longer knew, in the way of dreams, whether he was climbing or falling, trapped in a dark tunnel of branches heaving and pressing against him, and ...

Across the river there stood a tree – a lone willow, blasted by lightning in some inconceivably ancient past, for it was a mighty tree even in death – and its cousins lay scattered across the far shore.

The wreck of the enemy cavalry took cover by the dead tree. A warrior in a magnificent suit of armour and a golden helmet tried to rally them, pointing his bow across the river. A few arrows arched at them and fell short, and Srayanka smiled – a tired smile. He returned the smile and motioned to her, and she put a trumpet to her lips. Above the red swirl of dust he could see the last of a blue sky, and high in the sky an eagle circled.

'Charge!' he said. He gestured . . .

And they were in the river, bodies piled like gutted fish in the spring run of the Tanais, their blood making the froth of the river pink in the setting sun. They went forward, splashing through the river, the drops catching the sun like jewels and the cool water a blessing after a day of battle.

The shattered taxeis, the remnants of which had made their way back across, struggled to re-form, with a single officer, sword arm hanging useless at his side, bellowing for them to rally.

The man in the golden helm drew his bow, even as his companions left him . . .

Kineas was in midstream, his steel-grey charger stepping carefully because of the gravel and rocks, and then he felt a blow in his gut – sky – cold – water . . .

'You are waking the children,' Srayanka said. She sounded frightened. He listened to her cuddling the two babies and he felt – nothing.

He was a long time getting back to sleep.

In the morning, the horses were weak and difficult. There was little water in the camp and two days' travel until they could get more. The columns set off with a minimum of fuss or orders, as if two years of campaigning had been practice for these few days when every minute counted. The ground was dry grass and hard gravel, and they moved as fast as the state of their horses would allow. Srayanka looked pinched – she was losing fluid in her milk, and she was worried for the children.

'This is insane,' Kineas said to her. 'I ride to my death and you follow me to yours. The children – we must turn back.' Every word was an effort and his mouth felt like a drunkard's after a long night drinking.

'Turn back?' she retorted. 'Do you think me weak?' She turned around and waved a hand at the silent figures jogging along through the dust. 'Our children are as strong as they need to be.' She bent at the waist for a moment and then straightened. 'We must find water.'

Kineas rubbed his beard.

Four swigs of water later, they crossed a low ridge and, meeting with Nihmu, who had been left as a guide, they prepared to turn due east, away from the sun. The mountains remained on their right hand, and all that could be seen in the distance was a shimmer of heat.

Nihmu rode up to Srayanka and silently handed her a wineskin. It sloshed with water.

The column was halted so that everyone could change horses – the only relief any of them had – and every eye was drawn to the wineskin as if it glowed with blue god's fire.

'For the children,' Nihmu said. Her tone was curious – almost triumphant, or gloating.

Srayanka nodded and accepted the skin. Then she beckoned to Samahe – since Hirene's death, Samahe had become her hyperetes. 'Everyone take a sip,' she said. 'I'll have what's left.' She handed it to Samahe, who tilted it along her arm and handed it to Diodorus. Diodorus looked at it with wonder, and at her. But he, too, tipped it back briefly, before handing the skin to Antigonus, who passed it to Parshtaevalt – on and on, down the column. Kineas could follow the passage of the skin by the disturbance it made among the horses, almost as if a camel was walking among them.

When he changed horses, he chose Thalassa, because she was fresh, head high and seemed eager for him. It took him three attempts to get his leg over her back, he was so tired, and his Getae hack looked ready to drop. He could hear the sound of the skin coming back up the column. It filled his mind like something in a dream and the craving for the water drove all other thoughts from him. He imagined that the water was still cool, crisp, from some mountain stream that Nihmu had scouted.

'No one will drink,' Nihmu said by his side. The girl was so darkly tanned that she rivalled Leon's looks, and she had a straw hat over a linen wimple to guard her face from the sun. 'The water is for the children, and your people know it.'

Kineas looked at her, stunned to silence. He didn't think that he had the discipline to pass on a mouthful of water.

The water skin was already back to Carlus. Carlus looked

at it with obvious longing, but he didn't put it to his mouth. Instead, he handed it to Kineas. The skin was more than half full – some of the riders had taken a sip. But their discipline was remarkable, and humbling. Kineas took enough water to loosen his tongue in his mouth.

'We must have water tonight,' Nihmu said. 'Or many will die.'

Kineas looked at her. 'Why don't you find water?' he asked.

'I did,' she said. 'That water.' The wineskin was still in his hands, and he passed it across to Srayanka. 'It is a long ride to that water, lord. I can take you there. Ataelus will help. But you must lead.' Nihmu turned her head away to look at the horizon.

'Thank you,' Srayanka said. 'But do you think I could drink when all my people were thirsty?'

'All have had their fill, lady,' Kineas said. 'Now you drink.'

Kineas's eyes burned with unspent tears and Srayanka hung her head.

But she drank.

As she drank, her throat moving with the gulps of water, her drinking noises and the sounds of horses and conversation and Nihmu's light voice wove themselves like the border on a garment, so that in one moment they were disparate threads and in the next the voice of the god.

'*The time is soon. It is time to be complete.*'

Kineas stiffened, and the hair on his neck rose like the hackles of a dog, and his stomach recoiled.

None of them would forget that afternoon, because it seemed to go beyond a tale of hours. The sun beat down as if the gods had a burning lens focused on their column, and the heat was reflected off the scrubby grass like light from a bronze mirror. The horses took shorter strides and the dust of their passage rose to the skies like the smoke of a funeral pyre.

At the edge of dark, Kineas called a halt. The horses protested. He pushed Thalassa – still as brave as she had been at noon – through the throng to Diodorus. 'Two hours,' he said. 'Then we mount and ride on. The thirst,' he paused to rub his heavy tongue over his throat, 'it will not get any better,' he said.

Diodorus nodded.

Philokles waited until Kineas had dismounted and picketed his charger. Then he came up to Kineas and held out a cup. 'Drink, brother,' he said.

'I will not,' Kineas said. 'I will not drink your water.'

'You must command. And this is watered wine – the last from Coenus. Let us pour a libation to the gods and drink.'

Kineas took the Spartan cup and tipped a healthy portion into the dust. 'By Zeus who shakes the heavens and Poseidon who shakes the earth, Apollo, Lord of the Silver Bow, and Hera whose breasts are as white as the snow on Olympus, Athena wise in war, Ares clad in bronze, Aphrodite who riseth from the waves and Hephaestion the lame smith, Artemis the huntress, Hermes, god of travellers, who might relieve us in this waterless desert, and all the gods,' he said. And he drank.

Even as he handed the wine to Philokles, it went to his head, so that he threw his dirty cloak on the warm ground by Srayanka and before she had fed Lita, he was …

In the mud at the base of the tree amidst the terrifying silence of the dream's battle haze, a hundred maimed and bony hands reached for him. A knot of dead friends struggled back to back – Ajax and Nicomedes and Niceas still stood, but Graccus was gone …

He had the sword in his hand and he cut at the hands that tried to restrain him, and they flung themselves at him as he backed to the tree, and the stench rose through the dreamscape into his nostrils, so that all of the foulness of all the charnel pits in the world, all of the carnage of every battlefield, seemed to fill his nostrils, and above the sky was dark like the blackest storm at sea, and lightning forked across the dark iron of the heavens.

Something was on his back, something too horrible to contemplate, searching for his throat and his mind with its tendrils – hands – claws – and then it was gone, ripped free like the rising of a veil of mist, and he spun and fell to his knees in the muck. Immediately, he began to sink into the foul stuff.

'Get up,' said a familiar voice. 'Did I die so that you could fail?'

Artemis stood over him, her slit throat the least awful of the wounds around him. New forces were in the field, and the wall of silently screaming dead foes had been pushed back several strides. She wore the armour she had worn the night before Arbela, when she had danced the Spartan dances like a man and two thousand soldiers had called her name.

He rose to his feet. She turned her back to him, but she looked back as he set his foot on the trunk. 'I had a lot of friends,' she said with a smile.

And then he was climbing, flying, riding a nightmare beast that climbed for him, swarming up the trunk like a lizard or a misshapen squirrel, right into the top and up to the barrier of thorns and branches interwoven like a farmer's wall, and then he was mortal, no longer flying, bereft of his mount. He pushed his head into the branches and they fought him, but he gave a great heave, as Philokles might have done against a shield wall . . .

The arrow fell from the sky, burning like a meteor in the last of the sun and he fell . . .

Sitting on the ground as the alien spearmen pushed the javelin home in his guts . . .

Alone in the courtyard, cut off from his friends and so tired, as blow after blow fell on his head and arms, and then . . .

Standing over Nicomedes' corpse, each blow sending another foe into the dust with a clash of bronze, and the cry of the army, 'Apollo!', and he knew that victory . . .

An arm around her throat, she lashed out with feet, hands, everything, panic not quite winning over cunning, but the other hand held iron and it burned across her throat and warm wetness fell on her breasts and she screamed but no voice came and she fell into the dark . . .

Alone under the standard, and all around kin fell, protecting, covering, armour a blaze of gold . . .

The shock of the cold iron in his guts – killed in a winning fight – he might have laughed but there was nothing . . .

A child's cry ...

Screaming, red everywhere and pain like lightning in her flesh, waves that came so close that there was no rest and nothing but the lightning and the waves, moist waves of pain that carried her closer to the tunnel – an answering scream from beneath her feet, and the pressure lifted, but not the pain, and all her life pouring away between her legs ...

A child's cry – familiar – and death all around him, the iron tunnel gripping him with a rider's legs on the whole of his body, arms trapped. A child's cry ...

Standing frozen with fear as the man in the red-crested helm beats the file-leader to the ground – the sick noise as the man's spear crushes his breastbone and he rips it free, gore spraying – shield too heavy to lift to parry – frozen – the sudden ...

A child's cry ...

Light.

Three old crones and the end of a thread and the straight-limbed goddess with an owl fluttering by her shoulder, and she smiled ...

Light ...

He awoke to darkness and children crying.

By his side, Nihmu squatted, the thin hide of her leggings, worked with a thousand animals whirling in a geometric tangle of hooves and antlers and gold cones, tinkled at her shins and ankles. 'We must ride, lord,' she said.

'Yes,' Kineas said. He felt that he was speaking down a tunnel, an endless tunnel lined with sound and light and motion and life – too much life.

He turned to Srayanka, and there were tears in his eyes. 'I have done it,' he said. There was awe in his voice, and for the first time in his life, Kineas felt no fear.

Srayanka rolled to her knees from her cloak. She reached out and touched his face. 'Ahh!' she said. 'How the people will worship you.'

Kineas held her in his arms. 'Hush,' he said. 'Let's get these people to water.' His mouth was dry, but he could speak, and he could still taste the wine, and he gave the goddess a silent prayer and a smile in the dark.

They stumbled twenty stades in two hours, the worst time they had ever made, and then they rode another ten stades in a matter of minutes, because the horses could smell the water. This time, there was no holding them, no discipline, no attempt to stop the beasts or the people. Kineas gave Thalassa her head and she lengthened her stride, galloping the last stades in a few heartbeats. Even Kineas could smell the water. It gleamed like liquid pitch in the light of the new moon, a broad pond dug by the prodromoi, and they stood well clear as the horses rushed upon it and drank, more and more of them pouring in behind so that the first comers were pushed right out of the water and the weaker horses were knocked down. A mare screamed and her desperation drove other horses back, and her rider tried to get her to her feet, but the horses were mad with thirst.

'Here! Here! For more water!' Ataelus was shouting, over and over, because there was a second hole just a hundred strides away in the dark. Kineas had to drag Thalassa, usually the most obedient of horses, by her halter. He put both hands on the bit and pulled, abrading her mouth until he got her head up and away from the water and moving, and then she finally got the message that there was a second source of water and she let out a shrill cry and ran, leaving Kineas with his hands skinned raw, lying in the sand. Another mare following her lead stepped very close to him and a third kicked him where his ribs were hurt and he screamed, and then Ataelus and Leon were dragging him clear of the horses as many of the lead stallions and mares dashed for the second waterhole.

Kineas lay on the sand.

'Is he hurt badly?' Diodorus asked fearfully.

'He has lost his breath,' Philokles said. 'I think he was kicked.'

Both of them were very far away.

29

They emerged from the dry grass into the valley of the lake of the Jaxartes on the second day after the prodromoi found water. They had topped a ridge so shallow that they hadn't been aware they had climbed it, and looked down to see, not desert, but stades of water stretching away towards the mountains that now rose to the south. Horses had died, and more horses were ruined, most of them in the last rush to water and the brutal mêlée that followed – but not a man or woman or child had died. The horses had suffered, and their exhausted riders had to fight them, man and woman against horse, to drag them from the water before they killed themselves drinking.

Lot's people helped, having experienced the same just a week before. They had waited at the first water, hoping that Srayanka's people would catch up with them. Lot's wife was gone into the high country with all their herds and the young and old, and Lot appeared older. The loss of his daughters and the desert had put white in his hair, but it had not robbed him of courtesy.

'I apologize—' he said to Srayanka, but she cut him off with a quick embrace and a kiss on the cheek.

'Are we Greeks? You saw to your people and I saw to mine – and here we are.'

Lot smiled, but his smile faded as he regarded Kineas, who lay rolled in his saddle blanket, alert but mute.

'He was kicked,' Philokles said.

'He seems to hear everything we say,' Srayanka said.

Lot nodded. 'We had several in a bad way – always the ones who took the least water.' His tone left something out.

Kineas lay with an untouched Spartan cup of water in his right hand.

'Did yours recover?' Srayanka asked, as if the question were of little consequence.

'One did,' Lot replied.

'Of how many?' Philokles asked, and then repeated his question in Sakje.

'Out of four,' Lot said. He shrugged. 'I apologize again. But for Upazan, the king would have had Iskander at the Oxus. It is a heavy weight I carry.'

'Heavier than the loss of a daughter?' Kineas said, his head coming up. 'I have seen her, by the tree.'

All the commanders, Greek and Sakje and Sauromatae, stopped talking.

Tears rolled down Lot's face. 'No, lord. Not heavier than Mosva's loss.'

Kineas's eyes went over Lot's head, off into the blue sky. 'Death is not as you think,' he said. And then his head went down, and the light in his eyes dwindled, and he slept.

He was aware of the passage of time, although his awareness was flawed and he knew it, the way a man with a fever is aware that time does not pass for him as it does for his wife bathing his brow and cleaning the bed. He heard the reassuring voices of those he loved best, friends and wife, the babble and scream of his children, and he felt such passion for them that it was like physical pain, like a javelin piercing his chest straight to his heart.

He knew that a stranger had come, speaking a strange dialect, like Sakje, with many of the same words, but in a different tone with more music. He listened, but he didn't open his eyes for a long time.

When he did, he felt better and he could breathe without wheezing. He tried to sit up and gave a cry, curling into a ball, and Srayanka was there.

'Hush, Kineas.'

'I'm better,' he croaked. 'Oh, the ill luck of it! Right where the spear hit me.'

Srayanka stroked his hand. 'I have news,' she said.

'I heard a stranger,' Kineas said.

'A messenger from the queen of the Massagetae, bidding us

403

hurry to the muster. My husband is a famous warrior, I find. His fame carries even to the queen of the Massagetae.'

Kineas smiled and fell asleep.

For a day, he was aware of food, aware of wine, aware of Srayanka's caress at his cheek. He would hold his children and feel the piercing spear of love. He saw it all through the veil of dreams, and none of it had the immediacy of his thoughts, which raced and raced like a herd of deer run by dogs. It was not unlike his childhood experience of high fever.

One night he woke and Srayanka was weeping with the children in her arms. She looked at him and hissed, 'I am not a fucking Greek!' Then she lowered her voice still further. 'Come back to me! Better that you had died than that I have this walking corpse!'

And Kineas noted that what she said was true, in its way, but not important. I am dead, he thought. What did you expect?

Another sun, and another day in the saddle, his hips rolling easily with the gait of his charger, his mind far beyond the clouds. Around him they all chattered – so much talk! About him, about the weather, about the Massagetae and the Dahae and the tribes gathered in a great horde ahead of them, about Alexander's army across the river. And then it was dark, and he dreamed of the assembly of Athens and listened to Demosthenes and Phocion debate further support to Alexander, reliving the moment when he was summoned by the council to lead the richest youth of the city to support Alexander. The dream was as clear as the first experience.

He began to weep, because he had never thought to see Athens again, and because he missed it so much. How had he forgotten that the Parthenon shone so in the moonlight?

'What is death, brother?' asked a voice at his elbow.

He was weeping, and he could only just remember why. But the question was an excellent one. It engaged his mind so that his tears were choked off. He looked at the heavens and finally he said, 'The cessation of the body.'

'And truth? What is truth?'

Kineas took a deep breath. Again he was riding, and his

hips moved with a life of their own. 'Damned if I know,' he said, and his ribs hurt like fresh bruises when he laughed. And in saying, he became *aware* from the tips of his hair to the aches in his wounds. He was sitting on his Getae hack, legs clamped to its narrow back, and around him were thousands of horses, cropping the grass of the Jaxartes valley, and he was Kineas.

'What do you say?' Srayanka asked, riding up, her face lit with hope.

'I love you,' Kineas said. He reached for her and winced at the wave of pain.

She gave a little shriek like the one she sometimes uttered in passion. 'You have returned!'

'I was never very far away,' he said. He grinned and rubbed his beard.

'You climbed the tree?' Nihmu asked, full of excitement. It was night, and they were eating dinner in a camp at the edge of the Jaxartes valley.

'Be gone, bird of ill omen. Be gone with your barbarian notions of life.' Philokles made to shoo the tanned girl away from Kineas, like a farmer moving poultry in his yard.

'Shush, brother,' Kineas said. He smiled at Philokles. To Nihmu, he said, 'I climbed the tree. Now the tree is behind me.' He shrugged. 'I do not think that my tree and yours are the same.'

'Your death?' Nihmu asked.

'Is my business, girl,' Kineas snapped.

'And Iskander?' Leon asked.

'Is a very capable commander, with a fine army.' Kineas smiled. 'I have dreamed of him and I have thought about his army.' He shrugged. 'But he's across the river, as I understand.'

Philokles was polishing his helmet, using tallow and fine grit on a pad of linen tow. 'We've had brushes with his pickets every day since you went down, brother. I threw my best spear at Upazan just yesterday.' Philokles gave a mirthless grin. 'I find that all my wine-induced desires for peace vanish when I have a chance to kill.' He put the helmet down on the ground and put a felt cap on his head, then donned the helmet, transforming from philosopher to spirit of Ares in a few heartbeats. 'What is the point, Kineas? What is the point of all this marching, all this striving, all this killing? Did your precious tree tell you?' He pulled his helmet off, obviously dissatisfied with the fit. He stared at the lacings.

Kineas often found himself at a loss when debating with Philokles, but today the answers flowed into his mind like the Jaxartes in spate across the plains. 'Come, brother, you *know* the answer.' He laughed to see his brilliant and philosophical friend look at him so. He reached out and embraced Philokles. 'What would Achilles say to you, Spartan? What would Socrates say?'

Philokles drank water from a skin. He was blushing. 'They would say that the point was virtue,' he said.

Kineas nodded. 'Just so.' He took a deep breath like a man who loved the taste of air. 'Sometimes we kill because we are men of virtue and sometimes we abstain from killing for the same reason. Sometimes a man may choose to drink wine and another time he may choose to abstain. The doing of things is what earns the glory. We should need neither reward nor praise.'

Nihmu stared from one to the other. 'What are you talking about?' she asked with the annoyance of a young woman who thinks that her ignorance is being mocked. 'Is this a Greek thing?'

Kineas smiled and shook his head. 'Perhaps, and perhaps not, child.'

Philokles nodded. 'It is *the* Greek thing, child. The struggle for virtue.'

Kineas took the helmet from Philokles. 'You are the last man on earth to wear the Corinthian helmet, brother. What's wrong with it?'

'The lining is all worn out.'

Kineas nodded. 'Nothing for it but to pull the leather and sew a new one.'

Philokles nodded. 'I was being lazy.' He took his belt knife and cut the threads, and in one motion ripped the liner clear. 'Ares help me if we are attacked now,' he said.

Nihmu shook her head. 'I don't even know what you're talking about,' she said, and stalked off.

When she was gone, Diodorus joined them, with Leon and Srayanka. Ataelus sat heavily on the ground. He looked thin.

'Queen Zarina,' Ataelus said. 'For asking you.' He waved at the eastern horizon. 'For much messengers.'

Diodorus nodded. 'When will we reach her?'

Srayanka stretched. 'Two more days and we will reach the muster. Even going slowly. The horses are getting their coats back.'

Kineas nodded. 'I want to talk to Spitamenes first,' he said. 'He must be close.'

'Gods, is this some baqca thing?' Diodorus asked.

Kineas rubbed his chin and pulled his beard, enjoying his friend's discomfort. 'No,' he said. 'It's ten years in the saddle. Think of it, friend. When we were on the Oxus, Spitamenes was a hundred stades south of us. He never caught us on the Polytimeros. No one has said that Alexander caught him. We were all going to the same place. He can't be far.'

Philokles laughed. 'And we call Diodorus a fox. Well reasoned, Kineas!'

Ataelus grunted. 'Could have asked me. Fuck-their-mothers Persae at the second water today. Garait said this.' He shrugged.

Kineas turned to kiss Srayanka. 'I want to talk to the old bandit first. Then we ride to the muster.'

'The old bandit sold me to Iskander,' she said.

'I want to settle that before we ride into an alien camp,' Kineas said.

Srayanka rolled her eyes.

30

The next day, Kineas met Spitamenes. Garait located his
camp and Ataelus led him there. Darius was the inter-
mediary, and Kineas rode with a short train of followers to
share a meal with the last Persian in the field against Alexander.
Philokles joined them, eager to observe.

The Persian leader was tall and spare, with the greying
remnants of red-gold hair in his beard. He was a handsome
man despite a great beak of a nose, and he had an immediate
presence. He rode a magnificent Nisaean charger, and he was
deeply religious, so that even in the midst of his first meeting
with Kineas, he paused for prayers.

In his presence, Kineas knew that the man was a fanatic.
How could he be else? And confronted with the man, it was
as if his new-found wisdom was being tested against his old
hatreds. Spitamenes had sold his wife to Alexander for what he
thought of as a higher cause. The gambit had failed, and now
the Persian was sorry, but his apology had the distant quality
that indicated he would do as much again if it would serve to
push the hated invader off the sacred soil of Persia.

At his side sat Darius, translating freely, although Kineas's
Persian was of a high standard and many other men spoke the
same languages. But Darius did not look at Spitamenes with
worship, or even admiration. Early on, Spitamenes pointed
out Darius, who was greeting his friends and file-mates among
the Olbians. 'That one loves you more than his own country,'
Spitamenes said.

'We are guest friends and war-friends,' Kineas said. 'He has
saved my life several times.' Kineas was watching the Persians,
Medes and Bactrians around the fires. Spitamenes had fewer
than a thousand men and only the same number of horses. He
had lost the campaign that summer and his men looked the
part – dirty, tired, eyes dead. They sat on the grass with only
their saddle rugs for seats. They had no followers, no women

and very little chatter. They built their fires right on the grass rather than digging pits like the Greeks, so that the whole camp smelled of burning grass, and from time to time the grass would catch again and burn until a tired warrior stomped it out. They were dirty and yet they were proud, heads high, glaring at him as if he and Philokles were the personification of the enemy.

Spitamenes turned his head away, clearly displeased. Then he asked, 'Where is your beautiful wife?'

When Kineas visited the Persians, Srayanka stayed at home, as did all of the Sakje. There was nothing there but blood. No Sakje could forgive such an affront. 'In camp, sharpening her axe,' Kineas said.

Spitamenes nodded. 'She would do better to see to your children, surely?' he asked. It was not clear whether the question was honest or malicious.

'You did a foolish thing when you offered my wife to Iskander,' Kineas answered. He saw no reason to speak honeyed words. 'She despises you, and all her clan want nothing of you but your head.'

Spitamenes rocked back on his ankles. 'There is blunt speech!' he said. He rubbed his beard. 'I had hoped that we could be friends.'

Kineas laughed and ate more spiced mutton with his fingers. 'Let me remind you, lord, that you sold her as a hostage to Iskander – sold her, although she owed you neither allegiance nor vassalage.'

Spitamenes shrugged. 'She was to hand,' he said. 'The god requireth that I make hard choices for my people. She is the daughter of foreigners – why should I have stayed my hand?'

Philokles, sitting at Kineas's side, choked on a bit of mutton and covered his mouth with his hand.

'Your friend wishes to speak, perhaps?' Spitamenes asked. His eyes gleamed dangerously.

Philokles cleared his throat again. 'Your god should have a better eye to consequences, then,' he said in Greek. 'The lady has a sting in her tail and a thousand armoured friends.' Kineas translated.

'Do not blaspheme what you haven't the wit to understand, foreigner.' Spitamenes' tone hardened, and around him Persian noblemen handled their weapons.

Kineas took another mouthful of food. When he was done chewing, he said, 'Either Spitamenes is a man of his word, in which case this is all posturing and we should enjoy our dinner, or he is a treacherous cur, and we will die.' Kineas smiled at Spitamenes. 'And then Spitamenes will die. Don't you think my wife is out there in the dark?' Kineas shook his head as if he was a gentle father arguing with a favoured child, and then he went back to eating.

Spitamenes grew angrier at every pronouncement, but he was a man of honour and Kineas finished his meal unimpeded. 'I will not ask you to guest again,' Spitamenes said, as the Greeks mounted to leave.

'As you did not trouble even to apologize for the seizure of Srayanka, you'd be unlikely to get me to come,' Kineas said. 'Your time is over. The Sakje have the power to stop Iskander, or not, as they please. When you sent him Amazons as hostages, you lost them as allies – and you have done nothing this summer but lose prestige in every action. You are done.'

Kineas's voice had the sound of doom – of prophecy.

Spitamenes started as if he had stepped on a snake. 'Be gone before I regret my hosting!' he said.

'Keep from under our hooves, Persian,' Kineas said. 'If I find you there, I will end you myself.'

Philokles listened to the bloodless tone in Kineas's voice – not threat, but a statement of facts. Like the voice of prophecy combined with the voice of command.

Spitamenes frowned. 'I had heard that you were a prophet.'

Kineas backed his charger a few steps and nodded. 'Shall I prophesy for you, lord?'

Spitamenes said, 'I care not,' but his eagerness and hesitancy were there in his voice, and Philokles was left with the impression that Kineas was the elder of the two. And then the Persian asked, 'Will there be a great battle?'

Kineas nodded. 'Yes.'

'And will Iskander lose? Will I triumph?' Spitamenes asked.

Kineas was silent for a time – an uncomfortable time, with dozens of torchlit Persians surrounding him in the dark. At last, he said, 'Iskander will not win. But you will lose. I will die.' He laughed then, as if all of life was a joke. 'Your death is coming, but mine is near.'

'How will I die?' Spitamenes asked, pressing closer to Kineas's horse.

Kineas's face gave a spasm of fear, or revulsion – difficult for Philokles to read in the firelight. He looked at a man standing at Spitamenes' shoulder. 'Badly,' Kineas said. 'Ask me no more.'

Spitamenes turned away and growled something at one of his lieutenants. The crowd of torches dispersed. 'Go, before I turn on you,' Spitamenes said.

Kineas nodded. Then he backed his horse, checked to see that his friends were clear and rode away.

That night, they made camp in a stand of old pines at the edge of a high bluff along the Jaxartes. The grass had been cropped recently and Ataelus reported on a dozen Sakje camps around them. Kineas could see their fires, and he could see the fires of Alexander's army on the far bank and smell the smoke that filled the valley of the Jaxartes, which hadn't seen so many people since it first rose from the meltwaters of the Sogdian mountains when the gods were young.

Srayanka had built them a camp, or her household had, with a heavy hide as a shelter and a pair of spears supporting an awning of woven branches to give the illusion of privacy, right in under the supporting pines. It was a far cry from the luxury in which an Athenian officer might live, and yet it touched Kineas deeply – no one else had any shelter since the wagons had rolled north and west, and it had taken many hands to raise. There was even a fire pit with a circle of rocks and a small fire, fragrant with cedar.

She put a cup of wine in his hands after he'd seen to Thalassa, and he drank it in careful sips as he admired the ropework on the hemp bindings that held the spears – Sitalkes for sure. Then he took her hand and drew her close, and they kissed.

Philokles came into the little clearing that held their camp. He looked around as if puzzled, and Kineas could see he was drunk.

'Very nice!' Philokles said. He swayed a little.

Diodorus followed him up the trail, and behind him came Leon and Sitalkes and someone else moving in the darkness.

'Can I help you gentlemen?' Kineas asked, his voice redolent with the irritation of a man interrupted in kissing his wife.

Philokles turned his head away and gave a lurch and a burp. 'Excuse me, gentlemen. Not myself.' He grinned at Kineas. 'Didn't know you wanted to be alone. Missed you.'

Diodorus came up and put his hand on the Spartan's shoulder. 'Come away, Philokles.'

'Says he'll be dead soon. Then we'll never see him!' Philokles shook his head. He raised his cup. 'Godlike Kineas, share this cup of wine!' he said, and spilt some wine on the pine needles, though whether in clumsiness or deliberate invocation it was hard to tell.

Diodorus grabbed at Philokles. The Spartan glided out of his hands and sprang back, but in his haze of wine fumes he'd forgotten the two spears and the ropes, and he tripped. There was a crash and Philokles went down, and the whole shelter came down with him. He bellowed as he rolled through the small fire, extinguishing it.

'Hades! Philokles, you fucking idiot!' Kineas grabbed the Spartan by the arm and dragged him to his feet, sweeping the man with his hand to get rid of coals.

Philokles looked as if he'd been hit with a plank. 'Didn't mean – Gods! Srayanka! Sorry!' He pushed Kineas away roughly and began to try to gather up the pieces of the shelter. He stumbled and managed to pick up a single rope.

Sitalkes emerged from the darkness, and Temerix. Temerix took the Spartan's shoulder. 'Come,' he said in his heavy accent. 'Come, friend. We fix this. Come!'

412

Philokles wept. 'I only break things,' he cried as the Sindi smith pulled him along. 'I make nothing!'

Srayanka grinned. 'Sitalkes, make this right again,' she said. She turned to Kineas. 'He's hurt in his soul, husband. Go and help him.'

Behind her, Sitalkes had his fire kit out and was blowing coals to light, and Srayanka's eyes glinted. 'But don't take too long,' she said.

Kineas found Philokles by his own fire, with a clay beaker of wine in his hand and Temerix sitting by his side.

'I'm sorry,' Philokles said. He was more sullen than sorry, and his eyes were on the fire.

Kineas reached past him and grabbed the wine cup. He took a pull and then emptied the contents into the fire.

'Hey!' Philokles shouted.

'Do you love me, brother?' Kineas asked.

Philokles stopped moving. Then he drew himself up. 'Yes. Yes I do.'

Kineas nodded. 'I love you, too. Too much to watch you kill the hero in your breast with wine. That was your last cup, brother. Swear to me by all the gods and by my children that you will never drink wine again.'

Philokles was aghast. 'Never?'

'Never for any reason. Swear, if we are friends.' Kineas saw an amphora point-first in the ground, and he plucked it free. 'Temerix, is this yours?'

Temerix spat. 'Never bring wine to Philokles,' he said. 'Friend.'

Kineas tucked it under his arm. 'Mine now. Swear, Philokles.'

Philokles looked sly and sullen, two casts for which his face was not naturally formed. 'What if I don't?'

Kineas shrugged. 'Maybe I'll never answer another one of your cursed questions. Or perhaps I'll simply banish you and fight without you. But if you don't stop drinking wine, you are no companion of mine.'

Philokles came up. 'Fuck you,' he said, reaching for the amphora.

413

Kineas hit him on the chin. Then he put the amphora into the dirt carefully while the Spartan backed away. Kineas raised his hands. Philokles took another step backwards and stopped. He had adopted the guard stance of the pankration, hands open, held high to guard his face, his left hand stretched forward. Then he came forward, fast, reaching with his left hand for a grapple.

Kineas stepped forward, inside the left, and punched – one, two – staggering Philokles. He retreated a step and Kineas let him.

They stood facing each other.

Philokles bellowed, a shout of anger, almost the cry of a wounded man, and he charged. His two feints were not the feints of a drunk, and Kineas bought the second and in a moment he was on his back in the dirt, but he got his legs around Philokles' knees and rotated his hips, tripping the big Spartan and pulling him down. He got both of the man's hands in his own and they grappled, pushing for purchase with their feet and backs, covered in dust.

It was hopeless for Kineas to try to beat the Spartan in a grapple, but he continued to try until Philokles had his head and arm locked under his shoulder and the pain was enough to drive the breath from his body.

And then suddenly Philokles, who had him at the point of submission, sagged away in the dirt and lay on his back as if he'd been hit in the head with a plank. Then he rolled to his feet and held out a hand.

Kineas took it. Their hands clasped.

'I swear by Zeus and all the gods, and by the shade of my mother who died to bear me, and by the power of my love for you, Kineas, that I will never be drunk again in your presence, that I will never drink wine to excess. And if I dishonour this oath, may all the Furies shred my soul.' Philokles spoke in his sober voice.

'May the gods hear you, and support you in your oath,' Kineas said. 'But when I am gone, you must stay on this path. Or it will be your death.'

The Spartan and the Athenian embraced.

'I'm sorry!' Philokles said, and burst into tears.

'You need to stop being a soldier, brother,' Kineas said. 'It's the killing that makes you drink.'

Philokles wept for a while, and then he stood straight. 'What do people do when they don't drink?' he asked.

Kineas picked up the amphora. 'Experiment. You're the philosopher!'

31

And at last, after a year in the field, the army of Olbia, as represented by the hardiest three hundred men, and the Western Assagatje, as represented by four hundred riders culled by two summers of war, and the Western Sauromatae, as represented by Lot's two hundred, came to the gathering of all the Sakje peoples.

Queen Zarina had camped the bulk of her forces in a bend of the Jaxartes, secure that the water at her back was deep and cold, and that the mountains on her flanks were too difficult for any foe. In the vale of the Jaxartes, she had gathered thirty thousand warriors, and as many again lived in satellite camps, as close as a day's ride away or as far as ten days' ride, so that if the Sakje had been grains of sand spread across a parchment, it was as if the gods had tipped the parchment so that one corner of it held all the sand – tons of it – in one small area.

The grass was devastated, and twice the whole army had had to move. There were no deer to be hunted for fifty stades, no fish in the river, no wood for fires. Every tribe had sent away its weakest to their winter grounds to lessen the numbers, and even then the queen had to rotate tribes out on to the grass and back to the river to watch Iskander.

Across the river, the army of Macedon concentrated forces from camps along the Jaxartes, the Polytimeros and the Oxus into one single mass of men, horses and machines. The siege of Marakanda had been broken and only the thinnest garrison left. Oxen pulled the king's siege artillery up to his camp on the edge of the sea of grass, the greatest horde of enemies the Sakje had ever seen – and still the Macedonian officers stared at the dust clouds across the river and shuddered. Even odds against a foe who was mounted throughout her force.

North and east of Alexander's army, a smaller force – just two thousand men, Sogdians and Bactrians and mercenaries and a handful of Sauromatae – moved along the southern bank of the Jaxartes, searching for a ford, under Eumenes.

Kineas heard it all from scouts, from the Sakje, from Srayanka and finally from Ataelus himself before the last day of march was done. The sun was setting on the valley of the Jaxartes, and below them twenty thousand horses milled, every horse looking for the last clumps of grass along the river. Young men raced and shot bows. Women sharpened weapons and repaired tack. Tents of felt rose from some encampments, and others had a few wagons, but in the main it was a war camp and the people lay on the ground with the reins of their horses near to hand.

Ataelus waved at the whole sweep of the people, who covered the ground as far as the eye could see. 'The power of the Massagetae, the Sakje, the Dahae.' Ataelus wore a grin that eliminated his cheekbones. 'I was for boying here.'

Philokles rubbed his beard and watched, transfixed, while trying to take in what Kineas had just told him. 'So Alexander will try to turn the Sakje left?' he asked.

'Alexander will come right across the river,' Kineas said with finality. 'But my guess is that he will send a column to wrong-foot the Scythians on their left. And that's what Ataelus says.'

Philokles could almost see it. 'Ares,' he said. 'Right across the river here?'

'No,' Kineas said with a smile. 'There's no ford here. The queen chose her camp well. Upstream ten stades is where he will come.' He spoke with conviction, and Ataelus nodded.

The Sakje screwed up his mouth. 'Short ride,' he said. 'To battle,' he added after a pause.

'If you know all this, surely you can defeat Alexander?' Philokles asked.

Kineas shook his head. 'Do I look like a Sakje chief? I will not command here, Spartan. I can only share my views with Queen Zarina. Let's go and meet her.'

'But we may defeat him?' Philokles asked again.

Kineas halted his horse and leaned close. 'I have no idea, brother. I'm not a seer – I'm the commander of half a thousand

417

cavalry. So perhaps, despite your concern for the triumph of Panhellenism, you could shut the fuck up about the battle?'

Philokles laughed. 'You're nervous! I'd never have believed it!'

Kineas glared, but held his tongue.

Philokles laughed again. 'Let's go and meet the queen of the Sea of Grass!'

When the column was halted, they had to camp on a site that had already been used and abandoned by other contingents, and it took time to wedge eight hundred people and four times that many horses into the edge of the sprawling camp. The site was good and water was plentiful but the grass was cropped to the roots. Antigonus laid out the horse lines almost in the bed of the river, the only place where there was any grazing not already taken by other groups, and he doubled the horse pickets because Macedonians could be seen just a pair of bow shots away across the river.

Lot rode up from the Sauromatae at the back of the column with Lady Bahareh at his side. He clasped hands with Kineas. 'She and Zarina are old friends. We – Zarina and I – have traded some sword cuts.'

'Good,' Philokles said. 'We can all hide behind Bahareh.'

The Sauromatae spear-maiden grinned. She was as thin as a tree branch and her hair was the colour of iron. 'I'll protect you, little prince,' she said. 'Greetings, Lord Kineas.'

Srayanka took Ataelus and Parshtaevalt, and Kineas took Leon and Diodorus. Philokles never required an invitation. They took no escort and left their people cooking dinner. They rode hard for the queen's tent, just a dozen stades away around the next bend in the river.

After travelling more than four hundred parasangs from the Ford of the River God on the little Borysthenes to the upper Jaxartes, Queen Zarina was almost a disappointment.

Qares, Zarina's messenger earlier in the summer, was the first to recognize them. He ordered a group of adolescent girls to hold their horses and ushered them into the queen's tent, a magnificent construction in red and white. There were no guards, and the tent was full of tribal leaders and Sakje knights, as well as other Massagetae in simpler dress and a dozen slaves. If Qares hadn't been standing in respectful silence next to him, his whole attention focused on a short woman in a simple dress, Kineas might have mistaken who among the assembly was the queen. There were several women with regal bearing, two of them in armour, but the queen stood towards the edge of the group, looking at arrow shafts. One by one she looked down the shafts, making quiet comments to a child who stood by her with her gold-covered gorytos, until thirty were chosen. The discards were carried out of the tent. Kineas had time to observe her as she spoke in quiet tones to the child, and to a man of her own age who stood at her shoulder.

Zarina was a short woman with iron-grey hair in straight braids woven tight with gold foil, the only sign of her royalty that she wore on her person. On a lacquered armour stand behind her sat a coat of iron scales with alternating rows of gold, with a golden gorget as rich as Srayanka's and a golden helmet surmounted by a gryphon whose eyes were picked out in garnets. The child – clearly her squire – replaced the gorytos on the armour stand and brought her a long-handled axe with a double blade. She rubbed her thumb across the blades, first one and then the other, and smiled. As she smiled, she raised her eyes and in one glance took in Qares and then the group with him.

'You found them!' she said, stepping forward. The tent fell silent as she raised her voice and every head turned.

Srayanka went to meet her. She inclined her head – the closest any Sakje managed to a bow.

Zarina took both of her hands. 'You must be the Lady Srayanka of the Cruel Hands,' she said in Sakje. She had a deep, hoarse voice for a woman, but her tone was warm.

'I am Lady Srayanka. I have brought four hundred of my people to the muster, and my husband has brought two hundred Greeks, who are our allies. And Prince Lot,' she turned to invite Lot forward, and the Sauromatae lord bowed his head with a smile.

'Zarina and I are old friends,' he said.

'And bitter foes,' Zarina said. 'Sometimes.' Their eyes locked and the tent was silent. Zarina's tent – the entire tent – was alternating red and white silk panels, heavily oiled and almost translucent. The light from the coloured panels fell differently on the people in the tent – the queen was brightly lit under a white panel, while Lot was covered in red, like blood. He bowed again.

'So you have not followed that charlatan Pharmenax?' she said to Lot. 'Does he still call himself the king of all the Sauromatae?'

'Prince Lot has been fighting Iskander all summer,' Qares put in.

Kineas could see that the claim of an old enmity was founded on something. There was tension in her stance, and Lot was stiffer than usual.

'Only a fool would follow Pharmenax,' Lot said.

'I forbade you to go west,' Zarina said.

'I said I would return with allies,' Lot shot back. 'And I have.'

Bahareh stepped forward, distracting the queen, and the two embraced.

'But I forbade it,' Zarina said.

Kineas thought that she was speaking to Bahareh alone. The Sauromatae woman punched the queen's shoulder. 'He did as he said he would. Eh?'

Zarina's brows narrowed, but then her face cleared. 'So you have. Welcome!'

As if every breath had been held, there was a sigh throughout the tent and then conversation started again.

Queen Zarina beckoned and Kineas stepped forward in his turn. Close up, he became aware that she had the darkest green eyes that Kineas had ever seen on a human being. Her hands were as hard as a woodcutter's. 'You have truly come all the way from the Sea of Darkness?' she asked.

'Mother of the clans, we have indeed ridden from the Western Sea,' Srayanka responded. 'I promised to come, and I am here, though less than a tithe of our strength has come with me.'

Zarina waved her hand as if this loss of strength was of no

import. 'And the cities of the Western Sea sent a contingent? So that Greeks will ride to fight Greeks? This has been reported to me all summer and still I find it a wonder.'

Zarina's gaze returned to Kineas and gave him the sort of careful examination that a Sakje gave a horse she considered buying – or stealing. 'You are baqca,' she said. 'This I have heard.'

Kineas bowed. 'I am the strategos of Olbia,' he said. 'A war leader.'

'Hmm,' Zarina replied. Then she dismissed Kineas as other leaders were introduced by Srayanka – Diodorus, whose red hair and beard made the queen laugh, and Parshtaevalt, and Leon, whose dark skin she touched several times. Next came Ataelus. She raised an eyebrow. 'Surely you are of my people?' she asked.

Ataelus gave his Greek shrug. 'Many years ago I rode west, lady,' he answered. 'Now I serve the Lady Srayanka.'

Zarina pursed her lips and motioned for the next man to be presented, and Philokles stepped forward. She looked him up and down. 'You are a *Zpar-tan*?' she asked.

'I am,' Philokles answered, obviously pleased that here, at the edge of the known world, the barbarians still knew the word *Spartan*.

'Hmm,' she murmured. The two women in armour laughed – a tough-looking pair. One of them pushed past to feel Philokles' arm muscles. She nodded approval. 'That's what a man should look like,' she said to Srayanka. 'Why didn't you marry that one?'

Srayanka snorted. 'He didn't know how to ride!' she laughed.

Zarina laughed so hard she had to cross her arms on her gut. When she recovered, she was still smiling broadly. 'I welcome all of you to my camp,' she said. 'I'll see if my slaves can find space for you for dinner. Tonight we set the battle order. Are your horses ready to fight?'

Srayanka nodded. 'Ready enough. We miss the grain of home. None of our chargers are at their best.'

Zarina nodded. 'We're at the end of the grazing. Iskander is at the end of his. The fight must come soon.'

Dinner was simple and reminded Kineas of dinners with Satrax – spiced mutton served in the same bronze cauldron in which it had been cooked, and every man and woman dipping their flatbread into the pot. The mutton was delicious, but there was no wine and no oil. No one spoke. The gathered guests ate quickly and efficiently, and then sat quietly until Zarina rose to her feet.

'Now,' she said to her guests, 'we will discuss how to show Iskander our strength.'

The meeting of the chiefs of all the Scythians reminded Kineas that he was truly among barbarians. Everyone spoke at once – on and on. No considerations of tactics ever rose to the surface of the meeting, but rather, chieftains demanded precedence in battle – the left of the line, the right of the line, the position guarding the standard – based on ancient custom or hard-won privilege shouted and debated from one bearded warlord to another.

Queen Zarina appeared indifferent, watching her tribal leaders with obvious pride, sure of her strength. Kineas stood silent, with Diodorus, Srayanka and Philokles around him, whispering from time to time in disgust at the chaos and the arrogance.

Lot gave a wry grin. 'I'd forgotten what it was like,' he said.

Ataelus shook his head. 'Fight for too long with Greeks,' he said. 'Sakje for talking.'

'Do they know who Alexander is?' Diodorus asked. 'Do they think they can just ride around the plain and shoot arrows and call it a victory?'

Philokles had remained silent for over an hour. 'I admire these people,' he said, 'but no one here has proposed that we simply ride away and leave Alexander to starve on the high plains. Where is the wisdom of the Assagatje? Where is their Satrax?'

Srayanka pulled on a braid, fretting for her children. 'I had forgotten what we were like in my father's time,' she said.

'Truly, Kam Baqca and Satrax made us something greater. And you, my husband. The three of you made each leader see his place.'

'Perhaps if you spoke to the queen?' Diodorus said to Srayanka.

Srayanka shook her head. 'I am as much a foreigner here as any of you Greeks. I will go and see to our children. My breasts are heavy.' She kissed Kineas lightly.

Lot made a face as if he smelled something foul. 'I know Zarina of old,' he said. 'You won't find it easy to tell her anything. She esteems women above men, but not as much if they bear children.' He looked at Srayanka, who nodded agreement. 'She esteems men, but only for their strength, not their wisdom, even in war.' Lot glanced at Philokles. 'The Spartan might approach her with a message. She was impressed by his size and his name. And Lady Bahareh has known her for years.'

The chieftains went on shouting until the sun had set, and scouts came in to report that Iskander had moved bolt-shooters up to the banks of the river and was assembling bladders and rafts. Srayanka rode away. Kineas rubbed his beard and listened to the growing excitement. Rumours of Alexander's imminent attack only fed the shouting, and the queen watched with a tolerant amusement that proclaimed her more interested in being the warlord of these chiefs than in working to defeat the common foe.

Diodorus shook his head. 'They're going to get their heads handed to them. Ares' *balls*, Kineas – have we ridden fifteen thousand stades so that we can watch Alexander dispatch another horde of tribes the way he did the Thracians? Let us be gone – the rout will be ugly.'

Kineas was tired of standing. 'There is some god-sent irony,' he said, 'that we can all but see how Alexander will attack, and no one here cares to listen to us.' He shrugged and took his companions out of the great tent and into the gathering gloom of the Sakje camp, where three thousand fires twinkled along the curve of the river. The air smelled of horse and burning wood.

'We should ride back while the sun gives us a little light,' Kineas said.

'I would try to speak to the queen, if you gave me leave,' Philokles said. He glanced at Bahareh and Ataelus.

'When have you ever needed my permission?' Kineas slapped the Spartan on the shoulder. 'This is not as bad as you all seem to think. Their very chaos will serve them against Alexander. It is almost impossible to plan a battle against a hundred generals. New forces will ride on to the field all day, and each will commit themselves as they see fit, unbound by precedent or structure.'

'What would you have the queen know?' Bahareh asked.

Kineas was looking for their horses, tethered in a herd of magnificent horseflesh brought by two hundred chiefs. He was pleased that Thalassa held her own, surrounded by admiring Massagetae children and a dozen respectful adolescents. A severe-looking young woman handed him her reins and nodded. 'That is a horse,' she said. 'You sell her?'

Kineas grinned, his thoughts suddenly infected with an image of Thalassa's foals. 'Never,' he said in Sakje. 'But I wish you may find as fine a horse.'

They nodded to each other and Kineas used his spear to vault into the saddle, showing off for the children like a much younger warrior. He leaned down to Bahareh. 'Ask the queen's permission for us to ride north along the river to the next ford, to guard against a flanking move. Tell her we think that Alexander will send his best cavalry and his hardest infantry across with the dawn, tomorrow or the next day, and that he will send a force to cross upriver – to the north. Ask her to allow us to stop the northern thrust.' He caused Thalassa to circle, to the admiration of all.

'That's all?' Philokles asked. 'Alexander's coming across and we'll hold the northern ford?'

Kineas nodded. 'That's all. Trying to tell these people how to fight Alexander would be like trying to tell an Athenian how to argue. Any half-measures we push on them will only impede them.'

Bahareh looked at Kineas with respect. 'You are wise. I expected you to tell the queen how to fight.'

Philokles nodded. 'Wait for us. Either she will see us, or she will not. Either way we will be brief.'

Diodorus smirked. 'Show her your muscles and you won't be so brief, Spartan. All night, maybe.'

Philokles punched the Athenian in the knee, just hard enough to hurt. 'She values men in her bed to just the extent that I value women,' the Spartan said. Bahareh coughed in her hand. Philokles waved to Ataelus, who shrugged at Kineas and followed Philokles, and then his faded red cloak swirled and he was gone in the dusk.

Kineas rode his charger up and down. A boy came up on a tall horse, a captured Nisaean of which he was justly proud, and Kineas, in the grip of some daimon, accepted his offer of a race. Torches were brought and ten more riders materialized from the gloom, while Diodorus cursed him for a fool. 'Are you a boy? With a battle tomorrow?'

'Hush,' Kineas said. 'I am making a sacrifice to Poseidon.'

Diodorus pursed his lips. 'As long as you aren't just showing off,' he called, as Kineas rode to the starting spear.

The race was like swimming in darkness and fire from the first surge of Thalassa's hindquarters to the last pounding moments as the leading knot of them burst through the circle of light by the finish to a roar so loud that it rose above the debating in Zarina's tent like an offering to the Horse-God, to whom Kineas sent his prayer winging while the Sakje embraced him for his victory.

Diodorus sat on his charger, shaking his head. 'Are you twelve years old?' he asked.

Kineas shook his head. 'Let us make that sacrifice to Poseidon.' Kineas managed to convey that he wanted to purchase a goat and the animal was brought. A Massagetae baqca, resplendent in caribou antlers and a silk robe, led them past Zarina's tent to the camp altar. Kineas sacrificed the animal himself, slashing the beast's throat and stepping free of the blood with practised ease. He raised the hymn with Leon and Diodorus:

Poseidon Lord of Horses,
Thou lovest the clip-clop beat
Of hooves in hard-fought battle
And neighs to thee sound sweet,
And when our black-maned horses
The winning vase may gain,
Their swiftness cheers the ruler
Of the wildly tossing main ...

They sang to the end, Kineas grinning like a man half his age.
Philokles came up singing the hymn, and with him were many
of Zarina's commanders, and at the back of the group, Zarina
herself, talking and waving her hands at Ataelus, who wore a
deep frown.

Kineas stood by the altar with Thalassa beside him, surrounded by Massagetae and Dahae warriors, many of whom
reached up to touch his horse. He saw a girl clip a few hairs
from her tail and he was about to step in when he found
himself face to face with Zarina.

'Now I see how my young cousin could marry a Greek,'
she said. She nodded. 'Go north if that is where you see the
enemy, Kineax. I have heard the Spartan – I have understood.'
She shrugged. 'No queen has ever faced a battle this great
– with the whole might of the people. I am not a Persian,
to kiss and cuddle my chiefs until they go sullenly to some
carefully ordered place in the battle line. Nor am I the Qu'in,
with chariots and horses and lines of men like pieces on a game
board. I am the queen of the Sakje, and my chiefs will fight
like dogs for a place in the line. Do as you will – you are a man
of war. Those are my orders to you, as they are the orders I give
to every chief – you are a free man. Do as you will.'

As they rode back, Philokles rattled on about his time with her.
'Very much the sort of barbarian that Solon or Thales might
have admired. Utterly free.' He shook his head, barely visible
in the moonlight. 'I warned her that Spitamenes was coming.
She knows him. I gather that it is a marriage of convenience.'

'As long as he is on the right while we are on the left,'

426

Kineas said. 'If he comes in front of Srayanka, she will kill him and to Hades with the consequence.'

They reached their camp in the last glow of the western horizon. Fires were lit and warriors ate their fill. Leon waited until they took their horses out to the picket lines.

'We have food for two more days and then things will get tight,' he said.

'The whole host of the Sakje is in the same position,' Diodorus said bitterly. 'All Alexander need do is wait, and we will all melt away.'

'Two hours ago you were ready to leave,' Kineas said.

'I've ridden all this way,' Diodorus said, shrugging off his own mercurial comments.

'Alexander is in the same situation. He's converged all of his armies in the east at the edge of a desert, and he's spent the summer fighting partisans. He doesn't have the food stores he's used to. We'll fight him, tomorrow or the next day. My wager goes on the next day.'

Srayanka came up with Antigonus and the rest of the chiefs and officers, as if Kineas had called a council. They stood quietly, and Kineas smiled to think of the Sakje outside the queen's red and white silk tent.

'They're fine?' Kineas asked Srayanka.

Srayanka smiled. 'Would I wander out here to talk of war if my children were unwell?' she asked. She looked wryly at Samahe. 'I am becoming my mother. When young, she rode with the spear-maidens, but in middle age, she was a mother first and her hand grew light.'

Kineas took her chin and kissed her. 'I don't think your hand will grow light,' he said.

'Let Spitamenes come under it tomorrow and we'll see,' she said.

'Alexander is the enemy,' Diodorus drawled.

'Alexander was polite,' Srayanka said. She tossed her head. 'Hephaestion – that one I would geld, if only for Urvara's sake.'

Kineas felt his guts roil. 'I hadn't heard this.'

Srayanka shrugged. 'She's a tough girl. He did not break

427

her, and the young Olbian boy loves her, and she has healed. No more need be said. But Hephaestion ...' No one looking at Srayanka in the light of a fire needed to wonder if her hand had grown light. She cocked her head to one side. 'So, husband, do you see it in your head?'

There in the firelight, Kineas outlined his plan. He drew pictures in the dust with the tip of a bronze knife he'd found in the fire pit. 'Ataelus and I agree that Alexander will send a force north – either he will lead it himself or he will send someone he trusts. It's something he learned from Parmenion. It will be Philotas, won't it?'

'He murdered Philotas!' Diodorus said. 'Old age must be getting to you.'

'More fool he. Philotas was his best after Parmenion. So Eumenes, perhaps? The Cardian?'

'Craterus?' Philokles asked. 'I never served the monster myself, but I know the names. Why not Craterus?'

Kineas shrugged. 'Somebody dangerous, with good troops, probably all cavalry. In my head I still see Philotas.' He paused and poured a libation to the dead man's shade. 'They'll go north to the next ford – which Ataelus has already located – and try to push across into the queen's left flank. We'll meet them at the ford if we're quick. That's the best service we can do for this army.'

Everyone nodded.

'And if Zarina loses, we'll have a clear road home,' Srayanka said.

Kineas nodded. 'Yes.' He didn't elaborate.

'Let us say we meet this Macedonian and rout him back across the ford,' Samahe asked. She shrugged, looking around. 'Why do you look at me this way? We have been known to win battles in the past!'

That got her a laugh.

'Then what? Eh?' She looked around, defiant.

Kineas nodded. 'I really can't say. We could cross after them and return the favour, but I would expect that any fight will leave us too beaten up to turn their flank – and we're too few. We ought to be able to turn in on our own side, however,'

Kineas's knife point traced a black furrow along the Sakje bank of the line that marked the Jaxartes, 'and strike the flank of their main effort.'

'Our horses would be blown,' Srayanka said thoughtfully.

Diodorus had found a heavy basket to sit on. He leaned forward, the basket creaking under his weight, and he pointed a stick at the map in the dirt. 'What if Alexander's main effort is the northern ford?' he asked.

'Hmm,' said Philokles. 'How long would we last?'

Kineas shook his head. 'I wouldn't even fight, beyond some skirmishing to make the ford cost him.' He gave a bitter smile. 'We wouldn't last long.'

'No,' Diodorus said. 'And it wouldn't be worth spit, anyway. This Sakje army isn't a phalanx, Philokles. If you hit the Sakje in the flank, they just ride away and fight another day. If Alexander wants a fight, he has to goad them to it, fix them in place and then hit them.'

Srayanka nodded, as if she had held a conversation with herself. 'Listen. Let us fight like Assagatje. Let us move all our remounts to here.' She indicated a place just west of the ford, then pointed at Diodorus. 'If Diodorus's worst instincts are right, and Alexander comes north, we can fight in retreat, change horses and vanish. No pursuit could possibly catch us on fresh horses. Yes?'

All around the fire, the chiefs and officers nodded. Lot slapped her back. 'Cruel Hands, you are still the cunning one.'

She went on, smiling a very unmotherly smile at her husband. 'If we meet this flanking force and defeat it, we take the time to change horses – and we ride to the battle in the centre on fresh mounts.'

Kineas grabbed her and kissed her. They kissed, and the other leaders whooped and mocked them. When he left her lips, he shook his head. 'You kiss better than any of my other cavalry commanders,' he said, and she kicked his shin.

Diodorus looked at the map in the sand again. 'We should move tonight,' he said. He looked at Srayanka and shrugged, apologetic. 'Forty stades under a bright moon is nothing to us after the desert. And then there will be no dust to betray us.'

'Odysseus is, as usual, correct,' Kineas said. He and Srayanka exchanged a long look, because precious hours were being taken from them, never to be replaced.

'We will ride together, as we did when our love was young,' she said, and she began to choke on her words, but she fought through unbroken. 'I will ask you the names of things in Greek, and you will ask me the Sakje words, and we will forget the future and know only what is now.'

Philokles couldn't bear it, and he turned away.

Ataelus was already calling for horses, and Antigonus was passing the unpopular news, but the rest stayed by the fire. The night on the plains was brisk.

'I wonder where Coenus is?' Diodorus asked. He waited a moment, and then decided that Kineas had not heard him. 'Do you wonder—' he began, and Kineas turned.

'Coenus should be watching the sun rise over the mountains of Hyrkania in the morning,' Kineas said.

'Athena and Hermes, have we been riding that long in the desert?' Philokles asked.

Ataelus grunted. 'Yes.'

Diodorus thumbed his beard. 'Every time you kiss Srayanka, I miss Sappho more.'

Kineas slapped his shoulder. 'There are great days ahead,' he said. He felt sad and happy at the same time. And then, after a pause, 'See to Philokles when I am gone.'

Diodorus coughed to cover some tears that stood bright on his cheeks. 'It just hit me that it will be as you say – that you do know the hour of your death.' He sniffled. 'Are you sure?'

Kineas gathered him in an embrace. 'I know this battle,' he said simply. 'I die.'

'Philokles?' Diodorus asked, wiping his eyes with the back of his hand. 'Ares, it's Srayanka who will need us.'

'No,' Kineas said. 'She will be queen, and all the Sakje will be her husband. Philokles will have only you.'

Diodorus chewed his lip. 'You remember sword lessons with Phocion?'

'I think of them all the time.' The two men were still locked in embrace.

'I will be the last left.' He was weeping, the tears flowing down his cheeks like the muddy waters of the Jaxartes.

'So you must be the best,' Kineas said. 'When I fall, you command. Not just for one action, either. I leave you the bequest of all my unfought battles.'

Diodorus backed away, his hand hiding his face. 'I was never the strategos you were,' he complained.

Kineas gripped his neck. 'Two years ago you were a trooper,' he said. 'Soon, we will fight Alexander. You know how to command. You love to command.'

'Before the gods, I do,' Diodorus said.

'I leave you the bequest of my unfought battles,' Kineas said again.

'You should be king. King of the whole of the Bosporus.'

Kineas felt his own tears as he thought of all he would miss. His children, most of all. 'Make Satyrus king,' he said. 'I'm too much an Athenian to be a king.'

The other Athenian stood straight. 'I will,' he said.

They covered forty stades in a dream of darkness and the soft glitter of moonlight on the sand, and the hand of Artemis the huntress covered them. Ataelus's prodromoi waited at every obstacle and every turn, guiding them around a camp of Sakje in the dark, clearing them across a gully with a burbling stream at the base, and around a shaled hill that might have hurt the horses in the dark, until they came to the back of a long ridge running perpendicular to the Jaxartes. Ataelus rode up next to Kineas in the dark.

'For fighting,' he said quietly. He pointed down the ridge at the river as it bowed through a deep curve in the moonlight. 'Iskander!' he said, and pointed across the river, where a thousand orange stars shone in the foothills of the Sogdian mountains – Alexander's cooking fires.

They rode on for an hour, the column winding back to be lost to sight in the darkness over the big ridge. Twelve stades later, as Kineas reckoned it, they descended sharply from the path they'd followed towards the river, which they could hear but not see.

He rode down into the vale, heedless of possible enemy patrols, eager to see the ground as best he could, and Srayanka came with him, her household clattering along behind. They rode hand in hand, almost silent.

At the edge of the ford, they halted.

'Well?' Srayanka asked.

Kineas shook his head and grinned. 'For whatever it means, this is not the place of my dream,' he said. 'Too narrow.' He pointed across. 'No downed trees. No giant dead tree on the far shore.'

Srayanka exhaled as if she had held a single breath all day. 'So?' she asked.

Kineas looked at the sky. 'I speak no hubris,' he said. 'When the Macedonians come, on this field, we will triumph.'

They turned quietly and rode back across the ridge, to camp and perhaps to grapple a few hours of sleep from the last of darkness and the pre-battle jitters.

But not for Kineas. He lay awake, his body entwined with hers. He no longer needed sleep. He no longer intended to cede a moment to sleep.

The end was as close as the point of his spear.

32

'I want the enemy to see nothing but Sakje,' Kineas said. Srayanka nodded, as did Lot.

Sitting on his cloak, Kineas was fixing his blue horsehair crest to his helmet. He had an odd feeling, as if he had done all these things before so many times that he was an actor, playing the same part on many different days in the theatre.

All around him, the Olbians were polishing their gear and affixing their helmet crests, the hyperetes of each troop moving among them to inspect their work. Men used ash gathered from their last fire pits to put a fine polish on their bronze. Men skilled with stones put a fine edge on spear points and swords. A few of the Keltoi spoke loudly, but most were quiet.

Philokles sat on a rock, sober. He was combing out his hair. Behind him, the red rim of the sun rose above the distant mountains in the east.

Sitalkes, who had once been Kineas's slave, came up holding a pair of javelins, with long, thin shafts and linen throwing cords. 'I didn't think you had any,' he said, looking at the ground.

'May Ares bless you, Sitalkes!' The pleasure of a good weapon made Kineas beam. 'I hadn't even thought of it. Where did you get them?' He hefted one. 'They're beautiful!'

Sitalkes glanced at Temerix, who was watching from a distance, glaring at them under heavy brows. 'Temerix made the points. I set them.' He grinned. 'Good wood. Cut-down lances.'

The two heads were gemlike, gleaming blue-red in the first light, far better work than was usually expended on javelins. Kineas embraced Sitalkes and then walked over and embraced Temerix, who stared at the ground while being hugged and then laughed aloud when the strategos turned away.

Kineas thought that he'd never heard the Sindi smith laugh.

433

As ordered, Srayanka's people patrolled the edge of the river, their forms visible in a flash of gold or bronze or red leather. Most of her warriors were hidden in stands of trees on the near side of the Jaxartes, and a handful, the boldest, prowled the far bank.

The enemy force announced itself just before the end of the dawn, when shadows were still long on the ground and spear points winked against the last of the darkness. Their dust cloud showed them to be moving carefully, and their outriders made contact with Ataelus's prodromoi and drove them back easily. Kineas watched from a stand of trees on the ridge, his helmet under his arm, his reserves hidden in a fold of ground behind him.

At the water's edge, an hour later, two squadrons of Bactrians pushed Parshtaevalt unceremoniously across the river, brushing aside his heroics and the feverish archery of his companions in one quick charge that sent the Sakje fleeing for their lives. Srayanka was forced to reveal all of her ambushers to stem the rout. Her counter-charge stopped the Bactrians on the near bank and emptied a number of saddles, but the small size of her force was revealed.

The enemy commander came up with his staff and more cavalry.

'Eumenes,' Kineas said with satisfaction. He knew the Cardian immediately from his heavy athletic physique. The story was that Philip, Alexander's father, had seen the Cardian fighting in an athletic contest and drafted him on the spot. The Cardian had never disappointed the father or the son, and his physique, superb as it was, came second to his brain.

Eumenes rallied the Bactrians easily and his force began to deploy along the river, easily outflanking Srayanka's Sakje on both flanks. The enemy commander had men on fresh horses, and quivers full of arrows, and the Sakje began to flinch, giving ground from the riverbank and then abandoning the tree line altogether.

'Pen-pusher,' Diodorus said with disgust, referring to the Cardian's post as military secretary. They were lying in the gravel at the edge of the ridge. 'Caution personified.'

Kineas nudged him and pointed carefully, drawing his friend's attention to the bright flash of a golden helmet. '*He* won't be cautious,' he said.

Upazan was waving his lance, pointing across the river.

Upstream a stade or so, Ataelus's prodromoi burst from cover into the flank of a troop of mercenary horse, shooting at the gallop. The enemy cavalry detached some files to defeat them.

Across the river, Eumenes gave a sharp nod, as if the revealing of Ataelus's ambush had decided him. The Bactrian cavalry put away their bows. Upazan was already in the water with thirty armoured Sauromatae.

'Ares' balls, Kineas!' Diodorus rolled off the top of the ridge and got to his feet. 'He *is* coming across.' Diodorus sounded as if he'd just been invited to a particularly fine party.

Kineas shook his head. 'He ought to give it up. No point to a flank march that meets resistance.'

Diodorus stepped into the hand-loop on his spear haft and sprang on to his charger without touching her back, a dramatic mount that brought a rustle of approval from the Olbian troopers. He bowed from the saddle. 'To Hades with that. He's coming.'

Kineas rubbed his beard. 'Showy bastard,' he said to Diodorus and leaped on to the back of his second charger without touching the gelding's back. He grinned at Diodorus, who shook his head.

'Who's the showy bastard now, Strategos?' he asked.

Kineas took his spears from Carlus. 'Now for victory,' he said to the assembled Olbians and Keltoi. He touched his heels to the gelding's flanks and rode carefully to the top of the ridge, until he could once again see into the valley of the Jaxartes.

Just as on the Oxus, the Macedonians and their allies had formed on a broad front, intending to swamp Srayanka's thin force. Six squadrons of Bactrians, Sogdians and mercenary cavalry covered almost four stades along the bank, spread out because sometimes the banks were too high or the scrub too thick for cavalry. Eumenes' trumpeter blew a long call and then repeated it, and the whole force came across in a rush. It showed better discipline than Craterus's force had demonstrated, and Kineas's opinion of Eumenes the Cardian went up again.

Srayanka's household shot one volley at close range and broke, cantering to the rear, easily gaining ground on the riders coming across the river. The river was only dactyloi deep in most places, but horses wanted the water or they feared what lay beneath and they picked their way across.

Eumenes, visible in a purple cloak and a silvered bronze Boeotian helmet with a gold wreath of bravery atop it, sat peering under his hand, watching the ridge where Kineas sat on the back of his horse. He turned, shouting something at his hyperetes. Kineas felt like hiding, an irrational desire given that it was almost certainly too late for Eumenes to save his force from Kineas's trap.

Kineas muttered a prayer to Tyche that she not punish him for this mental hubris. Of course, it was all still in the hands of the gods.

The trumpeter raised his trumpet at virtually the same moment that Diodorus led the whole of the Olbian cavalry over the ridge at the trot and put them straight into a gallop. The ridge was nothing – a few men high at its highest point – but it was sufficient to add momentum to the Olbians.

Eumenes' trumpet call rang out.

Kineas watched as hundreds of enemy horsemen hesitated, in the river or just reaching the top of the bank. The signal was obviously a recall.

Kineas turned to Darius at his side. 'Tell Lot, *now*,' he said.

Darius grinned and pushed his horse into a gallop.

At his side, Philokles laughed. 'All morning,' he said, 'I have been dreading the fact that I would finally have to fight on horseback.'

'You're a fine horseman,' Kineas said.

'The best in Sparta,' Philokles said. He was laughing.

The Olbian cavalry struck the Bactrians and Sauromatae at the edge of the Jaxartes and blew through them, unhorsing dozens of men and knocking horses to the ground or into the water. Their wedge was scarcely disordered, and Diodorus led them on, right into the Jaxartes, an arrowhead pointed at the enemy commander.

Off to Kineas's right, Srayanka rallied her household with a raised hand, turned her horse under her like a circus performer in Athens and led them straight back at the enemy. Her household formed its wedge at the trot and she kept her force slow, so that they hit the shattered tangle of the Bactrians and stayed to kill them.

Kineas could see Upazan's helmet in the mêlée, and he saw Leon pushing to meet the Sauromatae boy. Leon downed a better-armoured foe with a spear thrust to the face, recovered to parry a lance thrust from an unhorsed man, and had to sidestep his horse to avoid being unhorsed himself. Sitalkes finished the man with the lance and Leon pressed in, but Upazan turned his horse, parrying blows from three Olbians, and ran.

Baulked of his prey, Leon reared his horse and threw his spear. It went over the Keltoi in front of him and struck Upazan squarely between the shoulders – and bounced off his scale thorax.

Eumenes the Cardian was looking around for support, and then he was riding away, followed by his staff, with Diodorus hard on his heels. The Athenian caught Eumenes' trumpeter at the edge of the rising battle haze and tipped him out of the saddle with a swipe of his spear.

To the north, the enemy's mercenary cavalry were across the stream and rallying on Srayanka's flank, coming forward at a collected trot in a strong tetragon. Unlike Eumenes, the mercenary commander saw his part of the trap in time to respond, and he wheeled to face Lot's Sauromatae on the flat ground a stade north of the ford, and both forces vanished in a towering cloud of dust.

Across the Jaxartes, Antigonus was sounding the rally call.

Kineas looked over the battlefield one more time. 'You can't have everything,' he said. 'The Sauromatae are in for a fight. Let's go!' He waved to his escort – the only reserve he had – and they were off, over the ridge and through the dust cloud of Srayanka's last mêlée. Her golden gorget shone like the sun, and he found her easily.

'I need to help Lot,' he shouted.

'Our horses are tired!' she called, but she sent dozens of her household knights to swell his ranks as they rode north along the Jaxartes. The mercenaries were holding their own, their backs to the river, visible through the battle haze like spirits in the underworld.

'Trot!' Kineas ordered.

He had fifty men, and they began to pull in on either side of him to make a wedge. He wheeled his horse to make sure – *sure!* – that he would punch into the mercenaries and not disorder the Sauromatae, and then the dust stole his sight and he was in a tunnel of sound and fury and fear. A spear came out of the scrum and tore into his Getae gelding's neck just as he threw his first – he never saw whether he hit his man or not – and then he was sword to sword with a Greek, and the Getae horse was sinking between his legs. He took a blow on his bridle gauntlet and hacked the man between his helmet and his cuirass and they went down together and he was punched off his feet by the next horse in his file riding over him. He curled into a ball, his side almost numb with pain where a horse hoof had hit him for the third time in four weeks. He tasted grit between his teeth and tried to spit. His own dying horse screamed as yet another horse trampled it and fell, and the weight of the horse's rump crushed Kineas to the earth, drawing a scream of pain from him.

But the gods did not utterly desert him, and the horse's weight was shared by his own gelding. They both rolled away, maddened, and yet no hoof caught him amidst the warp and woof of their tangle. He crawled a few feet clear.

'Brother?' Philokles asked. He reached down a strong hand and lifted Kineas out of the dirt and up on to his own charger's back as if Kineas weighed less than Nihmu. 'I would have sworn by all the gods that you had told me to avoid coming off my horse in a battle.'

Kineas put his hands around the Spartan's waist. 'Fuck yourself,' he said thankfully.

The fight was over before Kineas was rehorsed, and he was the only casualty. His bodyguards were deeply ashamed, as neither of them had seen him fall, and their apologies had all the drama the Keltoi could bring to any theatre.

Lot emerged from the dust and pulled off his helm. His golden armour was scratched in several places and his sword was gone. 'By the gods!' he said. 'That was a fight to remember. Who were they? Your cousins?'

Kineas watched the last of the Greeks crossing the Jaxartes, harried by Ataelus's scouts and still in good order. 'Greeks and Persians under a good officer,' Kineas said. His side hurt when he laughed or breathed. He had broken ribs.

'This officer?' Lot asked, leading a horse forward. The man on the horse's back looked defiant. He had bright blond hair and a heavy face.

Kineas didn't know him. 'Ransom?' Kineas asked Lot, with a grimace for the pain.

Lot shrugged. 'He was brave. I unhorsed him at the end – I thought I might keep him.'

Back at the ford, Srayanka and Diodorus's trumpets were busy.

'Where are you from, Hipparch?' Philokles asked.

The man looked from one Greek spear to the next with wonder. 'Amphipolis,' he said. 'You're all Greek!'

Lot spat. 'Eat my scrotum,' he said in Sakje.

'Listen, officer of Amphipolis,' Kineas said. He felt the goddess at his elbow. 'Listen, friend. Ride away. Go free. Your ransom is this – to go in person to the Parthenon and sacrifice to Athena.'

The Greek officer sat straight. 'I will do that,' he said dully. His elation at escaping death was slipping into an awareness of defeat.

'I'll just keep your horse,' Lot said, pulling the reins. 'Take him, lord.'

'Good!' Kineas said. He mounted the Thessalian gratefully, although he needed help and it hurt. He pointed back to the far ridge where the remounts awaited and touched Philokles on the shoulder. 'Let's go and find the others.'

They rode away, Olbians and Keltoi and Sauromatae, leaving one Greek cavalryman alone, dismounted in the dust.

By the time they reached the ford, Eumenes was gone and they could hear his men rallying on the flat ground above the Jaxartes, already three stades away.

'He won't come back,' Diodorus said.

Kineas watched the Macedonians from beneath his hand, breathing hard. 'Athena, I thought I was done for.' He kept watching. 'I'm inclined to agree. He's going somewhere else.'

Kineas looked back across the ford. 'How badly did we hurt him?'

Philokles shook his head. 'Thirty or forty men. A bee sting.'

Kineas nodded. 'Let the prisoners go – dismounted. They won't fight us again today if they have to walk.' He slumped. 'I need to wash in the river and I need someone – Philokles – to wrap my ribs so that I can ride.'

'We could just ride away,' Diodorus said.

Srayanka nodded. 'We turned them,' she said. 'No man can say we have not done our part.'

Kineas dropped from his horse to the ground and Sitalkes helped Philokles strip his armour. They tried to be gentle, but Kineas felt his vision tunnel and twice he cried out from the pain. Free at last of the scale shirt, he picked himself up and walked into the water. The cold helped him, as did the feeling of the grit running away. He splashed water on his torso, wincing as every motion of his left arm sent a pulse of pain down his chest and into his groin.

Srayanka held out a sheet of linen as a towel. 'All my maidens are jealous,' she said.

Kineas tried to smile. He felt better, but there were so many layers of pain and fatigue that he wasn't sure he could function. He had lost a great deal in the dust when his horse died under him.

Philokles took another length of linen from Leon and began to wind it around Kineas with the whole strength of his arms. Kineas couldn't breathe much, but the pain in his side diminished.

'I think we've done our part,' Diodorus said. He obviously didn't like what he was seeing.

'What was our part?' Kineas asked. 'We did our part when we stopped Alexander on the Oxus – when we rescued you, my lady. When we stopped Zopryon.' Philokles was binding his chest, winding it around and around his upper thorax. Kineas found it difficult to breathe, and Srayanka could see it.

'You are wounded. Take the children and the rest of the wounded and start west,' she said. 'We will yet cheat this prophecy.'

Kineas took the deepest breath he could manage and was delighted to find no pain at the bottom of the air, even as his twin vision saw things far away. 'Even now, Zarina is winning or losing this battle,' he said. 'Listen to me! She planned to line the riverbank. Alexander has his siege artillery. Guess what will happen! The phalangites will have room to claw a foothold on the bank. When Alexander leads his cavalry across, will the Dahae and the Massagetae hold?'

Diodorus shrugged. 'So?' he said. 'They'll run, and then they'll stop. Alexander will proclaim victory. Nothing will be changed. Isn't that what we've learned on the plains?'

Philokles mounted his charger – the same horse that Satrax had given him in the snow, a year and more ago. 'Now Kineas seeks to teach us a different lesson, my friend.'

Kineas took his children from Nihmu and kissed them both. 'You will protect them?' he asked.

'Until they begin to protect me,' she said. 'Goodbye, Baqca.'

Kineas turned for his horse. Philokles gave Kineas a hand and Srayanka pushed and together they got Kineas up on Thalassa.

'Get the horses watered,' Kineas said. 'All of them.'

Srayanka nodded, as did Lot.

Kineas sat silent for a long time, and gradually his friends, his staff, the chieftains and all around him became quiet.

He was about to speak when he saw the eagle.

He pointed off to the south. The eagle was rising slowly from across the river, clearly burdened by something – probably a rabbit. The prey's entrails hung down between the eagle's wings, unbalancing his flight. The bird turned and beat slowly towards them, wings pumping the air.

Among the Greeks and Sakje all conversation ceased, and every head watched the bird as it flew slowly, erratically, and as it closed, Kineas could see that the eagle had been feeding on the carcass of the rabbit, whose blood stained its white fur in streaks. The eagle rose again on a draught of warm air as it came over the bend in the Jaxartes where the officers had gathered while Kineas's wounds were tended. Then the eagle vented a raucous scream, pivoted on a wingtip and dropped the carcass of the rabbit, so that it plummeted to earth, making Thalassa shy and bouncing as high as a man's head before flopping almost at Kineas's feet. The eagle screamed again and turned away, leaving Kineas with an impression of fierce, mad intelligence from its golden eyes. Rid of the carcass, it flew like the wind itself, rose into the heavens and raced away.

The waves of pain from mounting had vanished with the eagle. He straightened his back and raised his voice. 'Listen,' he said. 'Would you leave a brother in a fight? This is not about *winning*. Winning – it is just as Diodorus has said. This is about *virtue*.'

'And you will die for *virtue*?' Diodorus asked, but his eyes were on the sky.

'Wouldn't you?' Kineas asked. 'You never left me in the agora that day, Diodorus. You might have run.'

Diodorus put his hand before his eyes.

Kineas took a painful breath. 'This is what we *do*, friends. Let's do it well.'

Srayanka kissed him. Then she rose, clamping her mare between her legs and stretching her spine.

'Sakje!' she shouted. 'Will you follow the king to battle!'

'Baqca-King,' they roared, a long, drawn-out roar like the sound of lions at the edge of night.

She was crying. Many of them were crying, but the dust dried their tears as they rode.

They rode five stades or more, seeing only the ephemera of battle – a fleeing rider, a wandering horse with its entrails dragging behind, screaming in pain. Time had flowed away under them like the rivers of the steppe, and it was afternoon, and despite fresh horses, they were tired.

And then they could hear the battle before they could see it, a cacophony of horse noise and metal that filled the air. Swirls of dust came floating over the low ridge in front of them as if ejected from the battle, or as if the spirits of the dead were fleeing.

Kineas stopped his horse at the base of the ridge. He waved to Ataelus. 'Go and be my eyes,' he said.

Ataelus gave a sad smile. 'For you!' he called, and he and his wife galloped diagonally up the ridge.

Kineas turned to the officers. 'Dismount. Have the troopers take a drink,' he said. 'When we go over the ridge, we'll have the Sakje on the right, the Sauromatae in the centre, and the Olbians on the left, where they are least likely to get entangled with the Massagetae or the Dahae.' He looked at them all. 'Unless Ataelus tells me something that shocks me, we will go over the ridge and straight into the maelstrom.'

Diodorus was ash-straight, sitting his horse as if on parade in Athens. 'What is our objective?' he asked.

Kineas raised an eyebrow. 'I intend to cut my way to Alexander,' he said. 'But failing that, remember what Zarina said. You are warriors. Do as you will.' He allowed himself a small smile. 'Obedient warriors in crisp formations!'

He won an answering smile from Diodorus.

He was considering a farewell speech – a classic battle oration – when he saw Ataelus careering down the ridge, Samahe at his heels. The man's body language screamed of disaster and Kineas abandoned his notion of a formal goodbye. 'Mount,' he called.

He waited until the slackers were mounted. 'Walk,' he called. He waved his arms to indicate that the Sauromatae and the Sakje should form arrowheads to the right as he had described. Srayanka reached out a hand – a hard hand with a doe-soft back – and they clasped hands like soldiers. 'Goodbye!' she said. 'Wait for me across the river!'

'Live long, Queen!' he shouted back in Sakje, and they were parted, her column forming to the right as his bore straight up the ridge.

Ataelus pulled up next to him. 'The Zarina's standard is down,' he said. 'The Dahae are leaving the field.'

'Ares wept!' Diodorus said.

And Kineas thought, *This is not what I saw.*

33

Even Thalassa laboured over the last of the climb, but before the sun had set another finger's-breadth, Kineas topped the ridge and the whole of the battlefield was laid out before him, a bowl of war covering eight stades or more from ridge to ridge. And what he saw shook him.

Nearer to him, Scythian warriors on the other slope of the ridge were retreating, shooting arrows, in the face of a heavy line of enemy cavalry – Macedonians and Greeks and Sogdians all intermixed. The Scythians were spread thin, and they gave ground quickly and never tried to rally.

Down in the centre of the bowl, the pikemen of the phalanx had established a line across the ford and had pushed on for some distance. A rubble of dead horses, visible even at this distance, marked the futility of the Sakje resistance. But there was just one phalanx – the other was visible, pikes erect, across the river behind the line of siege machines.

Only far away, at the limit of vision on the Sakje right, did the army of Macedon seem to be getting the worst of it. There, and only there, was the movement of the antlike contestants retrograde. Years of watching battles – and serving in them – had gifted Kineas with an instant grasp of the meaning of the hundreds of signs – sounds, motion, even the quality of reflection of light could tell you which direction a man was moving. The Macedonian left was losing. The rest of their army was at the point of victory.

Over all of it, the fog of Ares rose from the sandy ground to obscure everything but the wraithlike movements and the strongest glints of polished metal. The Sakje still glittered with gold, so that even through the battle haze, Kineas could estimate their positions.

Nowhere could he find Queen Zarina, who should have been in the centre. But just to the near side of the enemy centre, just behind the fighting, Kineas could see a purple cloak surrounded by aides. Even as he watched, Alexander was leading a wedge of Companions into the Massagetae nobles to his front.

And behind the Macedonian lines was the river. Dead trees filled the ford, and across the river, a huge dead tree towered over the field, stark and awesome, and Kineas felt the full weight of his doom. He shivered, and his side hurt – something liquid seemed to move *inside* his skin, and he swayed in the saddle. He began to turn his horse – he thought of how he might, after all his posturing, leave the field, flee with honour. Or without it.

I do not want to die! he thought. His breath burned in his throat and his heart seemed to pump out the last of his blood, so that he was cold.

The setting sun was red like the blood of a dying man, and it shone on his men as they crested the hill, barring any possible retreat, and they reminded him – more than reminded him – of who he was. They were strong, unbeaten, three crisp triangles that darkened the ridge so that there was immediate commotion in the Macedonian centre and the Sakje on the ridge before him panicked, assuming that they were Macedonians. He looked at his men – the Keltoi and former hoplites of Olbia, dressed in the remnants of Greek armour, with Sakje tack and Sauromatae armour here and there, many in barbarian trousers, some wearing Sakje hats in place of their helmets.

Just beside him, Hama grinned. 'Now for glory!' Hama called. He threw his sword in the air and it flew in a wheel of fire and Hama caught it by the hilt. All the Keltoi roared.

Thank you, Hama. Decision made, Kineas took a deep breath. Fear was deep in his guts, but there was elation there as well. There was even happiness, the happiness of a craftsman nearing the completion of a long and heavy task. To his right, the Sauromatae crested the hill and formed their ranks, glittering bronze and iron scales over every man, woman and horse. Gwair Blackhorse, the leftmost man in the front rank, turned and waved. The sun torched Lot's armour, but however bright his bronze and gold burned, Srayanka was the sun herself as she rode over the crest, her helmet and gorget too bright for him to watch.

Kineas's throat was heavy with all of it – pride, terror, joy. He could smell apples.

He left the point of the Olbian wedge and rode along the crest, sword in the air, until he was *sure* that all three wedges were fully formed and ready. If this were their moment, he would not waste it with a simple error. Their cheers followed him, and in the valley at his feet he could sense the change. They were too golden to be Macedonians. Even as he cantered back to his place, the ocean noise of the Sakje cheers began to come back from the centre, as the Massagetae realized that their long fight in the centre was *not* in vain. And the purple cloak flickered in the setting sun and the dust, but it was moving *back*.

Kineas pulled into his place, with Diodorus at one shoulder and Carlus at the other.

'Athena!' he called, and men laughed aloud – power flowed through him like the ichor of a god. And the Olbians – Hellenes and Keltoi together – sang Athena's paean as they started forward, and many among the Sakje and even the Sauromatae took it up, so many times had they heard it around campfires, standing in the rain or the biting heat of the plains, among the snows of Hyrkania.

> Come, Athena, now if ever!
> Let us now thy Glory see!
> Now, O Maid and Queen, we pray thee,
> Give thy servants victory!

The three wedges came over the crest at a walk. As soon as the horses felt the slope, Kineas let them move, taking the downhill side at a fast trot and then a canter, and he could see Lot and Srayanka at the point of their formations keeping pace.

The cavalry in front of him broke a stade before he could reach them. They had not had an easy day, galled by Scythian arrows and forced to climb the ridge. Now their world had turned upside down and they ran for the ford. Only the

Macedonian cavalry stood, then charged back, their tired horses making heavy work of the hill, and the Sauromatae in the centre crashed into them with a sound like summer thunder.

Kineas refused to let Thalassa have her head, and he pulled her up, keeping an eye on Lot's golden helmet as he used his heavy lance against the more lightly armed Macedonians, already disheartened to find themselves abandoned by their allies. The Macedonians held for a few heartbeats and then a few more, unused to defeat, fighting with their guts, and then they too broke, and the Sauromatae began to re-form their wedge on the move.

The chance of the hill and the ground had pointed their formations more at the ford than at the Macedonian pikes, who were already extending files and facing as fast as they could move to react – far too late, unless their king turned away from the centre to save them – and if he did, the battle was a stalemate.

Kineas could feel it.

He was off the last of the ridge, on the flat and in the battle haze. Off to his right, there were trumpets – Alexander calling his Hetairoi to save the battle. Kineas barked 'Take command!' at Diodorus and then 'Wheel right!' at Antigonus, who sounded the call. Kineas tapped Thalassa to a gallop and she leaped forward at his order, flying over the ground. Kineas raised his heavy spear over his head, showing all three formations their new direction, and the three triangles wheeled, staggered because of distance and reaction time. Kineas placed himself ahead of the Sauromatae. 'Wheel, Lot! Wheel right!'

Lot was becoming less visible in the dust, but he raised his lance and a moment later his trumpeter sounded.

Srayanka will hit them first, Kineas thought. He gave Thalassa her head and the mare skimmed the dirt, hooves scarcely touching the ground. How far away were Alexander's Hetairoi?

He saw the golden glow of Srayanka's armour first, and he pulled in as he came up. 'Wheel right!' he shouted.

She raised her long-handled axe in salute and her trumpet

rang out as Kineas closed with her, wheeling Thalassa. 'Alexander is right in front of us!'

She laughed, a sound of joy. 'Hephaestion is mine!' she shouted. 'Aiiyyeee!' and she gave her horse its head and the Sakje were off into the dust, Kineas already angling away to the centre. If he had pictured this correctly, the three wedges would hit the Macedonian Companions in three staggered plunges, like three sword thrusts.

He was nearly abreast of Lot when the red-cloaks came out of the haze. He turned Thalassa and settled into the Sauromatae formation seconds before the two triangles crashed into each other.

The explosion of noise as they impacted drowned out thought. Kineas never had time to throw his javelin, and Thalassa crashed breast to breast against a Macedonian horse that she couldn't avoid as Kineas ducked the point of the man's lance, and the two beasts went up in a flurry of hooves, standing on their hindquarters. Kineas's legs closed like a vice and he swept his javelin like a sword – the point caught between the Companion's arms, and Kineas leaned into it as Thalassa pushed forward on to four feet and the enemy trooper was down, unhorsed but probably otherwise uninjured. Kineas pressed in immediately. Now he threw his javelin into the man facing Lady Bahareh, recognizable from her heavy grey braids, and Kineas's throw caught him under the bridle arm and sent him into the dust and she pushed forward as well and there was another chaos of noise from their left as the Olbian wedge met the Macedonians.

Kineas was no longer a commander. He retrieved his spear from his left hand and got it up over his head two-handed as the men and horses pressed close – the two wedges were flattening out against each other, and the close-serried cavalry were reduced to fighting like hoplites, cheek to cheek with their opponents, their legs crushed between horses. His next opponent was still fumbling for his sword when Kineas punched his spear – shortened until his left fist was at the head – between face and cuirass. A blow rang off his scaled back and then another. He looked round at where a Macedonian had somehow penetrated their formation and he landed a blow with his butt spike, but it glanced off the man's cuirass. He took a blow on his raised arms – armoured arms, thanks to Srayanka's gift – and Thalassa, reading his body, backed up and kicked with her hind legs, both hooves striking home against the enemy's horse with the sound of an axe biting wood. Kineas thrust back again as a blow rang on the back of his helmet, and his butt-spike caught under the man's thigh, ripping his leg as his horse failed him, and they went down together. Kineas caught a glint of gold, a flash of a new enemy in his peripheral vision, and he swung the spear two-handed, straight from back to front even as he turned his head, and the whole weight of his cornel-wood spear crashed sidelong into Alexander's golden helmet, ripping it free against the chinstraps, and the king of Macedon sagged away, a dozen of his own troopers throwing themselves into the desperate press, but Kineas was on him and thrust again at the king's legs and scored deeply before two swords rang against his helmet – weak blows, but enough to drive him from his prey. He parried, got his spear-butt high and used it like a slave sweeping with a broom to parry, jabbing his point into faces and down into unarmoured thighs, so that men fell into the dust, but Alexander was slipping away, slumped in his seat.

The wall of Sauromatae was pressing forward now – Kineas could feel it. He was too far into the Macedonian formation but he could see Alexander just another rank away, Companions pulling at his bridle. He was hit – hit hard. Kineas took a blow in the side – the wounded side – pain blinded him and training made him lash out with the spear point to cover his agony, and a blow he never saw severed his heavy spear between his hands so that he had two pieces, but this was a moment for which Phocion trained you, and he lashed out with both pieces, raining blows on his opponents, his whole being focused on getting to Alexander, but his vision was tunnelling and he almost lost his seat when a kopis bit into his right side under his arm, scattering scales and drawing a new line of pain on his chest. Thalassa felt the change in his weight and reared, kicking, buying him precious heartbeats.

He dropped the halves of his spear and pulled the Egyptian sword easily from its scabbard. He couldn't breathe.

A long lance reached out from behind him and tipped a Companion into the dust, and he cut at his opponents, missing wildly but still alive, eyes clearing to his peril. He parried, and there were Macedonians on either side of him, so close that his booted knees were crushed against theirs, and his riding whip came into his bridle hand like a gift from Ares. He slashed back-handed to the left and then rammed the butt of the whip under the rider's jaw and turned back, the whole weight of his body and Thalassa's motion behind his sword, and he cut through the man's guard and his blade skidded down the man's shoulder and still had enough power to cut a long fold of flesh clear of his unarmoured sword arm. Kineas cut with the whip – one, two, three consecutive blows to the man's face over their locked weapons – and the man fell free, more flesh shredding off his arm as he went, and he screamed but he couldn't fall because the press of men and horses was so tight. 'The king is down!' shouted in Macedonian-accented Greek, and new strength flooded through Kineas. But with Thalassa's muscles straining between his legs, he couldn't move, trapped with the men he had put down, and the Companions just beyond the range of his sword were leaning far out over their horse's heads, trying to cut at him, and he had to parry to protect Thalassa's head. Thalassa tried to rear and Kineas hung on her neck to keep her down, afraid in this press that she'd lose her footing and fall.

'Take it!' over his shoulder. Again the lance struck over his shoulder and he risked a glance back – Lot was behind him. 'Take it!' he shouted.

Kineas didn't want a lance in this insane press. 'Cover me!' he shouted, parrying again to protect his horse, and the Sauromatae prince drove his lance into the Macedonian's unprotected head, killing him. And then Darius was there, and Carlus, and then Sitalkes, clearing his way through the press like a young Achilles, his helmet lost and his spear red and gold in the setting sun.

Darius did an insane thing, rising on his own horse's back and then jumping to the horse of the last man Kineas had dropped, moving like an acrobat. His sword licked out, blinding a man and then showering blows on his helmet until he ducked and fell away.

Carlus, on his elephantine horse, simply pushed through the press, and for heartbeats it seemed that he might unhorse Kineas in his eagerness. Next to him, at the edge of Kineas's awareness, was Philokles, raining blows without pause on his opponents like Ares come to earth.

Like a log jam in a Thracian river in spring, the Macedonians gave slowly. Thalassa went forward a short lunge – a single step. Kineas could only parry, his arms too weak to make the strong cuts required to put an armoured man down in the dust. But there were no blows coming at him to parry. Darius and Carlus had taken his place in the line. He hauled on Thalassa's reins and let Lot squeeze past him, thrusting strongly. Sitalkes cut down the trumpeter even as he set the instrument to his lips, and Sitalkes snatched the golden trumpet and raised it high, exulting, and died like that with a Macedonian lance in his side.

When another Sauromatae knight pushed past him, Kineas sagged and let them all past as the mêlée grew farther and farther away – a few feet, and then an ocean of sound away. He took a blow on the back from a Sauromatae who thought he was the enemy and he reeled, and the man apologized and rode clear with him, holding him against Thalassa's back.

'You did me no damage,' Kineas said.

'You are badly wounded,' the man said. Decorus – he had a name that sounded like that. Kineas couldn't get his head up.

'No,' he said. He was, in fact, wounded, somewhere under his shirt of scale armour. High on his left side, something wet had happened and there was a cut on his right side as well, and a lot of bruises. And breathing hurt again – more – more still. 'Go back to it, Dekris.'

'Thank you, lord.' The young man tipped his helmet down, pulled his lance out from under his thigh and looked right and left. 'Sounds more open over there,' he said, and plunged away to the left.

Kineas sat on his charger, alone, long enough to wish that he had a skin of water. Some random blow had cut the strap to his clay bottle. He got his head up, blew the snot from his nose and looked around. There was still no wind and the hanging dust made the air seem heavy and sick.

The prodromoi were still behind the fighting formations. While he took deep breaths, Ataelus came up, and Samahe, and Temerix. They competed to give him water. Temerix had some wine. He felt better immediately. Temerix gave him a piece of sausage with garlic in it – loot from some skirmisher fight, because the Sakje had nothing like it – and he wolfed it down. He hadn't eaten in hours – so he sat a quarter stade from the hottest cavalry fight he'd ever seen, sharing a sausage with his scouts. His sense of the battle began to return despite the dust.

The sun was setting and the air on his sunburned, dirty face seemed cooler. 'Thanks for the sausage,' he said to Temerix, who grinned. 'Let's go and win this thing,' he said, which sounded pompous, but that's the way it looked to him.

The mêlée had left him behind. The Companions weren't breaking – they were simply losing. All around Kineas, Scythian horsemen and women – not armoured nobles, but simple warriors from all the tribes – cantered up. Some peered at him. A few saluted him and called *Baqca*, and all threw themselves into the mêlée, often shouting for the prodromoi to join them. But the scouts waited with the discipline of two years of campaigns.

This, he knew, was what Zarina had meant. The Scythians had a lifetime of coordinated hunting on the plains. They knew when a beast was wounded, and they rode to the fight, every warrior choosing their own moment. His few hundred were now just the tip of the spear, and thousands of Dahae and Sakje were coming in behind them, riding into the war-storm to fire arrows or thrust with their swords. Many had changed horses after their initial panic, and they were comparatively fresh. The shock was over and they scented victory.

Kineas could smell it too, and it smelled like horse sweat and dust, and a hint of apples far away. Thalassa gave a cry and took a step forward – rare for her to move unbidden – and Srayanka came out of the murk.

'Aiiyee!' she shrieked and they embraced. And then she backed her mare. 'You are injured.'

Kineas just smiled at her. Then he reached out with his right hand and pulled her close, her gorget scraping dully against his scales, and they kissed like people who might have lost everything, despite everything.

'We could ride away!' she said when they parted. Her hand where she had embraced his left side was covered in blood.

'Too late, my love,' he said.

'I cut that fuck Hephaestion,' she said, as if passing the time of day. She handed him a javelin. 'A late wedding present,' she said. Her mouth thinned. 'Lot went down to the grass,' she said.

'Ahh,' he said, pain banished for a moment. Trumpets were sounding a recall. 'I put Alexander out of the fight.' He would mourn Lot later. And then he thought, I will join Lot soon enough, and he hurt, and it was wet, but he chuckled again. His grin was real. His fear was gone – really, he was already dead, and this last embrace was Athena's favour. He sat back on Thalassa, legs still strong. 'Let's finish it,' he said.

Srayanka's eyes locked with his, one last time.

'Take us!' Ataelus said at his side. 'Fresh horses!'

Kineas looked around. 'Form a wedge then,' he said, and Ataelus and Samahe barked multilingual commands and the scouts formed up. They advanced at a trot.

Side by side, Kineas and Srayanka pushed forward into the storm of Ares. The whole mêlée had motion now, and warriors made way for them as they pressed forward. All of their forces were intermixed, pressing forward with the strength of victory as the sun set red as a gaping wound behind them, blinding their opponents when it could penetrate the dust, and the daimon was on them all, and the Olbians shouted 'Apollo' and 'Nike' and few shouted 'Athena', while the Sakje and the Sauromatae began to shout something else – something that seemed wordless and built towards a word as they pressed forward, so that all the unfocused shouts began to be a word, repeated over and over, a thousand thin and tired voices making the voice of the war god.

'BAQCA!' they shouted.

And the sound carried him forward. He had time to think, This is what it is like to be a god, and he felt *Nike*, the euphoria of victory, suffuse him. And the Macedonians were breaking, having covered their retreat, exhausted, professional, superb, but now finished. Philotas might have held them longer, or Parmenion, but Hephaestion had already left the field with what he called wounds, and the thousand fickle spirits that warp even the best moved them to flow away.

Kineas broke through into the front rank and he threw his javelin, a long, high throw that caught the rump of a fleeing horse and stuck there.

'Good throw,' Philokles said. 'I find it little different,' he said, as if continuing an earlier conversation.

Kineas's vision was tunnelling from the pain of the throw, but he managed a smile for the Spartan. 'Hmm?' he said, as if they were standing on the porch of the megaron in Hyrkania, talking philosophy.

'A cavalry mêlée. Just the same. A lot of pushing, but with an animal doing the work.' Philokles smiled. His right hand was red, the wrist was red and the arm that held his spear was streaked with blood drips to belie his tone. 'I think I like it. A good way to fight one's last battle.'

Kineas laughed, and it hurt. 'You're a good man,' he said.

Philokles smiled. 'I can't hear you say that too often.'

The haze was clearing because the Scythians were too fatigued to pursue, and besides, the water of the Jaxartes was up to the hocks of their horses. Phalangites scrambled across the ford that they had won at such cost. Alexander's charge had saved them, but they had no order and they were done for the day.

Kineas turned his head and he knew them all – every man and woman – and he saw how the dream was true and not true. He looked to the front and he saw a beaten army, awaiting only the last blow. Just at the base of the great dead tree a lone horseman sat on an armoured horse, his gold-covered helm red in the last of the sun. He had a bow.

Leon's voice, away to the left, called through the red murk, 'He's mine!' and started into the water.

Diodorus said, 'Keep the line, by Ares!'

Kam Baqca was at his shoulder. '*It is time to cross the river,*' she said.

Kineas raised his sword, though the pain came in like the sea at flood tide. Above the red swirl of dust he could see the last of a blue sky, and high in the sky an eagle circled.

'Charge!' he said. He gestured ...

The next day in the full light of the sun, Srayanka crossed the river with thirty riders, all spear-maidens, their armour clean, their horses groomed and their hair adorned with circlets of roses and grass. Srayanka wore the sword of Cyrus, the hilt of jade flashing its own message in the sun.

On the enemy side, they met an escort of Macedonians who were not so clean, and she nodded to herself. The escort was led by the one Kineas had known – Tolmy – and he was wounded. She gave him only a blank face. They rode through a silent camp of Macedonians – silent except for the groaning of the wounded and the shrill pain of the horses. Those who could stared at her as she passed.

She led her column past the siege machines where un-wounded men stood ready, and past lines of tents and hasty shelters made of blankets, to where a dozen pavilions were pitched together, and Tolmy led them into a courtyard formed by the pavilions. 'The king will see you here. He is wounded.' He spoke very loudly, as if to a fool.

'My husband put him down,' she said, in Greek, and the Macedonian trooper's mutterings were as ugly as her smile.

She did not dismount, although Tolmy beckoned to her several times.

'The king awaits you,' he said.

'Tell him to come here. I do not dismount in a camp of enemies.' She raised her chin.

Her heart pounded in her chest, until she reminded herself that she had nothing to lose. She kept her chin high and eventually the flap of the greatest tent opened and Alexander emerged. He was pale, and he limped, and he immediately sat when a seat was brought.

'Only an Amazon would bring this courtesy, lady. Any other defeated king comes and kneels.'

Srayanka shrugged. 'I am kind, then. I will not ask you to kneel.'

Alexander's face was instantly a mask of rage. 'It is you who are beaten,' he spat.

She had a bag in her left hand. She opened it and threw the object it held on to the ground. It was Alexander's golden helmet. 'I might have put this atop a trophy such as the Greeks raise, across the river, and *nothing* could you do to stop me.' She nodded at his silence. 'Keep it with my thanks for your courtesy when I was a hostage.'

Alexander drew breath to speak and she raised her hand. 'Listen. I have not come to mock. You killed my husband – but I will hold my hand. You will not come across the Oxus or the Jaxartes, and the Sakje will no longer support the usurper Spitamenes, whom I hate. That is my word. Cross the rivers and die. Go elsewhere and conquer as you will.'

'I will conquer the world,' Alexander said. His anger was quenched already by his burning curiosity, his interest, his appreciation.

She spat back, 'Stay off the sea of grass, King.' She shrugged. 'Tell your slaves we came and gave you tribute, if you must. But stay off the sea of grass.' She drew the sword of Cyrus from the scabbard at her side. 'My people say this is the sword that Cyrus the Great King brought to the sea of grass. He left it with us. Come across the river and see what you will leave behind. I have spoken.'

She left him sitting on his ivory stool, holding his helmet. She didn't wait for her escort of Macedonians, who had dismounted, expecting a longer parley. She gathered her maidens and they rode clear, and no hand was raised against them.

And across the river, at the top of the ridge that towered over the ford of the Jaxartes, a big man, naked in the sun, made a pile of all the Macedonian armour that his friends had stripped from the dead. He wept as he worked, but he worked hard, and many hands helped. He built the trophy carefully, until it towered above the ridge, and the helmet that graced the top had a blue plume and the bronze caught the sun and burned like a beacon.

HISTORICAL NOTE

Alexander lost?

What kind of revisionist claptrap is this, anyway?

Alexander's record of endless victory was widely questioned in his own lifetime and there's no need to call an historian 'revisionist' if he chooses to believe that Alexander was fallible. Most of our sources on Alexander date from *long* after the events of his life but, rather like the gospels, we suspect that ancient authors (like Diodorus Siculus and Arrian and Plutarch) had access to contemporary works we have lost. Whether you accept this or not, it's worth noting that Peter Green, Alexander's best biographer (in my opinion) felt that Alexander was beaten on the first day at the Granicus and only Parmenion's direct intervention saved him on the second day.

By the same token, while some historians choose to accept Arrian's contention that Alexander won the Battle at the Jaxartes, I invite the reader to look at the sources with the jaundiced eye of the modern newspaper reader. Something went dreadfully wrong in the Jaxartes campaign – I think most historians would agree on that. Troops were sent home and defeats were experienced. Alexander did not, as it turned out, choose to conquer the steppes or even advance into them.

It is worth noting that Cyrus really did lose his life and his army to the Massagetae, and that Darius got into deep trouble against the Western Scythians. It seems unlikely that Alexander's army could force a decisive victory against the nomads, even if he managed to force a river crossing. Note that, even if you believe that he won the battle, he didn't advance one step beyond the battlefield. Compare that to his actions in other fields, and ponder ...

I think he lost – or rather, as the novel suggests, I think he failed to win.

For those relatively unversed in the period, Alexander's murder of Parmenion and the loss of the column south of

Marakanda are historical events, as are the 'treason of Philotas' and his subsequent torture and execution, the murder of several thousand Sogdian prisoners, and the riches and power of the Euxine cities and the Scythian tribes of the Sea of Grass. My website, *www.hippeis.com*, has a bibliography. For those who know these events well, I created my own timeline based on the superb comparison charts in the annex to Robinson's *History of Alexander the Great and the Ephemerides of Alexander's Expedition* (1953) which allow the reader to compare Arrian, Diodorus, Justin, Curtius, and Plutarch on an event-by-event basis.

AUTHOR'S NOTE

Very little survives of the Scythian language, and I am an author, not a linguist. I chose to represent some Scythic words with Avestan, and some with modern Siberian words, and some with Ossetic words, all with the intention of showing how difficult a language barrier is, even when many words share common roots. I have a very little skill with Classical Greek, and none with any of the other languages mentioned, and any errors in translation are entirely my own. I have translated some of the poetry on my own, and other passages I have paraphrased from nineteenth and early twentieth century translations – which were excellent! In particular, the *Hymn to Demeter* on page 56 is from Hugh G. Evelyn-White's translation. The extracts and quotes from Aristophanes' *Lysistrata* on page 196 are John Lindsay's translation of 1926. The *Hymn to Ares* on pages 354–355 is from Hugh G. Evelyn-White's translation. The poetry on page 371 is, of course, Samuel Butler's translation of one of the *Iliad*'s most famous passages. Page 426 features another Homeric Hymn; this my own (with help from Perseus!).

In addition, as you write about a period you love (and I have fallen pretty hard for this one), you learn more. Once I learn more, words may change or change their usage. As an example, in *Tyrant* I used Xenophon's *Cavalry Commander* as my guide to almost everything. Xenophon calls the ideal weapon a *machaira*. Subsequent study has revealed that Greeks were pretty lax about their sword nomenclature (actually, everyone is, except martial arts enthusiasts) and so Kineas's Aegyptian *machaira* was probably called a *kopis*. So in the second book, I call it a *kopis* without apology. Other words may change – certainly, my notion of the internal mechanics of the *hoplite phalanx* have changed. The more you learn …

461

ACKNOWLEDGEMENTS

I'm always sorry to finish an historical novel, because writing it is the best job in the world and researching it is more fun than anything I can imagine. I approach every historical era with a basket full of questions – How did they eat? What did they wear? How does that weapon work? This time, my questions have driven me to start recreating the period. The world's Classical re-enactors have been an enormous resource to me while writing, both with details of costume and armour and food, and as a fountain of inspiration.

In that regard I'd like to thank Craig Sitch and Cherilyn Fuhlbohm of Manning Imperial, who make some of the finest recreations of material culture from Classical antiquity in the world (*www.manningimperial.com*). I'd also like to thank Paul McDonnell-Staff for his depth of knowledge and constant willingness to answer questions – as well as the members of the Melbourne and Sydney Ancients for permission to use their photos, and many re-enactors in Greece and the UK and elsewhere for their help. Special thanks to Ridgely Davis (and Jack!) who took the time to teach me how to use a javelin from horseback. And years of thanks to the members of my own Hoplite group, the Taxeis Plataea, for being the guinea-pigs on a great deal of material culture and martial-arts experimentation. *On to Marathon!*

Kineas and his world began with my desire to write a book that would allow me to discuss the serious issues of war and politics that are around all of us today. I was returning to school and returning to my first love – Classical history. And I wanted to write a book that my friend Christine Szego would carry in her store – Bakka-Phoenix bookstore in Toronto. The combination – Classical history, the philosophy of war, and a certain shamanistic element – gave rise to the volume you hold in your hand.

Along the way, I met Prof. Wallace and Prof. Young, both

very learned men with long association to the University of Toronto. Professor Wallace answered any question that I asked him, providing me with sources and sources and sources, introducing me to the labyrinthine wonders of Diodorus Siculus and, finally, to T. Cuyler Young. Cuyler was kind enough to start my education on the Persian Empire of Alexander's day, and to discuss the possibility that Alexander was not infallible, or even close to it. I wish to give my profoundest thanks and gratitude to these two men for their help in re-creating the world of fourth century BC Greece, and the theory of Alexander's campaigns that underpins this series of novels. Any brilliant scholarship is theirs, and any errors of scholarship are certainly mine. I will never forget the pleasure of sitting in Prof. Wallace's office, nor in Cuyler's living room, eating chocolate cake and debating the myth of Alexander's invincibility.

I'd also like to thank the staff of the University of Toronto's Classics department for their support, and for reviving my dormant interest in Classical Greek, as well as the staffs of the University of Toronto and the Toronto Metro Reference Library for their dedication and interest. Libraries matter!

I now have a website, the product of much work and creativity. For that I owe Rebecca Jordan – please visit it. The address is at the bottom of this.

I'd like to thank my old friends Matt Heppe and Robert Sulentic for their support in reading the novel, commenting on it, and helping me avoid anachronisms. Both men have encyclopedaeic knowledge of Classical and Hellenistic military history and, again, any errors are mine. In addition, I owe eight years of thanks to Tim Waller, the world's finest copy-editor. And a few pints!

I couldn't have approached so many Greek texts without the Perseus Project. This online resource, sponsored by Tufts University, gives online access to almost all classical texts in Greek and in English. Without it I would still be working on the second line of *Medea*, never mind the *Iliad* or the *Hymn to Demeter*.

I owe a debt of thanks to my excellent editor, Bill Massey at Orion, for giving this book a try, for his good humor in the face of authorial dicta, and for his support at every stage. I'd also like to thank Shelley Power, my agent, for her unflagging efforts on my behalf.

Finally, I would like to thank the muses of the Luna Café, who serve both coffee and good humor, and without whom there would certainly not have been a book. And all my thanks – a lifetime of them – for my wife Sarah, to whom this book is dedicated.

If you have any questions or you wish to see more or participate (want to be a hoplite at Marathon?), please come and visit *www.hippeis.com*. And for those interested in further adventures, the website has an 80-page novella (and it's free) about the days and weeks following Kineas's death, called *Leon's Story*.

Christian Cameron
Toronto, 2008